HER AMERICAN CLASSIC

To Ivy
Enjoy
xxx

G J Morgan has been a Chef, a fashion graduate and now works in finance. His unpublished novella "Miss B Tee" has recently been adapted into a short film. His and Her American Classic are his debut novels.

HER
AMERICAN
CLASSIC

G J MORGAN

Matador
9 Priory Business Park,
Wistow Road, Kibworth Beauchamp,
Leicestershire. LE8 0RX
Tel: 0116 279 2299
Email: books@troubador.co.uk
Web: www.troubador.co.uk/matador
Twitter: @matadorbooks

ISBN 978 1788038 614
British Library Cataloguing in Publication Data.
A catalogue record for this book is available from the British Library.

Printed and bound in the UK by 4edge Limited
Typeset in 11pt Adobe Garamond Pro by Troubador Publishing Ltd, Leicester, UK

Matador is an imprint of Troubador Publishing Ltd

Thank you to all those at Matador and Troubador Publishing. You made the process of turning stone to diamond far less daunting than I thought it would be.

Thank you to my early readers: Taya Nicholls (my little Romanian pocket rocket/Business partner), Sarah Lawson (my cinema girlfriend) and Gina Hewitt (my lifestyle coach).

Thanks to Phil Burman (Dad number 2) for constantly being my technical support and turning childlike scribbles into a front cover. Thanks to Paul Burman for being the only person who could relate to the struggles of being a writer and when best to laugh or cry (mostly cry).

Thanks to Barbara Middleton-Chappell for telling me straight and making me realise I'd ran out of excuses not to start writing again.

Thanks and love to Jodi Ellen Malpas for taking time out from being a New York bestselling author and giving me invaluable advice on what to do when the last word has been written (turns out more writing).

Thank you most of all to my wife Krissy, my friends and family, for giving me hours and evenings and mornings and years to type away at my laptop. Without whom the novel would still be an idea on a hotel napkin.

PART ONE

Bantham/April/Shot 273

1

"Vince? Vince? Can you hear me?"

"Tommy?"

"What's going on?"

"Nephew's christening today. Got half my family here. It feels like fucking Little Italy. Can this wait till later? I'm kinda tied up."

"I wanted to tell you straight away."

"I can't hear you. What you say?"

"You're not gonna believe this, Vince. I've only gone and done it."

"Done what?"

"I got it, Vince. I got the shot."

"Serious?"

"I've just pinged it across to you."

"Give me a minute, let me just get this pancake batter off my hands and get someone to take over my frying pan."

I could hear him over the line, shouting Italian at someone, things rattling, the noise of his breath as I heard him pace around his house.

"Have you got the email yet?"

"I'm just loading up my laptop. Is it from the Awards bash?"

"No, after."

"Where? Max's hotel?"

"No, the place I thought."

"No fucking shit. Nice work."

"Has it come through yet?"

"Nearly, it's just finding a server."

He went quiet for a few seconds.

"Where is this place, some park?"

"Some bit of grass in the middle of Westminster."

"She looks pretty fucking pissed, man. They arguing?"

"Yeah. I couldn't hear them from where I was, but it looked pretty heated."

"And you're sure there was no one else there?"

"I'm positive."

The line went quiet.

"You still there, Vince?"

"You've only gone and done it, Tommy. You've only gone and fucking done it."

"Are they good?"

"Oh, these are good. Better than good."

"What do you think?"

"I think this is gonna make us a lot of green."

"How much will it make?"

"Did you get any video footage?"

"No."

"Shame. We'd get more dough if it wasn't stills. I need to speak to my office straight away. Like now. We need to get these on print ASAP, they're gonna want these sold damn quick. What time is it your end? Is it Sunday?"

"Sunday lunchtime."

"Well it's past six here. Why didn't you ring me last night?"

"Sorry, I feel asleep. I got back pretty late."

"We've lost a lot of time then."

"How much will this make us?"

"Taking off expenditure, sorting out my informers. It will leave us about 60%."

"That seems a lot taken off."

"Don't worry, Galella, you'll do well out of this."

"How well?"

"Your cut. About twenty gees."

"Sterling?"

4

"No, dollars. Sterling you'll be looking at just under twelve thousand give or take."

"Oh."

"You don't sound happy?"

"I thought it might make more."

"Hey, man. You did well. This is the fucking start, Tommy."

"Surely now we can stop? We got the shot. I've made enough to start over. That's all I ever wanted."

"This is far from over. This is finally starting. The girl is crumbling. She's been drinking all over Hollywood, her man Frank is over my side of the pond. She is ours for the taking. And it gets better. My sources tell me she is back down to Devon next week and it doesn't look like Frank is going back any time soon. She's got no security, no bodyguard. You can get close man."

"I can't get any fucking closer, Vince."

"You can always get closer. Cheer up, Tommy. This is a good day. You did good, man. You fucking stepped up to the plate. I'm a happy man."

"Good for you."

"Grab some balls, man. You just made yourself a lot of cheddar. That's money you can take home to your Mom and Molly. You should be fucking proud. You've become a man. And this is only the start. There is so much money to be had out of that girl."

"I'm tired, Vince. I'll call you tomorrow."

"Sleep well, my Prince. You did me proud today. Soon as I know money I'll holler at you."

"Night, Vince."

"I'm not sleeping tonight, man. I'm celebrating. I better go. I've got people to ring. Today is all about negotiation."

"What about your nephew's christening?"

"Fuck that. Baptism can wait. My nephew wants a cheque for his first car, not fucking balloons and cake. Besides, business comes first."

"Vince?"

"What?"

"Who is your informer?"

"My what?"

"Your informer."

"I got more than one, my friend, my little stool pigeons are all over. I got girls on perfume counters, men in baggage claims, some office clerk over at NBC. I got ears and eyes everywhere. All you need to know is, they are close enough."

"You must have a name? It's Sally, isn't it?"

"I ain't saying shit, Tommy. You can plot your little theories."

"Did this informer come to you?"

"Through my office, yes."

"They come to you?"

"They always come to us, Tommy."

"Are they making money out of Lilly?"

"No, it's never about money, well, not directly. Exposure is a two-way street."

"You must know something about them?"

"Niente. I ain't saying, Tommy. Why are you so fucking nosy all of a sudden?"

"Just finding it strange you can't tell me anything. We are partners in this. I should know stuff like this. It might help."

"Less you know, the less fallout if it all goes arse up. Anyway, man, I'm wasting fucking time here. Get off the phone so I can ring my office and make us lots of money."

"OK, Vince. I'm going home later today. Just for the night."

"I'd rather you didn't."

"I need a break. London has been pretty full throttle. I need to clear my head before I head back down South."

"OK, go rest your head. Back on point straight after, though. I want LG followed like a hawk, you got me, Tommy boy?"

"Got it, Boss. Let me know if you find out anything more about this informer of yours."

"Yeah, whatever. Now can you hang up so I can do my job?"

"You still flying over soon to check up on me?"

"Not now. Seems you can handle Lilly on your own."

★ ★ ★

I enjoyed checking out of that hotel, the bed that gave me back pains, sheets that turned my skin crazy, pollution that made me sneeze grey. Molly was pleased to see me, she looked taller, was that even possible, to grow in a week? I asked her what she'd been up to, she said lots, asked her how Grandma had been, she said tired.

In the garden I was shown courgettes, beetroot, spring onions, the chickens – the pair pecked around the lawn, I attempted to act like I wasn't petrified or that I'd prefer them roasted. Over dinner I let Molly root around my suitcase for her present from London, a Beefeater bear and a promise to take her to Hamley's when Daddy wasn't so busy or so poor, she seemed underwhelmed by both. Tried to put her to bed but it only made her upset.

"Don't worry." Mum came downstairs. "I wouldn't take it to heart. Funny age is terrible twos." She turned up the baby monitor, as we both listened to Molly fidget and sniff.

"Don't think age is the reason. You look tired."

"Speak for yourself, you cheeky bugger."

"OK, we both look tired."

"Least you can catch up on your sleep. Doesn't matter how much sleep I get, I can never quite catch up with mine." She passed me a tray of Ferrero Rochers. "Here, please finish these, I've still got three trays left over from Christmas."

I threw one into my mouth. "You want one?"

"Not for me. I've got a mouth full of ulcers to contend with." She sank into her armchair. "So, London. What happened?"

"A lot."

"You're going have to elaborate, Thomas. I've been stuck in this village most of my life. This is the closest I get to how the other half live."

"Your news first. How are you? And don't lie, not on my count."

"No news. More tests and results."

"They must know something though. At least I guess."

"I saw that specialist, had an ultrasound." Mum picked up her hairbrush, started brushing.

"And?"

"Said he could see some tiny black areas."

"What does that mean then?"

"Well, I then had a mammogram, followed by a biopsy. Said the lump may have to be removed, or worse, my whole breast. Seems to be an awfully slow process."

"Well, that's going to change soon, Mum."

"What do you mean, change?"

"I want to pay for you to go private. We'll look at what options are close by, how it will work logistically."

"That will be too expensive."

"Money isn't going to be an issue now, Mum. We need to get you better."

"Where has this money come from?"

"From all the things I've had to give up this last month. You deserve the best, Mum."

"I don't want the money, Tom."

"What do you mean, you don't want it? It's legitimate money, Mum. I worked hard. I earned it."

"Is it enough money? Can you stop now for good?"

"Not yet. Soon, a few more weeks away and this will be all be over. Me, you and Molly will be set. But it's enough to get you on the road to recovery, Mum."

"Look, you know how I feel about this whole situation of yours. I'm truly happy it's started to come good for you, you really deserve a bit of luck, a bit of fortune. But I'd rather not profit from another person's invasion of privacy. I appreciate it but I'd rather stick with the National Health."

"Mum, I thought you were OK with what I'm doing? We talked about this."

"I understand why you have to do it. I understand you have to do it. I understand it is what you need right now. But I don't want any part of it. Use the money for you and Molly."

"I want to use it for you."

"Then I will decline the offer again."

"This is fucking ridiculous. You'd rather die than take the money I've earned? The money which I have made legally and legitimately?"

"It seems that way, yes."

"This is a joke."

"Don't be mad. I'm happy for you. Use the money for you and Molly. Get her a new bike, put down a deposit on a house for yourselves. Go on holiday."

"I'm going to bed. I'm tired."

"Please, Tom. I'm not asking you to understand my reasons, but just accept them, that's all."

"Well I won't, OK? Just to be perfectly clear on this. I'm not going to accept your reasons."

And I stormed upstairs. I left the next morning. Said my goodbyes to Molly, which was fucking horrible, said nothing to Mum, which was even worse, more determined to get this whole saga over and done with. Just make the money and leave.

2

"You bloody stink, dog. Where have you been?"

"Nowhere. It's just his smell, old and fat, just like Alfred. He isn't very settled, bless him, too much noise."

"What's going on with all the cars outside?" I said, looking out of my window.

"Tell me about it. I've managed to keep your old room, you lost it at one point, Alfred nearly gave it away to some Joe, I gave him a clip round the ear, don't worry. It has gone a little bit barmy down here all of a sudden. Looks like it's catching on, this camera work, I wonder what they're taking photos of with their big cameras? Same as you, I can only imagine. Every guest house in South Hams is chock-a-block. Why can't they just stay at home and send us money instead? I want a life of peace and quiet. I'm supposed to be semi-retired."

"Have they said why they are here?"

"Nothing. They are more concerned with their laptops, using all our bloody electricity like it's bloody free. Keep asking for home fries, too, whatever the hell that is, Alfred isn't far off a heart attack and I'm not far behind him. Look, I'll leave you to sort all your bags out, you know where you're going," she said, handing me my door key. "Do you want me to bring you a pot of tea in about an hour?"

"Yes, please, Dot. Thanks."

"I'll do you some dinner in a few hours. Around six."

"Thanks, Dot."

"I've missed you, y'know."

"Missed you too. Oh, Dot you don't have any of today's newspapers lying about do you?"

"I usually have a stack left over from breakfast. I'll bring them in when I bring your tea. I've got a ton of mess to sort out, before they all come back demanding room service and alarm calls. This isn't a flaming hotel, it's a guest house, they must think I've got staff coming out of my ears. Oh, Tom, can I ask you a question before Alfred consults the internet, God forbid?"

"Sure."

"What's an over-easy egg? We guessed what sunny-side-up meant on our own."

"Fried both sides, Dot," I laughed.

"Why not just ask for things in plain English? Less of my moaning, you have a rest after your long drive.

"I'll try," I said disappearing down the corridor, knowing the last thing I would get would be rest, seeing the competition had arrived in droves.

★ ★ ★

I ate the last few mouthfuls from my plate, thick buttered toast, clotted cream, syrup, my arteries knew I was back on Devon soil. I walked back to my room, on my bed was the spread of newspapers. My photo was everywhere, Lilly was everywhere, so was Max. All of it, my doing, the debates, back stories, lies, truths, all of it because of me.

I could hear talking from outside, car doors being opened and closed. I looked out of my window, men loading or unloading, maps spread across car bonnets. For a second I found it funny, this sprawl of energy in the car park, watching podgy Americans work out where the hell they'd arrived or where to start, they were used to right angles and grids. Good luck, gents, I thought, welcome to Devon, a world of potholes and wrong turnings, roads that looked like paths. They didn't stand a chance, but I was wrong to underestimate them, they would be as hungry as me, if not hungrier, and probably a lot more qualified too.

There's a scene in the movie *Jaws*, just after one of the shark

11

attacks, when the whole world shows up on the beach, news vans, reporters, sport fisherman, all wanting a piece of this prize shark. And suddenly little Amity Island, a quaint little seaside town in Massachusetts with rocking porches and boardwalks, was turned into a feeding frenzy for the whole world to see. And somewhere in the endless blue ocean she was out there, this elusive great white.

Don't know who that made me in all this, I thought, Brody probably, feeding fish guts and chum, hoping she might bite. Or Quint, paid to bring her in, shooting yellow barrels at her, till she has no choice but to come to the surface. Either way I wasn't happy with the analogy, though it was pretty spot on. Truth was there was a bounty on Lilly's head, and every man and his dog had just arrived outside with all manner of gadgets and gizmos intent on being the one to catch her first.

What the hell had I done? I'd created this and it wouldn't be long till they found Lilly's cottage, if they hadn't already. I had to do something, but I didn't know what.

★ ★ ★

"Ludovic." I shouted over a car roof.

"I'm very busy. No time talk."

"I didn't know you were staying here."

"Me neither. Boss sent partner here. We share room now. He snores."

"I take it you are still after Goodridge?"

"Still yes," he said, busy with the boxes and bags in his car.

"Any luck?"

"Not yet. Why, you know something?"

"And why would I tell you if I did?"

"Because we friends. I scratch backs, you scratch backs."

"And how will you scratch my back?"

He leant in, he didn't smell good.

"I have weed. The best weed. Only best stuff for my friends, understand?"

"How much?"

"This much." He pulled a small bag out of his coat pocket, stuffed it into my hand.

"That's quite a small bag."

"You don't need a lot. So what news you have for Ludovic?" He closed his boot.

"Heard she is going to Newquay tomorrow morning for a few days."

"Nookey?"

"Newquay." I spelt it out as he wrote it on his hand.

"You lie, she filming this week. I know this."

"She is, tomorrow, but not for long."

"And what is in this Nookey place? Why she going?"

"She's going with friends, few of the guys off set."

"Chris Rogan. Muscle man, he going?"

"He'll be there."

"Max?"

"I tell you what else is in Newquay…"

"What?"

"Strip clubs."

"Strip clubs? You lie."

"Look it up, Ludo. Newquay is your sort of place."

"This place is full of titties and pussies?"

"Full of it, Ludo."

"You go Newquay too?"

"No, I've got to head back to London."

"I shall go. But if I not see Goodridge bitch there, I be angry at you."

"Hey, man. I can only go on my source. It's only advice, it's yours to take or leave."

"How far Nookey? Close?"

"A bit of a drive. About two and a half hours."

"Fuck this. That is too far."

"It's your call, Ludo. I'm just telling you what I know. All I know is, if I didn't have to go to London, Newquay is where I'd be heading right now. But one thing, Ludo, and I mean this."

"What, friend?"

"You can't tell anyone about what I've just told you, no one, not a soul."

"Trust Ludo. I tell no one, just partner."

"Shake on it."

"Shake, yes. Ludo tell no one."

"Good. I'll see you around. Have a good time. I'll tell you what, here's a twenty. Have a lap dance on me."

"Thank you. Enjoy weed. Very good. Promise."

"Remember. Tell no one, OK?"

"Ludo tell no one."

And I walked off, as did he.

I gave it one hour till the whole car park was on its way there too.

★ ★ ★

My plan worked, for the most part. The next few days most of the paparazzi checked out of the guest house and departed towards Cornwall in search of Newquay. Dot, confused by it all, but appreciating the few days of quiet it brought her, said she could now get on with all her jobs, get the place back in order.

And I was left with Lilly. Not that much went on, she barely left her house, not that I minded. I got to sit in my usual spot, under sun and shade watching hours pass by as occasionally I'd see her walk past a window, or every so often venture into the garden, barefoot and full of contemplation.

That was till Saturday. Saturday, it all changed.

My life and her's.

★ ★ ★

It started with a phone call.

"Tommy boy. You up?"

14

"I am now." I searched for my clock, my eyes still half closed. "Couldn't it have waited till later? "

"Well I thought you'd want to be the first to know that you've got eleven thousand dollars in your account."

"You being serious?" I said, sitting up.

"Hey, do I ever joke about money?"

"Thanks, Vince."

"No, man. Thank you. You earned it. What you gonna spend it on?"

"The obvious really."

"What, loose women and fast cars?"

"Yes, that's exactly what I'm gonna spend it on."

"What's going down today? Not had much news from you this week. It's all gone quiet on the western front."

"She hasn't done much."

"Well fear no more, Vince has more big news."

"Go on." I walked over to the kettle.

"Guess who's flying in from Paris to London. And guess who has ordered a private flight down to Devon."

"You're fucking kidding me."

"Lands around lunchtime. I doubt he's flying down there for cows and ice cream."

"Does Lilly know he's…"

"That I don't know. All I know is flight times. Let's hope she doesn't. Makes it more interesting."

"I don't think she would invite him."

"Your job isn't to understand her, it's to point your big black camera at her and press click. That's all your fucking job is."

"Aren't you curious?" I ripped a coffee sachet into a mug.

"I couldn't give two fucks and nor should you. What's this I hear about LG going to some place called Newquay?"

I laughed. I couldn't help it.

"Newquay was a false alarm, Vince."

"If things settle down my end, I'm gonna fly over soon."

"What, here?" I felt my stomach drop.

"In a week or so. Got some loose ends I gotta sort out here first but I wouldn't mind following LG around a bit, before she heads back home. I've been away too long as it is, 'bout time I got over there and showed you how it's done."

"You don't think I can do it on my own? I can do it on my own, Vince."

"Hey, man. You're doing a good job. But imagine the money we'll make when we are both hosing her down. The dream team, hey? She wouldn't stand a chance. I gotta shoot. Let me know how today pans out. I expect big things."

"See you, Vince. Talk later."

"*Buona fortuna*, Tommy." I looked at myself naked in the mirror, a half erection and a giant smile.

★ ★ ★

That was the first of many bombshells that particular Saturday, the money in my account, the pending arrival of Max. I rang Mum straight after, to tell her about the eleven thousand, I didn't tell her how much, but told her to take Molly out for the day, treat themselves to something nice, whether or not Mum was proud I couldn't tell, there were other things we needed to discuss more important than tainted money. She'd just gotten her biopsy results, came back clear, but Mum didn't seem too optimistic, she would still need monitoring over the next few months, more checks, more white coats. I offered to come home, drop everything, Mum insisted I stayed put.

I got to Lilly's not long after, she was already busy, cutting the grass with a mower as old as the house, looked like she was struggling pushing and pulling that ancient machine across the garden, and it wasn't a small garden either. As always Vince's prediction was right again, Lilly was preparing the house for guests, repositioning chairs, sweeping her patio, axing. It felt wrong to watch, not because she was in shorts and a bikini, but watching a girl battle with logs as big as her, whilst I sat and did nothing. But knowing Lilly, which I was beginning to, regardless of what man would have offered to help, she looked determined to complete the task alone.

A few hours later Lilly had ditched hard labour and was on the move. She had treated herself to a new car and I could hardly keep up, my Jeep was no E-Type and it was a pursuit Lilly was winning as she zigzagged through fields and hedges like she was Jackie Stewart. And what a glorious day for a race, green hills, blue skies, glorious sun. I could've followed her for hours, but it wasn't long till cliffs became white hotels and harbours.

After I parked the car I managed to catch up with Lilly who was in fierce negotiations with a butcher, before walking out with all the short rib in Salcombe. The town was unaware of Lilly Goodridge the celebrity; she was just another tanned ponytail as she looked at window displays, took photos of sail boats, helped a little girl crabbing out by the quay. This was a woman at ease, and I was at ease following her, we were sharing the same day out, just I was ten yards behind. I could live here, I thought, there have not been many places that I've said that about, but here was one of them. It was perfect, today was perfect, the town, the weather, Lilly.

Then I saw Ludo, the only frown in a street full of smiles, then I knew it would be spoilt, I just didn't know when or how bad. And worse, I couldn't even stop it, or get Lilly out of there before it was too late. It was disgusting what I saw, policeman and paparazzi turn paradise into panic, babies crying, fathers shouting, old people knocked to the ground, and for what? A few photos of a woman eating lunch.

When I got home I felt sick, lay in bed, angry at myself, angry at the situation, deliberated the many ways I could destroy my camera.

★ ★ ★

It didn't feel right to have to go back later that night. I'd have much rather stayed at home, and any other time I would have, left Lilly to her own devices, given us both a night off. But tonight, I had no choice, not with who was expected to show up, there was too much money to be made, and money aside I wanted to see how it was all going to play out, make sure Lilly wasn't facing Max alone.

I was back at Lilly's house just after it had turned dark, sat in my Jeep, poured a coffee from my flask, rode out the storm, didn't want to start my shift off by getting wet, or worse, damp, better to hang back. Besides it was a storm worth watching, that shook fences, loosened roof slates, that hit car windscreens like a round of bullets.

Any chance Lilly had of a garden party had been cruelly cancelled. Shame, I'd seen the work she'd put into it, watched her lug a kettle barbecue across the driveway, push that prehistoric lawnmower around the garden. Still it looked pretty, fairy lights lit up the patio and trees, through my binoculars I could just make out Lilly, she looked stressed, opening oven doors every five minutes, checking her watch. I looked at my watch too, it was getting pretty late for dinner, if Max was coming then it had to be soon, if he was coming at all.

I messaged Mum as I waited, asking if she'd had a reply from Cassie's folks yet. But Mum didn't answer, putting Molly to bed I expected. How long since I sent my letter? Less than a week ago when I was in London, they'd probably only just got it, I had to assume it would take more than a few days to cross oceans and freeways. Didn't even know why I expected them to reply, it wasn't like I wrote much, not that I gave them the answer they wanted to hear, but hopefully they'd be clearer on where they stood. I hoped it wouldn't make things worse, that wasn't my intention, I hoped my words put across the points I wanted to make, hoped it put them at ease a little. I hoped they wouldn't be mad that I didn't want to live with them.

Sometimes I thought about it, not LA, not Florida. I had a

friend who taught in Boston, that was an option I guess. I'd always liked the idea of Cape Cod, New York too. It would most likely be the East Coast, as far away from LA as I could get and still be in the same continent. I suppose Florida could one day be a realistic option, I could think of worse places to end up, especially having people who could help me get my feet off the ground, so I wasn't dismissing it completely, it just wasn't how I saw myself returning. I wondered how far eleven thousand would take us all, not far, wouldn't even last six months. I'd need more, double that, triple it. I'd need a few more front pages before I had any realistic option of emigrating with any real intent.

I looked back over at Lilly's cottage, the worst of the storm had gone, the rain now at a spit, the wind enough to rattle leaves, not the branches it was before. The house looked awfully dark, no Lilly, till eventually I saw a torch bulb pacing past windows and doors. A light must have blown or something, Lilly was probably under the stairs or some cupboard, looking for a fuse box. I waited for a few minutes, then a few minutes more, expecting light to resume at any point, but it didn't, so I too was left in complete darkness. I was tempted to turn my engine back on, light up the dashboard, but I didn't. Out in the middle of nowhere, dark meant just that, a black wall – if I turned my engine on I might as well have shot a flare gun.

I waited a little longer. I wasn't particularly scared of the dark, but I still didn't feel comfortable no matter how many times I'd done this before, there was an eeriness in those fields, sounds that only came out a night. Least before I had the glow of Lilly's house, now I was in Baskerville country, looking over both shoulders every time something with a heartbeat made a sound, something with four legs, something with wings, things that howled or growled.

Cassie loathed the dark, therefore our house in LA was never quite dark even at night, bed lamps, landing lights, the TV. There would always be something glowing in order for Cassie to get herself off to sleep without fear of what shadows might become.

I used to make a joke about it, jump out, creep up. She'd laugh, give me a whack, but her fear was genuine and I shouldn't have really taken advantage of it, regardless whether malicious or not. I thought about the crash, I hoped those last few minutes before she died she wasn't in the dark for too long, her eyes closed, still clinging on. I told her I was right next to her, I talked to her till the very end. Why did I still think of these horrible things? No good could come from it. Think of nice things, the good stuff, that's what I always repeated to myself, but most of the time it was the never nice stuff I remembered. It was all the rest, the stuff no human being should have to remember, the stuff you only remember when everything around is dark and black.

I needed to get out outside. I grabbed my stuff and crept quickly down towards the garden, it was a walk I knew well and the fifty yards was one I could do without a torch, though this hadn't always been the case, twisted ankles had made me learn quickly where to tread and where not to. Under the tree I started to set up all my shit, the tripod, the camera, my little fold-out chair, tried to get comfortable for a long night, get positioned, sort out my angles. I was planning on using my latest gadget, something I had picked up in London, the man behind the counter said they were like binoculars for the ears, up to a hundred yards, he said. I thought tonight would've been perfect, I'd have been able to listen to every single word, I couldn't see the meal adjourning outside in a hurry. I shouldn't have even carried them with me, lucky they were neither heavy nor large.

I heard a car, loud engine, angry tyres.

Max was here.

I took a deep breath.

Wished myself good luck, Lilly too.

3

Lilly screamed, an awful scream, the kind I'd heard before, the kind people made when you tell them their daughter had died, when there are no words loud enough.

Max was a prick, I'd watched him storm off, leave Lilly on her knees, watched him get into his car, he never even looked back. I'd taken off my earphones, I'd heard enough, I didn't need technology to hear a girl cry out every breath she had. I should have left, it wasn't right to watch. Lilly got up off the floor, walked slowly across the garden, her arms folded tightly across her chest, still cold, shaking, her footsteps tiny and slow. She stopped at the stream, her eyes fixed downward, motionless, it felt like I knew what was coming, what she was about to do.

I looked down at my camera, the hundred shots I'd taken felt heavy around my neck. I'd be lying if I said I didn't contemplate picking up that camera one last time, pointing the lens at Lilly one last time, the money it would make me and my family, the future it would give us. Suicide would make thousands and thousands of pounds, zeros that provided more than a nice day out, zeros that would change our lives forever.

All I had to do was take the pictures. That was all I had to do. Point and click.

4

I didn't jump, I fell, as if it made any difference...

Five.

... I'd never tried to kill myself before, which was surprising even for myself, knowing how complex and fucked up I was or am. Failed attempt at self-harm, though it wasn't a real attempt and there wasn't much harm done either. I barely even drew blood, I'd had worse paper cuts, think I just wanted to say I'd done it, make myself an outcast, make boys with guitars think I'm cute. I was listening to a lot of Billy Corgan around that time, a little Marilyn Manson too, so if anyone was to blame it was probably them, music was always to blame, that or video games. I wasn't even one of those girls that particularly liked suicide, or thought it cool or glamorous. Kurt Cobain, Ian Curtis, Elliot Smith. I thought they were arseholes, geniuses but arseholes, to be that selfish must take some real doing. To knowingly cause so much pain and leave so much pain behind, easy option for them, leaving nothing but hardships for everyone else...

Four.

... But life is hard though, unbearable sometimes, where support or advice or logic are neither asked for nor useful. Shame and regret can make rational people do irrational things, like load a gun, swallow a dozen pills, climb a wall...

Three.

... Funny thing was when I heard my name shouted, when I turned around, yes it was a surprise, yes it was shock, yes relief...

Two.

... But mostly I was just glad someone finally put down their camera, showed their face, stopped hiding. I just wasn't expecting him. His face full of fear, his arms stretched out, running toward me through the dark...

One.

... That was why I fell. Not because of what or why. Because of who I saw running to save me.

5

"It's bleeding pretty bad. Do you want me call someone? Lilly, are you OK? Do you need me to ring an ambulance? Talk to me. Say something. Can you walk? I'll take you back inside."

I heard him say all these things, but I didn't answer. I couldn't feel anything or say anything, not just yet. Even when he picked me up and carried me back inside, still I said nothing.

"Does that sting?" he said, putting a blanket over me. "I'm gonna try and find your fuse box, get some light in here, so I can see how bad your knee is."

He disappeared out of the room. Minutes later the house became bright again, too bright, as he came back into the room, he handed me a water, turned the light to a dim again.

"Do you want me to get you anything else?" he knelt down. "Some painkillers for your knee? I'll leave if you want me to. Do you need me to call someone?" He went over and stoked the fire, added a few more logs, turned dying embers back into a roar, as he sat on the arm of my chair, neither of us speaking. "Do you want me to explain?" he asked. "Explain why I was here. Do you need me to get something for you?"

"Tea would be nice," I said, my voice croaky, as he went out and came back in moments later, handing me my drink and a towel.

I turned the TV on and pressed play. Explanations and apologies could wait till another time, he deserved one, as did I. Easier to let actors and actresses do the talking tonight. I didn't have it in me, physically or emotionally I was past reaction. The title credits started to roll, a forest covered in white, sweeping score, a horse and his rider battling amongst the trees and snow.

The two of us, me and him, different couches, sharing our own different types of silence.

6

I'd been up for five minutes, woke up in a crumpled heap on the couch, my head throbbed, but my knee throbbed more. I made myself look down, it was mostly mud and blood, no swelling, just bruising, I'd seen worse but I couldn't remember when, my knee looked pretty fucked. I stepped in front of the fireplace to take a closer look at myself in the mirror, assess the damage, it wasn't pleasant, my face had taken a battering too, last night's make-up, last night's everything. I looked over at the other couch, he was still asleep, sat upright in his coat, arms folded, the snoring hero.

I limped my way to the kitchen, the room smelt of barbecue, the remains of dinner were everywhere, rib bones, corn husks, deformed candles. I boiled the kettle, opened the back door, sat for a while, sipped coffee, tried to gather my thoughts.

★ ★ ★

"Hi," he said, stood in the doorway
"Hi."
"Sorry, I fell asleep. I didn't plan to."
"It was a long night for us both. The subtitles didn't help either, I bet."
He smiled, though he couldn't look at me, his eyes everywhere but me.
"I'm gonna head off now," he said, his coat in his hand, "leave you to it."
"There's some coffee left in the pot. Thank you for fixing the lights by the way. Was it hard to do?"
"No, just had to flick a switch that's all."

"Will you show me how you did it, before you leave? Just in case it happens again." I passed him a cup of coffee.

"Sure."

"You fancy burnt peach cobbler for breakfast?" I said, taking a pie dish out of the Aga.

"Coffee is fine." He took a sip. "How's the knee?"

"Not that bad. My pride hurts more."

"I don't know," he smiled. "Your knee looked pretty messed up. My name is…"

"I know your name, we've met before. You can sit down by the way." I pointed towards the chair.

"I didn't know if you'd remembered."

"Awards show, right? London."

"That's right." He took a seat.

"I'm guessing that chance meeting had nothing to do with chance at all?"

"I'd like to talk about last night. About what happened. Talk about how I fit in to all this."

"Oh, I know where you fit in to all this. I'm gonna go and have a quick shower, then you can apologize and I can say thank you. I hope you like eggs, it's all we cook round here."

★ ★ ★

The shower stung, hot water on raw skin. When I came back down the stairs, I could hear him on his cell, I tried to pretend I wasn't listening as I took a seat, eyes behind my Wayfarers as I brushed out the last of the wet from my hair. I noticed he had already set the table, I could smell eggs and butter, bread becoming toast, I was being cooked for.

"Sorry about that," he said, putting his cell back in his pocket. "It's my little girl's first day at nursery today. Think she got a little bit upset by the sound of it."

"Is that like preschool? She must be, like, five, then?"

"She's three, well she will be in September." He went over to

27

the Aga. "I hope you don't mind me making breakfast," he said, stirring and seasoning.

"Shame for you to miss her first day."

"Tell me about it."

"Where's home? Near here?"

"Tiny village up North."

"When did you see her last?"

"Last Sunday. Flying visit, must've only seen her for about four hours. Still worth it though."

"When are you next due to see her?"

"Question mark. In a week, a week and a half. Depends on you, really. Where you go?"

"Me?"

"I go where you go, remember?"

"Well, if it's any consolation I haven't plans to venture too far away. I'm pretty much under house arrest now. Seeing all you fuckers have found me I'll never get a moment's peace, easier just to stay indoors."

"Sounds like I'll be here for a while then."

"And you think this is good for your daughter, this current situation, you being so far away, seeing her for four hours, not knowing when you'll be back?"

"No, this situation is far from good. But it's not forever." He walked over to the table, placed a pan of scrambled eggs in the middle of us.

"What, till you move on to the next troubled actress?" I said, helping myself.

"No, you're my first and my last, I can assure you."

Together we drank our coffee, we'd finished off the eggs and now I'd brought out the granola. I noticed him look at me as I poured myself a bowl.

"You're looking at me funny. Have I got something in my teeth?"

"No," he laughed.

"Go on, you've got to tell me what's so funny."

"It's not even that funny. I just read somewhere you had a nut allergy, that's all."

"Afraid not."

"This is weird, isn't it?"

"I'm used to weird."

"I'm not."

"I need to explain, don't I?"

"You do, but not yet."

"Not yet?"

"Let's enjoy breakfast first. It's a bit too early for confessionals." I took our plates and walked over to the sink.

"You enjoy the movie last night?" he said, bringing over the rest of the dirty mugs and glasses. "You feel asleep before the end."

"I've seen it like a billion times, don't worry."

"You like sad endings then?"

"Not necessarily. Not all the time. Just don't think all endings are always happy that's all."

"I always root for the bad myself. They normally deserve to win. They've normally worked harder for it."

"Well, you would say that."

"I'm not bad. Wrong side of good, but I'm not a bad person."

"Necessary evil I called you, didn't I?"

"You remember that?"

"I've got a good memory. Tour guide, right?"

"I was a tour guide in a former life, yes."

"What happened?"

"I got sacked."

"Nice work. How so?"

"Lost my passion for it. Got bored."

"Of tourists?"

"Celebrities, actually."

"I'm pretty bored of them too. Not much of a career change was it, tour guide to paparazzi?"

"I'm not paparazzi."

"You sure act like one," I said as I squirted washing-up liquid into running water.

"It wasn't planned, as I said, this won't be forever."

"What, till you get bored of me?"

"No till you go back home."

"Not long then, a few weeks. You don't fancy following me back to LA, then?"

"Don't think I'll ever go back to LA," he said, loading the dishwasher.

"Not even for me?"

"Not even for you, sorry."

"Do you wanna go in the garden? I can do the rest later. The sun is out, bit of a rarity in this country. Better embrace it whilst it lasts."

★ ★ ★

"Feels strange seeing it from this side," he said looking out across the garden. "Like I've gone from audience to stage."

"Perhaps I should hide somewhere and watch you all day. Give you a taste of your own medicine. Where is your little hideout?"

"Over by those trees," he pointed.

"I thought I'd searched over there."

"I'm good at covering my tracks. Lawn looks nice," he smiled.

"I guess you saw that then."

"Probably shouldn't use a lawnmower barefoot next time."

"You sound like my Frank."

We walked towards the stream, sitting on the cobbled wall, looking down at the water fizz and froth as bubbled under our feet.

"Looked far scarier last night. A much bigger drop in the dark."

"Still quite far down. You would've bust more than your knee if you'd fallen down there."

"Don't know what I was thinking. I doubt the current would've

30

been strong enough to carry me off, even if you hadn't been there. I probably wouldn't have drowned either, probably just broken a bone, got wet and cold, given myself a fever or something. Not the greatest attempt at suicide."

"Is that what it was? Suicide attempt? Sorry, I shouldn't be asking that."

"Lucky you were here to save the day, whatever attempt it was."

"If you wanna see far down, you wanna see the Humber Bridge. That's a jump you wouldn't get up from."

"Are we discussing suicide hot spots now?"

"I've not had the best year either. I've contemplated a similar jump."

"What stopped you?"

"I wish I knew."

We continued around the garden, a tour of sorts. Showed him my impressive herb collection, he said his mum would be jealous. We admired my herd of sheep, apparently he'd been introduced before, he'd even given them names, no wonder they never answered to me.

He stood at the mouth of the stream as we took it in turns to skim rocks across the surface. It appeared there was an art to it, an art I hadn't yet found and nor had he.

"Can I ask you a question?" he asked. "Off record."

"Go for it. I may not answer. We have only been friends for less than three hours."

"Why did you invite Max last night? I've been racking my brain and I just can't get my head round it. I just can't work out why he deserved a second chance."

"You think I was offering him a second chance? He passed second chance territory a long time ago."

"Is this the end then for you and him?"

"Probably not," I said as we took it in turns to throw our rocks.

"Shall I go?" he asked.

"Go where? Back to your little hideout?"

"Back to where I'm staying."

"What were you supposed to be doing today?"

"Following you."

I laughed. "What a ridiculous game we are playing."

"Look Lilly, if you want me to leave at any point then just say. I've overstayed my welcome as it is, feels like I'm crossing a line being here."

"Pinky promise the moment I feel you are crossing the line I will ask you to leave the building."

The doorbell buzzed, we looked towards the driveway, it was a white van.

"Looks like you've another one of your parcels."

"Who sends clothes on a Saturday?"

"Happens a lot, doesn't it, these free packages?"

"Too often. My bedroom looks like Macy's. I'll get us another coffee."

"No, I'm fine thank you. I'm gonna head off."

"Are you sure? I don't mind you being here."

"It's best I go." He started to walk towards the front gate.

"So, what happens next, Tom?"

"What do you mean?"

"Will my failed suicide attempt be on the cover of every newspaper tomorrow morning?"

"No, that can stay between me and you."

"And why should I believe you? Why should I trust you?"

He shrugged. "You're just gonna have to believe me."

"Please don't tell anyone about last night. I'm embarrassed enough without the whole word knowing. I'll pay you."

"No, Lilly, I don't want your money."

"And what do you want? Are you still gonna be in your little hideout following my every move?"

"My honest answer, I haven't thought that far, it's been a long night. I suppose so."

We stopped at the driveway.

"You gotta walk home?"

"No, my car is only up the road."

"Back to being enemies then, hey?"

"I don't know what we are, but not enemies, least not on my part."

"Thanks for last night."

"Any time. Thanks for the breakfast."

"Never know, if you here early enough tomorrow I'll save you some, wave you over. No point in both of us eating alone."

"I'd like that."

"What are you doing later?"

"Sleeping. Shower. After that, who knows? Back here I guess. Back to my little den."

"So, it goes back to normal. Me on one side of the stream and you on the other?"

"I think it has to. Doesn't mean you go jumping off bridges again."

"You could just knock, you know."

"Wouldn't it be awkward?"

"A little. I'd prefer to be spied on up close if I'm being honest, to my face, not behind some binocular lens, zoomed in on like a target."

"You don't have to do this, Lilly. Just because of what I did last night, it doesn't mean I'm owed anything from you. I know you don't like me. You have every right to ring the police and get me escorted off the property."

"I don't think I've decided yet what to do. This is a unique situation. You do what you need to do, and so will I. That's all I can say right now. But don't worry, I won't ring the police, I haven't the energy for an interrogation this morning."

Tom smiled, thanked me again as he walked out of my garden and up the hill, towards a car I couldn't see.

7

I felt better for a sleep, my body appreciated the mattress after a night upright on a couch. I didn't even get undressed, threw my bags down, threw myself on the bed, second time I'd fallen asleep in my clothes, but I was past caring. Woke up a few hours later to a knock at the door, Dot with a pot of tea and a handful of questions on last night's whereabouts. I lied of course, told her I'd stayed at a friend's, so technically there was some truth in it, she seemed satisfied with my explanation. She was more preoccupied with the mess of her sheets and the state of my clothes.

"Where does your friend live? In a bog?" she said complaining at the mud and grass, stripping the bed and then stripping me down to my T-shirt and pants, demanded I showered, said I smelt like a pond, before heading out the door with tuts and huffs.

Vince rang just after, too, full of questions, though he was harder to satisfy, but I lied the best I could, blamed the storm. A part of me wanted to tell him, I just wanted to tell someone, but I was right to keep it quiet. The worst person to tell would've been Vince, he would have turned it nasty, swung it to his advantage, I'd become an inside man, an agent. It was better he didn't know, I'd ring Mum instead, if I had to tell someone I'd rather it be someone who would be excitable for the right reasons and not for greed and wealth. Anyway, Vince asked to see whatever I had, said he'd be the judge on how good or bad the quality. I'd have to be diplomatic on what I'd send, think cleverly about what I'd give him, give him only enough so his sulk would last twenty-four hours.

God knows what I'd do next. My cover was blown. One thing was for sure it couldn't go back to what it was before, how could it?

Me with my binoculars, Lilly waving back, she was right, I might as well knock on the door from now on. Still didn't solve how Vince would make his money, eventually I would have to walk away, tell the truth or lie, either way my camera days were over.

But still, I would go back to Lilly, that was my plan. Why, I didn't know – in case Max came back? In case the paps turned up? I just didn't think she should be on her own, wasn't in the right emotional state to be left in a big old house in the middle of nowhere, just because she was smiling and looked fine, didn't mean she was.

Even if I didn't have the balls to knock on her door, better I was there behind a bush or tree, just in case she tried something silly again. I wondered when Frank or Sally were back, maybe Vince knew, if he didn't I was sure he could find out, till then I wouldn't leave or quit till they were, till she had someone there to look after her, to take over, make sure she was OK. After that I would go, tell Vince I was done and go back home for good.

In the meantime, she shouldn't be alone for too long. I ran a shower, in and out, put my clothes on just as quick, grabbed my car keys. Without my camera, I already felt a million times lighter.

8

I was sure Tom would come, I'd expected his arrival I just didn't know whether he would be behind a bush or on my doorstep. One thing was for sure, I didn't want to be indoors, despite my attempt at cleaning the house, it still smelt of failed barbecue and I didn't fancy staring at that stream any longer, puts you in a bad mood looking at the place you nearly topped yourself, staring at my noose only made me feel worse.

So, when I heard that knock on the door, let him in, us both standing there not quite sure how to deal with the situation, Tom standing there looking all awkward, like he'd run over my cat, the first thing I did was throw him a handful of towels, ordered him to take me to wherever he hides his Jeep.

"*Sugarland Express, Original Family Band, Wildcats.* Anything with Goldie Hawn in it. You?"

"*Shawshank, Rushmore, Pulp Fiction, Blue Velvet.*"

"I met Tarantino once. Toronto Film Festival."

Tom looked impressed. "No way. What was he like?"

"Talks really fast. He is pretty cool though. What can you say? He's Tarantino, he wouldn't be anything else."

"What did you talk about? Movies?"

"No, we talked about lunch boxes, actually."

"Please tell me you asked to be in his next movie."

"Hell, yes. Pretty much offered him a blow job in return."

"You didn't?"

"No, but I pretty much got on my knees and begged him. Disgraceful behaviour, really."

"Did he agree? To the movie, not the blow job?"

"Said he'd got some projects on the go. But as you may have noticed, I've not been in one of his movies yet, so I'm not holding my breath."

"That's pretty cool you met him though. Must be weird meeting your idols. Can't work out if that's a good or a bad thing."

"Mostly good. I've met a few arseholes, but most famous people are arseholes."

"Ever been star-struck?"

"All the time. Bumped into a Spice Girl at a basketball game, nearly wet myself. Met Melissa Joan Hart once, I think I actually did wet myself that time."

"I'll pretend I know who that is."

"Don't you have cable in England?"

"Cable? I came from a house with four channels."

"Well, anyway, I completely freaked out, made her sign my T-shirt, I told her I loved her. It was pretty awful to watch, I think she was pretty freaked out, I may have grabbed her arm."

"Have you met Goldie Hawn yet?"

"No. One day I will, though probably best I don't, I might do something regretful. What about you? Who would you like to meet?"

"Alive or dead?"

"Alive."

"That's hard."

"Dead then."

"Let me think." Tom pondered the sky. "Cash, Richey Edwards, Pollock. Milius. David Attenborough. Wait I don't think he's dead."

"No women? Interesting."

"Women are pretty dull."

"Not all of us."

"What about you?"

"I've always liked the crazy ones."

"They do make better dinner table companions. Is that your angle? The crazy one?"

"Not intentionally. My agent wishes I was crazier, he's already planning my autobiography. Says I need more peaks and troughs."

"You've done a pretty good job so far."

"I blame Hollywood. Always feels like someone else is winning. Better roles, more money, more billboards. Makes you do things out of character."

"Unless it is your character. Perhaps it just inflates it."

"You think I'm crazy, and Hollywood makes me crazier?"

"If it makes you feel any better. It made me crazy too."

"Perhaps I should see life somewhere a little less explosive. You know what it's like. You lived there, Tom. You've seen what it does to people."

"I loved Hollywood, actually. Hollywood treated me OK."

"Far from home, though. Don't you miss your family?"

Tom didn't answer, he looked busy with his eyes out front.

"What about you? You missing home? Missing your parents?"

"They're not those sorts of parents. My dad's always working, Mom too. We're close, but not too close."

"My Mum's not well actually, seeing lots of doctors and specialists. I'm hoping to go back soon, try to convince her to take it more seriously, get her some decent care. We fell out, she doesn't agree with my new profession."

"Not many do."

"Doesn't want to gain from any profit from it. Even if it means dying in an understaffed hospital to prove her point."

"I like your mom. She sounds ballsy."

"I still want to apologize, Lilly."

"What for, invasion of privacy? Trespassing? I could go on."

"Yes, those too. I wanna apologize for causing all this."

"All what? You didn't cause this circus, Tom, that wheel has been turning way before you showed up."

"But I still want to apologize."

"For what?"

"For London."

"That was you, was it? Peeking behind bushes in the middle of the night?"

"Sorry."

"How much did you make from it? Enough to help your mom?"

"If she lets me, that is."

"Then it was worth it, wasn't it?"

"I want you to get mad."

"The only person I get mad with is myself. I was the one to blame. I shouldn't have gone to see Max. I shouldn't have let him walk me home. I shouldn't have kissed him. I'm accountable, not you. It's all fucked up. I'm fucked up."

"Everyone is fucked up a little, just yours is documented."

"And that's what your role is in all this, is it, Tom? To document fuck-ups. My fuck-ups to be precise."

"Not just fuck-ups. Paparazzi document good things, too."

"Do they?"

"I admit it is very rare."

"Success doesn't sell newspapers. I wish it did."

"Well, I'm sorry either way. Fuck-up or success, I have no right to document either."

"Let's just agree that neither me nor you have to apologize for anything either of us has done before. Only what we do from now on. Does that sound fair?"

"Sounds fair to me."

"Hey, I recognize where we are now," I said, pointing to an ocean full of waves, begging to be surfed.

★ ★ ★

"And you 100% wanna do this?"

"Hell, yes. 100%."

"Feels risky," Tom said, his eyes looking at every angle, checking for colleagues. "We're definitely doing this?"

"Looks that way. Any sign of your guy?"

"Not yet," I said checking the rear view.

"You stay in the Jeep, I'll do a quick sweep to make sure we don't have any unexpected guests or followers. Try to look natural."

"OK, Spielberg."

Tom closed the door, as I buried myself in the hood of my jumper. I admit this had been a rash decision, like a lot I'd made lately. From garden, to Jeep, to beach without much thought process. I knew this was reckless, or it should have at least felt reckless, but it didn't feel that way, it just felt better than being sad.

I was thirsty. I searched for water, no luck, I checked the glovebox: a diary, a torch, a few photos, no water. I looked briefly at the photo, a woman and a little girl, his wife maybe, his daughter, his niece. I felt bad for snooping, closed the glovebox, returned to looking out of the window. Then there was a tap on the roof. It was Dave, all smiles and warmth. I wound down the window.

"You better be amped, miss, we got great wind. You picked a good day."

"Looks beautiful."

"No Dick Dale today. Where's big man?"

"Who, Frank? He's back in LA."

"Shame, would've liked to see him surf. No matter. Just you today then? I thought you said two over the phone."

"Two, yes. My friend is just walking back. He'll be here in any minute."

"Do you wanna come and we'll pick you out a suit? You shouldn't need gloves and boots today seeing as the sun has shown up."

"Do you mind if I wait till my friend comes back first?"

"Sure. I'll be over by the van sorting my shit out."

"Is it just us out there today?"

"Got a group of eight coming in a couple of hours. Few more

40

may turn up on the off chance. Just you two so far, though. You sure you don't want a lesson or do you two feel OK out there on your own?"

"We'll be fine."

"Looks like your friend is back," he said, pointing, as we both looked over at Tom trekking back down the dunes, big smile on his face, two huge thumbs up.

Five minutes later I was topless in a van, the smell of dog and damp wetsuits.

★ ★ ★

To his credit, Tom could surf, I was better of course, but not by much, we had enough skills to not embarrass one another. We'd surfed for a good while, till our arms hurt, pretty decent waves too, hardly riding giants, but enough to get the heart racing, but it didn't last long. After a succession of decent waves, the current shifted, like it had turned over in bed. Suddenly what a moment before was break after break, was now perfect calm, the ocean still, no more white fizz and froth. Gave me and Tom a chance to catch our breath again, sit on our surfboards, take it all in.

"I still can't believe I'm surfing with Lilly Goodridge. I keep having moments when I'm all right with it, then I start to freak out."

"Please no freaking out. Don't become one of those people that weird out on me."

"I'll try not to. It is hard though. You are pretty famous, you know. This shit doesn't happen every day."

"If you'd met me two years ago I'd just be plain old Lilly."

"You don't like being famous, do you?"

"And what is that based on? Our twelve-hour relationship?"

"Remember, I have read a lot about you. You're my specialist subject."

"I'm OK with fame. I know my place. They'll get bored of me soon, probably already have. How many photos have you taken

41

of me. Just you alone? I bet you've taken hundreds. And then multiply that by all the other paparazzi. Even I'm bored of me."

"Two."

"Two what?"

"I've taken two photos of you."

"I doubt that."

"I've taken hundreds. I've only had two photos go to print though."

"You serious?"

"Serious."

"You must be the worse paparazzi of all time."

"Completely agree."

I wiped my mouth with my arm, tried to get rid of the taste of salt. "You must've taken more surely?"

"I have taken hundreds, yes, but nothing of any value, nothing TMZ would find interesting. Most of the time I don't even bring my camera with me."

"You're definitely the worse paparazzi of all time."

"I'm not paparazzi."

"You are the anomaly, aren't you? What are you then? A stalker?"

"Not intentionally but yes, stalker seems about right."

"Don't worry, I've had stalkers before. Just promise not to fondle me in my sleep. Well if you do, at least do it quick."

"I promise not to fondle you asleep or otherwise."

"Joking aside. I don't really understand your purpose now, Tom. You are hardly setting the world on fire in this career of yours."

"Welcome to my world."

"What is it you want?"

"What everyone wants. Money."

"And what would you do with this money?"

"Start a new life."

"And how much would you need to do that? Ballpark figure?"

"I don't know. How do you put a figure on that?"

"Easy."

"I couldn't say."

"Well surely you agree your stalking days are over. I know where you hide out. I know who you are."

"My paparazzi career does seem to have become a little complicated."

"I could pay you off."

"Pay off what?"

"Give you enough money to leave me alone."

"I wouldn't accept."

"It would suit both parties."

"Not both."

"You sound like your mom now."

"I suppose everyone has a point they don't cross."

"I haven't found mine yet."

"I appreciate the offer, Lilly."

"Good, means you get to keep me company a little longer."

"Spy to pet in one fell swoop."

"Shall we head back in? My eyes sting and if I don't take the surfboard back over those dunes now I never will."

★ ★ ★

"That's an unusual tattoo," I said, talking to his back as we carried our boards back to land. "I haven't seen anything like that before."

"Chang Mai. Done with bamboo."

"Sounds painful."

"It wasn't actually. Carrying these boards is worse. You OK? Do want to stop again?"

"I'm OK. Ask me again in a couple of minutes," I said, out of breath. "Any other body art?"

"The one on my chest I got in LA. I've got one on my foot, a tribal thing. I don't like it to be honest."

"Where did you get it done?"

"Auckland."

"Bamboo too?"

"Chisel and mallet actually," sensing the deliberate sarcasm

"What's the one on the arm? What does it say? I can't see from here."

"Useless generation."

"Sounds very anarchic, Tom."

"I was sixteen in Skegness. I was rebelling."

"And what were you rebelling against?"

"Nothing. I just wanted to wear eye liner mostly."

"Didn't realize you were so international."

"That's me. Thailand to Skegness. Global jet-setter."

"Mine are far less exotic. Heart on the top of my leg, my friend did it. He was into body modification. It was a mistake to let him do it, but I was fifteen and impressionable. That's pretty much it. Unless you count all the piercings in my ears."

"You have a tattoo on your finger, don't you?"

"How do you know about that?"

"Can't even remember. Some website."

"Done your research haven't you?"

"What's the six mean?"

"Means I made another mistake."

"Least it was only a little mistake."

"Was it?" I laughed. I didn't even know why. "Can we stop now?"

"Sure," he replied, as we dropped our surfboards to the sand, looking towards the dunes yet to come.

Back at the van, the car park had filled, the nice weather had brought them out in droves. Dave looked busy, sorting out money, getting people in and out of wetsuits. Again, it was mostly men, big men with beards and bellies, naked or half naked, even saw a penis. Tom and I were exhausted, hands on our knees as we got our breath back.

"Tom!" Dave shouted through the bodies. "Not too bad out there, bra. Need to get up a bit quicker, stay low once you're up. Lillian, you just need to paddle a bit harder, build up your speed." He threw us both a bottle of water. It was gone within seconds, still couldn't shift the taste of salt.

"Hey, if you two fancy it tomorrow, I'll be here around ten or thereabouts."

I looked at Tom, he looked at me. We shared a similar expression, told Dave we'd let him know.

"Lillian." Dave came closer. "Do you mind if I ask you a little favour? Just in case we don't see you down here again."

"Sure," I said, attempting to unzip myself.

"Do you mind if I have your autograph before you head off?" he whispered. "My wife is a huge fan."

"How long have you known?" I said, feeling myself blush.

"All along, I'm afraid. Don't worry, your secret is safe. You're just another girl in a wetsuit as far as the punters are concerned. Oh, by the way fella." Dave was talking to Tom. "Someone was asking about your Jeep, man."

"My Jeep?"

"Said he was your friend."

"Did he give a name?"

"No, fella. Just asked who you were with."

"And what did you say?"

"Said I didn't know. He asked if you had an American with you too. He was a strange dude, Russian maybe, Polish. He didn't hang around for long. Don't think he likes you much, didn't seem too happy."

"Thanks for the heads up."

On the drive back to my house, my hair still wet, my eyes still stinging, I asked Tom who his friend was. Tom said he wasn't a friend. I asked if he was his partner, asked if we should be worried, he said no both times. I didn't know if he was protecting me or exposing me. I felt uncomfortable with both.

Back at the house I offered Tom a beer from under the sink.

"Sorry if it's a bit warm."

"Funny place to keep beer."

"Needs must."

My cell buzzed, I read it quickly.

"My agent. He's sending me a couple of scripts to look over."

Tom looked impressed. "You know what for?"

"Not sure. They sound quite a big deal."

"I don't why but when I think of agents I just think of *Jerry Maguire*. Show me the money and all that."

"What, my Ralph? You're not far off. There's not much Polo about Ralph. He's a slime ball but he makes me rich, apparently."

"Must be exciting though," he said. "Being sent scripts."

"You haven't read them."

"Nothing good then?"

"No, that's the sad thing. Nothing groundbreaking. Mostly predictable."

"There must be one, surely? They can't all be duds."

"They're all the same movie. No matter what film, I'm still down to play the damaged one, the one with problems. For me it's the same movie, just on a different location with different types of damage and problems. I must just have a face people like to see suffer."

"Or people just believe in what they are seeing."

"Great, so you're saying I'm both damaged and a bad actress. Anything else?"

"I'd just be happy to be in a movie, credible or otherwise."

"I shouldn't moan but I do. I know one of them is a Michael Bay production."

"Michael Bay? You'll be saving the world in some capacity then. Blowing up meteors or fighting robots."

"Either way I'll be in a short skirt."

"You don't have a very high opinion of yourself?"

"I can't act, silly. I thought you knew that."

"I wouldn't say it's imperative these days."

"Thanks for the boost of confidence."

"I didn't say you couldn't act. I'm just impartial. Besides judging by your popularity, being you seems to be working just fine."

"I'm just playing with you. I act OK, not the best but not the worst. You ever acted?"

"No. I'd be awful. Tried out at school, but it was painful. I think acting is something you are born with."

"I disagree. You know I went to acting school?"

"I didn't know that."

"Really? I thought that was public knowledge."

"Where?"

"Beverly Hills Playhouse. You gonna ask why I went?"

"I wasn't actually. I would've thought most actors did the same."

"You'd be surprised how many don't. They see it as a flaw, admitting that they aren't the finished article. Be like a doctor going back to med school. People assume once you've made the big screen then you're qualified, after that the education stops."

"Must have felt a bit weird, sitting amongst all those students. You being you and all that."

"It was more than weird, on my part mostly, they couldn't give two craps. They just treated me the same as anyone else."

"Did you get a lot of it?"

"Oh lots. I'm glad I went. I had far too many limitations before. I still have some, just not so many."

"You said 'went'. You stopped going?"

"I had to stop going. Got found out, started hounding the students, it wasn't fair on them so I just stopped going."

"Shame."

"Shame indeed. What about you? What's your story?"

Just as Tom went to answer, there was a knock at the door, startling us both.

"That's weird. I don't know who that'd be."

"Better check it's not the paps."

"Good idea," I said as I went to the games room for a closer look. "Fuck, it's Max."

"Max? What do you want me to do? Ask him to leave?"

"No, that'll make things worse."

Another knock on the door.

"Don't answer it."

"My car is outside. He knows I'm here. Tom, just go upstairs or something."

Another knock.

"You sure?"

"Go. I'll be fine." Tom dashed past me as I took a deep breath and opened the door.

★ ★ ★

"What are you doing here, Max?" I said through the gap in the door.

"I brought flowers."

"I don't want them, Max. Now isn't a good time. Can you please just go."

"You running a car dealership here? Jeeps and Jags."

I went to close the door.

"Lilly, please don't. I haven't come here for another fist fight. I've come to say sorry for last night. I was drunk and crass. I acted like a brute. I deserved that slap."

"Aren't you tired of apologizing?"

"Not when it's the right thing to do. Look, my flight leaves soon. I don't want things left like this. Please can I come inside, just for a few minutes?"

"Max, I'm not feeling great."

"I promise I will be quick as a flash," he said as I let him in, or he let himself in, I couldn't tell which.

"You fixed the electricity then I see. I'm impressed."

"Max, I'm really tired. I accept your apology, but I don't think we should see each other for a while. Whatever else you need to say, just say it and go."

"Look, when I head home I'm going to try and get my head round our next move, like I said, our situation is delicate, I need to understand how to let it play out. For the time being just leave the talking to me. I'll speak to Sally and your team, make sure we are all on the same page."

"I'll speak to Sally. Sally is not your employee, Max. I'll fill her in, not you."

"Less snarling, Lilly. I'm not starting a dogfight."

"Max, I want to make one thing crystal-clear. After that shit you pulled last night, there is no me and you, or ever will be. So, any plans you have to involve me in your grand schemes you best leave me out."

"Lilly, look…"

"No, you listen, Max. What I do from now on is of my concern. And whether I choose to be on your side or against you is my business. But don't think for one minute your career is top of my agenda. In fact, right now, watching you fail and plummet seems a lot more rewarding than seeing you succeed."

"I thought we could be civilized."

"I'm in a pretty far fucking place from civilized, Max. Now for the last time take your fucking bouquet and fuck off back to Tinsel Town."

Max looked at me, smiling, waiting for my face to change, which it didn't.

"If that's what you want."

"That is what I want."

"You might as well keep these. I doubt they'll let me take them on the plane." He placed the flowers on the side, as he noticed the two half-drunk beer bottles. "Didn't have to search too far in the end did you, Lilly?" he said, pointing at them. "Still cold, too." He picked one up, looking through the kitchen, up the stairs. "You call me when you're less busy entertaining."

★ ★ ★

Once Max's car had gone, Tom came back downstairs.

"How are you? That was pretty close. You think he knew someone was here?"

"Is it all right if you go too, Tom?" I was sat facing away from him, looking out across the garden. "I've enjoyed today, I really have, but I think it's a bad idea what we are doing. Thank you again for what you did last night, honestly, I can't thank you enough. But it's for the best we leave things as they are, end on good terms now rather than let things turn sour. I hope you understand. It's just better this way."

He said something back, that he understood, or that he was sorry, either way he left straight away, another door slammed, another man being asked to leave.

9

"Dot, here, hold my arm."

"I'm fine," she said mid-breath, trailing behind.

"You're not. Hold my arm."

"Tom, leave me be. I'm just old that's all, just takes me a little longer. I have done this before you know, more times than I can remember."

"I'm looking out for you. Don't want you going over the edge, that's all."

"I appreciate the concern, but as far as I can tell these cliffs haven't changed in the fifty-nine years I've been up and down them."

"Well, if you tumble to your death I won't be held responsible. Has anyone actually ever died up here?"

"No one I know. Though it's seen a few shipwrecks in its time."

"Really?"

"Probably why they felt the need to put up a lighthouse. Those rocks down there are a death trap. Seabed full of sailors' bones, I bet."

We carried on walking, watching, taking it all in. The sea looked rough but I couldn't hear it through the wind and birds. The ocean looked busy, tiny ships in the distance, tiny teenagers jumping off rocks twice their size. Through my binoculars I could make out a cluster of houses, roofless and abandoned. I was on the edge of England, about to fall off.

"Not a bad way to spend a lunchtime is it? Whilst most of the country are sat behind some desk looking at percentages."

"It's impressive, I'll give you that."

"I'm surprised you haven't brought your camera. You don't get much better views than this."

"I'm surprised Alfred let you come."

"He'll be in a sulk when I get back, no doubt, moaning about how hard he's had to work, how much his back hurts, the big girl. When are you going to tell me the real reason why we are both here today? Why I'm on top of the world, rather than at the bottom of an ironing pile?"

"I told you. Just fancied a day out."

"Just seems peculiar. A Monday seems a strange day to have off. In fact, you having a day off at all is very out of sync for you."

"Thought it would be nice, that's all."

"Everything is all right, though? No problems at work is there?"

"No nothing like that. Just felt like doing something spontaneous."

"Well, as long as you'd tell me if anything was bothering you. I'd like to think I'm someone you can confide in."

"Course I'd tell you. But I'm fine, Dot, honest."

"Back at work tomorrow then, or should I plan for more of your new unbridled spontaneity?"

"Ha ha. Yes, I'm back at work."

A family walked past, we exchanged smiles as their dogs sniffed the cliff's edge like they were about to jump off, before dashing back towards their parents' ankles.

"I'd like to see some of your work one day, if you'll ever let me. Never know, I could pick out a few I liked, get Alfred to hang them up around the house. I've always complained our walls lack a bit of activity. A nice seascape, perhaps, a pretty field. Be nice for people to look at whilst they eat their full English. Hey, after the lighthouse, do you fancy a pot of tea?"

"Sounds nice."

"Good. There is a place not too far. I know the owner. Warm ourselves up before we head back to civilization and chores.

Thanks for me bringing, Tom, it's nice to get out, I don't do it enough, seeing as it's all bang on my doorstep."

"It's been a pleasure, Dot."

"We should both give ourselves more days off like this, living here sometimes I take it for granted, it's not if as if I'll be able to climb up here forever. Thank you for making me remember, giving me an incentive to explore again. Feel like I'm a teenager again, bringing boys up here for views and a little bit of something else if they were lucky," she laughed.

We went quiet, taking in the view, breathing in the coastline, breathing out all that was in our heads.

"Dot, today wasn't really my day off. There's more to it than that."

"Oh."

"I'm not really a freelance photographer either."

"So, what's all the camera equipment for? Why are you here?"

"It's a long story."

"Well we have a long way back so now is as good a time as any," she said, linking my arm, heading towards the lighthouse, like we were looking at the end of England's chin.

★ ★ ★

"What you going to do tomorrow, Tom? I can't go walking every day, it will take me a week to recover from this one."

"I don't know. I really have no idea what to do next. Go home. It seems the right time to call it quits."

"I wouldn't give up too soon. If you've gone this far, you might as well see it through."

"I'm not knocking on her door, Dot. She made it clear that I wouldn't be invited in again."

"Then that will be her call." She sipped her tea. "And besides. us girls to tend to change our minds."

"I don't think Lilly will change hers."

"Then at least you'll be there when she does."

10

When England first got discussed, when the film got the green light and I got the part, Sally's initial idea was to have the three of us living under the one roof. Tried to sell the idea of us being one big family, dinners round the table, movie nights, and although it sounded tempting I pretty much put a halt to her plans from the off. Of course, she sulked for a few days, took it personally, but once she and Frank had sorted out alternative accommodation not too far away from mine, she soon changed her tune. To be honest it made little difference, they might as well have lived with me, the amount of time they'd spent here. Though, to be fair, that was mostly my fault, it was normally me asking them to come, or asking them to stay, most days we'd all be sat watching TV, or watching each other cook stuff. To a point where I felt a little guilty when it reached the natural time for them to leave, when all our eyes were half closed in front of the fire and the last thing they'd both want to do is get into their cold cars and drive back to their cold little houses and cold little beds. In reality, this house was a wrong choice. Far too big for just little old me, probably too big even if I had agreed for us all to live together. Someone obviously assumed I needed big rooms and lots of them, an assumption which happens a lot, when you're famous you get used to being offered more than you need and most of the time you take it. Most of the time the size of the house never bothered me, at night times, with all the creaks and shadows but otherwise the three of us coming in and out made it always feel like there was something to do or something to talk about.

I was missing Frank and Sally today, it was weird not having them around, I wasn't used to hearing my own thoughts and being in control of my day. I was in a strange mood anyway, girl problems that made my stomach go sideways and my hormones up and down. So, there I was, two days later, torn between being productive and being idle. So far, I'd been both, slouched about feeling guilty, attempted chores I didn't finish, but I enjoyed neither. Truth was, I was bored and it was hard to be bored knowing there was someone equally lonely watching me through a camera lens about fifty yards across the garden. Unless what I told him the night before scared him off. I hoped not.

11

The girl came over for a second time and asked me if I wanted anything to drink. I said I was fine, didn't want people to think I was taking advantage seeing as I'd already had the tour, already raided the buffet counter. I was trying to blend into the background, look as if being on a film set was nothing out of the ordinary.

I felt a bit useless sat watching, I should have been picking up some lighting rig or talking into a headset. Everyone had a purpose, carrying, discussing, pointing, scribbling. I was surprised at how calm it had been, being a fan of serious films with serious themes. I was prepared for intensity, actors suffering for their role, getting into character, channelling inner turmoil, every staff member being pushed to their physical and emotional limits. So far, I hadn't seen much directing, whatever direction was required had already been done. The room knew what to do, and when to do it, without prompting or pushing. I think I preferred the other extreme, though who's to say this method wasn't effective? I'd have to wait till I'd watched it in its entirety, on the big screen or on my TV. I still couldn't help but stare though, I couldn't help it, I was a movie fan, sweeping the floor looked important, a man analysing sunlight looked vital. Just to have a job on a film set was something loud to shout about and I was both jealous and intrigued.

The set was amazing, arches upon arches. You'd think an Englishman like me would be used to such grandeur. Lilly warned me on the drive here, that it would take a few visits, said she spent a week with her mouth open every time she walked into a room or garden, a fixed gawp upon every new ceiling. I couldn't see Lilly anywhere, I hadn't seen her for over an hour. She'd predicted there was a chance I would have to be on my own a lot today, I said I didn't mind, there was enough going on around me to keep me occupied.

It looked like something was about to happen. Extras were being handled, their outfits and hair being tucked in or loosened. Housemaids and footmen even looked impeccable. I tucked my shirt into my jeans, in a room full of curled moustaches and bowler hats, the least I could do was to be tucked in too.

A gentleman in suit and tails sat down beside me, started to mess with his cuffs and waistcoat, before finally acknowledging our proximity, nodding the way a lord might have nodded. I returned the gesture, it was all very dignified, like two kings holding court.

We sat for a while, him mentally preparing himself I expected, me pretending not to be mentally examining my new neighbour. I'd seen him on TV, I knew that much, just didn't know when or what in, he had the face of a bureaucrat, a villain, someone noble. It wouldn't have surprised me if he'd been in an adaptation, Dickens probably, one of those period actors whose voice was meant for a different decade, his beard a different century, a man born in the wrong era.

"Going over your lines?" I asked him, regretting it as soon as it left my mouth.

"Sorry, did you say lines?"

"If you need me to run through the scene with you whilst we wait, I don't mind."

"I think I'll be fine, young man. If I don't know it by now I never will."

"Is Lilly in this scene? Lady Alcot, I mean?"

"Yes. I'm about to tell her off actually. Lady Alcot has been frolicking in London with men of colour. I'm about to go all parental and stern. It doesn't come naturally, believe me."

"No children then?"

"Me? Heavens no. I'm as queer as a football bat. What's your role in all this?"

"No role fortunately. I'm just a guest. I'm a friend of Lady Alcot's."

"Young Lilly. Great girl. Marvellous attitude. Lovely breasts too which I shouldn't really say seeing as technically I am her father. So how do you know the delightful Lilly Goodridge?"

I paused, probably seconds, but it felt longer.

"I'm a photographer, actually."

"Oh, how splendid. You could take some of me. Or is just the young and pretty ones that you're interested at pointing your camera at?"

"Actually, I'm paparazzi. Or was paparazzi, I should say. I don't know why I just told you that, it was the one thing I wasn't supposed to do. Is it too late to pretend you didn't hear that?"

"You and I shouldn't really get on, seeing as I detest paparazzi. I'm lucky enough that they've stopped bothering me now. My days of hedonism ended in a field in Altamont, after that I started to behave myself, since then I'm deemed low profile. Means they leave me alone which is fine with me. Means I can walk my dogs without threat of my wrinkles getting anywhere near a front page."

"If it makes it sound any better, I've only been paparazzi for a month."

"Good for you. Awful creatures those people, well, they're not even people. Their cameras hanging from their necks like big black dildos, a statement of intent. And they're multiplying in numbers, moving around the corners and holes in filthy little groups. Little packs chasing innocent little darlings like my poor Lilly Goodridge. You know the collective noun for rats? A group of rats is called a mischief."

"Seems about right. Paparazzi are similar vermin."

"Don't know what the collective noun for paparazzi should be?" he paused. "A fuckery," he said, bursting out laughing. "A fuckery of paparazzi. I like it. And you can assure me you are no longer a threat to my Lilly?"

"Only her best interests are at heart, I promise. I'm Tom by the way." I offered him my hand to shake.

"Wait a minute. Are you Tom? The Tom?"

"Yes."

"Lilly was telling me about you this very morning."

"How much did she tell?"

"Well she failed to mention your profession that's for sure. Not sure if she's quite made up her mind yet if truth be told. How did this all transpire? She never said how the two of you met either."

"Luck mainly. Different circumstances she never would've even looked at me. I was the right friend at the right time."

"Then you don't know Lilly at all, young man. She treats people all the same. You should know that by now."

"Even paparazzi?"

"Yes, even paparazzi," he smiled. "Unlikely friendship, isn't it? The Actress and the Paparazzi."

"It is unusual, I guess. Opposite worlds."

"It's a theme tried and tested, Tom. We all love unlikely friendships. Foxes and hounds, ladies and tramps."

"So, I'm the tramp?" I laughed.

"Yes, in that scenario, yes, you would be the tramp. Is the tramp a little smitten for the lady?"

"I've only known her for a few days."

"That's a load of old piff. Time isn't a factor. Do you like the girl?"

"We're just friends. We're not even friends, really. We've spent a few days with each other, that's all."

"And now a second, now a third. Could it ever be more than friends?"

"That would that never happen. For lots of reasons."

"What reasons?"

"Well…"

Suddenly names were being called. A man came over.

"Looks like it's my turn." He was being ushered across the

room. "My turn to shine. Time to be the assertive voice of reason to my rebellious daughter." Now his jacket was being fiddled with. "I'm not sure of your intention with Lilly and it's not my business to get involved, my life is complicated enough. As long as you are both having fun and no one is getting hurt, the rest is just overcomplication."

"No one is getting hurt, I promise," I said, as he was escorted to his mark.

★ ★ ★

I think we finally left the set around six. In the Jeep on the way home food had been the only topic of conversation. A day of filming had left us ravenous, even me, though all I'd done was sit and snack.

"We could go to the Oyster Shack?" Lilly talking to the window. "I could so eat a lobster right now."

"It's not far from here, actually. Well, depending on the tide that is. May have to go the long route."

"Be nice for you to have a seat, Tom, seeing as last time you were in the bushes."

"That wasn't me, remember. That was Vince."

"Of course, I keep forgetting about your evil twin. Shall we go? I mean I'm not dressed for it, but I won't be alone, half the restaurant was in vests and shorts before."

"You don't think it's too risky? Paps will be out and about."

"How would they know? Is anyone following us?" she said looking over her shoulder.

"Not that I can tell. But still I think it would be safer to lay low. They are cleverer than you think. Eyes everywhere."

"OK, spoilsport."

The car went quiet, it was an easy silence, fields vast and green, rivers dotted with boats, it was a view that was easy to slip into, without the need to fill it with noise.

"Sorry for the other day, by the way."

"Sorry for what?"

"For asking you to leave. All that stuff I said."

"That's OK. You don't have to explain yourself."

"I just panicked a little. Got a bit freaked by this whole situation."

"I can understand that. I'm a little freaked out myself. What made you change your mind?"

"Just silly, me watching you, you watching me."

"How did you know I'd be watching? How did you know I hadn't quit?"

"You don't strike me as someone who quits."

"Well, I appreciate the change of heart. I've had a great day. An amazing day. But don't feel like you need to, if you want to have a day to yourself, or even a whole week. We don't need to see each other tomorrow if you don't want to, I won't be offended. If you need your space, just say. I don't want you to feel, like, pressured into hanging out with me."

"To be fair I haven't even thought about tomorrow. Still got the rest of tonight yet before that."

"That is true."

"I'm so hungry," stamping her feet playfully, 'what is it with this place? In LA food was the last thing on my mind, some days I had to remember to eat. Here my whole day is geared around when and where my next meal might be."

"Try my glovebox. They're should be something edible in there. I'm used to eating on the go."

"No food in here. Books and maps, I'm afraid," she said rummaging through. "What's this?"

"What's what?"

"Tom, you naughty boy."

"What?"

She'd found Ludo's weed, she held it up in front of me.

"It's not even mine, well it is, it was a gift, an unwanted gift."

"Don't worry, Pablo, I'm not the DEA. How long you had it?"

"Not long."

"Is it good?" she opened the bag, gave the inside a sniff.

"Not sure, I haven't tried it."

"You do smoke, right?"

I nodded. "You?"

"If the mood fits," she held the little bag in front of her. "I tell you what, Tom. Decision time. Either we go to the Oyster Shack, eat lobster, probably get hounded by paparazzi. Or we stay home and smoke some pot. Your call."

"Both are risky."

"Tom, come on, *Sophie's Choice* time. Lobster pot or smoking pot?"

★ ★ ★

"Are sheep clever?" Lilly sat cross-legged with one on her lap.

"Not especially."

"Do you think they know who I am? I mean, I feed them like every day."

"I guess they must do to an extent."

"They seem to like me."

"That might be the food, not you."

"No, they like me for more than my food." Lilly threw them more bread. "There's an emotional attachment."

"You do realize sheep don't eat bread?"

"These do. Especially Maude," she said, ruffling Maude's head as it chewed and chewed.

I burst out laughing.

"What?"

"You do know Maude is a boy?"

"Fuck off." She looked for genitals that weren't there. "I'm guessing Harold is a girl too. Better swap them round."

"Cool names, by the way."

"My mom was a big Cat Stevens fan." She passed the sheep more bread. "Well, that's the last of it," she said as we left the sheep to fight over crumbs, heading back down the garden.

"When are Frank and Sally back?"

"Not long. Monday coming."

"Five days."

"Yep. We better make the most of it. We won't be strolling round the garden half cut when Frank comes back, that's for sure. Not sure how long it will be till he finds you lurking outside either."

"If I'm here at all."

"You will be, won't you?"

"I'm not sure. Here, Lilly, come over here at minute." I walked over to the fence and started to climb. "I wanna show you something."

"I'm not dressed for scaling heights."

"I wouldn't class chest level as high."

"Well you aren't wearing my jeans, are you?"

Once over the fence I guided her through the cluster of trees, Lilly a few yards ahead of me, walking through the tall grass, meadows behind her, sun-dappled. I was watching a perfume commercial, a jeans advert. Looking at Lilly made me think of all things summer, made me want to drink Coke from a glass bottle, made me want to hold her hand.

"Where are you taking me, Tom? Is this the part where you murder me? I always knew it was coming. Though I always envisaged it being in the dark, not during a sunset. If you are, can you do it after we've had dinner, so I can die on a full stomach?"

"What is it with you and death? You're always bringing it up."

"Am I? Depressing isn't it? Fear of growing old, I suppose."

"I can't wait till I get old. That way I can sit and read all day, watch tons of movies."

"That bit I'm cool with," she passed me back the joint, it was nearly gone, "I'm just scared of how screwed up I'll be by then. I don't want to get to seventy and still be scratching away for the last tiny piece of fame, still have paparazzi at my door getting photo footage of my body ageing and deteriorating."

"That doesn't happen. Us paparazzi are only after the young

ones now. As soon as you hit fifty we'll leave you alone."

"I wish that was the case. You heard of Marla Miller?"

"Course. She's been in tons."

"I met her in London. You were there, remember?"

"That's right. You presented an award together. She had the room in stitches."

"Well, she is everything I'm scared about."

"In what way?"

"In every way. She is still having facelifts, I'm not even kidding. She still has an agent."

"Surely movie stars retire?"

"Not many. She says they're all the same. They still want that notoriety, they still want to be worshipped."

"Sad, isn't it? But you're not like her."

"Not now. Give me forty years and it wouldn't surprise me if I'm begging directors and surgeons for another crack of the whip."

"I suppose for some people, it doesn't matter what they have, it won't ever be enough. Fame is a drug, probably the worst of all is, it's legal."

"I just wish there was something I could do for her. Y'know, one last hurrah."

"And you think giving Marla 'one last hurrah,' as you put it, would be enough? Women like her will always want more. You could always twist someone's arm. Ask someone if she can have a part in something."

We came to the spot.

"So, what is it you want to show me?"

"My office," I said pointing over to the tree where I'd spent most of the last few weeks.

"Is this career day then, show and tell?" she walked over to its huge trunk, out of the sun and into the shadows. "I show you my work, you show me yours."

"I think yours is more impressive than mine. I can't compete with a film set."

64

"It's not that bad," Lilly knelt down and looked through the gap in the bushes and branches, towards the house lit up across the garden. "Looks pretty. I can't believe how close you are. I can literally see right into the kitchen. Could you hear any of our conversations?"

"Not normally, depended on the wind believe it or not, and how vocal you were all being. But no, most of the time I couldn't hear a word."

"I'm trying to think of any embarrassing things I may have done whilst you were watching."

"Well, there was the time you jumped off a bridge."

"OK, arsehole I walked into that." She nudged my arm.

"No embarrassing stuff really. Just normal things, quite sweet things."

"Like what?"

"Silly things. You dancing in the garden, goofing around with Frank. Private things that no one had a right to see."

"Must've felt uncomfortable."

"It did. The amount of times I wished I could've just come and sat with you guys. I mean watching you in the glorious sunshine, jug of iced water, reading a book. And there's me in the mud and shadows and sweat. You must have had some clue there might have been someone out there. You and Frank must've predicted you'd have visitors."

"Not me. I don't deal with that sort of stuff. But Frank planned for it I guess, he used to go out every once in a while, check no one was around. Glad he didn't find you. If you hadn't been here that night I'd be washed up in some ocean or river somewhere."

"I suppose that's the one positive of having a stalker. There's always someone two steps behind."

"Don't laugh, but that actually went through my head. That's probably why I jumped. Perhaps I knew someone would save me."

"What, you knew I was watching you?"

"Not you, but I sensed someone was out there."

"What, did you hear me?"

"No, never. But I just had this feeling. It's hard to explain, I just knew I wasn't alone. I still can't believe I didn't realize this was your spot. I remember Frank checking everywhere after those photos hit, including here."

"What can I say? I cover my tracks well."

"Frank must be getting sloppy."

★ ★ ★

"Do you actually watch movies from the present day? Or do they have to be made before 1960?"

She laughed. "Bad, really, seeing as I'm an actress and all. I should take a mild interest in present day, shouldn't I? Natalie Wood is so pretty isn't she?" Lilly pointed at the screen. "Warren Beatty's pretty hot, too. I'm going to grab us something sugary." She jumped up from the sofa across the room. "Weed brings out my sweet tooth."

"You want me to pause this?" I went to grab the remote control.

"Not on my account. I've seen it like a trillion times. Don't worry I'll pretend I'm surprised. I'll probably cry a little too, I normally do." She closed the door, leaving me in the dark with the curtains closed.

I put a few more logs on the fire, more coal.

"Here, cookies and pot. Doesn't get much better than that does it?" she said, sitting herself back in the dent of the sofa, passing me a plate.

"Homemade?"

"I could lie but I won't, Sally eats them, hides them away thinking I don't know where." She grabbed a lighter off the side table. "This is the last joint we have by the way."

"I don't think I'll have much more, Lilly, you have it. It's been a little while since I smoked like this, I don't wanna turn green and start yacking in your sink."

66

"And there was me thinking you was a seasoned vet." She took a drag, inhaled and exhaled. "So what did I miss?" she said, pointing at the TV.

"The father doesn't look in a good way. I think he's about to lose everything."

Lilly leant over and grabbed the remote.

"What you doing? I was watching that." Lilly was fast-forwarding the film again.

"I always skip the sad bits."

It was a strange movie to choose. Love against all odds, abortion, gossip, suicide, beauty. Perhaps this was Lilly's way of dealing with her own situation. One day she might tell me why she jumped that night, rather than making it into an anecdote we can both joke about. But it wasn't a joke, I saw the state she was in that night. She meant to jump and she knew what that fall might have led to. For now, I'd have to make do with half-truths and let the TV screen do the talking for her. Speak for yourself, Tom, I thought. I was hardly an open book, was I? Both as bad as each other. Desperate to tell the truth, but scared of what our sincerity might bring.

"I've been thinking," she said, mouthful of cookie. "Why don't you go home?"

"You want me to leave?"

"No, not now. I mean why don't you go *home* home?"

"Cos this is my job."

"I very much doubt this is what the job entailed. Anyways, Vince wouldn't know would he? It's not like I'm going to tell him and I know how much you miss home."

"I suppose I could go, couldn't I?"

"I promise I will be on my best behaviour. You won't be missing much. I will be under house arrest until your return."

"Sounds a good idea."

"I know. I'm full of them."

We went back to the movie, well she may have done, my mind was somewhere else.

I didn't want to go home, well I did, but not yet, not now. It should have been good news, news that any father who hadn't seen his daughter should have jumped at. But in all honesty, that wasn't how I felt. Selfishly, wrongfully, regretfully, I was enjoying my time with Lilly too much, this ride we were on was one I didn't wanna stop.

I was an awful person, a fucking awful father, and an awful son. Mum and Molly should have been my priority, not a girl I'd known for less than a week. I was embarrassed at myself, rather than planning my return home I was racking my brain for reasons not to leave when there weren't any.

"Or you could just stay? she said. "Or am I being selfish for saying that?"

"I think I should stay, too. At least till Frank is back. I can't leave you here on your own."

"What about your Mom? Your little girl?"

"I'll see them soon enough."

"Means I'm stuck with you till I leave then?"

"Seems that way."

She smiled, put another cookie in her mouth, sank deeper into the sofa.

★ ★ ★

The film credits rolled. I looked over at Lilly, she was fast asleep. I didn't want to disturb her, I checked my watch, it wasn't late at all, the day had just worn her out. I managed to move her legs off my lap without her waking and was about to put a blanket over her, when she whispered for me to take her to bed. So, I did.

Lifted her up, like I did Molly, carried her up the stairs, carefully, took my time to make sure I didn't wake her. I'd never been upstairs before, so I didn't know which room was hers, though it was easy to work out, I just followed the mess.

I rested her gently on her bed. I could've removed her clothes, sleeping in jeans was hardly ideal, but undressing someone who was asleep felt like too much of a violation, so instead I pulled her bed sheets over her, made sure she wouldn't be cold, made sure she had a glass of water.

I pulled up the chair beside Lilly's bed, her room was what I expected, busy, books half read, plants half dead, things thrown that should be placed, things damp that should be dry. For all her wealth and possessions, all the unopened boxes of free samples, the hangers of unworn clothes still in their bags littered around the room, Lilly still seemed to live out of a single suitcase, like she was always prepared to leave. Perhaps that's how all famous people lived, a life that takes them all over, a life where home doesn't really exist, just buildings with beds.

She was fast asleep now, tiny snores. I went downstairs, locked the doors, put out the fire, turned off the lights, wrote her a note, drove back to my hotel. Back to a cold bed when I'd just left one much warmer.

12

The room buzzed, the sideboard rattled, shook me awake, from under my duvet I threw out an arm, hoped it hit my phone.

"Hello?" My eyes were closed, my voice not quite ready.

"This is your wake-up call, sir. Rise and shine."

"Lilly?" I looked over at neon numbers. "It's, like, four in the morning."

There was a pause, a muffled response, kept cutting in and out.

"Lilly, I can hardly hear you? Where are you, outside? It sounds noisy."

"Sorry I was just overtaking. You're on speaker phone."

"Where are you?"

"Not entirely sure. I just passed a brown sign saying fifty miles to Heights of Abraham. What the fuck even is that? Sounds biblical? You could've warned me it was this far. Lucky I drive fast."

"Lilly? What is going on?"

"Aren't you being paid to follow me?"

"Is this a joke?"

"I've heard there's a little village up North. With a pond. Supposed to be nice this time of year so someone keeps telling me."

"You're insane."

"You probably should get a move on. I shouldn't really talk and drive. This whole left-hand side of the road thing requires maximum concentration. What's the speed limit again?"

"Lilly, you're breaking up."

"I'm going to stop soon. I need sleep."

"Lilly, you there?" I sat up in my bed. "Lilly?" But she'd hung up.

★ ★ ★

I waited outside the hotel just as Lilly's message told me. Despite the wind, the motorway still hummed, there were no cars, just a blur of trucks and lorries. The only people mad enough to be out that early were those being paid to be behind the wheel.

I recognized Lilly's licence plate, blacked out and inconspicuous, Frank's car blended in with every other executive car it was parked next to. I had visions of Lilly bringing the E-Type, lipstick-red, roof down. Thank God, she chose business class, even though it was early, eyes were everywhere no matter what time of day.

I'd left Dot a note. I didn't want her to worry if she found my room empty, she'd worry herself silly, think the worst. I'd just rung Mum, too, no choice but to wake her up, pre-warn her to expect royalty, knowing her she'd need time to prepare, prepare the house, prepare herself. She asked if we'd be sleeping the night, I said no, though no doubt bed sheets would be boiled and washed regardless, air freshener would be being sprayed, TV polished.

I checked my watch, it made me yawn. Four hours on the road, two more to go, I needed breakfast, caffeine, sugar, I needed a second wind.

"Hey, you?" Lilly shouted across a car roof, a rucksack in one hand, coffees in the other.

"Manage to sleep, then?" I said, taking her bag.

"I did, despite the mattress," she said. "No milk, right?" handing it to me.

"Thanks."

"Are you mad with me?"

"I'm not quite sure. I was at first, but it's worn off. Now I'm just nervous."

"I'm the one who should be nervous, Tom."

"It's no farmhouse. Mum's house is…"

"Good, my place is too big anyway. How long till we get there?"

"Couple of hours. You OK to follow me?"

"Cool. Just don't drive slow."

"If we get separated, remember we are coming off at junction 32."

"I'm not gonna remember that."

"Just ring me if you get lost, OK?"

"Admit this is a nice surprise, Tom."

"You could've warned me first so I could plan ahead. You've probably given my mum a heart attack."

"You think she'll freak?"

"At first."

"I'm more nervous than her, believe me."

"I doubt that. Come on let's go," I said as we got into our separate cars.

13

I nearly cried, when I saw Molly's face. She was in a ballerina costume so of course I fell in love with her straight away, looked nothing like her dad, the opposite, all blonde and tanned. On introducing me to Molly, Tom told her that I had to be looked after, that I was a princess too, Molly of course took this literally, so before I'd even put my bag down I was handed an obligatory wand and crown, forced to be worn and used, not that it required much effort on my part, I was used to acting rich and spoilt.

Next came the grand tour, led by Molly, she showed me the garden first, spent a good thirty minutes cross-legged in a pink shed, eating plastic apples and sipping invisible tea. Next was inside, again every room, the laundry room, Grandma's drinks cabinet, the cupboard under the sink, the medicine drawers. Tom's mom looked embarrassed, I could imagine it was quite a drama for her, having a stranger inspect her property on such short notice. She kept apologizing for everything, the noisy radiator, the faulty flush on the toilet, the fact she hadn't seen any of my films.

I kept looking over at Tom, he found the whole thing hilarious, at lunch I kicked him under the table, he deserved it, his little smirks. To be fair I was wearing a pink feather boa, it must have looked quite comical. I told Tom's mom she shouldn't have gone to so much trouble, the table laid out like the Ritz. Reminded me of my own grandma's cooking, lots of butter, lots of salt, lots of love. Wished I could've stopped yawning though, must've have looked so rude.

"Sleeping beauty needs some beauty sleep," Tom told Molly who wasn't happy I was going to bed whilst the sun was still out, informing her dad I would need to be kissed otherwise I'd never wake up. I hoped I wasn't blushing, the mirror told me otherwise. Tom showed me up to his room, told me where he kept the fresh towels, the nearest toilet, fire exits.

"Apologies for the room," he said, attempting to tidy around him. "It hasn't changed much since I was sixteen. I'm tidier now, actually, I'm not at all."

"Sure, you got enough books?"

"I ran out of shelves."

"You do realize there are such things as DVDs? Most people have made that leap from VHS. And I thought I was the film buff. You love shit movies more than me." She picked up a copy of *Tremors*.

"Do you want me to wake you up, or let you sleep through?" he said, putting a folded towel at the end of the bed.

"No, only let me have an hour or so. I didn't come all this way to sleep."

"When's the last time you slept on a single bed?"

"Probably when I was at college. It's fine, honest," I said still looking around the room, it was wall-to-wall teenager. "That's the coolest fucking poster I've ever seen." standing in front of a *Twin Peaks* poster, a Japanese *Twin Peaks* poster. "Where did you get it? Japan?"

He laughed. "Some store on Victory Boulevard. Cost me like fifteen dollars. I'm guessing the owner wasn't a cherry pie fan."

"Fifteen dollars. I'll give you fifteen thousand for it."

"It's not for sale."

"Twenty then?"

"I'm not budging, I'm afraid. Thanks for being so good with Molly. I think you're her new best friend. Don't think she's bothered by me anymore. I can't compete with an American princess."

"Ballerina too, remember. I'm the full package."

"You're also the first girl I've ever had sleep over." He leant against the doorway.

"Serious? Were you a late developer, Tom?"

"I'd say quality over quantity but I'd be lying. I'll leave you to it. Give me a shout if you need anything."

"Night, Tom."

"Night, Lilly. Thanks again for today."

"My pleasure," I said as he switched off the light.

I pulled the duvet over my head. I suddenly felt very aware I was half naked in Tom's bed, felt a little rude, a bit naughty, my boob was touching bed sheet, his willy had touched bed sheet. It was childish intimacy, playground romance stuff. Made me giggle, the room had turned me acne and braces, fantasizing over sex that was never going to happen. I closed my eyes, despite the attempt to darken the room it was still bright with midday sunshine, even though I was tired I couldn't sleep, stared at the ceiling, thought about everything that had gone on.

When I first brought up the idea of Tom coming home I genuinely had no intention of coming along. Hand on heart I never expected to be here of all places. It was only when I woke up in the early hours, with too much time to think, that I felt the need to step in, do something drastic, like drive halfway across a country to bring a stubborn father back to his family. And I knew he'd follow me, he said it himself he wanted to see the job through, that job involved being one step behind me.

It was a gamble though, could easily have backfired, anyone could've opened that door, his wife, his girlfriend, or in fact just his mom. I still felt like I was doing something wrong, stabbing a woman in the back. My guess was, and I hoped I guessed right, Tom was either divorced or separated. That was the most obvious, it was also the easiest to accept. But if there was a mother then where was she, why wasn't Molly with her. Alcoholic? Depressive? Violent? Addict? She could be dead, I thought, childbirth or cancer, adopted. This was ridiculous, my little conspiracy theories, I was sure Tom would tell me soon enough, instead of me guessing right or wrong. Not that it mattered, it shouldn't have mattered, we were friends, temporary friends till I flew home and he came back here for good. But still I couldn't sleep.

I could still hear muffled conversation underneath me. I knew downstairs Tom and his mom were probably talking about me, I didn't mind, I'd be talking about me too. It's not every day a big-time actress comes for lunch, or climbs into your bed, I thought, as I tried to drift off in a room full of warm sun.

★ ★ ★

"How are you so thin? You eat more than I do," said Tom's mom, stacking our dirty plates. "I thought you'd still be full from lunch. I suppose you'd like some pudding as well?"

I nodded, before finishing my mouthful. "Do you need help washing up in there?"

"Tom didn't cook so he's on plate duty. Leave us girls to talk. I've lots of questions, I'm afraid."

Tom stood up. "Don't cross-examine her too much, Mum, she's had a long day."

"It's cool, Tom." I said. "I expected questions. I have some too, myself."

"I think this little one needs a bath, Tom," Tom's mom said, smelling Molly's armpit.

Molly went to whisper in Tom's ear. "I'm sorry, darling," he smiled. "Lilly won't want a bath tonight. Just me and you this time."

"I'm nearly three, Lilly," she said.

"Wow. You are grown up. Your daddy will have to tell me what month so I know when to send all the presents."

"It's September, you know. I know about months, look," Molly said, pointing to a home-made calendar on top of a side table.

"I'd like to look through that later, if that's OK." Molly nodded as Tom led her through the kitchen with promises of spells and talking saucepans as I waved goodnight and Tom's mom went through to the kitchen.

I stood up and started to walk around the room. It was small but everything had its place, like a little thrift store, full of things to touch and ask about. I noticed Molly's calendar, '2010' scrawled in crayon on the front. I flicked through each month, it was quite sweet, Valentine's Day had a love heart, Easter had its eggs and so on.

Tom's mom came back into the room, handed me a bowl.

"What do all the crosses mean?" I said, showing her April.

"Molly crosses off the days that Tom's away. Sad really, it wasn't my idea, all her doing, but she seems to enjoy the countdown till he's home."

"Feel like it's my fault. I'm the reason for all the crosses."

"It's no one's fault, not yours or Tom's. It's just the situation, we all have to deal with it the best we can. You drink brandy?"

"I'm more of a port girl these days."

"My kind of girl." She went over to her drinks cabinet. "Tom says I drink too much. I don't think I drink enough." She poured us both a glass of port. "Whatever gets you through the night that's what I say," she said, sipping it as we stood in the middle of the room.

"Your house is like a gallery," I said, taking a mouthful of hot crumble. "I can't stop looking at everything. I could walk around for hours. Puts my place to shame."

"Please take some with you. I've got art coming out of my ears. Got a load more in the attic. I swap them around when I get bored of them. I think they're worth more than the house."

"What's this one?" I said, both of us standing side by side, looking over the dining table.

"'Le Rêve'. Not the original of course. Do you like it?"

"I love the colours."

"I might have to take it down soon seeing as Molly is getting cleverer by the day. I don't want the willy face fiasco happening all over again, like we did with Tom."

"Willy face?" I looked at the painting again. "Oh, willy face, I get it. Oh God, I can't stop staring at it now."

"What do you think of that one above the fireplace? Same artist, different muse."

I looked behind me. "I prefer willy face. It's bright and lively. The other one looks sad."

"Interesting. The sad one as you put it was actually Picasso's wife, Olga. The one you like is Marie Therese, his mistress. He met her when she was seventeen, he was in his forties. Love affair that lasted decades, he even had a daughter with her."

"Naughty boy, wasn't he? Did it have a happy ending?"

"Not really. He fell in love with another woman, and then another after that. Marie hung herself after he died. Artists are bastards aren't they? I should know, I married one. He wasn't too bad, my husband, one of the few."

"I would disagree but I've experienced artists first hand myself. Bastard seems the appropriate word. He was a director though."

"Still an artist, just a different instrument." Both of us were now moving toward the couch.

"I've never regarded myself as an artist," I said, finishing the last of the custard in my bowl.

"You create, don't you? You act, take on a role."

"I guess. Is acting creating?"

"Of course, it is, dear. Re-shaping one emotion into another. Doesn't matter if it's a paintbrush or guitar or a voice, everyone needs something to direct their creativity towards, joy, pain, love."

"She's very pretty," I said, pointing to the photo on the wall.

"She was. Has Tom told you what happened?"

"A little," I said, which was a complete lie.

"Life can be a shit sometimes."

"Where is she now?"

"Back in America."

"Where?"

"LA, I don't know exactly."

"Very far away from Tom and Molly."

"For now, it is the best place for them both, short term at least.

78

I do wish Tom would go back to America though, he doesn't suit here. He'd have a better life, as would Molly if he just went back."

"Tom doesn't talk much about her."

"Just his way of dealing with it. He doesn't like to be reminded, me, I think it's important not to forget, no matter how sad. Still gives me the shivers when I think about it. I lost a daughter-in-law, but I was close to losing Tom and Molly too. I'm surprised Molly and he walked away from it like they did. It was a big crash, that is why I'm so grateful, sad but grateful. She died instantly, that's what Tom told me. Which is a blessing, she didn't die in pain."

"When did this happen?"

"October just gone."

Just then Tom came through the door, a duvet and a foot pump under his arm.

"What you two talking about? Me, I bet."

We smiled, sipping our ports, as he started to inflate his bed for the night. I tried to work out how it was possible to feel so sorry and yet so relieved. And an awful human for feeling one more than the other.

* * *

It was agreed that night that we would stay an extra day. After such a long drive the day before, the thought of doing it all over again so soon made it an easy decision for us both. Just wished I'd brought more clothes with me, I had to get Tom's mom to wash my underwear, as I'd only brought a night's worth. Not to mention my lack of cosmetics, not that the village would've noticed, it wasn't the place fussed by greasy skin and a bad fringe.

The morning was nice, watched cartoons with Molly for a while on the blow-up bed, tucked up under a duvet for two hours of Mickey. I told her about Disneyland, all the times I'd been, it was now top of her birthday list. I didn't tell Tom this of course, he would've killed me for planting the idea of Orlando in her head. I could always pay for them all to go, my little treat. Not that

Tom would step foot back on American soil, and definitely not by September, judging by what his mom said the night before.

Me and her had just had a nice chat upstairs. Molly and Tom had gone for a walk to the shops, they'd been gone for a quite a while, though apparently, it's quite a way on foot, so we had the house to ourselves, sat on the bed, me in a borrowed dressing gown, applying the very limited make-up I had. Our heads wrapped in towels, waiting for our hair to dry.

We talked about lots of things, girly things like make-up and getting old, Tom's change of career, mostly we talked about cancer. Again, like the night before, she assumed I already knew of her situation. She was positive about it, though said she was fed up of looking old, said she had a bit of a cry the other week, a comment Molly made. I assured her Molly wouldn't have meant it, kids say the strangest things, it couldn't have been nice to be compared to a witch in a book, obviously hit a nerve. I did my best to cheer her up, asked her if she'd like me to do her nails and hair, a bit of pampering, a bit of colour. Made her feel more fairy godmother than wicked witch. It did the trick, she joked she should have had a daughter instead of a son, sometimes all women needed was lipstick and curls to feel back on track.

Downstairs as my underwear tumbled in the dryer, she made us tea, in a little pot with the cutest knitted tea cosy. We talked about Cassie a little more, how they met, what she was like, which Tom's mom knew very little about. I asked what their wedding was like, though according to her there wasn't one, at least not one she had been privy to. Tom and Molly came back not long after, a bag each, groceries in one, comic and chocolate in the other. Seeing as the weather was so nice we decided to take Molly out for the day, forced Tom's mom get some rest.

I went upstairs to get changed whilst Tom loaded up the car, tried to call my mom. Don't know why but I suddenly felt the urge to talk to her, spending so much time with a family made me miss my own. I was upset me and my mom never talked like me and Tom's mom just had, so effortless, so natural. I shouldn't badmouth my own mother, she does try, it's just so forced, our conversations had to be booked in, months in advance. Anyway, I tried to ring her, went to voicemail. Busy as normal, no change there then. Always too busy for me.

* * *

As Tom was upstairs settling Molly I lit a fire, a small one, watched the twigs and sticks spit before loading on a pyramid of coal. I looked out from behind the curtain, despite being relatively early it had turned dark quickly, the sun doesn't stay out long in England, early mornings and early nights, the opposite of what I was used to.

Glass of wine in one hand, I pottered around the room, eyeing the walls again, frames, family photos, art, cabinets, shelves, spine after spine of book after book. I picked one out, sat myself down, sprawled my legs across the sofa, till realized I wasn't in my own home. I couldn't stop yawning, putting a child to bed, all the whispered stories and glow lamps had left me rubbing my eyes too.

Originally, the plan had been to drive to the nearest beach, but just after setting off the skies clouded over, so armed with umbrellas and flasks of tea we decided to go to a country park much closer by instead. I'm glad we did, living in LA the only animals I ever saw were Pomeranians poking out of Mulberry bags, or cats in diamond collars. It was nice seeing pigs and sheep, rolling around in mud and filth like they were supposed to, as nature intended. I nearly bought a micro pig back with me, so cute, even smelt of bacon, not sure a pet was supposed to make you hungry.

"What are you reading?" Tom came through the door with a plate of cookie crumbs and a jumper for me.

"It's hilarious. Look at this guy." I showed Tom the book. "So much penis, so little dignity. I love his facial expression, too."

"Dad taught life drawing at some point, apparently. I guess that was research."

"Oh, you know this book, do you?"

"Know it? I had it hidden under my bed for the best part of five years. Got me through puberty."

"Hardly erotic. You can't see anything. Guess they didn't have bikini waxes back in black and white times. You manage to get hold of Vince?"

"No. Busy pestering celebrities I expect. What do you fancy doing tonight? I thought we could go to the pub."

"I can't be bothered to be presentable. I smell of farm."

"The pub won't notice, I assure you."

"Where is it? Far?"

"If you look at of the window, you can see it across the road."

"No. I'd still rather stay here. I've just got a fire going too and my butt is stuck for the night."

"OK, you win. I'm gonna grab something to eat. What about you? Or is that a silly question?"

"I could eat."

Tom got up. "Give me ten minutes, I'll rustle something up."

I grabbed the remote control and after several attempts I managed to turn it on. Suddenly my face came up on screen. Oh God, how embarrassing, I thought. It had only just started, I hadn't watched it since the first screening. My memory of the movie was mixed, awful film really, a photocopy of a dozen other romcoms. Still, I loved filming it in Boston, it was when Max and I had first got together, before the rows and the sadness. Walking hand in hand around Back Bay, under trees full of pink. I'd have to go back sometime, see if it was still so full of colour. Maybe next time I wouldn't have to take a pregnancy test, I spent the last few weeks of filming with my head down a toilet, worrying how I was going to tell Max he was going to be a father of a child he didn't want.

Tom came back in, put a platter of cheese and olives in the centre of the table, his mouth already full of cracker.

"How come there are only five channels?" I asked, still pointing it at the TV. "Am I doing something wrong?"

"No, Mum's just a cheapskate."

We both went quiet, leant over the coffee table, helping ourselves to the different colours of cheese.

"I was thinking about the whole Frank and Sally situation on the drive back," I said.

"Was that why you were so quiet?"

"I need some time with them before I introduce you."

"I'm being introduced, am I?"

"Course you are. I thought you would like to be introduced. Save all this hiding about."

"I'm joking, Lilly. Though I'm not gonna lie. Frank scares the shit out of me."

"I can see why. Me and Frank have lots to sort out, we didn't leave on the best of terms."

"What happened between you and him? Why did he leave?"

"Long story, actually it isn't that long at all. He thought I'd taken drugs when I hadn't, basically."

"Why didn't he believe you?"

"It's not the first time I've lied to Frank."

"What shall I do whilst you are smoothing things over with Frank? Should I stay up here for a while?"

"No. Unless you would rather stay here?"

"No, I'll come back with you. Otherwise it might complicate things with Vince."

"You could just tell him you quit. That way you can take Vince out of the equation completely."

"I did think that but it's not that simple."

"Why isn't it simple?"

"Cos if I quit, then he becomes my replacement. He's a lot more brutal than I am. You'll know your privacy is being invaded with Vince. I know for a fact he has at least two restraining orders."

"What are you suggesting we do?"

"Perhaps throw him the odd bone here and there. Let me take

a quick snap of you out shopping, go for a walk in one of the fields. A few of them should keep Vince sweet."

"I don't mind doing that. It's the not first time I've been on a prearranged pap shoot and it won't be my last."

"OK, that sorts out the short term." Tom took a wedge of cheese.

"Then next it's Frank and Sally? That's going be an awkward introduction. Frank hates paparazzi. Sally hates them too, thought she isn't too fond of people in general."

"Tough crowd then?"

"You could say that. It may take them time for them to trust you. God, I don't even trust you myself yet."

"You don't actually mean that, do you? You do trust me, don't you?"

"I wouldn't take it personally. I've had trust issues for years. People always letting me down."

"Do you trust Sally?"

"Strange question to ask?"

"No, I'm just curious that's all."

"Course I trust Sally. She's practically family. I mean, I can't stand her most of the time, so practically like my real family then."

"She scares me. Whenever I'd see her with you, she always looked angry at something. Do you think if I give her flowers it might help? Y'know, when I first meet her?"

"Probably not. Just tell her you're the one who made me famous. That's what she most cares about."

"I didn't make you famous, Lilly."

"Well, more famous then. If she feels you being around will increase my fame and reputation then she will love you forever."

"Bet she loves Max then."

"Strangely enough, she does. Not the man, but what he brings Brand Goodridge."

"Do you think I'm good for Brand Goodridge?"

"I'm the least concerned about branding, especially my own."

"Lilly. I was asking you a serious question."

"I know. I just don't know how to answer it."

We went quiet, concentrating on our cheeses.

"We need more crackers. Do you want a beer? Wine?"

"If you get any red I'll have a small glass." He headed off to kitchen as I pretended not to think of Tom's wife, her photo right in front of me. Felt like she was watching me fall in love with her husband.

14

"I'm having a bath, a long one that's for sure. "My top is stuck to the back of my seat, fuck knows what my bra is up to. How long have we been driving now?"

"Too long. My left foot's gone numb, too much clutch control."

"I'm bursting for the toilet."

"Again? Your bladder is worse than Molly's."

"Don't make me laugh, Tom. I'll piss myself, literally. How far off are we now?"

"Will be another five minutes."

"OK, talk to me about something to take my mind off wetting myself."

"What about? A babbling brook, a waterfall, a running stream?"

"Tom, if I wet myself you are cleaning my car. What are your plans for later? I really need to ring Sally. I've ignored her for two days, can't keep putting it off."

"Need to wash my clothes, watch a bit of TV. Boring stuff really. I'm pretty knackered."

"I should probably do the same. If ever you sell your story about me, which you probably will eventually, can you make me out to be a little more hellraiser? Orgies and drug-fuelled, rather than country parks and cheese nights. I've got a reputation as a wild child, I can't have people thinking I look forward to laundry duty and a good book."

"Shall we give ourselves a night off from each other tonight?" I said, trying to see her reaction in my rear view mirror, like I had the whole journey down. Pretending we were sat next to each other, when we were both behind separate steering wheels.

"Bored of me already, Tom?"

"You filming tomorrow?"

"They are, I'm not. I'm not scheduled back in all week."

"Are you in the movie much?"

"Seems not. I think once Jon has been in the editing room I'll be in it even less."

"How's Jon been? Is he still concerned about your lifestyle choices?"

"He hasn't said much since the shit in Salcombe. All I know is I'm keeping my nose clean and out of trouble."

We turned a corner, into a road that stretched further than we could see, Lilly's car behind mine, as she did her best to keep up..

"There she is." We could see the farmhouse for the first time. "You'll be glad to know your toilet is not far away."

"Sight for sore eyes isn't she? Wow."

"Pretty cool view, isn't it?"

"Tom, can you promise to take a picture of this before I leave? Bring your big expensive camera up here one day? I wouldn't mind a few around the house, the garden. Be nice to have some pictures for my apartment finally, I'm bored of stark. I think your mom's house has rubbed off on me. Who wants a house of magnolia and minimalism? Tom? Hello, Earth to Tom?"

"Lilly slow down. Pull over behind me a sec."

"What's wrong?"

"We have company."

I pulled into a grass verge beside a field, grabbed my binoculars from off the back seat and got out the car. Lilly was already walking towards me, dodging mud and horse manure.

"What am I looking at?" she asked as I passed her my binoculars.

"See that silver car parked about hundred metres from the back of your house?"

"Where?"

"There." I pointed. "By that gate, that cluster of trees. See it?"

"Oh, yeah, I see it."

"Strange place to park, don't you think?"

"It could be just a coincidence."

"Let me go and explore, just to be on the safe side. Like you said, it might not be what I think it is."

"Is it your foreign friend? Your weed guy?"

"Might be. I have no clue what Ludo drives. I have a vague memory his car was blue though, bashed up and old."

"Shall I come with?" handing me back the binoculars.

"No, you stay here. If you get any attention just drive off."

"I'm gonna find somewhere round here to wee," she said, looking over towards some bushes and brambles.

"Keep your phone close by."

"Be careful, Tom."

"I will," I said, walking into grass as tall as me.

★ ★ ★

"Is this the part where my house becomes a prison? Under house arrest?" Lilly threw an olive into her mouth.

"I don't know what it means. Could just be me overreacting."

"And you reckon it's not this Ludo guy?"

"I'm not 100% sure till I make some calls."

"It's game over either way. Doesn't matter if it's Ludo or some fucker else. If one person knows where I live then they'll all fucking know by now."

"Not necessarily. Paps keep their cards close to their chests. They all want exclusivity, the more eyes on you, the more their work drops in value. Like I said, it might not even be paps at all. Just cos the car was parked close and had equipment in the back doesn't mean it's them. I haven't seen anyone, remember, just the car."

"Tom, it's paparazzi. It's too much of a coincidence." She

sipped her drink. "What shall I do? Should I still go back home or not? I can't wait here all day. We could go back to your place?"

"No, there might still be a few paps hovering about. I'll think of something."

"I hate all that cat-and-mouse stuff. I came to England to get away from that. I expect that in LA, but I thought I'd be safe here. If Frank and Sally come back to cameras at my front door they'll make me move. Sally has already made it quite clear that the farmhouse isn't fit for purpose. She's looking for any excuse to turf me out."

"Turf you out where?"

"I don't know. Some high-rise tower like Rapunzel, security guards outside my room, military operations whenever I want to leave the house, driving in convoy like I'm about to be bumped off any minute."

"Don't freak out yet. Let me do some digging. Get rid of a few question marks."

I walked outside, rows of white cottages and thatched roofs, families trickled on foot to or from the beach, the sound of flapping flip flops, kids complaining of the walk, mums moaning, dads eyeing up the pub. I took another sip of cider, scrolled my phone for a number I probably didn't have. Turned out I did.

"How are you, man?"

"Who this?"

"It's Tom."

"What you want?"

"Where are you, man?"

"I'm somewhere. What you want?"

"A favour."

"Ludo out of favours."

"I need some more weed. That bag you gave me didn't last longer than an evening."

"I have no more for you. All gone."

"Come on, Ludo. You must have more."

"I saw your car at beach."

"When?"

"Few days before. Sunday. Goodridge bitch with you."

"I promise you she wasn't with me. But I know where she is right now."

"Where? I don't believe. You lie, Thomas. I stop believing. Newquay was lie. This is lie."

"I'm not lying, Ludo. Are you able to get hold of some more weed?"

"You prove you see girl. I find you weed."

I opened the pub door, aimed my phone at Lilly and took her picture. Sent it straight across to Ludo's phone.

"Where is this?"

"A restaurant in Kingsbridge, near the quay. Tapas place. The only one, you can't miss it. I'd be quick if I were you. I doubt she'll be here much longer, looks like she and her friends are just on dessert."

"If this is lie, Thomas…"

"It's not, Ludo, I swear."

"I go now."

"Oh, hey by the way, were you over by South Sands today? I thought I saw your car earlier."

"Not me, friend."

"You drive a silver Benz, right?"

"Not mine. I don't drive German. My father would cut off balls. Now let me go." He hung up. I went back inside.

Over at the table I could see Lilly chatting to the landlord, both of them laughing.

"Who was that?" I asked her, sitting back down. "You know him?"

"A friend. Anyway, panic over. I can go back home." Lilly looked pleased with herself.

"How so?"

"You aren't the only one capable of detective work. Just rang

90

my neighbour, forgotten he'd given me his number a few weeks back, something about blackouts and floods, best to have each other's numbers just in case we are in the dark or drowning. I just got off talking to him."

"What he say?"

"Car has gone." She sipped through her straw. "What about you? Still question marks?"

"Good news is, Ludo is now off on some wild goose chase."

"That's good."

"Bad news, the car is someone else's."

"And you say that was near where you used to park?"

"Pretty near, yes. That's why I don't think it's a coincidence."

"Well it is what it is. Nothing we can do about it. Listen I've had an idea. A short-term solution to our current situation."

"Let me hear it."

"Meet me here at five o'clock."

"Here?"

"You'll need an overnight bag, too."

"Lilly. What are you up to?"

"It's nothing bad, trust me."

"And when did you plan this?"

"Just now," she said, smiling behind her glass. "Whilst you were outside."

"You have been busy."

"Let's head our separate ways. Much to do. Places to ring." She threw me my car keys across the table.

"Where we going?"

"Somewhere safe." she said looking smug. "Oh, and you own a tux, right?"

★ ★ ★

"Here you go," she said, handing me the hanger.

"Thanks so much, Dot. You're a star. I owe you a nice lunch."

"Pleasure was all mine. I've been itching to use my new

garment steamer. I only bought it off QVC to annoy him indoors, but I actually quite enjoyed it. Quite therapeutic actually. Is it new?"

"Only worn it the once."

"Off the peg?"

"No, Savile Row."

"I should have known. You don't see lining like that on the high street. And where are you off to in such grand attire?"

"I'm not quite sure yet."

"With your lady friend, I assume?"

"A gentleman never tells."

"Well, you better be the gentleman, Thomas. Have you got her something nice?"

"What do you mean?"

"As a gesture. Some flowers. You can't turn up empty-handed."

"We're just friends, that's all."

"In my day, a man didn't dress up in tails on a Saturday night unless he was after something a bit fruitier than friendship."

"Times have changed, Dot."

"So you keep telling me. Though I don't think as much as you'd like to think. I best be off, got a pile of my own ironing to get through now."

"Dot, I really appreciate what you've done for me. Not just all the washing and ironing today but everything else. You've made a stranger feel very wanted."

"Just make sure you give us five stars on Tripadvisor."

"I thought you didn't want any more customers?"

"Three stars then," she laughed. "It's going to be sad when you go, Tom, for all of us, dog included. How long is it till you leave me for the North again?"

"Not long at all. A week, two weeks tops."

"Then you best make the most of it, Tom. Tonight included."

"It's not a date, Dot. People like Lilly don't date people like me."

"Well, from where I'm looking it seems she does now." Dot picked up my dirty mugs from off the side. "Does your friend still need a room anytime soon? You have been threatening me with his visit for the last few weeks."

"Not Vince's biggest fan, are you, Dot?"

"The man is a charmer, I'll give him that. But not charms that work on me, I'm afraid. Does he need a room next week? As I haven't got many spare."

"I need to ring him at some point. I'll ask him. Though last time we spoke he sounded pretty keen to."

"Well let's hope he stays put. I have enough rude Americans without adding one more. Try and put him off if you can."

"Don't worry, Dot. Putting him off was already top of my agenda."

15

I could already picture Tom's face when he pulled up outside the pub and I guessed that he wouldn't approve of my choice of transport. The E-Type was hardly subtle, and in light of the news of my new stalker, blacked-out windows would have been far more appropriate. But my little convertible was a lot more fitting. Where we were going was a place you turned up to with the wind in your hair and not a care in the world, arriving in style was all part of the experience. So, when Tom pulled up and took a glance at me in the driver's seat looking all *Thelma and Louise*, I was quite surprised how unconcerned he was by the car and how excited he looked about where I was taking him.

"I've a young daughter to think about, remember." He shoved his bag in the trunk.

"I don't drive that fast," I said, punching his arm.

"You forget I've been the car chasing you for the last few weeks." He folded his suit jacket carefully and draped it over the back seat. "You gonna tell me where we're going yet? Or am I about to be blindfolded?"

"All we be revealed soon," I said, putting my foot down, off through curves and bends, heading towards the most beautiful of secrets.

★ ★ ★

"Look, I'll take our stuff down," Tom said looking over the edge, a mile of steps. "I should be able to do it in one trip. How long we here for?" he said, feeling the weight of my bag.

It wasn't busy down below, still a few families making the most of the very little sand left, packing away their belongings, crushing sandcastles, the day was turning into evening, the tide was turning beach into ocean.

"Looks like squashed peaches, don't you think?" I said pointing at the sky.

"Edvard Munch."

"Showing off again, are we, art boy?" I said, tiptoeing across the wet, dodging little pools and puddles.

"Our taxi?" Tom pointed ahead of us, a taxi as high as a house, tyres bigger than us.

"Monster truck." Both of us smiling, excited by the absurdity of our transport.

Tom attempted to help the driver with our bags, but the offer was declined quickly, all part of the service he said, as we went to find seats that weren't there.

"Standing only, I'm afraid." he smiled. "Lucky you ain't got far."

"You cold?" Tom noticing me shiver.

"A little."

"Here." Tom pulled a woolly hat out of his coat pocket. "Put this on," he said, before gently pulling it over the top of my head, curling my hair behind my ears.

We thought we might be the only passengers as we waited for what felt like ten minutes but was probably more like two. Till a posh car drove down onto the beach and a well-dressed couple were escorted from car to tractor, as were their many suitcases and travel bags.

"That's how to arrive in style." Tom nudged me, watching Fred and Ginger move gingerly from sand to steel.

"Rather peculiar, isn't it?" The woman smiled at us, climbing up the steps. "Driving across an ocean."

"Better than swimming across, hey?" her husband laughed, as Tom and I laughed back.

"Right we are, ladies and gents. Hold onto your hats and

husbands," the driver shouted, starting the engine, as loud as it was angry, tyres quickly disappearing underwater. I took one more look at the mainland, already it looked smaller.

"I wish we had a camera." I nudged Tom. "Shouldn't paparazzi have a camera at all times?"

"It's my night off."

"And how do I know you haven't got it tucked away in that bag of yours, just in case?"

"Feel free to check." Our eyes turned back to our destination, not where we'd just left.

The hotel looked incredible, lit up like some ocean liner, like the world was covered in water and this was the only building left. We huddled together, the tractor battling against the waves, jolting and jerking, the spray of the ocean salty and cold.

"I think we're about to go back in time." I said. "Eighty-eight miles per hour."

"This ain't no DeLorean. More like a landing craft."

"Must be popular. I booked the last of the rooms."

"Room or rooms?"

"Room actually. There was only one left."

Tom didn't answer, but I knew what he was thinking, because I was thinking the same thing.

"Jo Baker room. I saw it as a sign."

"A sign for what?"

"You don't know Josephine Baker? She was like the Beyoncé of the 1930s. I learnt all about her at AMDA. I thought you said you did American Studies?"

"Please tell me that is a pub." Tom pointed ahead, a row of white houses, separate from the hotel. "You do realize I'm never leaving this place?"

"What's the date on the wall?"

"1336, I think," he said as we both squinted.

"You've better eyesight than me, Tom."

"How blind are you without your glasses?"

"How do you know I wear glasses? I guess you've seen me in the house haven't you? Am I allowed any secrets these days?"

"I won't tell anyone, promise. Your poor visual perception is safe with me." He nudged my shoulder as the tractor made its way upwards towards the hotel, as tyre finally hit concrete.

"Now that's one impressive gate." Tom helped me down the steps. "You look relieved?" as I jumped off the tractor.

"I prefer dry land. Hence why I don't fly or sail well."

"We nearly rented an apartment in Wiltshire Boulevard once." He inspected the railings of the gate. "Couldn't afford it, obviously."

"Where did you live in LA?"

"Somewhere far less Art Deco than this, put it that way."

The staff were already there to greet us, uniformed and polite as they helped take our luggage upward towards the entrance.

"Have you turned all 1930s yet?" he asked as we got closer to the hotel. "Tommy guns and pin curls."

"There is a strong chance I may talk like Judy Garland from now on."

"Well, Dorothy Gale," he said as they opened the door to polished parquet and wallpaper of shells, "I don't think we're in Kansas anymore."

He was right.

Black and white was for somewhere else. Tonight would be Technicolor.

16

"This is very me, Tom. Very me," she said taking in the view.

"Sure, beats my mum's duck pond."

"How pretty is our little cove? Our own secret beach. No chance of paparazzi round here." Lilly flopped herself on the bed, arms out like a starfish. "Have you read *The Beach*? Or seen the movie? Di Caprio was hot in that, he's hot in most things. Actually, don't answer that. You've properly been there yourself, haven't you? You've been everywhere. Bet you've been to that island, properly killed a shark too, lived in a hut and lost your mind."

I didn't answer. She knew my response already.

"Does the island really have a field of marijuana on it?"

"No and believe me I searched for it." I looked out across the cove from the balcony. "Reminds me of Maya Bay. How long we got till dinner?"

"Not that long at all," she said, checking her watch.

"How we doing this?"

"Doing what?"

"The whole sharing-a-room thing." I picked up a magazine from off the side, pretended I was cool and collected.

"I hadn't thought that far."

"You seen this?" showing the front cover to Lilly.

"Great. There's my cover blown."

"When did you do this interview?"

"No idea. Must have been a few months ago."

I flicked through to the article. There was Lilly, double-page spread. Photoshopped and flawless.

"Says here you're bringing out a fragrance soon."

"First I've heard."

"And you're writing a book, too."

"That's a lie."

"This whole interview is made up then?"

"Probably not all of it."

"Must be horrible. All the lies and make-believe."

"I'd rather they print happy and harmless rather than the other."

"Well this article makes you sound pretty happy," I said as I read through it.

"Trust me, I wasn't. I haven't been in a long while."

"Then why not tell them?"

"They never asked me."

"I find that hard to believe."

"Most magazines don't worry about the truth, they just want fluffy. What book I'm reading, my co-stars, what I eat. Least they make me look pretty."

"I'm gonna grab a shower, unless you wanna have one first?" knowing she probably would.

"If you don't mind. Unless you want a dinner date with damp hair." She got off the bed, went over to her bag, getting out what she needed. "I don't want you seeing my outfit either. It will ruin my grand entrance," she said, turning on the shower.

"Well, we wouldn't want that, would we? You better close your eyes too, Lilly. I don't want my grand entrance ruined either, though you've already seen my suit." I went over to the wardrobe, took out my shirt, took out the ironing board and iron, stood it up, plugged it in.

"Do you need anything ironing?" I shouted over the sound of running water.

"Tom, you don't iron an Alexander McQueen dress."

"My mother would disagree."

"You don't have to sleep on the floor by the way." Lilly said, walking back into the room, taking her complimentary robe off the back of the door. "I feel bad you always end up sleeping on some blow-up bed or hard floor. Just because I'm a girl doesn't mean I always get first dibs. I'm not a princess."

"Don't tell Molly that."

"I'm not messing, Tom. I don't expect you to sleep on the floor just because you are the man. This is the 21st century. Sisters are doing it for themselves."

"I'm trying to be a gentleman."

"We could always share? It's a pretty big bed."

"Don't worry. I've slept on worse floors than this, much worse. I'll be fine. You have it."

She didn't answer, disappeared back into the steam, as I ironed and swore at myself for declining an invitation most men would've accepted, regardless of whether it was a joke or a real offer.

★ ★ ★

"A Scotsman took a girl for a romantic ride in his taxi. She was so beautiful he could hardly keep his eyes on the meter."

"Englishman, Scotsman and Irishman walk into a bar. The landlord said, is this some kind of sick joke?"

It went on, me then him, him then me.

He laughed. "All we need now is an Irishman. Complete the set. You reckon there's any about tonight?" Itaking away myher bowl of chewed olive stones.

Me and the barman had been talking since I first took a stool at his bar, I'd gotten ready far too early, earlier than the whole hotel, so by my third cocktail he was already calling me Tom and swapping his best jokes before the room started to fill.

When I left Lilly, she was sat in her robe, duvet full of powders and brushes. Not that she even needed make-up, she already looked stunning, sat there cross-legged on the bed. God knows how stunning she would be when she was finished. She promised she wouldn't be much longer, but as I predicted, she was running late. I didn't mind, the waiting gave me more time to think, stare out the dinner menu over and over, when the last thing on my mind was ordering food.

I should have brought something for Lilly. Dot was right, it wasn't gentlemanly to turn up empty-handed. But I didn't have enough time, it wasn't as if I had time to get flowers and a corsage. Dot was right about a lot of things, tonight was more than friendship.

Technically I wasn't even married, not legally, not in the conventional way, but I made a vow, not to a vicar or my family, but a vow to Cassie. Even if Cassie wasn't there to answer it or repeat her vow to me, I had to assume she said Yes and I had to assume I was a married man still. I noticed the ceiling above me, stained glass, a dome as extravagant and as ornate as everything beneath it. The barman came over, I asked him for another drink, told him not to rush on my part, but he'd already filled my glass with another Tom Collins, which I downed as hard and quick as the ones before it.

A crowd had descended around the fountain and canopies as I left my stool for the quieter main reception out of the double doors. I could've died for a smoke, something to keep my hands busy and my mind from pacing. I kept telling myself I wasn't doing anything wrong, Cassie was dead and I was alive. I should be allowed to move on, I was allowed to fall in love again, wasn't like I had to be on my own forever, a permanent widower. And what could I do anyway? I was on an island, I could hardly run away, not that I should feel like I had to.

Tonight felt significant, I should tell Lilly how I felt. I saw myself in the mirror, a twenty-seven-year-old single parent with a dead wife and tons of debt. Who the fuck was I kidding? I had nothing to offer her apart from everything I had, which wouldn't be enough, not for the likes of someone like Lilly Goodridge. Just chew your food, Tom, laugh at her jokes, don't do anything silly.

"Would you like to be seated in the main hall, sir?" a waiter asked politely from over my shoulder. I was about to reply, but then I saw Lilly. I couldn't speak. No words.

"You know how to whistle, don't you?" she said, walking down to the stairs.

"That's Bacall, not Garland?"

"I know, dibshit. I was trying to catch you out. God knows who I'll be next."

"Well, whoever you might be later, you look amazing." I took her hand. "I mean your dress could do with an iron, but apart from that."

She whacked my arm with her clutch bag. "You look pretty handsome yourself. Like a true Gatsby."

"Sorry you've seen it before. It's the only tux I have."

"Any more than one would be a waste." I took her arm. "Sounds lively in there. Shall we go in? Be nice to sit near the piano. Front row seat and all."

"Apparently there's a live band later."

"You better be nimble on your feet. I want to dance tonight."

"I'll need more drink down me."

"Well, we won't get one standing in the entrance, will we?"

"Follow me, my lady," I said, leading her up the steps to the main hall, the beautifully set tables, the sound of a double bass, the sound of popping corks and fizz.

What the room was before, it wasn't any longer. Lilly was a vision in feathers and pearls, gliding through the bustle, the room didn't know how to handle her, she underestimated the impact she has on people, like the room had taken a collective deep breath, exhaling as she passed.

I don't think I could have been any more in love with her if I tried.

★ ★ ★

Dinner was delicious, small portions, lots of courses, food either cooked quick or long. I'd never used so much cutlery, so many forks and spoons, each more important than the last. The waiter took our desserts away, "Cheese will follow," he told us, Lilly's eyes lit up, the girl's savoury tooth was equal to her sweet.

The party had swelled with new arrivals, strangers introduced themselves to strangers, couples had become groups, excitement was in the air, a hotel at the end of the world, no inhibitions, no thoughts of tomorrow. What at the start was quiet and well mannered, over a few neon cocktails had turned everyone into free spirits and friends for life.

An old lady tapped Lilly's shoulder, complimented her on her hair, they chatted over the backs of their chairs before she turned back to her sorbet and smiling husband.

"That's made your night, hasn't it?" I said.

"It's nice to get a compliment."

"You must get them every day."

"Hollywood compliments don't count. You get too many, cheapens its value."

"You do look pretty spectacular tonight."

"What can I say? I'm a fashion chameleon. Dipping in out of styles. Borrowing and stealing. It's an art form really." She sipped her Martini.

"Speaking of thievery, I can't believe you stole all the complimentary shampoos. You could afford to buy the whole bloody hotel. Why steal bath soap? Do people even use soap these days?"

"They don't mind."

"They?"

"The hotel. They don't mind. Besides it doesn't feel like you've stayed at a hotel unless you steal something or make a mess."

"Is that so?"

"And I'm not as rich as you think, you know."

"Rich enough though."

"Few more career moves like this one and I'll be back at the Dream Centre. And I don't mean volunteering either."

"I doubt that, Lilly."

"It's true. It may look like I live this fabulous life but I never get to enjoy it."

"Why?"

"Cos, it always feels like it's about to be taken away."

I looked at Lilly over empty glasses and candles and I knew this wasn't for show, she meant what she was saying. It was a look I'd seen many times through my camera lens, not fearful, but the expectation of fear.

"I'd still rather be in your position than mine though. It's worse never having enough no matter how much you try, or how hard you work. It's always the same struggle."

"You must think I'm the spoilt little rich girl. It's a cliché but the more money you have the more you spend."

"What, cat manicures and florist bills?"

"Ha ha. My money all goes on people actually. Bought my folks a house, sorted my sister out, paid off all her student debt. Then there's the agents, publicists, security, overseas people."

"And they are all important, are they?"

"Apparently so. Though this movie won't do well, not because of the director or cast. It was just doomed from the start. Though to be fair no one said I should have taken this movie apart from me, so I've only myself to blame."

"Why is it doomed?"

"Big budget and low profit. That's why Max was so flavour of the month."

"How so?"

"His first film. My first film. Five million budget, hundred million profits. Small risks and guarantees. It's just a business trying to survive."

"You could just focus on independent films. Work with directors and actors you've always dreamt of working beside. Do one for your bank balance and one for yourself."

"That would be the dream. But I'm not seen in that way. I've gone too mainstream for the indie crowd."

"Actors are always reinventing themselves. Just takes the right script and the right direction."

"Well, I'm still waiting."

"Or you could just stop." I said. "Try something else. Go out on a high." I poured Lilly and then me more champagne.

"I can't. It affects too many people."

"Who, agents and publicists? I'm sure they'll move on just fine."

"No, my friends and family. Sally, Frank, my parents."

"Your job isn't to bankroll your friends though."

"I know that."

"And surely, you've made enough to able to live comfortably, live a good life. Probably never need to work again."

"I wish. My first movie I did practically for free. My others slightly more."

"What about all your endorsements?"

"They pay well, yes. But without movies, without gossip, without Max, they would all stop. Fame is relentless. Getting famous is the easy part, it's staying famous that's the problem."

"You're screwed then?"

"Pretty much."

"You could just try and enjoy it. Sounds crazy I know."

"I've tried that too."

"And how's that working out for you?" asking a question that required no answer.

The waiter brought over another bottle, topped up our glasses. I needed to slow down, have a water, I didn't want tonight to be a blur, I wanted to remember every last detail. But it was hard not to join in, give in to the excess, the jazz in the background was loud and upbeat, behind us guests danced and laughed, it wasn't a night for frowns. Every guest had the same look as Lilly and me, trapped on some mad, decadent island, where mad things might happen. Where any regrets were left on the mainland, even mine.

"OK, Dr Phil. My turn now," Lilly said with a wicked smile. "What about you?"

"What about me?"

"Plans?"

"I have no plans."

"I've got just over a week of filming and then I'm back off to LA."

"I know. I'm trying not to think about it."

"Well you need to, Tom. Have you made enough money out of me to start over?"

"Not as much as I'd hoped."

"Did you make any money out of those recent shots?"

"What, the ones of you in the country park? A little, Vince didn't seem that impressed. Not raunchy enough. I can see his point, you holding a kestrel was hardly front-page news."

"Why's this Vince so hell-bent on destroying me?"

"He's not after destruction, he's after wealth. Think he knows the paparazzi game has a short life span. He reckons he'll have to retire soon. Making his mark before everyone else jumps in."

"I can only see it getting worse."

"So does he. Soon everyone will be paparazzi. All it will take will be a decent cell phone."

"Great, so less privacy, more invasion."

"I wish I could tell you otherwise."

"Well on the plus side, Sally loved those country park shots, said the press lapped it up."

"Really?"

"Yanks love Brits. And they loved the thought of me turning British. Party girl turned nature lover. They dig that shit."

"Do you think Sally realized you weren't in Devon?"

"No, all she saw was green. And I'm not talking fields."

"Well, whoever is making the money from it, it certainly wasn't me," I said, taking a sip of my drink.

"How cute are those two?" pointing at the odd couple over

106

at the bar, one a giant, one tiny. "Shows you there is someone for everyone."

"You think some people get with anyone? Y'know, rather than being alone."

"I'd rather be an odd couple than no couple at all."

"It's not always that easy. Having a good life with the wrong person will only ever end up one way. It makes life easier, makes you financially and emotionally stronger being two, but it will only last till one throws their hands up and quits or finds someone right."

"Either real love or alone. Nothing in between."

"Yep."

She raised her glass. "Sounds like something we can drink to." Just then the house band stopped playing, the room turned quiet, all eyes turned towards the host.

"Ladies and gentleman." A man's voice rang across the hall, addressing the audience across table lamps. "And now for your listening pleasure this evening. Can you please put your hands together for the ever so beautiful and ever so talented Ruby Dubois."

We all clapped, watching as a woman, small and catlike, entered the stage and took her position behind the microphone.

"I'll be sad when this is all over, Tom." Lilly leant over.

"Me too. "I whispered back. "I don't know what I'll do with myself when it all ends."

"We've still got another week yet. We've still got tonight." Looking at me, the way any man would want to be looked at by someone so beautiful.

The lady began to sing, her voice warm, the piano soft.

"Would you like to… ?"

"I'd love to," she said, as men around the room led their partners to the floor and I led mine.

17

"These T-strap shoes are definitely not built for rock climbing," I said, struggling.

"We're not exactly climbing, Lilly. We're going downhill for a start."

I found this hysterical, I was finding most things hysterical as we walked down the pathway and through the dark and wind, Tom's jacket draped over my shoulders like a cape. I looked behind me at the party, still lit up in terrific yellow. The piano was doing its best to calm the last few guests down, not willing to let the night end. It felt too early to leave, which Tom argued was always the perfect time to leave. He was probably right, the party had peaked, couples drunk or sober, telling off or being told off, waiters bringing out hot chocolate and bacon rolls, hoping froth and carbs might fizzle out any heartburn or hangers on.

"Whose idea was this anyway?" I said, lagging behind. "We should be back in there. I've still got a few songs left in me yet."

"It was your idea, Lilly. And it was a good one. You need to sober up, otherwise I'll have to carry you upstairs again."

"Again?" as I linked arms with his. "When have you ever carried me to bed? I think I would've remembered."

"You fell asleep downstairs one night."

"I forgot about that. You could've left me, y'know. I'm quite prone to sleeping on sofas. I'll sleep anywhere. Or on anything. Or with anyone. Ha," she snorted at herself.

"You're the one who said you wanted to explore the island."

"Well I didn't know it was going to be this treacherous, or so fucking cold either."

"We can go back if you like? I don't mind."

"No, we've come this far. Besides I'm too windswept for party life. Is this safe? If they find our dead bodies down there on the rocks I'm blaming you, Tom."

"Look, I'm not keen on heights either. I'm probably more scared of being up here than you."

"Imagine I how I feel. My apartment is on a hill. The whole city is a fucking hill. Imagine being scared of heights and living on a fucking hill."

Tom smiled, it made me hold his hand a little tighter. I'd been holding his hand ever since we danced and I had no intention of letting go. I thought he was going to kiss me earlier, as we danced nose to nose, prepared myself for it, imagined what it would be like. Not kissing him was harder than kissing him and I very nearly did when he brushed my hair away from my cheek; instead, I rested my head on his shoulder until the song ended and my heart could beat normally again.

"Here it is."

"Here's what?" I said, looking around his body behind him.

"The pub."

"It's the size of mom's pantry and it's closed."

"Stop moaning. Here," he said, passing me my hot chocolate. "It's cooled down now." I took it in both hands, appreciating the warmth, as we sat down on a wooden bench. "Nabbed these too," he said, taking out two foiled parcels from inside his tuxedo. "Probably need my jacket dry-cleaned now. Smells of bacon."

"I'll buy you a new tuxedo," I said, my mouth full. "I'll buy you a whole rail of 'em."

"Not a bad view, is it?" he said looking across the horizon, putting his jacket over my shoulders.

"Pretty, though, all those little houses in the hills. You think anyone is sat looking at us? This crazy island. Our little Alcatraz."

"Probably."

"You sure you're not cold, Tom, just in a shirt? Here, have some of my drink."

"No, I'm fine. Think I have enough Tom Collins inside my system to keep me warm." He took a bite from his roll, as we both paused. No talking, our eyes outward across the sea as we chewed and thought. Black waves, black land, black sky, not even stars, not even a moon.

"Wish you didn't have to work next week," he said.

"Sucks doesn't it? I could ring in sick."

"Do famous people ring in sick?"

"I'm sure they do. I miss bunking off, I used to be pretty fucking good at it too, knew all the scams. Ferris Bueller had nothing on me."

"Would you actually do it? Ring in sick?"

"Probably not. Skipping Geometry and skipping a multimillion film production is a different level of truancy. I'm brave but not that brave."

"I see your point."

"And remember Frank and Sally are back in a couple days too."

"Don't remind me. Still can't believe we've only known each for less than a week. How fucked up is that?"

"Feels so much longer."

"It has been pretty full on."

"I don't think so. We've spent most of it watching movies and getting stoned."

"No, I meant full on as in I don't tend to spend six whole days with just one person. Especially not one I've just met."

"The whole thing has been surreal. Does it still feel surreal? Am I still the famous actress?"

"I still have the odd moment where I freak out, but it doesn't last long."

"Talk about extremes though."

"What extremes?"

"When I get on a plane and travel ten hours in the other direction, that will be the end. This will be over."

"Calm resumed finally," he smiled.

"And you're fine with that, are you? Never seeing me again?"

"I'm not fine with it, but I always knew that was the case. I never saw it finishing any other way. Think I'm just happy I met you at all, that I had the best few weeks of my life with you. I'm happy I had that."

"I'm not."

"There was never going to be any other outcome."

"Unless?"

"I know what unless you're talking about. And you know why I can't."

"I don't know, Tom. That's the thing. I don't know why you can't come back."

We stopped talking, I ate, took tiny sips of my drink, whilst Tom looked outward and downward.

"You wanna know why?" Tom said.

"I think I deserve to know."

"Surely you know already."

"And you think it's acceptable for me to have to guess why?"

"Would telling you change anything?"

"No, but it would help me understand why you are happy to let me leave, why you're happy for all this to be over. Cos at the moment I don't. I don't understand why you are willing to let this slip away. Your wife is dead. Not you."

He said nothing.

"I'm sorry, Tom. That was out of order."

"No, you're right, Lilly."

"About what?"

"All of it." He looked embarrassed. "Who told you? My mum, I bet. What else she tell you?"

"Only a little."

"How much do you know about Cassie?"

"Hardly anything. Bad car crash."

"You could say that."

"I can't even imagine what it must have been like."

"You never want to trust me."

"Least she died quickly, painlessly. I'm sure you get told that all the time. I know it doesn't sound much to hold onto. But it's something."

"Painless, who told you that, Mum again?"

"She said she died on impact."

"Well, she didn't."

"Why does your mom think that?"

"Because I told her. Because the truth is horrible. It's better this way. Like you said, dying quickly and painlessly is something for people to hold onto."

"And what about you? What do you hold on to?"

He didn't answer, eyes somewhere else.

"Who have you told about how Cassie died?"

"No one. And it will stay that way."

"You can tell me. It might help getting it off your chest."

He still didn't answer, took a few seconds before he could look at me.

"Cassie didn't die on impact."

"Did she know what was happening? Was she conscious?"

He nodded. "She kept crying, screaming in pain, screaming for me to help. But I couldn't get to her, she was trapped. I tried to get to her, tried to get through but I couldn't. I held her hand. That's all I could do. Told her she was going to be OK when I knew she wasn't. There was blood, so much blood."

"What did you do?"

"Nothing. Just kept hold of her hand. Told her to keep her eyes on mine, tried to stop her looking down at the blood and metal."

"And Molly?"

"Molly was in shock. I don't think she knew what was going on. But Cassie did, I could tell by the panic in the voice, she knew. The way she looked at me and Molly, she knew she was

112

dying. I was helpless, pathetic, I should have been able to save her."

"I'm so sorry, Tom."

"It's best to tell people she died instantly. It's easier for people to cope with, to cling onto when they are grieving. I couldn't bring myself to look them in the eye and tell them what I saw, and what she said. To tell them she was pregnant."

"Pregnant?"

"The doctors told me." Tom's face downward. "Four weeks pregnant. I didn't even know myself."

"Did Cassie know?"

"If she had known, she'd never told me."

"That's so sad."

"I lost my wife and child that day, Lilly. And I can't even tell anyone about it. I have to keep it built up inside."

"Did you get any help? Doctors? Counselling?"

"A little. None of it worked. The only thing that worked was this job, meeting you."

"I don't know how you managed to be so strong."

"I didn't manage at all. Took me a long time to get to where I am now. I don't think I'll ever fully recover from it. The things I saw in that crash, it'll never leave me, and nothing in self-help books or in medicine will ever change that."

"It will get better, Tom." I put my hand on his. "Every day it will get better."

"Can you see why the lie is better for everyone? Cassie died quickly and painlessly. And no one will ever know otherwise."

"You could have told me about Cassie sooner."

"I was protecting you from it."

"I don't need protecting, Tom."

"Well, protecting me then. I didn't want you to see me as a widow, to give me that look you are giving me now. I've seen it too many times. Just because my wife died doesn't mean every person I meet has to know. I just want to be Tom, not the guy everyone feels sorry for." Tom looked across the horizon, so did I, the ocean had turned darker. "You don't agree, do you?"

"No, I do actually. Lies are necessary sometimes. The world is a horrible place. I mean it's beautiful too, but there is so much pain and suffering, so much bad news. There is no benefit in her parents knowing the truth. Or Molly, it will just eat away at them, make things worse. And not everyone needs to know about Cassie, not until you want to tell people."

"Molly will ask questions one day. I can't keep lying to her."

"You can. Tell her you saw a bright light, a beam from heaven, angels took her away, whatever makes it easier to digest, whatever makes Molly able to lead a normal life, one filled with hopes and dreams and naivety, not memories that rot and fester, that make her weak and fragile."

"I can't lie to myself though. I know what happened."

"Oh, you can, Tom. You can. I lie every day."

"To me?"

"To you, to myself, everyone."

"Like what?"

"Small things. Big things."

"Like?"

"I don't know what you want me to say, Tom. I lie to myself about my relationship with my mom and dad, pretend it's OK when it's not. I lie in interviews, pretend I'm this happy, successful career woman. I lied to Frank about the coke that night."

"You told me you didn't take any."

"Well I did. If it makes you feel any better, I lie to myself too."

"Why do you need to?"

"My life isn't great, Tom. It may look like it is but my life is screwed up."

"What? Your parents?"

"No, not them. I can't blame them for everything. I'm equally responsible for fucking things up."

"Everyone fucks things up."

"Some fuck-ups are bigger than others."

"Like?"

I didn't answer.

"You can tell me?"

But still more quiet, more looking anywhere than at Tom.

"Did you know at thirteen weeks a baby can feel pain when it is aborted? Real pain, I read that somewhere once."

"Lots of people have abortions, Lilly."

"Safety in numbers doesn't make me feel any better. And is still no excuse. I stopped a beating heart, Tom. I terminated my own flesh and blood."

"You made what you probably thought was the best decision at the time."

"Best decision." I laughed. "It had fucking fingernails, Tom, toenails, it had a face, my face. And I let someone murder it."

Tom came over and sat beside me, put his arm around my shoulder, held me till my tears stopped.

"I'll never be happy, Tom."

"I'm tired of it though. Aren't you? I'm tired of being sad, feeling hard done by."

I nodded.

"I won't lie to you anymore, Lilly. I'm sorry for keeping so much back from you."

"I don't mind lies, Tom. Just try not to hurt me. I've been hurt before. I can break at any time."

"We make a great fucking couple don't we? Fucked up, screwed up. Lying to others, to ourselves."

"Please come back with me to LA, Tom."

"I can't."

"It wasn't LA's fault what happened? I need you, Tom. I can't do it on my own."

"I just can't. I'm sorry."

"Then I'll stay."

"Don't be silly, Lilly."

"I'll stay. Move to England."

"What about your family? Your friends? Your career?"

"I can do all three from here."

"You couldn't. It's too much for someone to give up."

"I'm not given anything up."

"You're drunk and it's late."

"Tom, I'm not that drunk and it's not that late."

He looked at me, smiling. "You're fucking wild y'know? I thought I was wild but I can't compete."

"I mean it though, Tom. I would move here."

"I know you would, that's why I can't let you."

"And you think not having your permission would stop me?" I leant over and kissed him.

Lips cold. Trembling hands.

18

Outside storm pelted thin glass, music was playing from our stereo, sweeping guitar riffs washed over the room, inside it felt silent. Lilly was still undressing herself, first her jewellery, the pins from her hair, I felt inclined to do the same, unbuttoned my shirt, took off my trousers, now I was laid on the bed, waiting as Lilly unrolled her tights, peeled off her dress. It was slow and intentional and it could have gone on for forever and still wouldn't have been long enough. In our half-lit room her body looked mesmerizing, the way her back moved, her curves, it was a temptation no man could refuse, so why was I talking myself out of it, why was I so petrified? The word 'marriage', the word 'vow', the name 'Cassie', the name 'Lilly', my heart filled with enough love for both, when neither should have to have been shared.

Breathing became a conscious decision as she removed her bra and laid beside me. I could tell she was scared, I was too, but I should have been strong enough not to be, she deserved better than indecision and I felt the fool being inches apart, eyes to ceiling, one bed and two people not sure what to do next.

The goddess and the coward.

19

I'd been nervous before but never like this. My hands trembled as I removed my earrings, my heart pounded as I unclasped my necklace, I consciously took my time, it felt significant, ritualistic, the removal of my clothes and make-up, my jewellery, becoming natural again, like an ancient tea ceremony. I'd never felt like this, never had sex like this before, so calm and meticulous. I knew how hard this would be for Tom, the conflict going through his head, but I wanted to be sure he was ready, let him have enough time to make his decision. For me, too; we were both as damaged and fucked up as each other, it wasn't the time for passion and impulse, it needed to be rational. Despite what the world thought and what everyone had read about me, including Tom, I hadn't actually slept with anyone since Max. And even though I'd kissed a few guys whenever they'd tried to take it to its next logical step I always found an excuse, not that I even understood what the actual excuse was. I just knew I wasn't ready, the thought of giving myself to someone again both emotionally and physically, like I'd forgotten how to do it, how to enjoy it, my body and my brain over-thinking it. Tom was the only person I'd met who would have the patience, who would understand how difficult it was and how fragile we both would have to be with each other.

I caught a glimpse of him in the corner of my eye, he was topless, tattooed, toned, how I imagined him unclothed. I'm glad he couldn't see my face, I was blushing, smiling too, a smile that hadn't left my face since our kiss on the cliffs. Tonight would change things, what happened next could make things unrecognisable and I was frightened by its extremes.

I removed my clothes, stripped myself down to underwear, as I laid beside Tom. I couldn't look at him, I wanted to, I just couldn't, lay there working out what might be going through his head. Maybe he wasn't ready, maybe this was a mistake. Someone had to say something, do something, two chess players fully aware of the danger and reward of who moved first.

We laid there for minutes, hours, I couldn't tell, the room felt different, the world felt slower.

Accidentally our eyes caught one another, I smiled, laughed, he smiled back, took my hand, kissed my head as I cuddled into him as tight as I could, his arms wrapped around me, rain and wind and music, but I'd never felt so warm and protected or so happy.

Nothing else happened that night, it didn't need to, we both knew the significance of what it meant, sex would have cheapened it and wonderfully and incredibly not making love had only made me love him even more.

PART TWO

The island/ April/Shot 268

20

The set was quiet today, I'd forgotten my love scene with Rogan, forgotten my handbag. I'd only been away for four days, but like returning from school after summer vacation unable to write or read, I was the same, scrambling around like the new kid, asking where everything was and where I should be.

Typically, despite wearing lingerie, it was still complicated to dress me, layers after layers, the sheer effort it must've taken to get a girl naked back in those days, finally getting his wicked way with her would've been a fair reward. Good luck to Rogan when they yelled "Action" and he had to work out how to get me out of the thing.

I looked over, Rogan had his arm around Jon, whatever they were talking about looked fucking hilarious. Rogan had that way about him, making everyone laugh, life just one big joke, probably why I could never take him seriously. I was sure every teenager on the planet would be jealous of me right now, abut to manhandled by such a specimen, but honestly the thought of him kissing me and touching me made me want to barf.

I would've preferred a larger crowd, too, the more people the less it insinuated something sexual was occurring. Jon disagreed of course, felt an intimate scene required an intimate audience. No girls too, just me and four men, though I didn't think the lack of females was preplanned, just an unfortunate coincidence. This was in fact my second love scene in my short career, my first feature Max had me half naked, doing all manner of filthy positions and making all sorts of grunts and wails. In the final cut it looked pretty harmless, a clever edit meant all the world saw was a few shadows and a glimpse of a nipple. But live, it was pretty intense, take after take, Max never said so but I think he liked watching it, and liked even more being able to live out the twisted fantasies in his twisted little head. I should have never got with that man.

My cell buzzed. It was Tom, telling me he missed me which was cute but completely unnecessary seeing we'd only left each other the night before, made me laugh though. Last night I was sharing a bed with Tom and now I was about to share one with Mr Chris Rogan. From one love scene to another, hey, always the hussy.

"When you flying home, Goodridge?" Rogan took a seat next to me.

"Soon. I think this weekend."

"Me too." He took a huge bite out of his apple. "Probably be on the same plane. I wanted a private jet but what can you do? Gotta fly coach instead which sucks dick."

"I'm sure you'll be fine in first class."

"Fuck first class. I should have my own plane. Air Force One, baby, all the way."

I bit my tongue, changed the subject. "You nervous about our scene coming up?"

He grinned. "Do I look nervous?"

"No not at all," I replied, wondering why I asked such a stupid question in the first place.

"Jon just gave me the rundown on how he wants me to have my wicked way with you."

"And what did he say? Just so I can brace myself."

"Oh, don't you worry." He took another bite of apple. "You just lie there and enjoy the ride."

"How's life as a superhero, Rogan? Must be hard to keep so grounded. How do you do it?" He could sense my sarcasm, he was dim, but not that dim.

"Hey, man. If you're happy doing shitty little movies like this for the rest of your life you go right ahead. I know where I'm going, sweetheart. Fucking global man. I'm gonna be on T-shirts, toy stores, lunch boxes. Live fast or last baby."

"Till another six-pack comes along."

"Can I give you some advice, Goodridge?"

"No."

"You need to drop the Winona Ryder act. Nobody likes a girl that doesn't smile."

"Is that so?"

"You're not even that hot any more, you're not that young and you're not that talented. The only things you're good for is fucking around or fucking up. If I was you I'd get the money anyway you can, darling, cos your movie career is on the way down, man, like straight to DVD."

"Fuck off, astro boy."

"What about *Playboy*? Whilst your tits are still facing upward. Some reality series like *Survivor* or *Dancing with the Stars*?"

"You're an arsehole."

"When I put on the costume, my cape, every girl in Hollywood is gonna wanna a taste of me. You included."

"Not me."

"I like a challenge."

"I suppose walking and talking at the same time must be quite a challenge for someone like you."

"See you in ten, Goodridge. Pucker up," he said, licking his lips suggestively, smiling; despite his perfect teeth he always had an ugly smile. He disappeared into a crowd of suits, a scoundrel amongst gentlemen, as I tried to work out how the hell I'd be able to get through the next few pages of script without ripping his dick off mid-scene.

Rogan later apologized actually, which I totally wasn't expecting, said he was having a bad morning, that he was an arsehole. I agreed, accepted his apology, asked him if he meant any of it, he said only some, with his smile and dimples, he had a face easy to forgive and guaranteed I wasn't the first girl to soften on his command. Weirdly, spending the rest of the day on set was actually quite enjoyable and him putting his hands through my hair and kissing my neck was something I wouldn't mind doing again. Still didn't mean I particularly liked the guy, but girls are girls and being given attention by someone as handsome as him, it was hard not to go all dumb and ditzy, not that I'd tell Rogan, or Tom for that matter, it would inflate one ego and deflate the other.

★ ★ ★

I'd got back off set about an hour ago, I already felt shattered, pretending to have sex was even more hard work than having sex. Wasn't even like I could rest, I still had to make the farmhouse look presentable, get rid of anything that resembled a fun time. Finished, I was now in the games room, jumper pulled over my knees, mug of fennel tea, looking out over the driveway for a certain car to park in front. Waiting like it would make it sooner, though sooner implied I was excited. I may have been, but I was other things too, mostly I was fucking terrified.

I'd never really used the games room in the way it was intended, always found it cold and bare. It wasn't a room with me in mind, a foosball table and a few battered board games were wasted on a girl with weak wrists and an empty brain. I liked the armchair I was sat on though, its leather cracked and soft through age rather than design, it was easy to sink into.

I'd never noticed the pictures before, I stood up and walked over to each wall. Whoever owns or owned the house looked like they'd had a great life here. In fact, not just here, everywhere, they'd done so much, seen the wonders of the world. Smiles on boats, smiles in vineyards, deserts, smiles on temples. And it was a recent happiness, the photos were black and white, but it didn't look nostalgic, like they could have been here last year or last week. I would like to meet this family, they looked fun, looked like they had stories. Sometimes I wondered where they were now, whether they were down the road or on some other continent, sipping drinks I'd never tasted and food I'd never dare try. I should get out and about more, get out of my comfort zone, get out of chic hotels and off sun loungers, start exploring more than cocktail menus. Places I would never have dreamed of going, places a little more dangerous. Africa, Japan, South America, places where Tom and I could disappear, where even paparazzi wouldn't dare follow. I was jealous of the family on the wall, jealous of what they owned. This house wasn't mine, sometimes I had to tell myself that, my bed, my Aga, my garden, they weren't mine at all. It was all borrowed, as was the little idealistic life I'd made for myself here, it would all have to be given back. In a week I'd migrate back West, back to an empty condo and a life too busy to really enjoy.

My cell buzzed. Tom, asking me again if I was sure I didn't want him there for moral support, to which I replied I didn't. Another message, telling me my hair looked nice, I told him that he should go. Another message, telling me to keep clear of the window, telling me he'd do one more sweep of the house before the heavens opened. "Be safe," I told him, and I meant it.

I kept forgetting there was more than one out there, that I was being watched by more than just Tom. Despite my advice, Tom was still adamant to locate his rival and hell-bent on catching them in the act. I was past caring, whoever it was lurking around in bushes wasn't causing harm, whatever secrets they had, they were keeping them close to their chest, whatever they were up to, they were doing it quietly with no impact on me or my career, at least not yet, 'yet' being the word that worried Tom the most. He's been on the phone to Vince a lot, so he told me, trying to get to the bottom of any scandal that might be coming my way, but according to Tom there has been little or no coverage of me at all across the pond. The world has finally lost interest, at least for the time being, even Vince, who apparently was 100% not coming to check up on us after all. I'd never met the man but the fact he'd found something more money-making than me was a huge relief to both me and Tom, meant we could breathe easy till I finally had to fly home. I should count myself lucky, my time in England could have been a lot worse, the threat of paparazzi was worse than the reality, maybe I'd overestimated them, thought them finding my farmhouse was a sure thing, though a lot can happen in a week.

I wished we were back at yesterday morning though, mine and Tom's little white island, down the steps to our little mermaid cove where we had our breakfast. Afterwards we walked to the top of the cliff, the roofless ruins of a chapel, a hundred seabirds, a thousand miles high. It was the perfect place to tell each other how we truly felt, but I didn't and neither did he. Mostly we just talked about what happens next, with neither knowing really how to answer.

One thing for sure, if I was going back to LA then things would have to change. My time with Tom had made me realize how much of my talent I was wasting and taking for granted. I knew I was fucking up, I wasn't making movies I was proud of, I needed to change that, make more of a stand. Needed to stop talking about quitting and start taking control of my shit. When I got home, things were going to be very different, a shift in focus, projects for me not anyone else, credible films made by credible people, ones that got people talking, ones that slow-burned before they set fire, movies people either loved or hated, movies that bombed or triumphed and did both spectacularly without apology or explanation.

Most probably it would ruffle a few feathers back home but Tom had that effect on me, made me feel determined and certain of myself, made me grounded. Whether everyone would agree with the new radical version of myself, I didn't know, but people would have to get on board, top to bottom, publicists, agents, those closest to me, Sally and Frank included. Sally being the one I was most reluctant to tell.

Tom said a strange thing yesterday as we drove back from Burgh Island, we were talking about Frank, how I met him, what he was like, talked about Sally and out of the blue he asked me if

I trusted her. I said yes of course, and he changed the subject, but I could tell there was a reason why he asked. And even though he didn't say it, I guessed by the sheer fact he asked, he wasn't sure if he trusted her himself.

I thought I heard a car, got out of the seat to see if it was them. It wasn't, I sank back into my chair, tried to maintain my resolve whilst I still had it built up in my system, hoping it wouldn't wear off by the time they arrived.

★ ★ ★

"Come here, girl." Frank grabbed me, lifted me up off my feet. "Let me take a look at you." He checked me up and down. "Not a scratch or nick. Just as I left you."

"You been working out, Frank?" I said, feeling his arm. "You look like a grenade."

"No, just lugging Sally's luggage around. Let's just say we were way over weight allocation. Cost us a small fortune." He stood back again. "I've missed you. Can we just forget everything that happened before? Fresh slate. When you're my age it doesn't serve you too well to hold a grudge."

"Sounds good to me. I was an idiot. It all got blown out of proportion."

"Can't we do all the peacemaking inside where it's less monsoon?" Sally appeared from around the back of the car. Shades and her cell phone, her heels dashing across gravel with her handbag over her head.

I followed her back to the doorway, as Frank quickly sorted out the suitcases.

"You looked tanned, Miss Sally."

"Don't know how, I've been stuck in an office for the last two weeks. I've got a fat chance of getting tanned here, have I? Never feels right stepping off a plane to grey skies. Especially when I've just left blue ones behind. Hardly a welcome home, is it?"

"Sorry no banners. I'll look after you, don't worry," giving her a big hug. "Take it easy tonight, get you both over your jet lag. Run you a nice bath. Turn that frown upside down."

"Better be a hot bath. This is no sort of temperature," she said, disappearing down towards the kitchen.

"Mad dogs and Englishmen, hey?" Frank ran inside, shaking the wet from his head and luggage, as I closed the door behind them. Thinking about one Englishmen in particular mad enough to still be out there in the rain and cold. Wondering how it was so easy for me and Frank to slip back into familiar comfort, whilst it always felt like me and Sally had fallen out or were about to. Like I always needed to brace myself for defence or attack.

21

Last night was fucked up. I'm not quite sure where to start. Still trying to make sense of it, how so much could change in twenty-four hours, how two islands could turn me into such opposite extremes. To think just the night before me and Lilly were sat dining by candle light, the sound of double bass. Though barely a mile off shore the distance between ocean and land was enough to make us feel untouchable. We were both fools for thinking once back on the mainland that anything would've changed. It all started on the drive home, once Frank and Sally had finally arrived, looked like they weren't going anywhere for quite a while, so I decided to call it a day, hit the road. When about halfway home out of the corner of my eye I noticed something familiar on the other side of the road. I had to do a double take when I first saw the licence plate, pulled the car over quickly, checked the scribbled note in my jacket pocket. I quickly found a decent spot to park, somewhere I could sit and watch, close enough to not be noticed, near enough to chase. Then it was just a case of waiting.

It was already late, which didn't help. I'd just been sat outside Lilly's house for the last few hours watching nothing move, the last thing I wanted was watching something else that didn't move. But that was what I did, sat and stared at a parked car, the sun going down behind it, the clock above my steering wheel going from seven to nine, hours longer than they should have been and the longer the time dragged, the darker the night, the more I wanted to catch the guy red-handed. Staying alert felt hard work, this wasn't like the movies, coffee and doughnuts, someone to talk to as you staked out, talk football, talk about our wives, our sex lives.

Surveillance when done alone required patience, when I had none, concentrating with heavy eyes, the fact I hadn't eaten since lunch. I could feel my fists clench, I could smell blood, I could already imagine the reward of finding him, Lilly's face when I told her, the hero I'd become.

What happened next was embarrassing, launched myself across the street, pinned the guy up against his bonnet, screamed in his face, swore and spat, demanded answers. The guy looked pretty shaken up, I didn't notice his wife and kids behind him, they looked pretty scared too, made his two little girls cry, they couldn't have been much older than Molly.

Turned out the car was a rental, he'd only picked up the keys the day before, only just arrived in Devon on the train, showed me railcards and paperwork to prove both. I apologized of course, over and over, to him and his family, gave him my phone number, told him to bill me for his cracked glasses, wished them a nice holiday, drove home and drank a couple of bottles of beer, lay in bed trying to work out what had just happened, what it all meant.

Next morning, bright and early, I was the only person stood outside the car rental shop, the manager looking quite surprised as he opened the gate and switched off the alarm, made a joke about first customers getting a free machine coffee. Of course, he told me nothing, asked him questions that I knew he would not be at liberty to answer, watched as his face changed from smiles to stern once he realized I wasn't interested in his fleet of cars on the forecourt. Whoever the car's previous driver, the store manager wasn't going to tell me, he was pretty damn clear on that as he ordered me out of his office.

I told nothing of this to Lilly, as far as she was concerned there was nothing to worry about, so I shouldn't worry either; after all, what had any of this proved? In fact it may have just proved that whoever used to be here, wasn't anymore. Or it just proved that whoever was here was still here, the only difference was, they knew I was looking for them.

22

The next morning Frank had resumed his familiar position back at the stove, eggs in a skillet pan, coffee in a cafetière, just like he'd never left. It was a morning that felt too early for all of us. Last night was fun, more fun than I'd expected, started off calm, they both had long baths, ate the pie I'd cooked them, talked about our times away from each other. Frank by his own account had done very little, which I could tell by his face was his idea of pure bliss. Sally was all work talk, she filled us all in on my career, where it was going, the direction it was heading. I agreed, any bold plans I'd dreamt up before their arrival had been replaced with nods and smiles. I didn't have the energy for a battle, not on their first night back. I was happy just to accept whatever direction I was being pointed in, as along there would be no raised voices, better I chose my moment wisely, once things were settled. We ended up getting through quite a few bottles, jet lag meant Frank and Sally were far from tired, I had to excuse myself around midnight, left them with the last of the Merlot and the number of a taxi firm. I think they left around one.

"When are we gonna talk about the sports car sitting in the driveway? The one under the sheet." Frank chewed his toast.

"I wondered when you'd spot that."

"When? Why? How much?"

"Just over a week ago. Cos it's the coolest car in the world. What was the last question?"

"How much?"

"A lot."

"How much a lot?"

"Over fifty."

"Lilly." His eyebrows all twisted

"C'mon Frank. Admit it's cool."

"It is cool, Lilly. Completely unnecessary and stupid. But it's pretty far out I must admit. What is it, like a 1.5?"

"What, you looked already?"

"I had a sneaky peek under the hood this morning."

"We could take her out after I finish work."

"Best you keep it under the sheet. If Sally asks I'll tell her it's a lawnmower."

"What's that about lawnmowers?" Sally walked into the kitchen, eyes on her cell.

"Lilly mowed the lawn whilst we were away, that's all. You want coffee?"

"Yes, lots of it. Feel like I've done ten rounds with the Klitschko brothers."

"Wine or jet lag?" I asked.

"A little bit of both. What about you, Frank?"

"You know me. Ready to blaze a trail," he smiled. "You want toast, Sal?"

"No, liquid lunch today. You had toast today, Lilly?"

"No," I lied.

"Good. You do look a tad rotund," she said, sipping coffee, oblivious to either insult or my reaction. "I've just booked the flights home for us. We've got to go to New York first, darling. I need you to meet up with some people of mine. Important people." She took another sip. "What, Lilly? Why are you frowning?"

"Can't we fly straight back instead?"

"No can do. We'll only be there a week, two weeks tops."

"What day we flying?"

"June 6th. God knows what day that is. My brain is still fried. Sunday rings a bell."

"Less than a week. Fuck."

"Don't pull that face, Lilly."

"I'm not pulling a face."

"Don't tell me you're still all green-fingered."

"I like it here. That's nothing to be ashamed about."

"Or proud of either. You must prefer back home, no more rain, no more mucky England."

"I like both, Sally."

"Anyhow you'll love New York. I'll show you around. None of that tourist bullshit. The real New York. Knocks spots off this little ghost town."

I looked at Frank. He smiled behind his coffee.

"Right. Shower, Lilly. Busy day today." Sally inspected the fruit bowl.

"You two fancy going for a drive later?" I jumped on Frank's back. "I've found some really cool places I know you'd like. I mean, it's no Manhattan, but I like it."

"I'm game." Frank moving me into a headlock.

"You two stop messing about. Get ready. And no, Lilly, you're too busy for chauffeuring."

"What am I busy doing?"

"Don't you even look at your own schedule?" said Sally, throwing me an apple. "Filming for a few hours."

"Good, so a short day."

"I wasn't finished. I need you home for just before five. Some homo won a radio show. He gets to ask you ten questions via webcam."

"Sally. You can't say homo."

"Well, he's a super-fan and he's male. Chances are he pitches for the wrong team. You do seem to attract the queer folk, don't you?"

"I'm not even going to answer that."

"Don't worry, I've already vetoed any questions I don't like. He'll be harmless, those sorts normally are."

"Why not let him just ask his own questions?"

"Lilly, don't start. What time is it?" she checked her watch. "Right, car is picking you up in an hour. Be ready."

"I don't mind driving. I've been driving loads since you've been away."

"Absurd. The car will pick you up in an hour. Can't have you driving around with your top down like Diana Rigg. Don't think I didn't notice, Lilly. That car outside is going back."

"That's not your decision, Sally," I heard Frank say from behind me.

"Frank it's impractical."

"Even if it is, it's still Lilly's decision."

"Yes, and I'm not going to watch her waste it."

"I'm going to get ready," I said, leaving the two of them to fight it out between themselves. I hadn't the energy, took myself upstairs.

Outside my window I looked out across the garden, checked if I could see Tom, which I couldn't, checked if I could see anyone else. Whoever was out there was either not there at all, or better at hiding than I was at finding.

23

The lady passed me a paper bag of warm bread as I gave her the last few quid in my denim jacket, before finding somewhere in the sun to sit. I didn't feel like Dot's breakfast today, which was no offence to her, just tired of being waited on, where every meal felt like I was at a restaurant, my drink topped up, my dirty plates taken away, a bench and a good view was a nice change. Kingsbridge looked peaceful today, like it hadn't yet woken up. You wouldn't have thought it a Monday morning, there were no people in suits rushing to work, no beeping traffic, there were more boats than there were cars. It was a village where everyone walked or sailed, where people had time to do both just as slowly. I tore a piece of bagel, took a gulp of orange juice, felt like I was abroad, my legs a few metres from the quay, the warm sun on the back of my neck, as good a time as any, I thought.

I'd been putting off ringing Vince for the last few days, normally he rang me, but from the last time we spoke he sounded like he had bigger things on his plate. I very nearly confessed the last time we spoke, had this mad moment where telling him about me and Lilly seemed a good idea, one that would end up with a pat on the back, as opposed to a stab.

As much as I told myself I didn't care, that Vince wasn't a true friend, deep down I still felt like an arsehole for what I was doing behind his back, for all his flaws he had thrown this job my way, he'd put money in my pocket, he didn't deserve to be lied to. In all honesty, I was more afraid of what he'd do with the information rather than what he'd do to me, I got take a fist, a bloody nose, but I couldn't handle him taking it public, which was the reason why for now it was best he was kept in the dark.

He took a long time to answer and when he did he sounded put out.

"Oh my God, man, I'm sorry," realising my mistake. "I completely forgot the time. I haven't woken you up, have I?"

"It's fine, it's fine. I was just in the shower." I could hear scrambling around.

"What time is it where you are?" I looked at my watch. "Must be about one. So sorry. How comes you are still up and about?"

"Less about my late-night washing habits. Let me take a wild guess and predict that Lilly is filming today."

"She is an actress, Vince. She is here to make a movie you know."

"What about Frank and Sally?"

"What about them?"

"The fact they arrive later."

"How d'ya know about that?"

"You told me, dumbass."

"I doubt they'll get to here till gone five and I reckon none of those three will be straying too far tonight. I think this rest of the week is gonna be a similar flavour, I can't see there being much action here before she leaves."

"It is what it is."

"You not mad? I thought you'd be sending me home seeing as there is no money to be made. Doesn't seem like anyone is sticking around, everyone with a camera has flown back home with their tail between their legs."

"Better you see it through. You never know, one thing the girl has proved these last few months is she's unpredictable."

"You want me to stay on till she goes I guess?"

"Might as well see out the fourth quarter. I always finish things I start, no matter the result."

"Bet you're glad you didn't come in the end. Would have been a waste of money and time."

"And you know I hate wasting both of those. How's your mom?"

"OK. Not great. Still lots of tests. Be easier once I'm home."

"Not long now."

"Did you manage to find out anything about our new competition?"

"Nada. I still think what you saw was a coincidence. There's a lot of Silver Mercs on the planet. I wouldn't worry too much anyway. It doesn't change our game plan."

"I suppose whoever is snooping around Lilly, the good thing is so far they haven't bared their teeth yet."

"You keep me in the loop. Let me know as soon as you are on the move. Look, Tommy, I gotta go."

"At one in the morning?"

He didn't answer.

"I'll call you in the next few days, Vince."

"Best I call you. I'm in and out of stuff this week."

"Speak soon, Vince."

"Don't lose sight of the prize, hey. Wherever she is, you need to be."

"Sure."

"Say it back."

"I heard you, Vince. Wherever she is, I need to be."

"Good," he said, as I tried to enjoy the rest of my breakfast, the rest of my view. Vince always had a way of making me feel shit, rushing breakfast or rushing off, either way I felt guilty.

24

"This is awesome Frank. I so needed this," I said mid-mouthful. "You want my gherkins?" handing them to Frank.

"Don't you get ketchup over my upholstery, you." His lap was covered in napkins as a precaution.

"Where's Sally again?"

"Some conference call. I didn't ask, she looked stressed and had lots of notes. That is never a good sign." He took a slurp from his straw.

"She seems pretty hardwired today."

"She has a lot on her plate. A lot of things are up in the air in regard to what you do next."

"Making sure I'm not getting screwed over, I hope."

"You aren't getting screwed over. The opposite in fact, that's why she is so stressed, sifting through contracts and small print, getting you the best deal possible."

"She doesn't have to be so hard on me all the time though. Despite what both you and her think, I can fend for myself."

"You know what she is like. She just wants perfection."

"Perfection is unobtainable. Hence why I'm sat here eating drive thru when I should be eating carrot sticks."

"She isn't doing it to be mean. She knows the game is fickle, she doesn't want the size of your butt to mean another girl edges in front."

"You don't think it's just because she's never had children?"

He laughed as he chewed. "No, I don't think that at all."

"You think she's lonely?"

"If she is, she doesn't show it. Most of the time she's too busy too care." He ate the last mouthful of his burger, screwed up the wrapper. "How comes you're so full of questions about Miss Anquist all of a sudden?"

"Just wondering what makes her tick. She's a hard one to work out."

"One of a kind, that one."

"You don't think she'd do anything behind my back, do you?"

Frank frowned. "What would make you say a thing like that?"

"Nothing, just something someone said."

"Who?"

"No one."

"Well this 'no one' is way off point."

"So, I have nothing to worry about. I can completely trust Sally?"

"You shouldn't even have to ask, Lilly." He still looked mad, slurping his shake. "You be careful who you talk to. A listening ear can be a running mouth. You finished?"

"Yep. All done," passing him my rubbish. "Sorry, Frank, I need to… " letting out a humongous burp, sweet and fizzy.

"That was impressive," Frank smiled, starting the engine and driving out of the car park into five o'clock traffic. "Let's get you back. You have a date with the webcam, remember?"

"What we gonna tell Sally? She'll smell it on us, and she'll wonder why we won't touch our dinner."

"We've only had burgers, Lilly. We haven't committed murder."

"I know, but you know what she's like. She'll make a big drama out of it."

"Her dramas never bothered you before."

"Well, they do now. Frank is that car behind following us?"

Frank checked his rear view. "Don't think so, why?"

"I swear I saw it back at the drive thru." I tried to catch sight of the driver. "It's a silver Merc, right?"

"That's not a Merc."

"Oh."

"You seem a bit jittery today. Something up?"

"Nothing's up, Frank. Just think it should be you keeping an eye out for stuff like this, not me."

The car went quiet, radio low, the rain showed no signs of stopping, I didn't look at Frank, I knew that comment was below the belt, but in all honesty, it was what I was thinking.

"You sure you're OK? You seem different," he asked me.

"Do I?"

"I can't put my finger on it."

"In a good way, I hope."

"No, actually."

"Wow. Cheers for that, Frank. You know how to cheer a girl up."

"I'm just being honest. You seem on edge this last few days, looking over your shoulder, quick to snap. That isn't like you."

"Isn't a girl allowed an off day? I've got a lot on my mind round now."

"Did something happen whilst me and Sally were away?"

"No."

"You sure nothing is up? You can tell me anything, Lilly, you know that."

"No, but sometimes I wish you took your job more seriously, Frank. You're my security, not my lunch date."

He didn't answer. He put his foot down. We both kept an eye on the car behind as it became smaller and smaller, till it wasn't there any longer.

★ ★ ★

Later I rang Tom, asked him if he was any closer to finding my newest stalker, even made him ring Vince, who in my eyes was still the prime suspect, let Tom try to catch him off guard, put him on the spot, get him to make a mistake. Tom wasn't too happy about it, said he'd spoken to him the day before, said there was nothing to catch out.

Tom messaged me an hour later.

I told you. It's not Vince.
How do you know for sure?
His wife answered his cell. So, unless she is here too, it's not
Vince.
Fuck.
Lilly, can we meet somewhere? I miss you.
No.

25

Tuesday was shit, argument with Sally, argument with Rogan, argument with Frank. Wednesday, I just got up and went to work, tried to keep out of everybody's way in case I said something stupid again. The only person I hadn't argued with was Tom, but that was only because we hadn't talked much. Felt like we hadn't fallen out, but something was definitely off, something had changed, mostly on my part. Just struggling with what to do next, I was in this weird head space where I knew I either needed to commit to him 100%, or run in the opposite direction. I was used to the running, it's what I do best, but commitment has always been something I've found trickier. Might explain why I've been so much of a bitch this week, torn between the biggest grin or largest frown.

Today was Thursday, another long day, my head hurt, my jaw ached, I was all kissed out. Rogan was on top form today, had me in stitches, it felt good to laugh, made me forget about all my decisions. Everyone was in high spirits today, last day on set, so lots of patting on the back, lots of champagne corks. I think the fizz had gone to my head and worse still there was more fizz to come later.

I'd just arrived home, the driveway was busy with vans and more vans, this last week they just kept turning up outside, arriving empty before driving off filled. I watched from the window, Sally delegating and directing, orchestrating my possessions' safe return overseas, she looked agitated. I didn't know where half of it had come from, I'd brought so much, but worn so little, packed like every night I'd be attending a ball, when in fact I'd spent most of the time here in bra-less in baggy tees. Sally ordered Frank to help with the lifting, ordered me upstairs and in her exact words said I needed to try and make sense of my bedroom, whatever that meant, making things into piles, turning mess into order.

I didn't even want half the stuff, I was grateful for all the clothes, but it was too much for one person and guaranteed when I got to LA I'd be given even more. I told Sally to give them to charity, no person should own so much, it was a waste to have much beauty hanging up in a darkened wardrobe. Sally disagreed, of course, said it would be criminal to give Marc Jacobs away to some crack whore or street rat, she had a point, the last thing an addict needed was haute couture. I could auction them, choose a cause I believed in, give them a big cheque they can use rather than wear.

★ ★ ★

My cell buzzed, it was Tom. He'd just got here having followed me from filming, asked me to sneak out. I said I was busy packing.

My cold response was intentional, I was purposely separating myself from Tom, preparing for my departure, giving my heart a chance. I'd done a lot of thinking these past few days, about me and Tom. One thing was for sure, I was in love with him, madly and deeply, but if he wasn't ready to come to America and if I wasn't serious about moving to here, then really what future did we have? Our relationship wouldn't survive. I mean I had thought about moving here and I'm sure I would love it, but in doing so I'd be pretty much writing off my career and saying goodbye to my family and friends. It was a big ask, that was problem, it was big ask for either me or Tom, one of us would have to give up so much, too much. Right time, wrong place, that was the fact of the matter. It would be easier if I just told Tom the truth, tell him what we had was over. I walked to the window, opened it, let the warm breeze fill my bedroom. I couldn't see him, but I knew he was there.

My cell buzzed. Tom telling me I looked beautiful, that it was a nice evening for a walk. I thought briefly about his invitation, jumping over the fence, giving him a hug, letting him take my hand as we walked through the meadows and fields. I hadn't seen him in days, I wanted his company again, but it would only make things harder. I decided not to reply, turned my cell off, concentrated on my clothes piles.

"Close the window, Lilly. The last thing I need right now is a draught. Here, get this down you." She passed me my drink.

"What is it?"

"Berroca for you. Lemsip for me."

"Still not feeling great, then?"

"Can only breathe through one nostril but apart from that, I'm fine. Trust me to get a blocked nose during a mini heatwave." She looked around the room. "Looks far more bedroom than clearance sale now, doesn't it?" She sat at the end of my bed. "Now, the majority of your clothes I've sent back to LA. But obviously we'll take your main suitcases with us to New York. If you need anything in particular I'll send someone to get it for you."

I nodded.

"Why, thank you, Sally," she said dramatically. "Thanks for organizing it all for me. Thanks for spending several hours organizing it for me, Sally," rolling her eyes.

"It is your job, you know."

"What, sorting out your dirty laundry? I don't think that was ever in the job description."

"You know you love it, Sally. I've never met anyone who loves multi-tasking as much as you. You ever thought about being a wedding planner?"

"Not till recently." She smiled. "Probably pays better. And I'd take a Bridezilla over an actress any day of the week."

"Sally, what am I going back to?"

"Back to?"

"America. What am I going back to when I land? Just so I know what to expect. Is it still me and Max?"

"Afraid so. Don't think that will go away soon either."

"Why?"

"Well, neither of you are talking. Without answers the press like to make up their own."

"And what answers are they giving?"

"Depends if they are Team Lilly or Team Max. Depends on who they class as the victim. At the minute, the majority are siding with Max."

"Why?"

"He's declaring his love for you."

"He's what?"

"Doesn't seem interested in other girls. Anytime you come up, he's nothing but gushing praise."

"You spoke to him recently?"

"No actually, which is unusual for him. Do you want me to call him?"

"No, let him do whatever he is scheming."

"Well, whatever scheme you think he is plotting it's certainly working to our advantage. You'll both do well in all of this."

"We're Taylor and Burton. Is that what you are saying?"

"If you are both clever enough."

"Sally, this isn't a chess game for me. This is my life."

"I know, Lilly. And I intend to make it the best life it can be."

"With Max or without?"

"Lilly, can I be honest with you?"

"You're asking my permission now. Wow."

"Lilly, the fact of the matter is, as much as I hate to say it, Lilly Goodridge on her own is not as interesting or as marketable as when it's Lilly and Max."

"I'm not interesting on my own. Is that what you are saying?"

"I'm just telling you the truth, Lilly. You and Max need to work as a team, if you want to sustain a long and prosperous career."

"We're not on the same fucking team, Sally!"

"Doesn't matter. As long as you are both playing the game then everyone wins."

"I don't believe this. I'm going to grab a shower. Get ready for tonight."

"Oh yes, the wrap party. Where is it again?"

"I've got it written down somewhere."

"What will you wear?"

"I don't know yet."

"Shall I pick you something out?" going over to my clothes rail.

"Sally, I'm sure I can dress myself."

"I only help you do this because I care," already passing me hangers to try on.

"Your care sounds more like control."

"That's not fair. I care for you like you were one of my own."

"But I'm not yours."

"Lilly, don't be like that."

"I'll be ready in an hour. Shiny and sparkly just like you want me to be."

"I give up with you sometimes. I really do." She stormed out.

Thirty minute later she was straightening my hair. Neither of us talking.

26

"Well as long as you feel up to it, Mum. It isn't a requirement for Molly's day to be so hectic."

"I do for it the both of us, Tom. I don't like being housebound either."

"Just don't tire yourself out. A few hours watching TV isn't going to harm her. Or you."

"OK, less of me and my frailties. How's things with Lilly? Still all doom and gloom?"

"Afraid so. She's… "

"Wait a sec, Tom. My name is being called from upstairs. I think someone is still constipated." Mum put the phone down. I couldn't quite make out the exchange but it sounded important, I heard clapping

"What's the big news?" I said, intrigued. "Sounded celebratory. Has she gone for a shit finally?"

"No, but she has just sat on it. In the last two days, she's gone from being petrified of it, to sitting on the potty. I'm very optimistic that any day now and she'll do the deed."

"Tell her she's a good girl. Text me when she finally does."

"She better go for a poo soon, otherwise I'll have to take her to doctor's. I might feed her fig syrup, that will get things flowing in the right direction. You were saying about Lilly and your disagreement."

"Nothing to report. Still the same."

"She's probably finding the whole thing difficult. Just let her do things at her own speed."

"Mum, it's Thursday. She flies back on Sunday. That's three days. We haven't got time to take things slow."

"It's only America. The world is a small place these days. Just because you'll live on different continents doesn't mean it won't work. In this modern age, especially."

"Being a voice on the end of a phone would hardly be a relationship."

"Then you need to act fast, Tom. Talk to her."

"I've tried. I message her every day, but she barely responds."

"Then you must think of a way of getting in front of her so she has to respond."

"I can't just knock on her door. Not anymore. I don't know who would answer."

"You're creative, Tom. I'm sure you'll find a way. Is there no way you speak to her face to face?"

"Not without Frank and Sally around. I'll think of something."

"You always do."

"Any news from Cassie's folks? Any letters?"

"Sorry nothing here."

"I don't like how quiet it's gone their end."

"There's probably a logical explanation for it. I wouldn't worry yourself about it."

"Lou might be mad I rejected his invitation."

"Would you still reject it now? Since the whole Lilly situation."

"Florida isn't Hollywood. Might be the same continent, but it still would be too far."

"I still don't see why you and Molly can't just move back to LA."

"I told you, Mum. I haven't enough money to start over."

"Tom, your girlfriend is a multi-millionaire probably."

"One, she isn't my girlfriend and two, I'm not no freeloader."

"Better to be a freeloader, then lose her forever. I get the impression money has nothing to do with it. Even if you had the money, you still wouldn't."

"I would."

"Well, prove me wrong, Tom, prove me wrong. What is there

for you here? I don't think staying put sounds that attractive either. You need to find a town or city. Scunthorpe, Grimsby, Sheffield, somewhere with a heartbeat, somewhere where you can find decent work."

"No, Mum. That isn't an option. I can't leave you, not with how you are."

"What if we move together? The three of us."

"Seriously?"

"I've lived here long enough. The house drives me mad now, too many things I dislike and I haven't the time or the money to change them. I'm bored of the quiet, too. Need a bit more noise and excitement and youth."

"Mum. You need to rest. You're still not 100% well."

"I'm sure they have cancer in these other cities too, they'll know how to deal with it."

"Mum stop saying cancer. We don't even know it's cancer yet."

"Well anyway one hospital ward is no different than the other. Besides if I'm going to be stuck in bed, I'd rather be stuck with a different view for a change and not that bloody pond."

"We'll see. Let me get home and unpack my suitcase before we start selling up."

"Oh, and remember later tomorrow I'm going to hospital again. Different doctor this time."

"What time?"

"Four. Don't worry, I've Molly sorted, she's staying over at next door's."

"I should be home, Mum. I hate the fact I'm not home."

"I'm fine, Tom. They said I'll be in and out. Can you tell Lilly I finally got around to watching one of her films the other night? It was on late on Channel 4, had to record it, watched it in two halves. Loved the film, really sad in parts, especially the ending. Beautifully shot, a lot of breasts too."

"Sad endings and semi-nudity is her forte."

"Make sure you tell her."

"If she speaks to me."

"Have you told her about Cassie yet?"

"I have."

"You still mad at me? I genuinely thought she already knew."

"No. I should have told her way before you did. Surprised she didn't run a mile."

"But she didn't, Tom. Take solace in that. She didn't run."

"Not till Sunday. Then she'll run a mile. More miles than I can count."

"I bet my left nipple she doesn't." I heard a cry. "Tom, I better go, I think Molly's tummy's hurting again. I better see to her. Call me later, OK?"

"Will do. Give her a kiss from me."

Mum hung up the phone, I made myself a coffee, turned on the laptop, started browsing through airline websites, scrolling through the cheapest flights to LA, pretending I had the balls to do anything apart from watching Lilly leave.

27

"Jon. Can I ask you a question?"

"Why of course, young lady," he said, cutting his scallop in half.

"You've never actually told me why you cast me for this role?"

"And darling, why would you want to know a thing like that?"

"Humour me please. Another anecdote you can add to your list."

He looked to the ceiling, squinting his eyes like it was up there somewhere. "If memory serves, there was no audition."

"Not a good sign so far."

"Don't take it personally. I did a shed load of crazy substances in the eighties; my long-term memory is nearly as bad as my short. Can I try some of your bouillabaisse?"

"Had you seen any of my movies?"

"I think it needs a bit more salt," he said, taking his spoon to my bowl. "Everything in this restaurant needs salt. Seasoning must be contraband in this part of England. What was the question again? No, I hadn't I'm afraid." He wiped his mouth with a napkin. "Don't look so glum. If truth be told, Lilly, there wasn't much thought process. Someone handed me a list of potentials for the role and I picked you."

"Based on?"

"Based on merit of course. Even though I hadn't seen your movies didn't mean I was incapable of reading. I knew your reputation, what you were capable of. I knew how much the screen loved you." He poured some more wine for himself and then me. "What have I said?"

"Nothing I didn't already know."

"Don't think for one minute I'm belittling your talent, darling. You have a naivety and a power that can never be taught. You either have that or you don't. And you have that star quality, Lilly. You do."

"But can I act?"

"You don't need to act, darling. You're you."

"I'm an actress, Jon. I get paid to act."

"You get paid because people want to watch you, there is a big difference. You focus too much on your limitations. You just need to work with good directors with good scripts. The rest will come naturally."

"I'm typecast," I smiled.

"Again, you're focusing on the negative, sweetie. Some of the most well-known faces in cinema were typecast, and all the better for it. You think an audience wants to see Stallone in tailcoat and breeches, Jon Wayne flying a spaceship? Take Chris Rogan for God's sake, look at him." We both peered across the table at him, he was mid-soup. "For all his failings, he knows his place in the game. Knows what the audience wants. Bravery and biceps."

"But an audience must like actors who can adapt, transform for a role, come out of their comfort zone."

"It's all balls and a complete ego trip, a fad. Losing weight, putting on weight, beautiful women making themselves ugly. It will pass, I assure you." He put his knife and fork down. "What's brought all this on, Lilly? All this self-doubt?"

"Ignore me. Let's talk about something else."

"You still having a bad time in the press?"

"No, they've left me alone for the time being. Just been thinking about my career lots. Don't quite know what to do next. Doesn't help that I've done such a bad job for you."

"If you think you've done a bad job, darling, then that is an error on my part as well as yours. My type of direction doesn't suit everyone."

"I know when I've given something my everything. And I haven't given that to you."

"You're too harsh on yourself."

"I'm my worst critic."

"The only criticism that hurts is the criticism you agree with. Here, have some more wine."

"I think I might quit, Jon."

"I don't believe you."

"I've thought about it a lot recently. Go back to dancing. Go back to drop-in centres. Help people. Quit whilst I still have some dignity."

"Dignity is overrated. Though you must do what you must. It would be a crying shame of course."

"I know it sounds like madness. But deep down I know it's the right choice. There's other things now I want to focus my life on. People I want to spend my time with."

"Then I shall call a toast. A quiet toast between me and you."

"Don't, you'll make me cry, Jon."

He leant in across the table, almost nose to nose. "Do anything, Lilly, but let it produce joy." And we clinked our glasses.

"Is that one of your own again, Jon?"

"Not this time, Lilly. Can't take the credit for that one. Good luck, Lilly. I mean that. In whatever you do."

The waiter came over and started taking our plates away.

"I'm going to grab some fresh air." I got up from my chair. "Make some room for my blade of beef."

"I'll order us some more Barolo. Hopefully you'll go out retired and come back an actress again."

"Jon. The way my brain is at the moment, that wouldn't surprise me."

★ ★ ★

Outside I lit up another cigarette. I was being naughty, I blamed the girls, once I was offered one on arrival, it was always going to become two. I could think of more favourable places to smoke, but a few paparazzi had set up camp out by the front, so the manager had kindly let me use the staff hang-out, instead of festoon lights and heat lamps I was out amongst the bins, the sound of chefs and the smell of cooking. Another type of backstage.

I was glad I came in the end. I nearly didn't, had to drag myself, but like most nights doomed from the start, after a cork had been popped I soon forgot my bad mood.

I took one last drag, stubbed the butt under my shoe, about to go back inside.

"Hey, Lilly."

I turned around. It was Tom. White shirt, black tie.

"What the fuck? You made me jump."

"Sorry."

"What are you doing here?"

"Would you believe me if I said it was a coincidence?"

"What are you doing here?"

"I'm eating here too. I'm sat a couple of tables away from you. Table for one in the corner. It must look so depressing."

"You're spying on me."

"I just wanted to see you."

"You could've just asked to see me. You don't need to sneak around."

"I'm sorry if this looks bad. I only had good intentions. Can we please talk? Not now, but after the meal. I think we both have things we need to say face to face, not over the phone."

"I don't know, Tom. Everything is a little fucked up right now."

"Have I done something wrong?"

"No."

"It feels like something's changed."

"Like I said, I don't know. I'm confused."

"You think me and you was a mistake?" he said.

"Not at all, no."

"Then why do I feel like I'm being let go?"

"I'm sorry, Tom. I don't know what you want me to say."

"Do you want me to back off?"

"I'm not saying that."

"Then what are you saying? You're not making sense."

"I can't give you any answers right now."

"I need you to tell me how you feel. I'm going crazy."

"That's how I feel, Tom."

"Do you want to be with me?"

I looked at him, a man on his last legs, on his feet, but on his knees.

"Yes, I do want to be with you. More than anything. But this will never work, Tom. It just won't."

"We'll find a way. I know I said that I wouldn't… "

"I think you are an amazing person. You are an amazing dad. But me and you will only ever end badly, end up with one of us getting hurt."

"Yes, it's a gamble. All relationships are a gamble."

"My heart can't take a gamble, Tom. And I don't think yours can either."

"You're running away again. Is that your default position? To flee when things get hard. What about all we talked about?"

"Tom, I need to go back inside."

"There's more that needs to be said. Here is the wrong place. What time will you be home later?"

"No, Tom. It's better this way. It's better it ends now. As friends, not enemies."

"Why are you so complicated? Is it intentional?"

"Bye, Tom."

"Please don't do this."

"I'm doing this for you. I'm poison, Tom."

I felt a tap. It was Rogan.

"Everything all right here, Lilly?" he said, putting his arm over my shoulder.

"Yes, this is my friend Tom. He was just leaving."

"Come inside. Everyone is waiting." he said, giving Tom a look up and down, a warning shot.

"Bye, Tom. I'm sorry."

"You're sorry? We still need to talk. I need more of an explanation than 'I'm sorry'."

"I think she made herself quite clear, dude." Rogan pushed Tom's chest away, as we started to walk back inside. I didn't look back but I knew it would take more than a whispered apology to stop him from giving up just yet.

Back inside, Rogan ordered the table of round of shots. I knew how this night would turn out after downing that first Sambuca and quite frankly I couldn't think of anything I wanted more than to order another round and then another.

★ ★ ★

I knew it was stupid, from when I offered Rogan to come back to mine, to when I let him open another bottle, for not stopping when he put his hand on my leg. I was in the bathroom, sat on the toilet, working out my escape, or more his escape. Could just say I was tired, I thought, which wasn't a lie. could just say I made a mistake. God, he was so beautiful, most men aren't, handsome but not many were beautiful, his skin was so perfect, his eyes. He talked to me like I was being undressed, and worse still I felt inclined to do the same. He was dangerous, he knew what he was doing, though so did I, we didn't even live close to each other, in fact the opposite, out of the way opposite. He knew and I knew what sharing a taxi meant and although we'd only flirted so far, it was getting to the time of night when one of us would have to advance or withdraw, time to either make excuses or make out.

I looked in the mirror. My reflection blurred, my eyes blotchy and red, but nothing handbag make-up couldn't hide. I looked again, not at my features but at myself. This was a terrible decision, whatever the initial intention, even if I felt it would produce the right outcome, it was still an awful decision, one fuelled by alcohol, fuelled by the desire to fix myself or damage someone else, I didn't know which. Was it coincidence I'd brought Rogan back, knowing Tom would follow? Was I that bad a person? Was it the only way to make Tom give up? I was drunk but not that drunk I didn't know what I'd done and what I was about to do.

I opened the door. Candles were lit that weren't lit before. Sexiest man on the planet pouring us both more wine.

Oh fuck.

I was stupid for inviting him back, yes, stupid for letting him stay, and there was still plenty more opportunity for stupidity to come.

Lots more.

28

Go home Tom. This is pathetic. Have some fucking backbone and at least let it end with some dignity. Pull the car around and go home, get some sleep, next morning just pack up and do what I should have done days ago, get back up North where I belong, not sat in the dark staring at shadows and silhouettes. What was I even waiting for? I followed them home, I saw them both giggling and laughing as they went inside, I knew what was coming next. If this was Lilly proving a point then it was working. So, unless I planned on knocking the front door down and taking on a man twice my size then all that was left was to leave. Forget Lilly, forget this house, forget I ever came here, forget falling for someone again. Get back to my family, to reality, not this far-fetched fucking fantasy.

I looked down at the envelope on the passenger seat, what a waste of money, tickets that wouldn't get to see an airport either here or across the Atlantic.

29

"Dot, I'm not ill."

"You've got a temperature. You need rest and rehydration. Here, I've got you some magazines and some Lucozade." She fluffed up my pillows, tidying away old plates and cutlery.

"Dot, I just need sleep not mothering."

"And what time did you finally get in your own bed last night?"

"I don't know. I ignored the clock when I got back."

"You live life like an owl."

"Vampire sounds cooler."

"Do you mind if the dog sleeps in your coffin with you. He's had his tail between his legs all morning. Bad weather brings out his bipolar." Tripod was already spread across the floor by the side of the bed. "Looks like every man and his dog is departing on Sunday. America is going home en masse. I assume your lady friend has something to do with that."

"Bet you're happy. Back to peace and quiet."

"Oh, I won't see peace and quiet till after the holiday season. Besides, peace and quiet is overrated, I'd rather be boil-washing bed sheets then spending a whole day with him indoors."

"You and Alfred talk, surely?"

"The old man? He's OK really. We ran out of conversation in the early nineties. We share a bed but very little else. You promise to visit though, still? Bring your mother and little Molly. I won't charge you."

"Dot, I wouldn't expect to be given a free room."

"You'd be my guests, not my customers. Before I forget, I'll bring your tuxedo up later on. Sorry it's taken so long. I've been up to me eyeballs, as you well know. You'll be pleased to know, the pockets no longer smell of bacon."

"Thanks, Dot."

"You never did tell me about the tuxedo night with your lady friend. Was it a success?"

"It was."

"I'm going to need more than that, Thomas. Apart from reading my Mills and Boon, having you here is the closest I get to romance."

"A gentleman never tells."

"Very commendable. I've raised you well."

There was a knock on the door. Alfred stood with his clipboard and trolley, stressed and calm in equal measure. "I better get off, Tom, I'll be back at lunchtime with my home-made cure. My turkey and split pea soup beats anything you get over any pharmacy counter."

"Here Dot. I've got something for you by the way."

"For me?"

"For all your help, this last month." I stood up, walked over.

"Don't be silly."

I handed her an envelope.

"You don't have to give me anything, you silly sod."

"You'll have to get Alfred a tuxedo," I said, watching her read it. "Can't have him turn up in one of his old jumpers."

"Don't know what to say," she said, just as Alfred appeared behind her.

"I highly recommend you order a Tom Collins. Though don't have as many as I had."

"I feel a bit overwhelmed," she said, staring at it like she'd just won a lottery, showing it to Alfred, who looked at it like he'd lost. "Come here and give me a big hug."

"Are you crying, Dot?"

"What if I am?" she smiled, wiping her eyes with a tissue. "Do you need some fresh towels whilst my trolley is outside?"

"No, Dot afraid not. I've decided I'm going to leave today."

"Leave?" she looked shocked. "Why?"

"It's just time to go."

"You said Sunday. I wrote it down. Sunday 6th."

"I know I did but things have changed."

"What has changed?"

"Lots of things."

"Has something gone on with Lilly?"

"You could say that."

"I thought you said it was a success? Your romantic night away."

"I thought it was too, but I don't think I was ever right for her. She's made that quite clear."

"In what way did she make it clear? Did she tell you this?"

"I think sleeping with someone else is pretty clear-cut, Dot."

"She never? When?"

"Last night."

"That sounds very unlike her. You must be so cross."

"I'm not her biggest fan right now, to be honest."

"Well, don't do anything that you'll regret."

"Like what? It's not like I've got thousands of photos I could sell to the highest bidder. It's not like I couldn't sell my story for millions of dollars."

"You wouldn't."

I didn't answer.

"Why don't you go and see her? Talk to her. Try to get to the bottom of this. Has she tried to contact you?"

"She's messaged me twice this morning. Rang me a couple of times too. Not that I've answered any."

"You see? It means that it isn't over, Tom. Go on. Go and see her."

"No, Dot. It's best I pack and get out of here. That's the right thing to do."

"I think you are being silly, Tom."

"No. This is the only smart thing I've done since I got here."

30

Red wine had always given me the worst headache, regardless of whether it was cheap or the best that money could buy, the end result was always the mother of all hangovers. The Sambuca should take some if not all the responsibility too.

I had no idea of the time, the sun was out, I knew that much, I heard keys rattle too and the front door being opened and shut, that was about an hour ago. There was a cup of coffee next to my bed, it was still hot. Frank or Sally or both, or even burglars, polite burglars, either way I wasn't getting up just yet.

I checked my cell. Ten o'clock and no messages, not sure whether to feel relieved or depressed. I closed my eyes regardless, I must have fallen back to sleep, when I woke up my coffee was cold and someone was opening curtains.

The first thing I knew I had to do was speak to Tom.

★ ★ ★

"Feel any better for having a shower?" Frank said from behind his newspaper.

"Not particularly." I crept across the room, flopped down on the sofa, putting my legs across his lap. "Cleaning my teeth three times didn't help either. It's Friday, isn't it?"

"Last I checked."

"Just to recap. I'm not working today, am I?"

"Not unless you are filming on your own."

I closed my eyes for a bit, zoned out as Frank turned pages.

"I'm gonna book a holiday soon." I sat up. "For all of us."

"And where are you planning on taking us?"

"Anywhere. Far away. New Zealand, Thailand, Japan."

"Have you seen your calendar for the next few months? You haven't get a day off till Thanksgiving by the looks of it."

"Lucky me."

"Busy means you're doing something right."

"I wish I could believe that."

"I see you're full of joy today aren't you, Miss Sunshine? You want a pancake stack, turn that frown upside down?"

"I think I'll need more than home-cooking for that to happen."

"You go upstairs and get dressed for the day, throw some jeans on, brush your hair. I'll make a start on breakfast."

★ ★ ★

"What have you done now then, Lilly?" passing me a carton of juice like I was capable of pouring. "You look like you caused a mischief last night."

"What makes you say that?"

Frank leant across the table. "You've been checking your cell every ten seconds."

"Nearly did something silly, that's all."

"Nearly?"

"Yes, very nearly."

"I like the word nearly. Shows you knew when to stop. That hasn't always been the case," he said, sifting flour, cracking eggs, pouring milk.

"Can I tell you something, Frank?"

"What?" I'd seen that look before, like he was bracing himself.

"Can you promise you won't say anything to Sally?"

"Lilly. I am not promising nothing till I know what it is."

"Frank. Swear it."

"You're not pregnant?"

"No Frank. But thank you for questioning my birth control."

"Tattoo? You didn't get caught drink driving again?"

"Frank, shut up a minute."

"Now I'm fucking nervous," he said, turning the bacon, flipping pancakes.

"How would you feel if I said I was thinking of giving up movies?"

Frank didn't look amused. "Run that past me again."

"How would you feel if I took a break?"

"I think you'd be out of your fucking tree, that's what I think. For how long?"

"I don't know, a few months, a year."

"What did you do last night, Lilly?"

"What I did last night has nothing to do with this. I've been thinking about this for weeks."

"And you want my consent? My approval?"

"I want your opinion that's all. Frank, be careful you're... " pointing at his frying pan.

"I think it's a mistake, Lilly. I've heard Sally talk, I don't think you realize just how huge you will become. I'm talking big. Huge."

"That's why I need time off. I'm not ready for that level of stardom."

Frank didn't answer, took his eyes back to saving his pancakes from the bin.

"If you are worried about your job, Frank, please don't worry. I don't want you to worry about money. I will make sure you are covered."

"That's a hell of a thing for you to say to me, Lilly."

"I didn't mean it like that. I just meant that I would make sure you are sorted in the interim."

"I'll do just fine, thank you very much," handing me breakfast. "I get paid for what I earn and I would never expect a handout."

I started to eat my breakfast, tiny bites, as Frank sipped his coffee.

"This is happening then?"

I nodded, mid-mouthful.

"When?"

"I don't know yet. Soon hopefully."

"How long for?"

"I don't know. Till I feel ready, I suppose."

"What if you never are?"

"Then so be it." I looked at Frank, he looked pretty sad. "But that isn't my plan. I'm not giving up. I just need some time, need to slow things down."

"You're positive on this? You understand what you may lose by doing this?"

"I know the risk I'm putting on my career."

"I wasn't talking about your career," he said, as we heard keys rattle and Sally come in through the front door.

"She'll understand," I whispered.

"You honestly think that?" Frank said under his breath.

"Think what?" Sally barged through the kitchen.

"Oh, nothing."

"Let me take a look at you," grabbing both my cheeks, staring into my eyes. "Let me assess the damage. How bad?"

"Bad."

"Do anything that I should know about?"

"Nope."

"You sure? I'd rather know now."

"Positive. Can I look through your bag? See if you have anything to get me through the morning?"

"Help yourself. *Mi bolsa es tu bolsa.* There's some Naproxen, should be some Tramadol too. Tramadol kicks arse. You won't shit for a week, but it gets rid of headaches, gets rid of most things. Catatonic and carefree, my kind of drug."

"You eaten?" Frank offered her pancakes.

"A small one please."

"Lilly here was talking about treating us all to a holiday." Frank smiled. "You reckon we could squeeze it in? I think we deserve it."

"I don't disagree. It's a nice thought but I don't think it plausible. A weekend away, but nothing longer."

"You not really a holiday person are you, Sally?" I said, downing a mouthful of tablets with my OJ.

"They are OK in moderation."

"So, if you had some time to yourself what would you do?"

"I'm easily pleased. A good bottle of wine and a book."

"No, I mean what if you had a proper vacation. Some real quality time just for you. No work, just time to unwind, do things for yourself."

"I don't know, do I? I'm a work person, Lilly. Holidays put me on edge. Too much time to think. It isn't good for the body to be docile. My parents learnt that the hard way."

"Your parents?"

"They both worked till they were into their early seventies, both fit as a fiddle. You know what happened when they retired? When they had time to themselves?"

"What?"

"They died, that's what."

"And you think your body would shut down?"

"Not shut down, but I wouldn't cope well with time on my hands. My mind is troubled, Lilly, full of bad things and negative thoughts. Best I don't give it time to roam. I will always work. I will always give up my life to work. That's why I love this job. I mean I moan a lot, I'm stressed a lot but I wouldn't change it for the world."

"You assume time for yourself means being idle. Having a break doesn't mean you can't be productive, you can still be busy."

"I beg to differ."

"What about you, Frank? If you some time just for you?"

"Might stay with my family in Washington for a bit. See how Chillum Heights has prospered in my absence. After that, who knows? Not a lot, surf, eat, sleep. I've always fancied building something, like a tree house, my own boat."

Sally's cell buzzed, she took it from her jeans pocket, gave it one look. "I need to take this," she said, walking into a different room.

I looked over at Frank. "I'm dead in the water, aren't I?"

"Yep."

"I'm going to hell for this."

"Yep."

"You're not helping, Frank"

"Sally's a big girl. She'll hate you for a bit, but she'll calm down. I can't imagine she'll be unemployed for long, there are plenty of troubled actresses out there in need of a governess. Question is, when you decide to come back in the game, whether Sally will too. When you gonna break it to her? Tell her about this long vacation of yours?"

"Soon."

"Before or after we fly back?"

"Before, as long as I grow big enough balls to tell her by then."

"Might be a long flight back with Sally ignoring you."

"That's if I fly back."

"You're staying here?"

"I might be. I need to sort some things out. It's all a bit up in the air."

"Sort what things out?"

"Just people I need to talk to."

"Who?"

"Just someone."

"You're being very vague here, Lilly."

"I met a guy, that's all."

"What guy?"

"Just a guy."

"When?"

"After you left."

"Please tell me he isn't the reason for this sudden change of direction."

"He doesn't even know I'm doing this. This has nothing to do with him."

"Seems an awful coincidence to me. Who is he?"

"I'd rather you meet him before you start making judgements."

"That doesn't sound promising." Frank took my empty plate. "Jesus, Lilly. Anything else you wanna tell me today? Anymore revelations?" just as Sally marched back into the kitchen.

"What's wrong with you, Alquist?" I joked, hoping it would crack a smile.

"You tell me, Lilly," she handed me her phone. "What the fuck is this?"

I looked at her cell. Photos of me, lots of photos of me.

"Is this how you keep busy when me and Frank are away?"

"How did you get these?"

"Where even is this?"

"That's a hotel."

"And here?" scrolling through her cell, showing me a photo of me in Tom's garden.

"That's a friend's house."

"What friend?"

"A friend, that's all."

"And please tell me this isn't you smoking pot."

"It was only once, Sally, I swear."

"Who took these?"

"I don't know."

"Don't play dim, Lilly."

"How did you get these? Who gave you them?"

"How and why aren't important right now. You need to explain yourself, Lilly. I need to understand what the hell you have been doing."

"She's met someone." Frank stepped in. "She's met a guy."

"Who is he?"

"His name is Tom," I said, looking at Frank, wondering why he wasn't fighting my corner.

"And who is Tom? What is Tom?"

"He's a friend."

"And how did you meet this Tom?"

"We just met."

"What does he do?"

I sat down. "Sally, who sent who these? I need to know."

"Right now, I don't know, Lilly."

"You don't know?"

"It's anonymous. I have no idea who sent it. I have no idea who else may have been sent it either."

"What's so bad about them? OK I smoked some pot, but the rest are harmless."

"Lilly, read this email. Read what it says at the top."

I looked at her cell again.

"What does it say?"

"It says these are just a warning."

"A warning, Lilly. Whoever sent this has more and it looks like there is worse to come. I'll ask you again, Lilly. What else have you done?"

"Nothing." I felt myself starting to cry.

Frank put his arm around me. "Tell us about this Tom."

"Tom wouldn't send these."

"How much do you know about him? How did you meet him?"

"He's paparazzi. I mean he was paparazzi."

"Oh, for fuck's sake, Lilly." Sally's face was red. "You fucking child."

"It's not like that. He isn't like that."

"Lilly is there a chance… " Frank's voice calm and low, '… the tiniest of chances that this Tom might be playing you for a fool?"

"No, 100% no."

"He has no reason to use you for his own gain?"

"I bet it's Max. I bet it's some evil fucking paparazzi. It's not Tom."

"Can you be 100% it isn't this Tom?"

"Tom loves me."

"People will say anything to get what they want."

"How do I know you didn't take these?"

"This is absurd. You've finally cracked up. You hear her, Frank? She's finally lost it."

Frank put his hand on my shoulder. "Lilly, listen to yourself. Sally wouldn't do something like this."

"How can I trust anyone anymore?"

"Lilly, you need to tell us what you have been up to. This could affect your career. I might not be able to fix it if you don't tell me the truth. This is a vital time for us."

"I'm not telling anyone anything, least of all Sally. I know what you are up to."

"Lilly, where are you going?"

"Somewhere."

"You can't just leave. This needs sorting."

"Then sort it. Until then I'm trusting no one but me."

"Do you want me to come with you?" Frank went to grab my hand.

"That includes you, Frank. I'm sorry." I ran to the front door before anyone could stop me or follow.

31

Her driveway was empty.

I watched the house for about an hour, someone was in, lights were on, the chimney smoked. I checked my phone, Lilly hadn't attempted to contact me since the morning, I tried ringing her, now it was my turn to be ignored.

It wasn't the weather to sit and wait either, heavy clouds hung low above trees, I was about to be rained on, I already felt like shit, my nose blocked, my throat sharp, I didn't have the stamina to wait it out much longer.

At her front door, there wasn't any part of me that wanted to turn back. I'd had all night and all day to go through what I wanted to say to Lilly, I knew what I wanted to ask, I even knew how she'd answer. But it was an answer I wanted to see for myself, wanted to hear the words come from her mouth, not the ones in my head. After that I could leave, fill my car with everything in my room and never come back.

I took a deep breath. The door had a bell, instead I knocked.

She looked mad when she saw me, but not mad enough to make a scene.

"You better come inside," she said calmly.

She already knew who I was.

★ ★ ★

"You said sugar, didn't you?"

"One please."

"Sugar is worse than tobacco, you know. Has the same toxic effect on your liver as alcohol. There four teaspoons of sugar in a can of tomato soup, you know that?" passing me a mug, sitting down on the sofa opposite.

"I do all three, I'm afraid. Smoke, drink, sugar. I don't touch tinned soup though."

"Well, more fool you."

"Where is Lilly? I thought she'd be here."

"She was. But now she isn't."

"When will she be back?"

"Soon I expect." Sally paused to sip her drink. "Anyway, gives me time to find out about you."

"There's not much to find out."

"Oh, I believe there is. I hear you are paparazzi."

"I'm not paparazzi."

"You take photos of famous people, yes?"

"Not people, just Lilly."

"Sounds like paparazzi to me."

"Lilly is my first job."

"Harassment is harassment, Tom. Doesn't matter if it's your first or last. Who is paying you? Agency?"

"A man. You know him. Vince."

"No, I don't I'm afraid."

"Well, he knows you."

"I know lots of people, Tom. Is this Vince paparazzi too, or just some pencil pusher?"

"Yeah he's a pap. A pretty ruthless one."

"Show me one who isn't. Why send you to do his dirty work?"

"I keep asking myself the same thing. Maybe cos he was tied up back home. Probably because I'm the only British guy he knows. I don't know. I didn't want to take photos of Lilly. I want to make it clear that I had no choice. Situation arose which meant it was an offer I couldn't turn down."

Sally sipped her drink. "Tom. You had a choice and you made it."

"I didn't want to take photos of Lilly."

"But you did."

"Yes, I did. But not for long."

"And then you met. How?"

"I was just in the right place."

"Right place, right time, hey. Aren't you the hero? And then you wormed your way into Lilly's arms."

"No."

"She is an easy target. She trusts people. She falls in love easily. Of course, you knew all this and you took advantage."

"It isn't like that."

"Then what is it? Enlighten me. She is your fast ticket to a fortune."

"Not at all."

"What then? You want us to take your bait. You want us to beg. Is that your grand plan?"

"What are you talking about?"

"Don't play that game, Tom. I've been around long enough to know when someone has made their first move."

"I'm not playing any game."

"So why send me the photos?"

"I haven't sent you anything."

"Do I look like I have the patience for this? What is it you want? How much to make you go away?"

"Sally, hand on heart, I have no clue about these photos. Show me them."

Sally got her cell out, passed it to me, sat quietly as I scrolled through.

"I didn't send these, I swear."

"Then who did?"

"I think I know."

"Who?"

"Someone I haven't been able to catch."

"I think you are lying."

"My guess is, whoever sent these photos has more."

"No shit, Sherlock."

"Photos of me and Lilly, I bet."

"Doing what?"

"Things that sell newspapers."

Sally finished her drink. "And so begins the love triangle. A very profitable love triangle."

"Look, I wanted to make money, but not by exposing myself like this. I don't want to be famous, don't want my face on front covers."

"Everyone wants their five minutes, Tom. Don't make out you are any different."

"You have a low opinion of me, don't you?"

"I have no opinion of you. All I know is, Lilly makes bad choices. And I'm the one left to sort out whatever is left behind."

"And how should we tackle this situation?"

"Let me make this clear. There is no 'we'. There is us and there is you. All I care about is Lilly. I don't care where you end up in all this."

"I'm on your side."

"But I'm not on yours."

"Does Lilly know about the photos?"

"Course she does. I showed her."

"And what did she say?"

"Not a lot."

"Does she think I'm involved in all this?"

"I didn't have time to ask."

"She thinks it's me."

"Don't flatter yourself. She thinks it's everyone, including me."

Just then the front door banged shut. For a minute, we both thought it may have been Lilly, we both got out of seats, there was a moment's relief, but it wasn't her, it was Frank, looking at me like we didn't need an introduction.

"What the fuck is he doing here?" his teeth snarled, his fists clenched.

"Tom, this is Frank. Frank, this is Tom."

He looked at Sally. "Did you invite him?"

"No, he invited himself." She poured him a drink. "Frank, sit down, you're giving me indigestion."

I stood up to shake his hand, introduce myself.

"I'm not in the mood for pleasantries, boy."

"I'm not part of this. I've nothing to do with these photos."

Frank sat down. "Right now, I couldn't care less what you did or didn't do. All I wanna hear from you is where she is."

"I know as much as you do. I've only just found out she's missing."

Sally stood up. "Well, wherever she's gone, she's taken her passport with her."

"Let me help you find her," I asked.

"We don't need help."

"Three people searching is better than two."

"That may be, but I still don't trust you."

"Look, I know you don't believe me, but I'm not involved. Why would I be here if I was involved? It makes no sense."

"He has a point, Frank." Sally smiled. "Besides, he's too innocent to be dangerous. Just young and dumb and caught up in something too big to get out of."

"Thanks. I think."

"I wasn't being complimentary. You said before you might know who's behind this. Someone you hadn't caught yet."

"Just a car I'd seen a few times."

"That's not a lot to go on." Sally was pacing. "This could be paparazzi, but it seems far too thought out for them. What about Max? He's capable of shit like this."

"It's possible," I said. "Things weren't left well the last time he was here."

"He was here?" Frank looked pissed. "When?"

"Just after London."

"Why?"

"Sounded like Lilly wanted to keep the peace."

"And did they?"

"No. They didn't keep the peace at all."

Frank wasn't impressed. "That girl is a liability sometimes. She really is."

"And was this before or after you and Lilly became acquainted?"

"Before."

"So, Max isn't aware of this little holiday romance?"

"No. Not that I know."

"There is not a lot Max Salter doesn't know. My bet is he is involved."

"Who gives a fuck who is involved or not? Finding Lilly is the only concern."

"I would not worry yourself, Frank. She's a big girl. She knows where we are. She's just sulking."

"I don't think she is as strong as you think," I said.

"Oh, you do, do you? You've known her seven days."

"I know enough. I know she is capable of doing silly things. Doing things without thinking."

"And you think we don't know that?"

"Well, did you know she tried to kill herself? Tried to fling herself off that bridge."

Neither of them answered.

"I'm not sitting here waiting for bad news, assuming she will come back."

"Where are you going, Tom?"

"I don't know yet. But I'm not sitting here." I got to my feet. "Please, regardless of whether you trust me or not, if Lilly comes home, please get her to contact me. Please."

Sally looked at Frank. Frank looked at Sally. Any anger they may have felt towards me was outweighed far more by worry.

"We will."

"And I'll let you know, too. I'll make sure she calls you guys."

"Look man," Frank stood up, "I'm coming too. I can't just sit around doing nothing. It doesn't need two of us to wait for her here. Sally can stay just in case she comes home."

"Frank I'd rather... "

"I'm not asking here. I'm telling. Now where we going?"

"The only place she's felt safe," I said, both of us heading towards the door.

32

"I recognize this place." Frank pointed through the glass towards a blur of sky and ocean.

"You've never been here. Well, at least not with Lilly." I noticed Frank's smirk. "I can see why it's familiar. You were just over there," I said, pointing behind us. "Bantham Beach. You were all quite hungover if I remember correctly."

"And where were you when all this was going on?"

"Behind some sand dunes initially. Though after a while I got brave, at one point I was pretty much next to you." Frank looked pissed. "How would you have known I was paparazzi? I just looked like everyone else."

"That's no excuse. I get paid to know, not to sleep on a beach with a sore head whilst some mad fucker gets close enough to do something silly."

"I wasn't going to hurt her."

"Others would. There's a lot of bad people out there. People who aren't all there upstairs. Obsessives, stalkers."

"I used to be a tour guide. I've met quite a few fanatics up close."

"You don't know the half of it. I've seen the things they write, what they ask her to do, the threats."

"You can get restraining orders, surely?"

"And you think that will stop them? These people aren't bothered by legalities. Some don't even value their own lives let alone someone else's privacy rights."

"And Lilly has fans like that?"

"Course she has. They all have. I just have to make sure that the Oswalds and the Chapmans of this world never get close."

"I'm no maniac."

"But I have to assume everyone else might be. Or assume there are people capable of doing such things."

"Doesn't sound a nice way to live. To live in fear."

"In her profession, it's the only way."

"Then she's in the wrong profession."

I pulled into the top of the hill, parked the Jeep, turned off the engine. Burgh Island hotel straight out the windscreen.

"You think she's there?" Frank sniffed.

"If she's still in Devon it's the only place I could imagine she would be." I looked over the rows of roofs. "Can't see her car though."

"If she's in Devon, that is. Or England for that matter. Have you rung the hotel?"

"No. But we could try."

I got my wallet, trying to find the telephone number.

"What shall I say? Does she just use her name or something more creative?"

"Creative?"

"When she books hotels. Y'know, like Mrs Quack, Dixie Normous."

"No, she doesn't do that I assure you. I don't think any self-respecting adult would do that."

"What then? Goldie Hawn? Monroe?"

"You're asking the wrong guy. I'd just try her name. Goodridge or Goodmanson."

I found the number, dialled it and rang.

★ ★ ★

"What they say? I take it that was a firm no?" Frank said, finishing his cigarette.

I nodded.

"Let's take a walk over there anyway."

"What time is it?"

Frank checked his watch. "Seventeen forty-seven hours."

"What?"

"Nearly six."

"We better move quick. Before the tide comes in. If we're quick we can walk across. You want to borrow my jacket? I've a spare one in the boot, weather looks like it's turning nasty."

"I'll be fine." Frank slammed the door. "I'm used to colder." He was already off across the car park.

I'd found some change in my pocket, put the ticket inside the windscreen before catching up with Frank. He was already at the bottom the steps, hands on hips as he surveyed a deserted beach. Footprints led the way from mainland to the hotel, many had walked across the wet sand today, but we would be the last. The tide was nearly in, the pathway of puddles and footsteps that would soon be seabed.

"Beautiful, isn't she?" I said. We both looked out across, the hotel lit up, majestic and grand.

"Pretty special," said Frank as he took off his shoes, rolled up his trousers to his knee.

"What's Goodmanson? Like a code name?" as I did the same.

"It's her real name, dumbass."

"I take it someone didn't like Goodmanson too much?"

"A bit too *Helter Skelter* for some."

"And there was me thinking I knew Lilly inside and out."

"Well, Joe Friday," Frank smiled. "Looks like we're both screw-ups. Let's make a move before we sink or drown."

We walked in silence. The wind was against us, whistling, our eyes squinted, our mouths covered.

"You said Lilly tried to jump? Was that true?" Frank asked through the muffle of his scarf.

"Yes."

Both of us were shouting to be heard over the weather.

"And you stopped her?"

"Yes."

"Did she say why?"

"Not straight away."

"What night did you meet her?"

"After she got back from London. The night she invited Max over."

"I shouldn't have flown home. I should have sent more security."

"Why did you leave?"

"Cos I was stubborn. I should have believed her, or at least pretended to."

"Do you believe her now?"

"I know she took drugs that night. I could see it in her eyes. I know when she is lying."

"Then why did you come back?"

"Cos I'll always come back."

"No matter what she does?"

"Lilly will always self-destruct. It's more a question of when and how much devastation it will cause."

"And you weren't mad?"

"I was mad. Otherwise I wouldn't have left. But I couldn't stay mad. She doesn't do these things intentionally. You follow someone around long enough they will fuck up eventually. Even me and you. Lilly is no different, the difference is the whole world is waiting for it."

"Then why not be honest? Why accept her apology if you knew she was lying?"

Frank didn't answer. He changed the subject. "How was she after? After the bridge? The night she jumped?"

"Better."

"Better how?"

"It's hard for me to compare. I haven't known Lilly that long as you know. I can only go on what I know about her from the last four weeks."

"And that is?"

"She hasn't been happy in a long time."

"About what, her career?"

"Yes. But other things too. Sounds like she has had a tough twelve months."

"She told me she wanted to quit the movie game today."

"She's pretty conflicted. Different days we talk about it she draws different conclusions. One minute she's talking scripts and acting classes, the next she's talking about buying a boat and learning to sail."

"Well, she was pretty adamant this morning." Frank coughed hard, and then coughed again. "Is any of it your doing?"

"Lilly wouldn't do what I told her even if I begged her."

"Ain't that the truth," he coughed.

"I know you and Sally don't believe me, but I'm not Lilly's enemy. I'm a friend."

"Just a friend?" Frank raising an eyebrow.

"Right now, as of this moment, I wouldn't even say we were that."

"But you want it to be more?"

I didn't answer, walked on, it had started to rain, not heavy, but rain nonetheless, rain that made you walk a little faster, bury your head, move with a purpose.

"Can I ask you a question, Frank?"

"I may not answer but go ahead."

"What would you say if I told you I know who the informer is? The one providing my boss with every little detail, Lilly's every move."

"I'd say it's none of your business."

"It's Sally."

Frank said nothing.

"Don't you care, Frank? Doesn't that bother you?"

"It would bother me if there was any truth to it."

"It is true, Frank. Why would I lie?"

"Do you have proof?"

"No."

Frank laughed. "What a fucking joke."

"I know it's her."

"Based on what?"

"Frank, I'm not telling you this to be vindictive or smug."

"Then, why are you?"

"I don't think Lilly deserves any more turmoil."

"That's fucking rich. You and your profession are fucking bloodsuckers."

"You may not like me or trust me but you gotta believe I'm on Lilly's side in all this."

"This conspiracy theory of yours. Who else have you told? Please tell me you haven't told Lilly?"

"Lilly has her suspicions already."

"And I'm sure you were more than willing to stoke that fire, hey kid?"

"I want you to talk to Sally. Get her to stop."

"I'll do no such thing," he laughed. "You're pretty cock sure of yourself, Tom, I'll give you that."

"You won't talk to Sally?"

"You deaf? I said no."

"Then I will."

Frank turned, squared up to me, nose to nose. "No, you will do nothing."

"Then Lilly carries on being hounded, her privacy invaded. Lilly unhappy."

"Lilly will be hounded regardless of who the informer is, or was, or is going to be."

"Yes, but at least the informer wouldn't be someone she knew, someone right under her nose. It's a pretty cold-hearted thing to do, for Sally to do this behind her back. Lilly thinks of her like a mother."

"You don't have to worry. The situation had been sorted."

"Sorted?"

I looked at Frank. He looked right back at me. It took me a few seconds to realize.

★ ★ ★

"Why?"

"Because that was what I was told to do."

"By who? Let me guess, Max Salter?"

"Max wants control. Over himself, his people, his staff, the people closest to him."

"I don't believe you. You're saying this to protect Sally."

Frank sniffed. "That woman needs protection from no one."

"You know it was him that sent the photos today?"

"If it was I would be the last person he would tell. Let's just say mine and Max's working relationship has come to an end."

"He fired you."

Frank laughed again. "Believe me he would have fired my arse months ago. He hasn't been too happy I stopped playing ball."

"Since when?"

"A while. Just before we came out here, after he laid a hand on Lilly. After that, any loyalty I had was only with Lilly."

"So why quit now then?"

"Lilly needed me here, soon as we get home I'll make my excuses, leave quietly with no fuss or bother."

"What, so Max can find another replacement?"

"Something like that."

"I guess Sally is an informer too? If you're on Max's payroll then so must she be."

"She may be on his payroll but she is no informer."

"Lilly will find out about this. About what you've done behind her back."

"She won't find out."

"You're not gonna tell her?"

"I wasn't planning on it, no."

"So, Lilly will never know. About you or Max?"

"It's for the best."

"For you and Max it is."

"Hey, I know I'm an arsehole but you don't know me well enough to judge."

"You're right, Frank, I don't."

"You don't think this is hard for me? Lilly is my fucking world. It will kill me walking away."

"But that is what you are doing. You are walking away."

"I have no choice."

"You could stay. Fuck Max. Protect Lilly."

"I can't."

"So instead you protect you and Max. How brave."

"I'm guessing you will tell Lilly anyhow."

"I should, but I won't."

"I'm surprised."

"So am I." We went quiet, eyes forward. "You might be right though, Frank. Lilly shouldn't know. I don't know what good would come from it."

"Lilly will be OK, you know. She's stronger than a lot of people give her credit for, Max included. She's able to look after herself."

"Lilly won't see it like that."

"My days were numbered regardless. I'm an old man. Surely she understands that one day I will have to step down? Informer or not, I'm too old to protect her. Too old to do my job."

"I don't think Lilly gives two fucks if you could do your job or not. She just wants you close by because you're her family."

"I can't be with her forever."

"That's the problem, Frank. Forever is how long she thought you'd stick around."

33

I nearly drowned once – I was three years old, no armbands. I decided to jump into the deep end of my uncle's swimming pool. I was saved of course, Uncle Walter to the rescue, coughed up a load of water, Mom and Dad were so mad, my drowning had made them look bad in front of friends and family. "Never drown again," they said, like the first time was deliberate.

Another time I bust my head open dancing in my mom's heels, slipped and fell onto the corner of our kitchen table, spent hers and dad's anniversary in A&E, bet you can guess how pleased they were about that.

Fourteen years old, ran into a door chasing my sister, completely fucked my face up, my whole school thought I'd had a nose job.

What else? Cut my little finger opening a tin of dog food, two stitches, scar like a fish hook.

I looked down at my knee, the last of the scabs had gone, just a graze. It looked worse at the time, that mad jump off into the river, my moment of complete madness or complete sanity, depending on opinion, anyway add that to the list of injuries – twenty-two, attempted suicide.

Weird the flaws you're left to stare at. Marvel at how the body has fixed itself, when at the time, soaked in blood or gasping for breath, it all looked beyond repair.

★ ★ ★

I was out of the bath now, washed and dried, finished inspecting myself, my cuts and scrapes. It had helped, the therapeutic process of examining my skin, washing it thoroughly, at least it had stopped me crying, seeing as that's all I'd done since arriving at the hotel.

I was outside now. From up high I could see all the commotion down below. Despite the weather the beach was still busy with children and adults and dogs, laughing and yapping. It was hard not to be jealous, the fun I wasn't having, I may have had a luxurious room and a luxurious view, but it all felt a waste doing it alone.

I'm surprised I wasn't followed, think I was even too quick for Frank, by the time he probably scrambled to his car I was already long gone. Kept checking my rear mirror, but all that was behind me was road and exhaust fumes. I dread to think how fast I drove, I knew these roads like the boulevards back home but that was no excuse and though I felt elation when I finally reached the hotel, I regretted the speed at which I'd arrived.

Thank God, this place had a room, I didn't have time to ring ahead, didn't even have time to pack, grabbed a bag and ran. I must've looked such a fool, everyone else on blankets and towels, families lunching on the sand, me storming past with my luggage, dour-faced, eyes red and focused solely on the hotel in the distance.

My room was nice, bigger than the last visit with Tom, lots of sofas, my own garden overlooking the world. Then again, my demands were different this time, asked for the most expensive room they had, told them that privacy was paramount. The lady at reception smiled, showed me down a corridor. I declined her tour of the room, opted for wine instead. "Red or white?" she asked. I said both.

I hadn't ventured out of my door since. I could've walked down to the pool, I could've headed down to the Mermaid Cove, taken a dip in the sea, played billiards, gone in the sauna even. I didn't feel like seeing anyone, just wanted to be alone, sat on my veranda looking downward, my ivory tower, working out what to do next.

I was tired of thinking, working out theories, who committed what and why. The long and short of it was, someone was lying and plotting, could be someone close to me, could be someone I'd never even met, that's why I ran, just wanted time to digest it all, think it through. Sally wanted instant answers and instant decisions, I thought it best to leave, get some fresh air, breathe.

So here I was, fresh air, breathing, thinking it through. With neither answer nor decision of who was innocent or to blame. No wonder I was so messed up, sat on my own, on this little green island, in this big white house talking to myself, scratching at the walls like some mad lady in a straightjacket. The only difference was, I was being served ridiculously good wine.

Must be how queens feel, I laughed, as I contemplated being sociable.

★ ★ ★

"Hell of a view isn't it, miss?" as a pot of tea was placed in front of me. "I say, it's a beautiful view, miss," he said again.

"Oh sorry. I was miles away." I looked up at the barman stood beside me, waistcoat, hair slicked back.

"I make sure I find time at least a couple of times a day to take her all in," he said as he started to pour me tea.

"Are you dropping me a subtle hint?" I said, pointing to my empty wine bottle.

"No, not at all. Thought you might need warming up. It ain't sunbathing weather." He put a blanket over my legs. "If you don't mind me saying, you do look rather familiar." He studied my face. For a moment, I thought my cover was blown. "You were here last week. I remember serving you. And your man too. Tom Collins for him, I recall. Martinis for yourself. Followed by enough tequila to sink a ship. It's lucky you're still alive."

"Were we that bad?"

"You drank my top shelf dry. No harm. Sign of a successful evening. That's what I like about this place. There's a certain order to it. Order at the beginning, chaos in the middle, then back to order. Just like a mystery novel."

We both looked out across our private cove. A few people paddling twenty yards ahead, a man asleep or reading. In the distance, the mainland, tiny spots and moving blurs of people enjoying the same tranquillity as us, but without the same degree of privacy.

"How long have you worked here?" I asked him.

"Too long. Not long enough."

"Mad island, isn't it?"

"Not mad. Different. Eccentric. Everyone needs a wee bit of escapism."

I laughed. "Escaping sounds ideal right about now.

"Forgive me. You don't mind me talking, do you? You're my only customer. I think everyone has retired for midday naps."

"No not at all. I appreciate the company. You think they can see us up here? Y'know, from the beach. All those people on their holidays."

"Na. Too high. But I bet they are trying to. Wouldn't you if you were down there? Wouldn't you want to know? I know I would. You're staying at the top of a grand castle. And all those down there have to look up and wonder."

"You think?"

"I know so. Where's your man from the other week? Is he down there somewhere with the riff-raff or is he inside the hotel? Billiards Room I bet?"

"He's somewhere."

He looked over his shoulder, checking his bar.

"What is it you do, if you don't mind me asking?"

"I'm an actress."

"How very grand. A fabulous life to lead, I can imagine."

"It is. Most of the time. It's harder than you might think."

"Doesn't seem hard from where I'm standing. Cocktails and romance seems pretty fabulous to me," he smiled, pulling up a chair beside me. "I'm joking, of course. I had a friend back home who worked the theatre for years. She worked every hour under the sun, I can only imagine how hard it must be, harder than making cocktails and pots of tea. I couldn't do it; one character is enough for me, thank you very much."

"Did she ever make it on the big screen, your friend?"

"No, not even close."

"That's a shame."

"She wasn't too fussed. She was just happy acting, she couldn't care less if she was on the West End or the top floor of a corner pub. As long as she was performing, she was happy."

"She sounds cool."

"She is. She was. She died not long ago. That was a hell of funeral. Pints of heavy, singing, a few rammies. Just how she would've wanted it. Must be an amazing profession to be in. To give people so much joy."

"It is. But your job must give people joy too."

"Depends how drunk I get them. Joy and despair aren't too far removed when alcohol is involved. I think your line of work is far more rewarding than mine."

"I don't think all people see it like that. Some would say the last thing this planet needs right now is more dancers, more actors, more artists."

"Only the uneducated think that way. Art makes us human. There are so many restrictions in life, scientific rules and laws we are governed by. Everyone needs a creative outlet."

"What's your outlet?"

"People. I love people."

"Not cocktails?"

"Don't get me wrong, I love my job. I love making cocktails, but that's just science, mixing chemicals, changing taste and colours. More rules and laws I'm afraid. My outlet is people. Yours is acting."

I sniffed and smiled.

"What's so funny?"

"If you'd asked me this morning, I was about to be a retired actress."

"Has something dramatic happened between breakfast and lunch to cause such a change of opinion?"

"You could say that."

"And is there likely to be a change of opinion again? By dinner or supper?"

"Most likely."

"Keeps you on your toes at least."

"I wouldn't recommend it. It's a volatile way of surviving."

"But still you survive."

"And what about you?"

"What about me?"

"Are you surviving?"

"I've done OK. I've had successes, failures too, and I can't take credit for either. Strangely the big decisions in life are the ones it's best to plan the least, most weren't even planned at all. Working here, for example."

"I'm intrigued."

"You should be. It's quite a story. One that now I can look back at fondly. At the time, it was far more complicated, lots of drama and twists."

"Drama and now calm."

"For now, yes. But you know what they say about calm and storms."

"Are you predicting drama for yourself?"

"Always, but calm to follow. It works both ways. Hence why decisions shouldn't always be thought through, sometimes a little impulse is required." He looked behind him. There was movement around the bar. A couple dressed in beige. "I best get back inside. I shouldn't leave the bar unattended. Even if it so quiet today. Leave you to the view and me to serving more Americans."

"Poor you."

"Me. I love it."

"Really?"

"I never take for granted the magic of this place. I've been here years, they only get to sample it for a day or two. Every customer deserves to be treated like only they exist. Like they're a Hollywood star. Even if it is just for one day."

"Well, you certainly do that. Thank you."

He smiled, his mouth closed. "Let me know if ever you need anything. More wine, more tea, more blankets."

"I will. I promise. Oh what is up there?" pointing to the top of a cliff, at half a dozen people as small as pins.

"The old chapel. A good place to take stock of the world. Though not the sort of walk I'd recommend if having wine for breakfast and lunch. It's a long way to fall and last time I checked, Superman isn't on our payroll." Said with a smile, offence not to be taken, which it wasn't.

I watched him walk back inside the hotel, I could already hear him embrace his new customers like long lost friends. "Beautiful view, isn't it?" I heard him say, like he just had to me.

I laughed to myself.

Every job had its script.

It took another pot of tea and a complimentary shot of grappa before I realized that Tom was not involved in all this, deep down I always knew it wasn't him, but at that split second I saw the photos, everyone close was guilty.

My guess was it was Max, it was far too timely to be paparazzi, this little twist had Max written all over it, I could picture his face, his cigar being lit, smoke fumes and a big grin. This was a man whose job it was to toy with tension, to know how to create it, build it, know the exact point or page at which his audience should be knocked off their seats, when they should boo and cheer.

I wasn't going to give him the pleasure of a reaction, though knowing him he knew I wouldn't give him one. There was more to this though, movies were a blood sport and a decent director was fully aware of the need for a little sadism. Any decent movie, the protagonist will get their happy ending, but they will have to suffer in the middle, that was for damn sure, they'll have to lose, or bleed or die, or defeat the antagonist, but they will win.

So why was I worried? Whatever Max was planning for Act Two, I might possibly come away from it unscathed, but that didn't mean that others would be so lucky. I had to get to Tom, explain things, prepare him for what might happen next, tell him to brace himself.

I checked my cell, a list of missed calls, mostly from Tom. I tried his number, let it ring and ring. I needed to fix this and quick, speak to him before he did something stupid like leave or stay. I was sure Max had escape routes for both.

34

"And then she lamped him one. Slapped him silly."

"She did that?"

"I saw her do it, man. She doesn't take any crap, that girl."

"I get that impression." I turned the heating down in the Jeep. "You warm now, Frank?"

"I'm warm, but I ain't dry, that's for sure. You?"

"Same."

"You still feeling bummed?" Frank checking his cell.

"I could've sworn she'd be there. Thought they'd at least let us through the gate."

"It wouldn't have made a difference. If you stay on a private island, there's a strong chance you want your privacy. Even if we had found her I'm damn sure we wouldn't have been welcomed with open arms. Knowing Lilly, it's better this way, let her come out when she's good and ready, on her own terms."

"I guess so. Least me and you got to bond, hey?" I joked, when I wasn't sure me and Frank were in joke territory yet.

"Who said we'd bonded?" he coughed.

"We are still enemies?"

"I'm just yanking your chain. Don't take it personal if we don't hold hands just yet. It's my nature to think the worst of people. I'm used to protecting things, buildings and front lines remember. I ain't so good when people are involved. Don't quite know how to behave apart from attack or defend."

I smiled. "You're just looking out for Lilly. I can understand why your guard is up."

I took a quick glance at the clock, it was earlier than I thought, the sky was the wrong colour, gave the impression there was no day left.

"How did it come about?" I asked. "You and Lilly?"

"Nothing special. I worked through an agency. Security, hired thug. Politicians and billionaires mostly."

"Sounds a luxurious way of living."

"It was. I had some fun times, stayed in some amazing places, got to see the world using someone else's wallet."

"Any hairy moments?" turning on the windscreen wipers.

"Plenty. The richer my employer, the more people wanted their money or power."

"That must be the draw, though. Why else would you be a bodyguard if it wasn't for a life of danger?"

"The younger me would agree. The time I got the call to work for Lilly I was just about to accept a job for Union Pacific over at Salt Lake. Nine-to-five pencil-pushing."

"Bit of a career change. Bullet vests to rail roads," I said, putting my foot on the brake as a tractor pulled in front of us.

"Fancied a different speed. Danger is a young man's game. Just wanted something to top up my Marine Corps pension till I could forget work entirely and focus on important stuff like good beer and decent waves."

"Then why didn't you take the job in Salt Lake?"

"Few days before, one of my friends at the agency rang me in a panic, said she was in a spot of bother. Some young actress with a reputation for sacking folk had gone and sacked another. I owed her a favour, they needed someone fast, that someone was me. I just thought of Lilly as another pay cheque, so when Max asked me to keep tabs on her, I thought of the money rather than the person I was protecting."

"Lilly likes to sack people then?"

"I think they sack themselves. Lilly may have given them the push, but from what she tells me the guys she fired were amateur at best. They weren't fit to handle her."

I laughed. "You make her sound like a wild dog."

"Oh, she's wild. There's a mean streak to that girl. Selfish side, too. Stubborn."

"Loyal though."

"Very. She's a very complicated girl. I've seen many a side of Lilly. Some I wouldn't want to see again if you know what I mean. She's hard-shelled that one."

"Most people are, one way or the other."

"Don't know where it comes from? I know her parents' divorce affected her pretty bad."

"Divorce?"

"Her biological mother ran off with some party boy. Moved across state. Lilly was just about to start junior high. Never saw her again."

"How could her mum do that?"

"Bad people are bad people. Don't think her dad handled it very well, breakdown, remarried pretty quick. He made some bad choices."

"Like?"

"Nothing major. Just little things that can mess with a daughter's head. Not spending time with her. Letting her become an adult way too soon."

"Makes sense of why she is like she is."

"She's changed a lot. When I first met her she was all over the place. Fame came quick for Lilly, I don't think she knew quite how to handle it. Drank a lot, partied too much. Far too much."

"Till you came along."

"Not straight away. Took time."

"And what made you so special?"

"I think I was just honest with her. Told her straight."

"I bet she loved that. The iron fist."

"We had our fights at first. She just needed to get things out of her system. After that she was sweet as pie. But there's still that nasty side to Lilly. I don't see it often, but it hasn't gone away.

Probably why she ran off again. I think she knows how bad she can turn when things get too real or too close. Running away seems her defence mechanism."

"What's the deal with her step-mum and dad now then? Some days they're one call away from child welfare, the next they're Parents of the Year."

"They're OK. Met them a few times. They're just preoccupied."

"With what?"

"Themselves. They're Hollywood people. Her dad's still waiting on his big break. Her mom too."

"Her step-mum's an actress?"

"No, though she likes the idea of being an actor's wife, that's for sure."

"She sounds lovely," I said, watching the tractor in front, contemplating overtaking the damn thing.

"They're nice people. Not a bad bone between them. Just not too good at being parents."

"You got your own kids, I take it?"

"No, never lucky enough on that front. You?"

"Girl."

"I always wanted a girl. Boys you can leave to find their own way. Girls you actually have to father." He looked out the window. "I always wanted a girl."

"I think you already have one of those. Do you think we should ring Sally? Let her know we are on our way back."

"I still can't get a signal out here. You?"

"My battery died ages ago. Is there a charger anywhere near you, Frank? I normally I have one."

Frank started to rummage, under his seat, the glovebox, as the tractor took a right and I could finally put my foot down, make up for lost time. Both of us ready for home.

"She won't move here, Tom. I know she's filled your head with the idea. But it won't happen."

"I kinda gathered that a long time ago."

"What next then?"

"More than likely she'll go her way and I'll go mine."

"And what if, by some miracle, that doesn't happen? Say she wants you as much as you want her?"

"That won't happen, trust me. Not based on the last few days, not based on what's happened today either."

"Lilly is prone to change her mind. What if she does? You have a choice here, Tom. End things happy. End it quick. Before people start making drastic decisions liking quitting careers and upping sticks."

"I don't have that choice, Frank. Lilly has taken that decision out of my hands already."

"You might be right. But if she hasn't then you might have to. Could you do that, Tom? Could you end it with the big and famous Lilly Goodridge? Have you got the balls to do something like that?"

I didn't answer,

"Is that a yes?"

I nodded, convincing neither Frank nor myself.

35

The lady at reception asked if there was something wrong with the room and I did my best to assure her I wasn't leaving early on their part. I could see her point, I'd checked in at lunchtime and I was leaving before dinner, a full night's charge for four hours' stay. She offered to reduce the cost, which was unexpected. I declined of course, left them a substantial tip and a glowing reference on their visitor log. I'd made a mistake, not them, I should never have come, the least I could do was scribble a few adjectives down on paper before I sped off again, not that I was entirely sure where I was speeding off to.

I looked down at the map drawn by the landlord I'd met ten minutes before, then back at the crossroads I was facing. It was hard to work out if I was lost, all I knew was, what started as pretty little rows of cobbled houses now just looked like one dark alley away from a murdered American. Thank God, a group of guys pointed me in the right direction, even offered me their fish and chips, which I was too cold and hungry to decline.

★ ★ ★

I rang the bell and heard a bark so prepared for a dog. Rang it again, another bark, but again no dog, just the threat of one. Eventually I could see movement, someone chewing and smiling as they rattled the key chain, opening the door, letting the heat of indoors pour into the cold street.

"Sorry darling, I was mid-mouthful." the lady said. "No one normally knocks at this time apart from the Jehovahs."

"Oh sorry. I can come back in a while if it's…"

"Don't worry," she said, pointing at her plate. "It's only last night's shepherd's pie. What can I do you for you? A room?"

"No, I'm looking for someone actually."

"Oh well, I'll try to help."

"Do you have a Tom Smyth staying here?"

"Do you mind me asking who you are, sweetheart? Y'know, guest confidentiality and all that."

"I'm his friend Lilly."

"Lilly?" her face beamed. "*The* Lilly? I've heard a lot about you."

"Really?"

"Oh lots. Nothing bad of course. I'm afraid he isn't here. Been gone since the morning."

"Did he say where he was going?"

"No, he never does. He was supposed to be ill. Went to go and check on him, but as per usual he disappeared. To be fair he's never here. Uses this place like a *bloody* hotel he does." she laughed. "Have you tried ringing him, dear?"

"I have. Think he might be ignoring me."

"That doesn't sound like Tom at all. Would you like me to try for you? See if I can get hold of him?"

"Yes please. If you don't mind. That way I know if he's ignoring everyone or just me."

"It's no bother. Take a seat," she said, letting me inside, where I felt instantly warm. "I'll grab my handbag and put my glasses on."

I sat on the chair nearest to me, angled my legs so I didn't trample on the dog. I stroked its head, ithe seemed to like it, started panting and sniffing, licking off the last of the chip salt and vinegar, as I tried to ignore its breath and spit.

"Right, here we go, found the bugger," she said, holding her cell phone out in front of her like it was the first time she'd ever used one. "I've got his number on here somewhere I'm sure. Ah ha, got it."

I watched her try to ring him, cell to her ear, the ringing tone, over and over.

"Looks like he's ignoring the both of us," I smiled.

"Phones aren't the most reliable of equipment down this neck of the woods either, signal is pretty hit and miss, so I rarely use mine, as you can probably tell. Do you want me to leave a message for him behind my desk? I should be up a few more hours watching my soaps."

"If you could. Tell him to ring Lilly as soon as he gets back. Or come see me. I'll be at home."

"Have you got anywhere you can go till then?"

"I'll be OK. I can walk around for a bit, go to a pub."

"Nonsense. Not in that weather." She pointed outside to the dark and rain. "You'll catch your death and I'll be held accountable. I'll get you a drink, hold out here till outside looks more agreeable. Never know, Tom might be back any minute. I've come to learn that rain always brings him home pretty quick."

36

We pulled into the drive. Sally was already at the doorway, arms crossed, trying to look through my Jeep windows in search of a third person.

"Any calls your end?" Frank said from under his hood.

"I just got a message actually." she said. "Quick, get in before you get soaked."

"Why didn't you ring me? What's it say?"

"Says she is fine."

"Is that it?"

"Better than nothing."

"What about the Max situation?" I asked.

"Nada. If it's him he's keeping quiet. If it is him, just cos he's the prime suspect doesn't mean he's guilty. I got takeout, few cold pizzas inside if you're hungry."

I wasn't sure if the invitation was aimed at one or both of us.

"You got time for pizza, Tom?" Frank asked. "Feel privileged. Sally inviting paparazzi for supper is unheard of."

"Could I use your phone? I need to ring home. My mum was in hospital today, better get the medical report."

"Sure," he said, as the three of us made our way inside. "Me and Sally will be in the kitchen. You can use the front room if you'd like a bit more privacy." They went off towards pepperoni smells and I headed to a phone and a roaring fire.

★ ★ ★

"Hi, Mum. You OK?" I said, not sure why I was whispering.

"Still alive, yes."

"Is Molly already in bed, I guess?"

"She's staying next door tonight, remember?"

"I forgot. How did today go?"

"I've had better days, Tom, I'm not going to lie."

"Anaesthetic isn't nice."

"No, that went fine. Ever so quick."

"And what did they say?"

"Well, I've officially got cancer."

I couldn't speak.

"They say my lump is now a tumour. Grade 2."

"Is that bad?"

"It's not good, I know that much."

I could tell she was crying, or trying not to cry.

"What happens now, Mum?"

"I've got an operation next week. Remove the lymph nodes, whatever they are." She was sobbing. "I can't stop bloody crying. What's wrong with me?"

"Look, I'm gonna drive back tonight."

"You don't have to do that, Tom."

"I should have never come back in the first place, Mum. I've been wrapped up in my little world down here. I've been selfish. I should be with you."

I expected Mum to tell me not to, to tell me to stay like she always she did. But she didn't, not this time.

"How long will you be?"

"By the time I get home you'll probably be in bed."

"Just come back as soon as you can."

"I love you, Mum."

"I love you too. See you soon. Bye."

I went through to the kitchen. Frank was at the stool eating pizza straight from the box, Sally busy with her phone.

"Sure you don't want any of this?" Frank pointing at the last few slices in front of him.

"Something's come up. Gotta go straight home tonight."

"Where's home?"

"A long drive away."

Frank looked pleased. "I know it's hard now but it's the right thing to do."

Sally looked up from her phone. "You've gone all pale. You OK?"

"It's been a hell of a day, that's all. Not sure how much more I can take if you know what I mean."

"Ditto on that," she said, returning her attention back to her phone, walking off with it to her ear, leaving me just with Frank.

"Hope things work out for you, Tom. This is for the best."

"Thanks, Frank."

"Lilly will be fine, I assure you." Getting off his stool. "I'll make sure she is safe."

"See you around, Frank. Good luck."

"You too, friend."

We shook hands, knowing it meant a whole lot more than just shaking hands.

37

"Feels like only yesterday he turned up. Tom and his other half," she said, pouring more tea into her cup and into mine.

"Other half?" for a moment thinking she meant a woman.

"American fella. Nice on the eye. He was only here a few days."

"Vince?"

"That was his name. Vince."

"What was he like?"

"We barely spoke. He was on his phone mostly, he was nice enough, looked angry most of the time, a little rude and cocksure, but I've had ruder Americans. Sorry, I don't mean to offend."

"Tom doesn't speak too highly of him either," I said, not meaning to talk with my mouth full. "Thank you for this by the way. Delicious."

"You're welcome. If I knew you were going to turn up I wouldn't have cooked last night's leftovers and I certainly wouldn't have used effing gravy granules."

"Don't worry. I was raised with boxes or packets. Mac and cheese and minute tapioca. This is a luxury for me." I took another mouthful of food, forgetting to chew, forgetting manners. "What time do you think Tom will be back?"

"It's hard to say. He comes and goes. I'm normally in bed by the time he gets back."

"I'll stay here a little longer, if you don't mind, that is. If he's not back then, I'll call it a night."

"Stay as long as you need to. You have got somewhere to stay tonight I take it?"

"Yes. Well, no, sort of. It's a bit complicated."

"Well one thing this place isn't short of is beds."

"Oh no, don't worry."

"Do you want anything else to eat?" noticing my plate empty, cleaned bone dry.

"No, I'm fine, thank you."

We both went quiet. For the first time, it felt a little awkward, we sipped our tea. Someone came through the door, past main reception. He was holding a camera, looked like paparazzi, felt my heart sink. He briefly looked across at us, Dot then me, I tried to look away. Don't think he realized who I was, went off down the corridor, obviously wasn't expecting celebrity, not on his front door, not on his own territory.

"You and Tom courting then, I assume?"

"Courting?"

"Sorry, I shouldn't be asking such personal questions."

"I don't know what me and Tom are. It's complicated."

"A lot of things are complicated for you, aren't they?" She laughed to herself. "It will be a shame to lose Tom. I'm going to miss that boy when he leaves me. He's been a breath of fresh air, that one. But these things have to end, don't they?"

"They do."

Dot yawned, apologizing straight away.

"Would you like me to leave? I don't mind. Think it's fair to say wherever he is, he won't be back soon."

"Sorry, I would stay up with you but my alarm is set for 4am, hence why eight o'clock is deemed as a late night in this household. Be a shame for you to not see Tom though, seeing as you've made the effort to come all this way."

"It can't be helped."

"I shouldn't really do this, but I'm sure Tom wouldn't mind just this once."

"Mind what?"

"Do you want to sit in his room whilst you wait. Least that

way you can put your feet up, watch a bit of telly. Can't make you leave now. You'll drown in that rain."

"Are you sure he wouldn't mind?"

"Can't imagine he would. I can't see the harm. Think it would be a nice surprise." She stood up, picking up the tray of plates and cups. "Follow me and I'll show you to his room."

Walking behind her we made our way through a corridor, past door after door, rights, then lefts, the house was endless and, luckily for me, empty.

"Here we go. This is him." Taking a big bunch of keys from her pocket.

"Are you sure he won't mind? Don't want him to feel like I'm invading his privacy." I asked, realising how ridiculous that sounded knowing Tom's occupation.

"Well if he moans, tell him to moan at me, not you," Dot said as she opened the door. "If you need anything, just ring on the phone next to the bed. Press zero. Can't promise I'll answer, mind."

"Thank you, Dot."

"If you get bored you could always give the room a good going over. That boy is many things, but tidy isn't one of them," she said. "I'll leave you to it, sweetheart." She closed the door, leaving me stood in the middle of the room, not knowing quite what to do with myself.

I looked around me. Dot was right, the room was a mess, half packed, half on the floor. I stepped over a pair of jeans, over a pile of T-shirts, made some room for myself to sit on the edge of the bed. Picked up a book off his bedside table, it looked boring, 30 million copies sold, maybe I should read it seeing as I was one of the few who hadn't. There was a little photo of Molly too, which was sweet. A diary which I could've easily flicked through and very nearly did.

Bored quickly, I walked around the room, investigated equipment, investigated my reflection in the mirror across the room. I filled the kettle, found a herbal tea bag, wandered the room as it boiled. There was a big folder titled LG, I had to assume it was about me. I looked inside, only quickly. More maps mostly, drawings of the farmhouse, lots of notes, photo after photo, press cuttings. It should have weirded me out, the level of intrusion, the sinister volume of detail, the homework of a serial killer. But this was just Tom's job, or was his job.

I noticed a large envelope on the side, a little note stuck to the corner.

To Lilly. So you don't forget. Tom X

I know I shouldn't have, but I opened it, instantly I smiled, they were the photos I asked him to take for me, the ones I'd forgotten I'd even asked for. One of my garden, the little stream, the bridge, my lambs and sheep. One from far away, way up from the top of the road, must've been like a mile away, the farmhouse looked wonderful, all the fields and trees, the house and its big white walls and smoking chimneys. One of Burgh Island Hotel too, taken from the mainland, sat there on the island like a pearl. God knows when Tom had taken all these, of all the things he'd done behind my back, this was by far the cutest. I kept looking at them over and over, they were beautiful. Felt myself starting to cry, it hadn't hit me just how much I was going to miss it here, the people, the person I'd become. How soon they would just be a memory, a picture on a wall, or in a photo album, made me both grateful and sad.

As I went to put the photos back I felt something else in the envelope, something stopping me sliding the photos in clean. I tipped the envelope upside down, out of it fell an airline ticket, London to LA.

It was then I heard keys rattle in the door. I had to stop myself jumping into his arms.

38

The drive back to my hotel was quick, gave me just enough time to plan my departure. This wasn't how I wanted my last day to look, so quick and abrupt, I'd had plans to leave my room spotless, take Dot out for a nice walk on the beach, a long lunch, perhaps take one last drive around the place, soak it all up. But life didn't always work out that way. I'd leave her a note I thought, give her the courtesy of a thank you at least, or ring her in a few days' time, explain it all so she'd understand and wouldn't take it personally, which I was sure she would.

My hand kept trembling, had to grip both hands on the steering wheel, focus on the road. Two words going through my head.

Cancer and death. Cancer and death.

The two inseparables and despite other words, like early days, more tests, curable, stage two, they all sound muted. You hear the word cancer, everything that comes after is white noise. Hopefully the drive home to Mum would sort my head out, allow me to become logical again. Didn't want Mum to see me like this, rattled and scared, she needed hope on her doorstep, positivity, this wasn't a time for despair. Any fear I had would have to be gone, left here, left on the Jeep, left on the motorway.

I parked the car, ran through puddles, ran past reception, the hotel was asleep, no Dot, no guests. I'd have to pack quickly but quietly. I took out my keys, opened my door expecting dark.

39

Somehow, I found my way back to my car, soaked and crying and cold, I stared out in front, the sound of rain on the windscreen. What before I thought quaint and charming, little tea rooms, little house and little windows, now it just looked somewhere that wasn't home. I sat there, ten minutes, thirty minutes, long enough to get warm, find some energy, the thought of facing Frank and Sally tonight made me contemplate Burgh Island again, get a good night's sleep, face them tomorrow.

What stopped me I didn't know. I needed them more than I feared them, that was all I knew.

"We've finally gone and done it, guys." Frank's head in the fridge. "We've finally run out of eggs. Nothing left but glass jars I'm afraid," he said, putting jello on the table, as the two of us took it in turns to spread our toast.

"How you feeling? Get much sleep?" Sally's mouth behind her coffee.

"Not bad considering."

"You feel like talking about yesterday yet?"

"I suppose we have to at some point, don't we?"

"Bit of a strange day, wasn't it?"

"You could say that."

It went quiet, eating, drinking.

"Did you know Frank and Tom are now blood brothers?"

"What? How?"

"We're not best friends, Sally." Frank coughing.

"How?" I asked, still a little freaked out.

"He knocked on the door. Sally answered it." More coughing.

"Then what?"

"Sally let him in."

"What did you say to him, Sal? You didn't scare him off, did you?" looking at both of them.

"If you must know, he and Frank went looking for you."

"Where did you look?"

Frank put down his newspaper. "Tom had a hunch you would be at Burgh Island."

"Let me get this straight. You and Tom drove to Burgh Island and got the tractor across to the hotel."

"We walked actually."

"Then what happened?"

"You weren't there so we left."

"But I was there."

"It wouldn't have mattered. We weren't allowed past the gate anyway."

"Then what happened?"

"Not much. We drove back here and then he went home."

"Did he seem OK? Was he angry?"

"He was a little angry. He said he had to ring his mom. He went straight after."

"And that's it?"

"Pretty much."

"Did he say anything about me and him. How he felt about me?"

"No, he didn't."

"You're telling me you spent a good few hours with him and he didn't say anything about me and him."

"We didn't talk much really."

"I find that hard to believe, Frank, sorry. He must have said something. Told you about how we met. Or how things might change when I fly home. Frank, be honest."

"Lilly. If you need to talk to Tom, you need to speak to him, not me."

"I tried. I rang him like five times last night. I rang him this morning. He's not answering. Did he say if he was leaving?"

"Said he had to drive home."

"Did he mention LA? Flying?"

"Not to me."

"Frank, be honest, you scared him off. Filled his head with whatever it took to make him hate me."

"I did none of the sort. I've had enough of this interrogation. I'm going to the can for a bit of peace." He left me and Sally to finish breakfast.

"You need to eat, Lilly." Sally passed me more toast, trying to calm things. "Long day today. Long flight. Not long till we have to head to the airport."

"Can't wait."

"Less of the sarcasm please, Miss Goodridge. You should be happy you're going home."

"I'm not going home, though, am I? I'm going to New York for some reason no one has bothered to explain."

"Today's attire is not coincidental then. Are you in mourning? Is this the reason for head-to-toe black? Protesting?"

"If only black came in a darker shade." My sarcasm was deliberate and intentional.

"I thought you loved New York?"

"I do. Just not now."

"You could at least sound a little bit more excited. Even if you have to pretend. Just for my sake."

"Excited for what? Sounds like I'm going back into the fire."

"Stop being so dramatic."

"What's the situation with this latest batch of photos of me? Are they out there?"

"Not yet."

"Oh good. Least I've got a few days of tranquillity before the madness starts."

"There's something I need to tell you about that."

"What? It's not bad, is it?"

"It looks like this all stems from Mr Max Salter."

"I'm not surprised. Have you spoken to him?"

"No. I'm just waiting on how he wants this to play out."

"I'm not getting involved. He can do whatever he needs to do."

"Might be wise to tag along. There may be logic behind the madness."

"Are you for real?"

"Please don't tell me this sulking is all over Tom."

"What do you think?"

"Come on. You'll have forgotten about him by the time we land."

"I love him, Sally."

"Oh please. I've had longer shits than your so-called love affair."

"Me and him aren't going away if that's what you think."

"I'm sure of it. I'm sure Max has lots in store for you and Tom. Never know, your bit of rough may do well out of this."

"Are you on my side?"

"I'm always on your side."

"Really?"

"What do you expect me to say? This isn't the part where I say "Way to go, Paula, way to go." You think falling in love with a dropout is something I would condone?"

"I expected you would support me, that's all. Even if you don't agree."

"That isn't me. If you want someone to agree and nod then you need to hire someone else."

I went to storm off.

"Where you going?"

"Where do you think?"

"Running away? Aren't you bored of that by now?"

"You could always stop chasing me. Ever thought of that?"

"Lilly. Where you going?"

"Don't worry. I'm going upstairs." I grabbed my cell, already looking for Max's number.

★ ★ ★

I tried Max.

If he was in LA it would be around four in the morning, if he was even in LA. He could have been anywhere, across state, across another continent, could even be here.

I sat on my bed. Tried to think back to my last meeting with Max, the things each of us said, how things were left. Nothing good could've come from whatever plan he had. I had to hope it wasn't going to be too painless, but I couldn't see any other explanation other than to cause maximum devastation. What other reason would there be, where that wasn't the sole intention? Unless Sally had gotten it all wrong, though she very rarely did. Jeez, I hoped that was the case. Other enemies I could cope with, enemies behind cameras and laptops, if it was Max it would be personal and vindictive. Max always said enemies were the best teachers, the one thing he taught me was perseverance, how never to give up. But what would he gain from it? Exposing me like this. Apart from to embarrass me. Surely, he knew this wouldn't change things? Surely, he didn't think this would win me back? Why would he even want me back? If his aim was to have me and my new English fling plastered across every magazine and internet page then why would he even want me back? I'd be used goods, dirty and damaged. He must have another reason, I just couldn't work out what it was.

I tried again and again and again, till I ran out of time, till the clock told me England was nearly over.

40

We were at the airport. Departure lounge and a delayed flight. About an hour so far, though I predicted more delay to come.

Just before our car arrived to pick us up, Frank, Sally and I took a walk around the house, spent some time in the garden, one last lap of the house before we left. Made me nostalgic, made me want to return when I hadn't even left. When the driver did arrive to pick us up, knocked on the door, I very nearly didn't get in the car. Had to fight every bone in my body not to stay, it felt wrong to leave with so much unsettled. I'd always predicted this day would be hard, but I always thought, regardless of whether Tom and I were over or just starting, at least I'd know which one.

"Should keep us occupied till they replace the engine," said Frank, placing a tray of drinks for me and Sally, some pastries, trash to read.

"Don't joke, Frank. Some of us don't particularly like air travel. Stupid comments like that only make it worse."

"Here. Read this." Frank offered me a magazine.

"The last thing I want to read about is gossip right now. Frank, you don't have to serve us. They have staff for that."

He didn't answer, started to sugar and stir his coffee

"Please cheer up, Lilly." Sally sipped her champagne. "There will be some amazing places we should see over the next few days. I'll try my best to make sure we have some slack in the diary so me and you have time to shop and eat. New York won't know what's hit 'em."

I smiled.

"First thing I'm doing is grabbing a dog." Frank licking his lips. "Chilli, mustard, sauerkraut, the works."

"I was thinking more Greenwich Village, Frank, not some sausage cart. Who are you busy texting?"

I looked up, realising she was talking to me. "No one."

"You've been staring at that thing since we got here. Watching it isn't going make it ring." She picked at her bagel, removing salmon from cream cheese. "Hey just take it for what it was. You lived in another country for a few months, met lots of new people, even had a little holiday romance. That doesn't sound too bad, does it?"

I didn't answer.

"Sally, just leave her be." Frank, trying to defend me.

"Frank, I'm not having this silent treatment all the way to New York."

"She's hurting. Give her some space."

"Don't play Oprah here, Frank. I know you think the relationship was doomed from the start, too, so don't act all innocent."

"I'm just saying let her deal with it in her own way."

"What, by ringing Tom? Making things worse? Do something stupid?"

"Guys," I interrupted. "You're doing it again. Talking like I'm not in the room."

Frank huffed, picked up his newspaper, spread it across his lap and his face. "I'm not getting involved in this anymore. I'm out."

We went back to silence.

"I'm not ringing Tom, you'll be pleased to know. I'm trying to get hold of Max."

Sally suddenly perked up. "Good idea. Try him again. I'm intrigued to see what he says for himself."

"If I ring him it'll be my choice not yours." I got up, heading off towards perfume shops and handbags, with no intention of buying either.

41

"Can we feed the ducks, Dad?"

"We haven't got any bread, darling."

"Birds shouldn't eat bread, silly."

"Who told you that?" as we crossed the road onto the grass verge around the pond.

"Nanny did. Makes their tummies full."

"What do you normally feed them?"

"Seeds from Nanny's pocket. Do you have any?" sticking her hand into my jacket.

"Sorry. Just my phone and some keys." I could see Molly's face crumple. "Don't worry, I'll make sure my pockets are fully stocked tomorrow."

"I'm cold."

"Me too," I said, picking her up and crossing the road, letting ourselves back in. "Let me take your boots off."

"Dad, I can take them off myself, look." She sat on the floor, removing each boot from each foot, before dashing off inside the house, jumping onto my mum's lap.

"Molly, be gentle," I said taking my own shoes off. "Remember what we just talked about?"

"Just be a bit careful, darling. Nanny is still a bit sore."

"Dad said you have lumps?"

"Yes, doctors had to do some checks on me. Try and make me better."

"Where?"

"Here." Mum putting her hand on her chest.

"Would you like some Calpol?"

"Yes please."

Molly had already dashed off towards the kitchen.

"You had a phone call by the way." She looked pleased with herself. "Lilly."

"What did she say?"

"Wouldn't you like to know?"

"When she call?" I asked, sitting on the edge of the sofa.

"Just after you left."

"I should ring her now."

"You might be too late. She was just about to get on her plane."

"She's going home then?"

"Yes. Though I think she would rather be here with you by the sounds of it."

I smiled.

"You relieved?"

"Yes. Thought I'd blown it."

"Well you haven't. Least by what I've just heard."

Molly came bursting in, telling us off for not following her. I tried to call back Lilly, as Mum attempted to walk to the kitchen.

"Tom, make us all a hot chocolate. Seeing as I've not got long left, my diet is now firmly out of the window." She leaned against the door frame, like the walk from one room to another was a walk too far. "She not answering, I take it?"

I nodded.

"Must be in the air by now."

"Or on the phone."

"You make us those drinks, Romeo," she said as Molly fed her an empty Calpol spoon. "Then I'll tell you everything she said."

220

42

It was a relief to speak to her, it wasn't Tom, but his mom was close enough, filled me with enough hope to last the journey. I started to make my way back to Frank and Sally, browsing at sandals and sunglasses, even bought a book, a thick one, Tom would be impressed.

The voice on the speaker told me and the rest of the airport that my plane was now boarding. When I got back to Frank and Sally they were already getting all our things together, when Sally saw me she started waving me over frantically.

"Where have you been?"

"Shopping." Showing them my carrier bag.

"It's the last call. We need to get a move on fast. Did you ring him?" Sally said, putting her bottle of water back in her bag.

"Yes."

"So?" she said, looking excited. "What did he say?"

"Spoke to his mom actually."

"You spoke to Max's mom?"

"No, Tom's mom."

I could tell Sally wasn't happy, nor Frank as he started to drag our hand luggage through the crowd.

My cell buzzed.

"I'm gonna take this. It might be Tom."

"We haven't got time."

"Wait, it's Max."

Sally grabbed my bags. "I'll tell the hostess. They won't take off without us, I assure you. Frank, let's both get all the stuff over at the desk." I managed to answer it in enough time to hear Max at the other end of the line. To hear his apology or his list of demands.

43

"Would you like some more grapes, madam?" the gentleman asked me.

"Sorry, I've ruined your fruit bowl, haven't I?" He didn't answer, smiled, took away the remains of the grape vine, returning with a fresh bunch for me to pick at once again.

Typical of Max, he'd hired a suite in a hotel that disappeared into the clouds, always the show of wealth, the constant need for grandeur. We had Central Park just blocks away, little quiet corners we could've met in, little benches under trees, free of charge too. No, Max choosing here was intentional, it had a purpose, a display of power and intent, felt like a businessman about to be wined and dined, or worse still, bumped off. If I had my own place I'd have asked to meet there, somewhere less formidable, on my own turf, but Sally's apartment would've been a bad idea. Besides, I didn't want Frank anywhere near Max, I'd worry what he might do, or Sally for that matter, hence why neither was aware of today's little engagement and never probably would be.

Max was running late, sent me a message, stuck on Lexington. God, I wished he would hurry up, waiting made it ten times worse, even though our previous conversation was short and brief, it still filled my head with the required amount of doubt to make sure I showed up.

It was hard to hear him over the commotion of the departure lounge yesterday. I asked him if it was him, if he was the one at the bottom of all this, he said yes. I asked why, he said he couldn't say yet, told me to meet him, I said no. He laughed, "Meet me tomorrow, four o'clock at the Carlyle," he said. I told him no again, tried to stand firm. And again, he laughed, told me it was in both mine and Tom's interests before hanging up. Hence why I was here, jet-lagged, worrying and waiting.

I'd spoken to Tom, which was one positive. Once I got out of the airport and into an SUV unscathed, the first thing I wanted to do was ring him, this time thankfully he was home. We both said things that needed to be said, things felt fixable, thanked him for the photographs, I didn't mention him flying to LA. He asked about our situation, if anything else had come to light, I lied and said no. Wished we could've talked longer, though Sally ushered me away, meeting across town, execs to impress. We said our goodbyes, promised I'd ring him again later, when we both had more time to get things off our chests, work out the next time we could see each other.

I picked another grape, sipped more water, another excuse to go to the toilet, pee in luxury, look in the mirror, psych myself up. The restrooms were something else, the whole hotel was something else, velvet walls, Manhattan skyline, it didn't deserve to be associated with Max, to be the backdrop where evil got to see out its awful schemes.

The gentlemen came back over. No grapes this time.

Mr Salter had arrived. Now it was him waiting for me.

44

Max took off his suit jacket, and ordered the nearest staff member to fetch us drinks and some privacy.

"Thank you for coming today on such short notice."

"Like I had a choice."

"You had a choice and you're making the right ones so far." He sat down opposite me across a heavy table. "How does it feel being back on home soil?"

"Who took the photos, Max? I'm guessing it wasn't you. You've never been one to get your hands dirty. Leave that to some other expendable."

"Why does it matter who took them?"

"For when I file my lawsuit."

Max laughed, elbows on the table, smiling.

"You think this is funny, arsehole?"

"I'm sorry, I shouldn't laugh, it's just hard to take you seriously when you're mad."

"Are you at least going to tell me why?"

"Not yet. I'm enjoying the show you are putting on for me."

"Is there a reason you chose now to threaten me with whatever else you have on me? You could've threatened this weeks ago. It seems pretty shitty timing just when I'm about to come home."

"You know me, Lilly. I like things drawn out, I like people to get settled in their seats. Besides, I didn't want you making any rash decisions."

"What, like staying with Tom?"

"It was better I stepped in."

"What I do with Tom is none of your concern, Max."

"That is where you are wrong, little lady. Your actions have consequences. Your actions reflect on me. So yes, how you conduct yourself and who you surround yourself with isn't something I take light-heartedly."

"And this is your reaction?"

"You expected one though, surely?"

"You know what, Max? At first, I did, I expected that you would do something juvenile like this, make a noise, cause a scene. But you know what, I also hoped you'd just leave me alone, let me get on with my life, least have the decency to realize how fucked up you made me and just let me be. But I never thought for one minute you would sink as low. How did you even find out about me and Tom?"

"It was obvious."

"And why is it any of your business who I see? When are you going to realize, Max? Me and you are over. I don't love you anymore."

Max laughed, hands behind his head. "Lilly, this is business."

"You keep saying that."

"Because it's true."

"You wanna know the truth, Max? You need me because without me your career is over. That's what I think."

"I agree, Lilly."

"Then just fuck someone just like me. I'm sure they're a dime a dozen. Go on, go and groom your next reprobate."

"If only it was that simple."

"It's easy, Max. Find someone new, break her spirit, turn her into an emotional wreck. Screw her up emotionally and physically. Then leave her in a crumpled heap."

"That's unfair, Lilly. I loved you once."

"Yes, Max, you may have loved me, but you can love someone too much. Crush them with it. Suffocate them with it. And some girls want that, that type of love. That type of control. But not me. Go and find someone new, Max. A more beautiful, younger and more talented Lilly Goodridge. I'm pretty damn sure they exist. The press will forget about me and you very quickly. Trust me."

"I wish that was true, but again, it's not that simple."

"Then what is it you want, Max? Why the fuck am I here?"

Max stood up, unbuttoned his suit jacket and took himself over to the window, admiring the view, admiring his reflection.

"Lilly. Remember that day we met?"

"Max. I'm not here for nostalgia."

"Humour me," he said, smiling. "I knew right away you would be a star. That first time I saw you in that tiny little dance school. You wanna know why?" he started to wander the room like it was a gallery. "You know why I knew you were going to be a star? Because I knew every part you would play, you would always be Lilly. No matter what role, what director, you would always play you. And any director that doesn't know that will fail. Hence why your subsequent movies have failed and your latest movie will fail no doubt also." He sat on the table. "Some characters are too big and too complex to change. You know a superstar when every single movie you watch they will only ever play themselves. Everything else, the plot, the cast, the wardrobe. It's just for show. A ruse." Max sat back down.

"Sounds like a curse, a shackle."

"Only if you fight it. Not if you embrace it."

"What is it you want, Max? Why am I here?"

"I have a proposition for you."

"I'm not getting back with you, Max."

"And you've made that pretty clear. I don't want love from you Lilly either, just to be clear."

"What do you want?"

"I want success, for both of us. Alone we can't do that."

"So, what's your proposition? You want to expose me and Tom. Then what?"

"Well it depends how you answer my next question really."

"Go on."

226

"It's a simple question. I just want a yes or no answer."

"Get on with it, Max."

"Would you be the lead in my next feature?"

"What? You caused all this shit, just to ask me that? You could've just rung me. Spoke to my office."

"Yes or no, Lilly?"

"You expect me to answer that? Where? How long? I've not even seen a script."

"Would it matter? Does any of that matter? The question is, would you work with me on my next feature. Yes or no?"

"No. You've wasted everyone's time today, Max, including your own."

"That's what I thought you'd say."

Max took out his cell.

"Max who are you ringing? Max?"

He ignored me, got up, walked back to his chair, told whoever else was on the other end of the phone to come in.

"Max. What the fuck is going on?"

"As I said, Lilly. This is business."

My agent walked through the door. Suit, briefcase, a smile hard to read.

"Ralph, what are you doing here?"

"I invited him," Max said, as Ralph sat beside him.

"Who gives you the right for you to contact my agent?"

"Lilly, you forget he's actually my agent too. Technically he was my agent first if you remember?"

"Ralph, what the fuck is going on?"

He looked uncomfortable. "Max invited me here, told me to bring all the required paperwork." squirming in his chair.

"And you didn't think it appropriate to contact me first?"

"Max told me not to. I'm sorry."

"And you do everything he tells you to, right?"

Ralph didn't answer.

"Just to let you know, Ralph, you are fired, you hear me?" I said, pointing at him. "Whatever shit this is about, I don't want you as my agent. After this, we are done."

"Lilly, claws down." Max smiled. "You've aired your lungs. Take a deep breath. Compose yourself."

I poured myself some water. Continuing to stare at Ralph as he attempted to avoid eye contact.

"Go on then, Max. Do your little sales pitch. Then I can decline and get the hell out of here."

"I'm not selling, Lilly."

"It feels that way. You two sat there like some fucking tag team."

"Lilly. I'm gonna be honest with you."

"I doubt that."

"Shush now, darling. You need to hear this."

"Just say whatever it is you want to say, Max."

"Over the last few months, as you know, whilst you've been scurrying around some English countryside I've been in discussions with various studios about my next picture and in those last few months I have been offered several offers to direct, all of which I've declined so far."

"Why was that, Max? Not enough money?"

"No, in fact the opposite. Too much money."

"Then why turn them down? Grab the money and run."

"You know me, Lilly. I don't make movies for money. You know I'm not driven by pay cheques. I need to be excited by a project. It needs to grab me by the balls."

"Why's that, Max. Cos you are the big Oscar-winning director? Cos every other movie is now beneath you?"

"No, Lilly, because I want to make movies that will be remembered. Be revered."

"Because you want more trophies, Max, that's why. What is it with you big-time directors and your need for accolades? Whose dick's the biggest. That's what all this is about."

"Lilly, let him talk," my agent piped up.

"Shut the fuck up, Ralph. You job is to stay quiet and keep the pens warm."

"Lilly, quit with the cuss words. Otherwise you'll have to leave."

"Just get on with your little saga, Max. I'm dying to know what happens next. Does it have an end or like most of your films is it going to last three hours with a long drawn-out middle?"

Max knelt down, so we were eye to eye. "I think you should cut the profanity. You'll probably want to listen, it affects you quite a bit." He stood up again, going back to his chair.

"As I was saying I hadn't been offered anything that excited me, until I met an investor who liked what I brought to the table. And he offered me something exciting. Something perfect."

"What?"

"Do you ever think about why our first feature was so popular?"

"No, I don't Max. I'm too busy to sit and ponder personal glory."

"Because it was perfect, Lilly, that's why. Perfect cast, perfect plot, perfect timing. And because of you." Max smiled. "Let's be honest with ourselves here, Lilly. The following movies both me and you have made have been poor in comparison. And if I'm being brutally honest we are both at a career crossroads. We are off the boil. If it wasn't for our volatile relationship we wouldn't be being talked about at all."

"You may not be happy with your career choices since you won all your trophies. But I'm happy with mine."

"Your movies are forgettable, Lilly. And mine too. I can't think of anything worse than being forgettable."

"And what did this investor offer you? I'm dying to know, Max."

"He offered me the funding I needed to finally make my sequel. Taken longer than expected. But now there is finally a light at the end of the tunnel. The only problem is you."

"Me?"

"They will only offer me funding and allow me to direct this feature if you are on board. If you reprise your role. Star as the lead again."

"Max. I appreciate the offer, and if it was any other director I would jump at the chance. I love that character. I love her storyline. I loved what you did with the first film. Like you said, it was perfect."

"Then say yes, Lilly."

"No. I won't work with you again, Max. I'm sorry. Too much has gone on."

"And you realize your response will mean the movie will never be made?"

"Unless someone else directs it."

"Which I won't let happen. It's my story, my baby. No one else's."

"Regretfully, yes. I'm sorry, Max. Surely you must understand why?"

"I don't think you understand the severity of your actions, Lilly. How many people this will impact."

"Just use another actress. Rewrite the script. Write my character out if it."

"You are the movie, Lilly. I can't write you out of it."

"Look, I've given you my answer. Can I leave now?" I went to stand up.

"How much do you know about Tom?"

"Excuse me?"

"How much do you know about Tom?"

"Fuck you, Max."

"Answer the question, please. How much do you know about him?"

"I know he's honest."

"No money. Unemployed. He's spent half of this year chasing you whilst he leaves his cancer-stricken mother to look after his only daughter. Not to mention my photo evidence of him smoking pot. His hymn sheet doesn't make for great reading, Lilly."

"You fucking hypocrite. I wouldn't be surprised if you snorted coke in the back of your cab on the way here."

"Yes, but I'm not dumb enough to get caught doing it, that's all."

"How dare you, Max. The things you've just said don't make him a criminal. You've twisted it to sound worse than it is. You're digging to find dirt you ain't gonna find. He isn't doing anything wrong. He has never done anything wrong."

"Wrong? Tom ain't no saint. You know he got stopped by the cops, breathalysed?"

"When?"

"Couple years back. Driving around LA early in the morning. Luckily, he was under the limit. Dodged a bullet that night. Likes a drink as much as me that one. Makes you wonder if he was drinking that day he crashed his car and killed his wife."

"He didn't kill his wife, you arsehole. The car collided into him, he told me. He would've been breathalysed and questioned as part of the investigation. You're just clinging onto anything you can get your hands on Max. It's pathetic, even by your standards."

"Seems a coincidence though, doesn't it? Wonder if Cassie's parents would find it coincidental? You think they are happy that Tom has snatched away their only grandchild? Him running off with her halfway across the world."

"Tom is Molly's father. He didn't snatch her away. He has a legal right to look after his own child."

"You are right, Lilly. But would the State see it that way?"

"Tom's a good man. A decent person. A great father. What have you poisoned Cassie's parents' minds with? What have you said to them? Tom has written to Cassie's parents. I remember him telling me."

"Do you know what a Declaration of Paternity is, Lilly?"

"Of course I don't."

"Well, neither does Tom by the looks of it." Max smirked.

"What does that mean?"

"It means he has no legal right to Molly."

"He's her father, Max. Course he has a legal right."

"Might take a lot of aggravation to prove that, though. Blood tests, courtrooms, lawyers."

"Then I'll buy the best lawyer money can buy, Max."

"Hey, and maybe you'll win. But maybe you won't."

"Is this even legal, Max? What is happening in this room today?"

"All I'm doing is warning you of the danger. Which could easily be avoided if you just do this movie with me. Tom can continue living his little life in England. With little Molly and his dying mother."

"And that's all I'd have to do. Just make this movie with you."

"Not all, Lilly, I'm afraid. I want you to end things with Tom."

"What?"

"I want you to end it with Tom."

"And get back with you I suppose? You're unbelievable, Max. You really are. You honestly believe I would get back with you after this stunt you are trying to pull?"

"Not physically, not emotionally. Just visually. We can continue our separate lives. But as far as the press, the world media and Tom are concerned. We are back together and couldn't be happier. This won't work if Tom is in the picture."

"You're sick and twisted."

"No Lilly. I'm just determined, that's all."

"You can't do this." I stood up. "Ralph, he can't do this. This is blackmail."

"The only legal document so far is the film contract," Ralph butted in. "Everything else is just being discussed between these four walls."

"And what's in this for you? Your 10% I guess. A big payday.

You're supposed to be on my side, Ralph. I pay you a salary to be on my side."

"I am on your side. This deal will make us all rich. And make you a global superstar. It makes business sense to accept."

"Fuck you," I said, feeling myself launch for him. "I can't believe this is happening."

"We'll give you ten minutes." Max walked over to the door. "We'll grab some fresh air. Give you time to weigh up your options."

"I'm not doing it, Max. You think you've won this game but you haven't."

"We'll be back in ten minutes to get your final response. And please don't ring Tom. And don't run off, Lilly. If you run off or talk to him then I have to assume you've made a decision not to sign the contract. And you know what that would mean for poor little Tom."

"I could still speak to Tom? Be friends. Give him a decent explanation on why me and him won't work."

"I'm afraid that's not possible."

"Why not?"

"Because you might slip up, change your mind. It's a bad idea."

"Then what? Just stop talking to him. Ignore him."

"Yes. Cut all communication."

"Easy as that, is it? You're fucking evil."

"He'll get over it. How long has he known you, like, a month?"

"I love him."

"You fall in love too quick. I'm sure you can fall out of love just as quick."

"I love him, Max. More than I ever loved you. I want you to know that."

"How sweet. I was counting on you saying that. It's made today a hell of a lot easier for me. Sacrifice is so much easier when love is involved. Ralph, can you please give Lilly the paperwork?"

"I'm not signing this without my lawyer, Max. I'm a fool, but I'm not that foolish."

"I couldn't agree more. Like agents, we both share the same lawyer."

"Is he outside, too, I guess?"

"He is."

"You're a snake."

"He's already had time to view all the small print. It's all pretty standard. I'll bring him in after you've had time to make your decision." Ralph handed me the contract and a pen.

"Max, I'm not doing this. I'm not making your movie."

"Think carefully. A lot is at stake. Be a good girl and sign. Let's not make things difficult."

"Max, I need more time."

"No."

"How do I know you want to expose Tom anyway? Even if I do everything you say?"

"Ten minutes, Lilly. I need an answer."

45

"Tom, I can see here you are twenty-seven but you've only had the one employer. And as far as I can tell you have never had a job in the United Kingdom."

"That's right, yes."

He scanned his notes. "Interesting," he said, showing little interest at all.

"I worked for just over two years for the same company back in LA."

"Oh yes," he said, turning to the previous page. "Hollywood Star Tours."

"I was one of the top guys."

"But still no references. I've no proof on whether you were a top guy or not. In fact, I haven't got proof of anything in front of me." He huffed. "What about before? Talk me through when you left education."

"After university, I travelled. Worked a few odd jobs in various countries, bar work, fruit picking, cleaning."

He smiled, scribbled at his paper. "Says here you left Hollywood Star Tours around July last year. That's quite the gap of unemployment. Nearly a year."

"I worked in insurance, but only for a few weeks."

"What happened?"

"I had to come home, back to England."

"And did you find work here?"

"I did some agency work briefly."

"Doing?"

"Warehouse work for a few weeks. Cab driver briefly."

"Anything else?"

"I've working with my friend since Christmas."

"That's not written down here is it?"

"It wasn't a real job as such. Just helped him out you could say."

"Was it paid work?"

"It was. Not a salary as such. Cash in hand."

"Cash in hand?" He wasn't impressed. "Cash for what?"

"It's hard to say. It was target-based you could say."

"Targeted on?"

I took time to answer. "I suppose you could say journalism. I worked with cameras mostly."

Adjusting his tie, he considered his notes, flicked through my CV, my cover letter.

"I'm not going to lie to you, Tom. It's pretty light reading and I'm struggling to understand your journey from fruit picker to tour guide to warehouse operator to photographer and now telesales. Why are you here today, Tom? Why this company?"

"I feel like a different challenge. Like you said, my career has a been a mixed bag. I want to lay down some roots. I want to be able to provide for my family. This isn't my dream, no. But that doesn't mean I won't give you my 100%."

"But for how long? How do I know I can invest in you, train you to our high standards? Put yourself in my shoes as an employer. You've never had a career, most jobs you've had have lasted months, sometimes weeks. You may have transferable skills, but nothing you can prove on paper. How do I know you won't give up in six months and move onto your next venture? I don't want to waste your time or mine and we certainly don't want to waste our money providing with you all our skills and resources only for you to go off on another adventure."

"I wouldn't be here if I wasn't serious. I know my résumé isn't great, but I assure you, I'm timely. I'm hard-working. I do as I'm told. That has to stand for something, doesn't it?"

"That's not enough here, Tom. The ethos is to aim higher. We want people who exceed. Who deliver more than is expected. To live our brand values. Not just arrive on time and be a nodding dog."

"You ask for a lot for fourteen grand basic."

"We do," he said. I was already imagining the big red cross he was drawing through my application.

★ ★ ★

It went on, me explaining myself, selling my soul to the corporate brand, being asked a serious of pre-scripted questions, designed to test my flaws and weaknesses, an example of when I'd last influenced someone, when I'd embraced change, when I'd overcome a difficult situation. My answers were poor, made up on the spot, I knew I hadn't got the job before the survey started, the smug look on his face, he disliked me from the moment he heard 'university' and 'gap year', not to mention the words 'single' and 'parent'. He didn't ask why, luckily, all he heard was 'inflexible' and 'childcare', why I was a single parent was of little concern.

He said good or bad, I'd hear from him in the next few weeks, though I didn't count on it. At first, I felt triumphant, happy I hadn't measured up, but back in the car with time to think it over, I knew I'd let everyone down. If I was serious in making a go at this I had to be better prepared next time, plan my responses, learn how to sell myself.

Mum agreed.

That evening we sat searching for jobs again, slim pickings with small salaries. Found a few possibilities, tweaked my CV, completely rewrote my covering letter, sent them back out there, then I just had to wait. And if I got some responses, got a phone call telling me when and where, then I'd need to prepare more than ironing my shirt and polishing my shoes. I had to make myself sound employable, become the actor, play the part, as at the moment I had as much chance of finding work as I did hearing from across the pond.

The rest of the week was interview after interview, more positive responses, better feedback, but still the same outcome. There were jobs out there at least, lots of opportunities, just not intended for me. Very nearly got a job in a local newspaper, beat reporter, in fact they said it would have been mine to have, if the position hadn't been promised to one of the boss's sons. To be fair, the money was awful, OK for an eighteen-year-old with no outgoings, but not someone pushing thirty. There was always getting back behind the wheel of a taxi again, the one thing I knew I could do was drive around in circles, I wouldn't need an interview for that.

★ ★ ★

We waved at the lady whose name I'd already forgotten. I attempted to ask Molly questions about what she thought of it all. Did she like the sandpit? Cushion corner? The sunflowers outside? The slide? But she was preoccupied, a group of young mums had a few of those handbag dogs, they were yapping and sniffing. Think one of the mums even smiled at me, she was about my age, probably just being friendly, probably me getting the wrong impression. Anyway, Molly now wanted a dog, one she could hold and paint its nails, something else alive to be added to her birthday list, flesh and blood rather than batteries and bubble wrap.

It had been a long day for Molly and by the time I got her in her car seat her eyes were closed before I got into second gear. I hadn't enjoyed today, we'd visited three day nurseries in total, they all were nice, not much between them, all within twenty minutes of Mum's village, all the staff friendly, the facilities what I'd expected. I hadn't enjoyed today because it hadn't sat right, gave me an awful feeling in my gut. There was a horrible reality to it all, that I would have to work full time again, that for Molly one of those nurseries might be her new home for most of the working week. I looked out of the car window, so far removed from my time in Devon. Gone were the views of meadows and coastlines and ball gowns. Now I was back to grey, bus fumes, roadworks, overdrafts. I checked Molly out in the rear-view mirror, still asleep, she deserved better than being offloaded and a better future than the view outside.

Back at home, Molly had set up a small veterinary practice in the front room as me and Mum peeled potatoes at the kitchen table.

"I don't like the idea of putting down roots here either, you know, Tom."

"It is what it is."

"I wish you'd let me sell up. Start afresh. I've always fancied Spain. Port de Soller. Great food, great architecture, fantastic art."

"If anything, if went abroad we would be worse off. Not all healthcare is free."

"Tom, you don't have to follow me. Just because I'm ill doesn't mean you are now my carer."

"I'm afraid it does. I could hardly leave, could I? Leave you to go through all this alone. You're having a lump removed tomorrow, Mum. We all need to stay put."

"It's my cancer, not yours."

I took a handful of potatoes skins to the outside compost bin.

"If Cassie was still alive and that crash had never happened, I would still have cancer you know."

"Mum, what point are you trying to make?"

"You would still have been living in Los Angeles, with Cassie and Molly, and I would be here. I would've had to fight cancer on my own regardless."

"No, you wouldn't have. I would've flown back."

"Would you?"

"Course I would've. Would you have flown to the States if you found out I had cancer?"

"I hate being a burden, you know that."

"It's one of those things, Mum. We just have to get on with it."

"Tom. Can I ask you a question?"

"Sure," I said, lighting the ring of the gas hob.

"If I was dead, what would you do? I mean, what would you and Molly do next? Where would you go?"

"Mum, seriously?"

"Please, Tom. Humour me. Where would you go?"

"I don't know, do I?"

"You must have an idea."

"I don't, Mum. Don't think you being alive or dead makes my choices any easier. I've got too many question marks. All I know is, I wouldn't be here. I wouldn't be in this village. I suppose I wouldn't want to live anywhere. I'd just grab a suitcase for me and Molly and just go off somewhere. India, Thailand, anywhere. Just roam. Point at a map and go."

"You've always been one to be on the move. I had visions of you never marrying, living day to day, turning up in twenty years with grey dreadlocks or worse, a bloody sitar. Cassie must have been some woman to keep you in place. Was she the same as you? The travelling hobo?"

"No, not at all."

"You two didn't have much in common, did you?"

"Except Molly."

"For some couples, a child is the only common ground required."

"We did talk about it once, the idea of upping sticks, well I did. A travelling friend of mine was about to embark across South America, asked me to tag along, told me to bring the whole family. Six months on the Amazon, me, Cassie, a one-year-old. Sounded pretty wild."

"I take it Cassie wasn't too enthusiastic by the whole idea."

"You could say that, yes. To be fair, looking back on it I can see why. Molly wasn't in good shape around that time. It was stupid of me to even have suggested it."

"What about now? Does it sound as stupid as it did then?"

"I don't know, Mum. Molly starts school soon."

"There are other ways to be educated, Tom."

"You sound like Dad."

"I know. Sounds hypocritical, but even though he was a teacher he always felt the classrooms and curriculum were far too restrictive. Felt children learnt more from touch and smell and experiences. I don't think education through travel is that radical any more anyways. Maybe in my day and age but not now."

"It's not just about education, Mum. There's lots of things to consider."

"You think Molly would prefer stability. Somewhere to call home, to make friends, to have pets. Rather than being a vagabond."

"I'm not saying I don't want to build some foundations. I've just no clue where it should be yet. Doesn't help not having a clue about me and Lilly either."

"You need a contingency plan, Lilly can't be relied upon, which I wish wasn't the case."

"Just wish she'd speak to me."

"Look, over the next few days we'll start looking seriously at all our options. Whether to stay put or sell up. To stay in England or think further afield. Work out what is best. But at least we have a starting point. We are both in agreement that it's not here."

Mum knelt and opened the oven door slightly. The room filled with heat, a waft of spitting sausages.

"Cassie would've hated today," I said taking the grater out of the cupboard. "She was always against day care and childminders. Parents both working full time. She always believed mothers should be the ones doing the mothering, not strangers. She wouldn't approve of me putting Molly into some nursery five days a week."

"Well, sometimes life isn't that easy. Sometimes you have to go against your principles."

"What did you and Dad do?"

"I stayed at home. I didn't go back to work till you were in your teens. Only had your father's wage. They were hard times. Really hard."

"I never noticed," I said, as I grated and mashed.

"We hid it well. We went without for a long time."

"Thing is, Mum, I've done the maths. With your widow's and state pension, with me currently out of work, the bulk of our outgoings will have to come from what's left in savings from my work with Vince."

"How much?"

"I don't know. Taking away the money I've spend on food and petrol this week, her new coat. I'm guessing around ten thousand, maybe less."

"That's a lot of money for three months' work. I can see why people do such work. A lucrative business."

"On paper, yes. But unless I add to it, all it will do is go down and down. I need to earn."

"Those day nurseries won't be cheap."

"Tell me about it. I'll lose most of my wage."

"Hardly sounds worth it. Money will go in and then straight out again. Not easy being a single parent. I thought the government would be doing more to help you. You must be able to get some support. I mean, child benefit, jobseeker's allowance, you might even get something for being a widower. May even be backdated."

"Mum. I don't want handouts."

"It's not a handout. You're entitled to it."

"It means I'll have to sign on, meet with someone, send proofs. I'll be begging, basically."

"It's not begging, Tom. And yes, you're probably right. You may have to meet with someone and talk through your situation, so they can understand what you might be entitled to. And sending proofs is no hardship. Probably need a birth certificate for Molly, probably want to see proof of what you've been up to since you came back to England. We'll have to check online, see how it all works. It might tide us over till we know where all our futures lie."

"I don't even know where Molly's birth certificate is."

"You brought it back with you, surely?"

"I can't find it, Mum. I thought I brought it back."

"You need to get that sorted."

"I know. I've got a number of a county office in LA. I need to ring them. I've got some other stuff I need to check out about Molly and Cassie."

"Stuff?"

"Legal stuff, paperwork. I left in a hurry. I just need to get my shit in order."

"I'm surprised you aren't receiving any widower's pension for Cassie?"

"I just assumed as we were never married that I wouldn't be entitled. That's the stuff I've got to find out."

The phone rang. Mum answered it, hanging up moments later.

"I take it that wasn't Lilly."

"Unless she's now in PPI Claims. That's another reason to leave this country. If I've months left to live I'd rather spent it strolling on a beach rather than arguing about being missold something I've never even had. And don't worry, Lilly will call. She's a busy actress, remember? Busy being famous, not like she's sitting at home with her feet up."

"That's what worries me. She's back in her real world now. Looking back at me and England might not seem as attractive as it once did."

The phone rang again.

"I'll get it, Mum. Probably be PPI Claims again. I'll make it clear not to ring again. We need to ring BT, get them to block these cold calls."

I picked up the phone.

It wasn't Lilly. It wasn't PPI Claims either.

It was a voice I didn't expect.

Cassie's father.

46

It shouldn't have been such a surprise, though it was still a shock to the system. My months away in the English countryside had gotten me used to quite a lethargic way of life, where things got done when they were ready, things done at their own speed, it had turned me soft. This was a wake-up call, back to work, I wondered if Sally had done this purposely, made such a manic schedule, a boot camp of endless work duties, make me hard again, get me back into shape as quickly as possible.

Sally did actually warn me that I would be pulled from pillar to post whilst in New York, but I didn't predict the extremes of one city and three locations in one day. Sally talked me through it in detail at the celebratory dinner she'd thrown for me the night before. Told me in depth what to expect and where I needed to be, but I was barely listening. I chewed my food as toasts were made and glasses were clinked, another one of those happy occasions when I couldn't have been unhappier. It wasn't Sally or Frank's fault, to them it was celebratory, a time for pats on the back and high-fives, defining moments, they kept saying, role of a lifetime, and they were right, it would take everything I had and more. If I could act, then this would be the time to prove it, I didn't know if I could do it, honestly and truthfully, I didn't know if I'd be capable of putting up such a front, over such a long period of time, lying every day to Sally, Frank, the world, Tom. I had to, though, I couldn't fail at this, had to see it through. Otherwise none of it would've been worth it.

How long had I been on my feet now, I thought to myself. Shoot began at five, now it was dark. The morning started with

Rockefeller's. I've never been great with heights, especially before sunrise and without a decent breakfast, 9/11 sprang to mind, which was never good when seventy floors high in the middle of New York, I kept looking out for planes. I got a bit upset would you believe, my dad knew someone who went down in the South Tower, being so high made it all too real, the horror of it all. I felt quite vulnerable up there, tried my best to look unaffected, look sexy and confident, wondering if they could edit out my nerves, seeing as they could remove wrinkles and cellulite, I was sure fear and exhaustion could be Photoshopped just as easily.

Next whisked away to Manhattan harbour. The Captain warned us of the weather, said it might get a bit choppy out there as we stepped onto his schooner, didn't think I would actually throw up, not that anyone noticed. One thing us models and actresses knew was how to vomit in secret, managed to find a toilet below deck to spare any embarrassment, make-up girls worked a minor miracle turning my skin to any colour other than green.

Now I was in Queens, back on dry land, not back at the ground level necessarily but the garden rooftop terrace of a swanky hotel was a height I could cope with. Despite my bad mood, I still appreciated the view across East River, being under a bridge never looked so fucking cool. Biggest bridge I'd ever seen, made me feel small, sometimes humans amazed me with what they were capable of. New York was an amazing place, full of man-made miracles, skyscrapers, statues, bridges, but even that couldn't make me smile. For all that the city could offer I still wished I was somewhere else, with someone else.

I looked over my shoulder, the crew frantically setting up the last shot of the day, moving lamps, checking cameras, testing light. I didn't quite know how I'd gotten through today, caffeine mostly, Renata the photographer was full of relentless energy, as was the crew, rubbed off on me, gave me a boost I didn't think I had in me, especially considering the last few days I'd had.

My feet were throbbing, various shoes throughout the day,

ornate and expensive, yes, so my toes and ankles were officially ruined, all over was pretty fucked actually, head to toe. Prodded and poked all day by my dresser. My outfits had been beautiful, this one in particular, small and tight, my hair sprayed high and pinned, my jewellery heavy. I looked amazing, but now I just wanted to be comfortable, I was tired of being pulled in and up. Now I just wanted to have a bath and go to bed, let my fat roll and frown.

A girl, Alex, came back with a coat which I put on immediately. We'd spoken briefly throughout the day, what her accent was, where she got her dress, where she got her bangs cut. She invited me out later, bar, club, gonna be a late one, she said, wild. She was the sort of young that could survive on zero sleep and despite me declining, she gave me her number anyway, just in case, she said.

I noticed Sally cutting her way through the crowd, stepping over props, cat-like.

"I'm getting déjà vu," she said, scanning the surroundings. "I remember blueberry mojitos, but very little else."

"Sign of a good night. You should order one, Sal. See if it jogs the memory."

"Only if you have one. Drinking alone is alcoholic. Drink together and it's socializing."

"Sorry, I'm on the tea I'm afraid. Too cold. Frank not with you?"

"He's in some meeting with management."

"Management?"

"Going through your schedule. Just working out logistics, safety, y'know, bodyguard stuff."

"What's happening tomorrow? I'm assuming it isn't a day off."

"You've got most of the day off actually."

"Thank God."

"In the evening, I'll need you for a few hours. There's a meet-and-greet and I think it would really boost your profile if you were there to attend."

"Can I say no?"

"You can say no. But… "

"Don't worry. I'll be there."

"Friday is the biggy though. Jimmy Fallon."

"I haven't seen you this excited since I got you an iPad."

"You know how many people watch him each week? It's like half the planet. We'll need to prepare for it beforehand, obviously. I'll speak to Max to make sure we are all on the same page, but the plans are, so far, you'll reveal the big news on the show. Should get everyone's tongues wagging. Don't worry we'll let you know what you can or cannot say."

"Are you around tomorrow? I fancy therapy."

"Retail, I hope."

"To start with."

"I've got a lunch meeting, but apart from that I'm free. Meeting Max, funnily enough."

"To talk about me, I suppose."

"Indirectly. I just thought it best I meet with them so I can set up a time line. Get our heads round both our calendars. Whisper is they are looking to start filming around late Feb, early March time."

"I wish it was sooner. That's like half a year away."

"March is pretty good going in my book. This has been in the pipeline a long time. Sounds like it was all set up ready to go. Scripts, locations. You were the final piece of the puzzle."

Sally's cell buzzed, though she didn't care to look or check who it was.

"I'm so happy you've decided to take on Max's project. This could be the movie, Lilly. The one that people will talk about for years to come. You must be so excited. I know I am."

"It was an offer I couldn't turn down."

"You're damn right, Lilly. The contract's amazing. Hell of a pay cheque, not to mention all the added perks. Max has made sure you'll be well looked after."

"How do you mean?"

"Let's just say your entourage might be expanding slightly. Own private chefs, personal trainer on set, life coach, extra security."

"Great. I'm Mariah fucking Carey."

"Enjoy it."

"You don't think Max will try and push out Frank, do you? They've never seen eye to eye."

"I hope not, but now you've mentioned that it wouldn't surprise me if he tries to replace Frank."

"Max might even try and replace you, Sally?"

"He can fucking try," she snarled. "I'll make it clear tomorrow that me and Frank are here for the long haul."

"Please. And tell him I'm perfectly happy with the team I've got now. It's done me well so far. If I need someone to sort through my M&Ms he'll be the first to know."

"I'm still surprised by all this. It's all happened so quickly. I wouldn't have imagined this in a million years. It's fate, isn't it? All that stars and planets and shit. Everything coming together at the right time."

"You mixed up your meds again. You've gone all utopian. I'm not sure it suits you, Sally."

"You know what I mean. Y'know, like a higher power. Like, for all the planning and predictions, life already has it all mapped out."

"This wasn't fate, Sally. Max knew what he was doing."

"But did he ever think you would say yes? If you'd have asked me back in England what you'd be doing now, I wouldn't have expected this. You and Max together again, well, working together, I mean."

"Well, like I said. It was an offer I couldn't really refuse."

"Well, however he managed to persuade you, I'm impressed with his methods."

"What does Frank think? I've not had much time to talk to him."

"You know Frank. He's hard to read."

"He is acting a bit weird though, isn't he? It's not just me, is it?"

"Frank has always been weird. But yes, his weird levels have increased. Certainly quieter, if that is even possible. It's the whole Max thing. You know he's not his biggest fan. He needs to grow a pair. Move on like you."

"Me?"

"Yes you. I think it's brilliant that you can put the past behind you. I know a lot has gone on with you and Max and I know it will make working with him difficult at first. I'll be there for you every step of the way. I'm so proud of you, Lilly, for looking at this as a career opportunity and not letting emotions get in the way of good business. You've really grown up. Put all that went on in England behind you, all that talk of emigrating, put all that soul-searching behind you. Get back to what you do best."

"Go Team Goodridge."

"Are you being sarcastic?"

"I can't tell anymore," I said, sipping my tea.

"Surely you see how ridiculous it all was? He was a nice boy, but a simple boy, with simple aspirations. Your life will always be too big for someone like Tom. The poor boy would've drowned."

"*Hora dorado, personas,*" Reneta shouted. "Golden hour, people."

"Time to shine, Lilly," she smiled, 59th Street Bridge behind her, a sunset of metal and orange.

★ ★ ★

My cell buzzed.

You up?
No x

Seconds later there was a knock at my door.

249

"Couple next door are trying to break a record."

"Gross," I said, letting him in.

"Can I crash here till the baby-making is all over?" Frank sat beside me on the bed. "You eating this?" noticing my room service.

"It's probably cold by now."

Frank was already halfway through it with his fork. "What you watching?"

"*Deadliest Catch*. Those guys don't get paid enough."

"How was today?" he said, chewing.

"Long."

"Don't worry. Few more days to go now. What are you and your folks getting up to on 4th July?"

"The usual. Tons of meat, slaw, banana pudding, pecan pie, beer. Try and get a good view of all the fireworks, normally head towards the Bowl. What about you?"

"Good bottle of whisky and the remote control." He yawned.

"You had a long day too?"

"Not especially. Just tired. Want my own bed now. The novelty of fresh towels and bed linen has officially worn off." He dipped asparagus into hollandaise. "I need my armchair, my own bathroom, my own coffee. You?"

"I'm not sure how to feel now. I went through a stage where I was quite looking forward to going back, but I think I've gone full circle. I've gotten used to be waited on, beds being made, my clothes washed. I know one thing though."

"What?"

"I'm gonna move out of my apartment."

"You haven't been in your new one that long. Where?"

"Not a clue. Somewhere less show-home, something lived in, with a big garden and lots of space."

"Sounds familiar."

"I doubt I'll find Devon in Beverley Hills."

"You have enough money, you can find anything in Beverly Hills."

"I'm not rich yet."

"I wouldn't be so sure." He smiled. "You spoken to your folks?"

"About?"

"Your big movie news."

"Only briefly. Think Dad is already pricing up a new Harley. Why is Sally meeting Max tomorrow?" I said, changing the subject. "Should I be worried?"

"I wouldn't read too much into it. It's nothing sinister. Just think they need to walk through the next twelve to eighteen months. Boring stuff. Distribution overseas, media tactics, dealing with the press, getting the world enthusiastic about the film."

"Probably involve me spending large amounts of time in the same room as Max."

"I wouldn't disagree there. You're the star and he's the director. You better get used to it. Hey, but you knew that would be part of the deal. Otherwise you wouldn't have signed."

"Just because I signed doesn't mean I have to like Max. I just have to work with him."

"And that's all he wants? Just to work with you?"

"Probably not. He'll do his best to romance me, sweep me off my feet."

"And will he be successful?"

"Probably. You fancy a beer?"

"Why not, hey? I'll get 'em." Frank got up, lumbered over to the mini bar, taking out a couple of Buds.

I took a sip. "God that tastes good."

"Hits the spot." Frank propped a pillow behind his back.

"We got any more?"

"Not unless you fancy hitting the miniatures."

"Feel like doing something wild. We could trash the room, throw a TV out of the window."

"Me? I'm gonna watch TV, finish my beer, go to bed. What you do next is up to you."

"Don't be surprised if you wake up to carnage tomorrow. I may have totalled my room."

"As long as it's not me cleaning it up I don't care what you do. It will be Sally you'll have to answer to. You sure it's worth it?"

We both leant back against the headboard.

"You think I'm stupid doing this, don't you? Working with Max again?"

"No actually."

"You don't? I thought you hated Max more than I do."

"I think it makes sense. I may dislike the man, but still doesn't change the fact it was the right move."

"You don't sound 100%."

"I understand why it makes sense. I just can't for the life of me understand how it made sense to you."

"Like you said. It was too good to say no to."

"Just be careful with… "

"You don't need to tell me that, Frank."

We took a gulp of beer.

"You seem quiet these days."

"Do I?" he looked surprised. "Overworked and underpaid. I'm getting too old for this."

"Too old for what?"

"Everything. Just want to sit and pass the time."

"Don't retire on me just yet. Not when things are about to go a hundred miles per hour."

"Trust me. You'd be in better hands with someone else."

"I'm sure I would."

"I can't work forever, Lilly."

"I'm not asking for forever. I'm just saying not yet. You promise?"

He didn't answer. Took another gulp of beer as we both sank into the bed.

"You promise, Frank?"

"I'll do my best," he smiled. Eyes on the TV. Crab pots and heavy seas.

★ ★ ★

Witching hour again. Ever since I signed the contract with Max, it was like this. Days were worse, but nights were a curse, too much quiet. I was on my own at least, had to send Frank back to his room, he wasn't impressed being pushed out of the door mid-snore. I did try to budge him on his side, move him so the bed could be shared, but the lump wasn't to be moved.

I heard a helicopter overhead, New York was just getting started, car horns, dogs, sirens, now helicopters, the Upper East Side sounded agitated, wanting attention or getting it. I thought it might stop, thought it might subside as time sneaked further towards the morning, no such luck. I never knew noise travelled so far, or so high. Not loud enough to deafen, but loud enough to make me search for earplugs I already knew I'd forgotten to pack. I could've complained, but what would it have solved, not as if I could go any higher, my apartment was top floor. I could've rung down for earplugs, but I didn't, I was too embarrassed to ask.

I opened my bedside drawer, I could've sworn I'd brought Zantac. Why was I so drunk? Must be my empty stomach, me and Frank had only the one beer, well, a shot of vodka too. The fizz of beer was still in my tummy, as was the alcohol in my bloodstream. I wasn't drunk, but I didn't feel sober either, a horrible middle to be in. Outside there would've been far more easy and accessible alternatives that the Big Apple would be able to accommodate and a younger version of me would've pursued such alternatives – would have got up, grabbed some clothes, found somewhere dark and neon, smoke-filled, loud, become a shadow for a few hours.

I thought of the girl earlier today, her invitation, it would've been so simple to ring her. It wouldn't have taken much to get dressed, speed across town. I didn't even remember her name, that wouldn't have mattered, I wasn't after friendship, just didn't want to be alone, just wanted to feel anything other than headache. Fill myself till I didn't feel so empty, music, liquor, chemical, whatever cure it took.

Perhaps that is what it would take, something to take the edge off. Not just for tonight, but to see me through the next few weeks, months, years, see me through to the end of Max's little plan unscathed. Ring my doctor, get him to prescribe everything legal, ring someone else to prescribe everything else. That wouldn't be a good idea, me and drugs had a love–hate thing, I loved them, they hated me.

I could hate Tom instead. Build him up as the villain rather than the victim, better to think of him as blameable. The man who crashed his car, killed his wife, trespassed on my property, a bad father, a bad son. Tom wasn't my problem and his mother and his child were not my problem. I shouldn't have had to pay the price for his mom's cancer or who his daughter should live with, those were his problems, not mine. I could have pretended I'd never met him, pretended he'd never existed, hundreds of miles away it wouldn't be that difficult. It would be sad at first, but he could be forgotten quickly, if I buried myself in my work, found someone new, our time together could just be something to look back on fondly, no regrets and no hard feelings. So why couldn't I do that? Why couldn't I accept that? Why couldn't that be enough?

Because it wasn't the truth and Tom was none of those things. He loved his wife, his mom, his daughter, he did what he had to, to make a living. He wasn't to blame in all this, neither of us were, he at least deserved an explanation, even a fake one. I'd nearly done it, you know, several times, pleaded with Max to let me speak to him, even wrote Tom letters though they all ended up in the trash.

None of this made sense, if Max wanted drama, headlines, then it would better just to expose me and Tom, it would get people talking, sell his goddamn movie. Maybe that was the plan, no matter what I did from then on, we would be exposed regardless. Or maybe, just maybe, he didn't want to see me with anybody else. The rest, the movie, the plan, perhaps he just wanted me back and this was the only way he could make it happen.

Screw this. This was fucking torture.

I threw on some clothes, grabbed the first cab I could find, found the nearest place that sounded loud. Did whatever it took, numbed my senses, partied till there was little party left in me. By the time I got back New York was finally waking up, though neither of us had really slept.

47

"What's it like?" I whispered, though I didn't need to, Molly was preoccupied with her fork and peas, the peas currently winning.

"What's what like?" Mum chewing. "It's hard to explain."

"Does it feel like dying?"

"No. It's like nothing is wrong, but the sheer fact you're told there is, means you feel obliged to act the part. I don't think you're allowed to smile and laugh. You have to look broken and beaten."

"Does it hurt at all?"

Just then the waitress came over, asked us if our meals were OK, which they weren't particularly, not that we complained.

"It hurts sometimes, yes."

"Where? Your chest?"

"No, all over. My bones. Like I'm suddenly heavier."

"I can't imagine what that must be like."

"Have you ever had a check over?"

"No. You think I should?"

"Well my brother had it in his bowel. Then there's your father."

"Dad had a heart attack, though?"

"Yes, but brought on by his lymphoma."

"I thought he'd beaten that. I remember talking to him on the phone about it."

"He did, several times. But there is only so much one body can take."

We chewed our food.

"Sorry, Mum. Death is hardly ideal dinner conversation."

"I feel better for talking about it."

"People go strange when death is involved. Cassie became nameless for about two months. Became a 'she' for a long while."

Mum laughed. "Mine has already become an 'it'. 'It' or 'thing,' most people call it. Pete across the road won't even give me eye contact. One friend can't even speak to me without breaking down into tears. Silly really." She took a sip of water. ",I need to visit the ladies' room before I have to undo a belt loop,." walking off down the middle of the restaurant.

she said, 'I ed,I regretted loading my plate. Beef, pork, Yorkshires, crackling, stuffing. Endless food, food we could have cooked far better at home, for half the cost. But, hey, it was a special occasion, I tried to ignore the carvery fumes that hung in the carpets and ceilings, pretended the toilets didn't smell of gravy. A Sunday Roast when it wasn't even Sunday.

"You OK, Mol?"

"It tastes squishy," she said, pointing at her vegetables piled high and pale.

"Eat the broccoli," I said, though even they looked the wrong shade of green.

"I'm full up, Dad."

"Me too."

"Can I have… "

"You said you were full, little madam. And you haven't finished your… "

"A bowl of ice cream won't hurt her." Mum sat back down at the table. "Besides, today is a celebration. Balloons and ice cream are a given. Even for the adults. I'm surprised you are starting so soon. They don't waste much time, do they?"

"It's not like I have to work my notice. From what they've told me the first month I'll mostly be in training."

"Close by, I hope."

"I'll be close for the first week. After that, Wakefield, apparently."

"That's not close at all."

"I'm promised a hire car which is good. Though it might mean I'll be in hotels on and off."

"You'll need a couple of shirts and ties. We'll pick some up on the way home. Asda do a shirt and trouser set, I'm sure. Not to mention a good wash and shave."

"You're not a fan of beards are you, Mum?"

"You look like Abraham Lincoln."

"I was going more NME."

"Well, I don't think your new employer would appreciate either."

The waitress came over, she took away our plates, promised us the ice creams would be a few minutes.

"This isn't how you saw things panning out, is it?" Mum said, wiping her mouth with a napkin.

"No, not really."

"This place is hardly helping, though we have got balloons." She pointed at the one tied to the back of my chair. "And at least this new job will give you something to focus on other than you-know-what."

"I'm OK, honest, Mum. I know you think I'm not. But I'm fine."

"Well, I know being a bank clerk isn't your dream job. Or being stuck with me. But if it means anything, I'm proud of you anyway."

"Thanks Mum. I'm proud of you too."

"Me? Why?"

"The way you're dealing with all this. Not letting it get you down."

"I haven't much choice, Tom. But thank you anyway," she said, just as the waitress handed out our sundae bowls of ice cream. "You said 'it' by the way. Remember you can call it 'cancer,' it's not a dirty word, remember?"

"Same goes for Lilly too. She's not a dirty word either."

"I beg to differ," she said as we took our spoons to our

desserts, working out how to get past the sprinkles and the spitting sparklers.

★ ★ ★

Later, belly still full, I ironed my new shirts, the TV being ignored, as I wished for bed when there was still plenty of evening left. I looked over at Mum laid on the sofa, her head down, pencil sketching, the room felt tiny, the house, outside, everything smaller.

"Fuck this, Mum. Let's do something drastic."

"What?"

"This isn't it."

"Isn't what?"

"Let's go. Get out."

"Go where?"

"I don't know but just not here. Not this."

"We talked about this before, Tom. You told me it was a bad idea. Persuaded me to stay here. You said give it a go."

"I know what I said."

"What's changed? Why tonight?"

"This future isn't yours, Mum, and it certainly isn't mine. We're kidding ourselves if we think it is," I said, folding up the ironing board.

"I'm not disagreeing, Tom. I told you I wanted out."

"I should never have applied for this job, any of them, should never have put Molly in that nursery."

Mum put her pencil and paper down, sat up. "Whatever we do though, Tom, we do 100%. Promise me that. If we do this, me, you and Mol, then we do it properly. No half measures."

"Even if it kills you?"

"Even if, yes."

Mum looked excited, a smile I hadn't seen in a while. "Will I need to find my passport?"

"I think you might, yes."

"Good. I might as well leave a tanned corpse. What's brought this on? A drastic way to avoid ironing I expect."

"We can't afford this, you know."

"We can't afford not to either, Tom."

PART THREE

Mum's/Nov/Shot 14

48

"We need to wash your hair tonight, madam. It's knot city."

No answer, brain focused on cartoons as I brushed out tangles and kinks.

"Dad, why isn't the sound on?"

"There is no remote control. You'll have to lip read, sorry." Molly looked confused. "Like this," as I mouthed 'I love you,' as she did the same back.

"Can I wear pink today?"

"No. I've got a nice white dress for you."

"Please."

"Molly, you can't wear pink."

"Why can't I?"

"Your pink dress is dirty and mucky."

"I'll wash it."

"With what?"

"Stain remover."

"How do you know about stain remover?"

"I just know. I'd like some for Christmas."

"You want stain remover for Christmas?"

"Please can I wear pink? Pink is my favourite."

"Sorry, Molly. Today is not a pink day. Look, I'm wearing white," I said, pointing to my shirt.

"Why?"

"Because some days the colours we wear are important. Some days aren't meant to be pink."

"OK, Daddy. I will wear white today. But tomorrow can be pink?"

"Yes. We'll both wear pink tomorrow, I promise."

"Boys don't wear pink. Can I wear my tiara today?"

"No."

"Can I have plaits today?"

"What about just a ponytail? Make Daddy's life easier."

"Plaits are prettier."

"You hungry? Shall we go out for a bite to eat before we get there? We've got time."

"Yes. French fries, please. Ketchup. And Coca Cola."

"Molly. You're not allowed fizzy drinks."

"Nanny lets me."

"That's a fib, Molly. Nanny never let me have fizzy drinks when I was little so I know for a fact she wouldn't be giving them to you. Right, pass your hairbands please."

"Nanny sings when she does my plaits. Can you sing please, Daddy?"

"I'll try." I said, not quite knowing where to start with either request.

★ ★ ★

She reminded me of Cassie, how she ate, wolfed it down as though, if she didn't, then someone else would.

"You eat too many chips, young lady," I said, stealing one from her plate. "Do you want to turn into a potato?"

"Yes."

"I'll have to peel you, boil you up, deep-fry you. I'll do you a deal, eat something green off of my plate and I won't turn you into French fries." Molly leant forward, took a handful of salad.

"Nanny says I shouldn't eat the salad here."

"Look I'm eating salad." I took a bit of vegetable, put in my mouth. "Am I being sick?"

"No," she said, nibbling cucumber with caution.

"You look pretty today. Do you think I did a good job with your hair?"

"It looks funny," she said, laughing.

"Does Daddy look pretty today?"

"Yes. Like a Prince. Can I paint your nails again?"

"Princes don't wear nail varnish."

"They do. I've seen them."

"Where?"

"Here. At the night times."

"That wouldn't surprise me." I smiled to myself.

"What?"

"Nothing. I was making a daddy joke." I took my wallet out of my pocket.

"I know a joke." Molly still analysing her salad.

"Go on."

"Doctor, Doctor, I feel like a sheep."

"And what does the doctor say?"

"That's too baaaaaaaddd."

I forced a laugh. "Who told you that?"

"Nanny."

"I should have guessed." The waiter came over, Molly asked him if he was an elf. The man smiled, despite his Christmas hat he wasn't full of festive cheer.

"What about dessert?" staring at the back of the menu.

"Sorry, sweetheart. We're not going to have time."

"I always have dessert. Nanny says if I eat all my dinner then I can always have a treat. And look, I've eaten all of the salad now." She showed me her plate.

"There'll be lots of desserts and treats afterwards. Besides, I don't want you getting seasick."

"I won't."

"Well I've got a memory of a certain young lady being sick on a boat quite recently after too much sweet stuff."

"The driver was going too fast."

"Come on, Nemo. Let's head over to the beach. Hold my hand tight, OK?" My voice was hard to hear over the traffic, as we ran past the scooters and tuk-tuks, dogs and trucks.

"Will there be a coffin? Will there be a body?"

"There'll just be an urn, probably."

"What's an urn?"

"It's like a stone bottle."

"And what's inside?"

"Ash and flower petals."

"From the burnt bodies?"

"Yes. And they let it float away on the sea."

"When I die I want to be in a tomb, in a pyramid. I don't want to be burnt. I want to be wrapped up in bandages, with all my jewels and crystals."

"That sounds expensive."

"And a canopic jar."

"A canopic jar? What have you been reading?"

"Please," squeezing my leg. "Promise."

"I promise to bury you in a pyramid. Now let's hurry up. It looks like something holy is about start."

"There's a lot of people, Daddy." She gripped my hand a little tighter.

"They love a funeral here, that's for sure," I said, as we started to take our shoes off. We stood far at the back, behind the rows of chairs and backs of heads.

"What are they all doing?"

"Praying, I guess."

"The urn is very small."

"There isn't much left after you've been burnt."

"Does it hurt being burnt?"

"No, silly. You don't feel anything when you're dead."

"Did Granddad get burnt? Is he in an urn?"

"Molly, you're talking too loud. You are supposed to be quiet at funerals, remember?"

"Why?" she whispered.

"Because you are. Because people are thinking about things. People are sad."

"Are you sad?"

"Molly, no more questions. Just watch and listen."

"I want Nanny."

"Molly, shush."

We continued to watch, behind us motorbike versus motorbike, in front sad faces and sullen silence. It was strange this yin and yang, one side *Mad Max*, the other a quiet paradise. That was Thailand after all, spoilt, unspoilt, about to be spoilt.

"Who is in the urn?"

"No one we know."

"Oh." She looked confused.

"We've met her daughter though. The lady who runs the guest house. Look, she's over there in the front." I pointed. "Can you see her?"

"Yes. I like her, she lets me stroke her cat."

"Remember what we said about cats? They are different than back home."

"Why are we here, Daddy?"

"You'll have to ask Nanny that."

"Where is Nanny?"

"That I'd like to know."

"Look there she is." Molly pointed at Mum who was making her way through the crowd, trying to keep her balance and her hat on her head, as she walked barefoot across the sand.

"What have I missed?" she said, out of breath.

"Chanting mostly. How did it go?"

"Brutal."

"You should have got a taxi."

"I enjoy the bus."

"Nanny. Daddy wants to know why we are we?" Molly asked, now sat on the floor covering her feet in sand.

"To pay our respects. What's happened to your hair, Molly?" looking at me. "Looks like old rope."

"Daddy did it."

"When we get back I'll do it for you."

"Can we go soon please, Nanny?"

"Soon, darling. Ten more minutes." Molly continued to dig.

"You OK, Tom? You look angry at me."

"I'm fine."

"You don't look fine."

"If this is what you feel you need, Mum. Dragging us all around more temples and processions."

"These are my dress rehearsals. Try before I buy," she laughed.

"It's not funny, Mum. You should be putting all your energy into your chemo. Not the planning of your elaborate funeral."

"I think this is my favourite so far. Nice being outdoors, not so crowded, calm."

"Mum. I'm being serious."

"So am I, Tom. I don't take dying light-heartedly. When I die… "

"*If* you die," I interrupted.

"*If* I die, I want it to be perfect. I want it done properly."

"Haven't you ever heard of Google? It's quicker and means I don't have to keep wearing this bloody linen suit."

"It's not the same." Mum took her glasses out of her handbag. "We won't be long."

"Good, one thing these Thai funerals aren't is short."

"Stop complaining. Let me see the floating of the ashes and then we'll go, promise. We need to finish packing before we head north. I'll miss this place."

"Be nice to have a different volume, don't you think?"

"Too loud for you, darling?"

"No, too British. I'd just prefer somewhere a little more authentic."

"I like the noise."

"I know you do. I've seen it first-hand. Mum, you're not eighteen. This wouldn't be what a doctor would recommend."

"I doubt a doctor would recommend any of this, Tom. I had

to fight tooth and nail for them to let me fly, make them sign all their forms. We both knew this was what we needed. Yes, it isn't the norm but what would you prefer, white sands like this, or white rooms back home?"

"You know my answer, Mum. Here, obviously. I just think sometimes you need to slow down. Remember your illness."

"I don't want to be reminded of it. I want to drown it out."

"Just make sure you listen to your body, promise?"

"I will. I like to be around youth, Tom. It's contagious, makes me feel young, makes me feel better. But I do agree with you, I think Nai Yang will be a nice change of pace, nice it's so close to the airport too. How long till arrival?"

"Next week."

"I'm looking forward to it."

"I'm a little nervous."

"Well, you shouldn't be."

"You OK, Mum?" I asked her, as she took a deep breath, hands on her knees.

"I'm fine. I can take a deep breath you know. It doesn't mean I'm about to keel over."

★ ★ ★

We stayed for another twenty minutes or so, till Mum had taken mental notes and Molly was starting to play up. It was a short walk home back to our apartment, the three of us, well four if we included the stray chicken squawking at our feet.

"Can I see my friend when we get back, Nanny?"

"I think they left this morning, Molly."

"Oh," she said, looking sad.

"Hey, why don't you and your dad go for a swim when we get back? Give Nanny time to pack our things."

"I don't want to go. I like it here."

"You'll like where we are going even more."

"Are we going back home to England?" she said, looking hopeful.

"No not yet, darling. We're here for a good while longer yet."

"But you said about airports?"

"Someone's coming to visit, Molly."

"Who?"

"Someone special." Later that night, as I read the last of my book I noticed something in the doorway, something sulking.

"What's wrong Mol?" She was stood, teddy in one hand, looking all grumpy and dishevelled. "Do you wanna come and lie with me for a bit?" She nodded, climbing on top of me and nestling into my chest, her hair her all wet and sticky. "Is your fan on?" She nodded, rubbing her eyes. "You're soaking."

"I had a bad dream."

"What about?"

"Can't remember."

"I bet you're pulling your blanket over your head again." She smiled. "Don't worry, it's not your fault, I think it's hereditary. I know someone who used to do that too."

"What are you reading?"

"It's a daddy book, bit boring."

"Is it about kissing and cuddling like Nanny's books?"

"A little bit. I tell you what, as a special treat, would you like a midnight feast?"

"Yes please," she said as I carried her over to the kitchen and sat her on the worktop. "You promise straight to bed afterwards?"

"Can I have a story too?"

"No stories. It's extra late, even Nanny is in bed. Right." I looked at the options. Noodles and hot sauce. Savoury things, not much for children. Thank God, I found chocolate spread.

"Daddy, what's happening with our house?"

"It's being rented, darling."

"Rented?"

"Renting is like borrowing. Some people are borrowing it till we come back."

"Like sharing?"

"Yes. Like sharing."

"They won't mess up my room, will they? Or play with all my toys?"

"No, your room will be exactly how you left it."

"How long are we sharing it for?"

"Quite a long time. Till next year."

"We've been on holiday for a long time."

"I know. Are you still having lots of fun? Do you want to go home or stay?" She didn't answer, her mouth full of sandwich. I knelt down, started to search through the fridge, eggs, a half jar of salsa, milk about to turn. It was clear we barely ever ate in.

"Did you enjoy the funeral today?"

"It was boring."

"Most funerals are."

"Have you been to lots of funerals?"

"A few, yes. Do you want a drink?"

"Yes."

"Yes, what Molly?"

"Yes please," she said, her mouth covered in chocolate. "How many funerals, Dad?"

"I'm not sure." I passed her a bottle of water. "It's not something you keep count on."

"I don't want Nanny to die."

"That's a sad thing to say, Mol."

"The doctors need to fix her."

"They are trying to."

"Promise me Nanny won't die."

"I can't promise those sorts of things, darling."

"Please promise."

"Sometimes sad things happen, Molly."

"Like when next door's rabbit died?"

"Like when the rabbit died, yes. Sometimes beautiful things have to go to heaven." I gave her a big cuddle. "But hey. Nanny is getting a lot better. Taking lots of medicine."

"Mummy is never coming back is she?"

"No, sweetheart. That's right."

"Don't worry, Daddy. I don't get sad anymore, do I? I'm a grown-up now."

"You're allowed to be sad, you know."

She didn't answer.

"You're probably too old for Nutella now. Seeing you are all grown up." I picked up her. "Probably best if I eat the last triangle."

"You're silly."

"Your mummy would be very proud of you. I love you, smelly pants."

"I love you too, Daddy."

"And you happy we came here still?"

"My tummy hurts, Dad. Can I have a story?"

"Funny how your tummy hurts went you want something."

"Please."

"Just one," I whispered, carrying her back into her room, the blast of cold fan and mosquito spray, the smell of chocolate from Molly's cheeks.

Two hours later. A single scream. I barged through her door, she was sat upright, crying, frightened. She'd been sick, everywhere, over herself, her blanket, the floor. Mum was already up, stripping the bed, though neither of us was quick enough. Round two was all over the hallway, ten minutes later, round three. At least the final time it was down the sink, though by that stage there was nothing left to be sick, just the noise, her stomach emptied of whatever bad that was inside. Poor thing puked up everything she had, gave her a quick wash, a glass of water, gave a her a few minutes to take it all in, it had been quite the ordeal. Mum was in the next room working quickly to put her room right, fresh sheets, mopping the floor, new pyjamas.

"I want to go home," she whispered into my chest. "I want my old room. I don't like it here. I won't eat salad ever again," she said.

I kissed her head, took her back to her bed, shushed her till she went back off, it didn't take long, she was exhausted.

Mum and I chatted a little, had a cup of tea, discussed who was to blame, salad or chocolate, or both, either way both would be banned. Just before we took ourselves back to bed we poked our heads around Molly's door, checked she was OK, which she was, sucking her dummy, out for the count.

This wasn't a place for a four-year-old, I thought, as I stared at a spinning fan. Things moved too fast for little girls used to empty fields and duck ponds, for all its clear oceans and white beaches, life here was still filled with hidden danger, roads, diseases, con artists, insects, food. I just assumed Molly would be fine, her body and stomach would cope with it all, take it in her stride, lap it all up. Didn't stop to think that mine and Mum's paradise may not be hers. And worse still, we never even asked.

49

She asked me if I'd ever go back to England, and the magazine that millions read, as did I, would see my answer printed clear as day, three words, short and sweet, *I hope so.*

But that wasn't the answer I gave.

Far from it.

I remembered it had been a bad morning, couldn't find a particular sweater, stubbed my toe on a stack of boxes, period pains, out of milk, a new home where nothing knew where to be, including me. A series of shit events, that individually I could deal with, whilst grouped together I could clearly not. I was not in the mood for visitors and I certainly wasn't in the mood for questioning, luckily the guest due to arrive was a good friend who wouldn't judge my mental state or the conditions I was forced to live in, at least not out loud.

Her name was Frances Bernard and she was everything you'd expect a Frances Bernard to be, just what you'd expect someone who worked for an international women's magazine. But don't be fooled, behind the Chanel and the Wayfarers and the quick tongue and the emotional distance was quite possibly my most favourite person on the planet. In fact, she'd even promised to aim her bouquet purposely in my direction when she got to fling it over her shoulder in a few months' time – not that that was any guarantee of marriage, seeing as her throwing was probably as bad as my catching.

For some obscure reason, I'd agreed to let her interview me at home today. Franny thought it had some significance, all the boxes and bubble wrap, conveyed a change, a new me, thought it would make for an interesting theme for both me and her audience. A popular format she said, trust me she said, not that I saw it myself – didn't the world know enough about me without knowing the colour of my kitchen units? But hey, she was the expert, she was good at what she did. I trusted her thought process having always come off well in whatever she had printed.

She arrived with her little team just before lunch, cheek kisses in the doorway, I apologized instantly for not having anything to offer them to eat or drink. Of course, she put them to task, sending one poor girl off to fetch us Japanese whilst the rest scurried off around the house and pool looking at angles and lighting and whatever is was they checked for. Meant me and Franny could have a quick chat before we had to put our work faces on.

We talked for a bit, mostly about her, panicking about being ready for a winter wedding, worrying about big things and small details. Who could blame her? The woman advised on health, beauty, relationships, fashion, how to have better sex. Her wedding, her hair, her body, the weather, all of it needed to be perfect. No wonder she looked thin, though she said I looked thinner. Still, the weight of expectation would crush any woman, so as much as I could I tried to offer advice I wasn't suitably qualified to give, attempted to make her see past table flowers and glassware and focus on what the day really stood for and eventually after bento boxes and bridal affairs it was time to get down to the matter of business.

Even before we started Franny admitted this wouldn't be hard-hitting journalism, an excuse to have a pretty photo of myself and make my life sound unobtainable. The world was more concerned about my thoughts on heavy knits and trench coats than what I thought about oil spills and tensions in China, and for once I was relieved.

Franny sat down opposite, got herself prepared with pens and pads and voice recorders, reassured me again not to worry, said she would go easy on me, told me to pretend we were just in my front room, she joked. As predicted and pre-warned she did ask about

Max though, in fact the bulk of the interview was concerning our rekindled relationship and I fed Franny the lies I'd rehearsed in my head the night before, even managing to convince myself that what me and Max had become was wholehearted and sincere, just like I'd managed to convince half the planet and my close friend sat directly in front of me.

"England, Lilly. Excuse my ignorance, having never ventured outside of Bond Street, but what is there to do down in Devon? I have visions of mud and pigs and men with beards."

"No pigs and beards. There was mud. Lots of sheep too."

"How awful."

"Not one for Mother Nature, Franny?"

"Animals are fine if groomed and trained. It's mud and beards I have the issue with. But you're glad to be finally home, I bet?"

"I don't think glad is the right word."

"Happy? Relieved?"

"I don't know. Not relieved."

Franny looked surprised, offended. "Sounds like you didn't want to come back."

"I did. It's just I enjoyed England. I enjoy LA. The two don't have to compete."

"OK, Hannah Montana. So, you're more comfortable in Hunter wellies than in your Jimmy Choos all of a sudden. But what else did your time in England teach you?"

"Taught me not to take good weather for granted. Taught me that I'm a better cook than I thought. That I need to get out and about, see more of America. Taught me I'm more capable than I give myself credit for. How to enjoy the simple things. To be comfortable in my own company. To let my guard down."

"You've come back a changed woman."

"You could say that. I know now what is important and what things aren't."

"England was an education then? Does LA fit into this new ideal of yours?"

"LA is so fast sometimes we all forget to slow down. I think I'm gonna try and lie low, keep my head down, definitely not party like I used to that's for sure."

"New home, new man, a quiet life of mud and cooking. Sounds like you are nesting?"

"I assure you I'm not."

"Do you think you and Max will have children?"

I looked at her, hoping she'd take the hint, which she didn't.

"We've only just got back together. It's far too soon. It would be irresponsible."

"Was it hard being away from Max and your family?"

"I was so busy with work, I didn't have much time to think."

"Must've been lonely. The only Yank in the village."

"We had a great cast. Made me very welcome. I wasn't lonely."

"Did it bring you together, that time apart from Max? Absence makes the heart grow fonder so they say."

"I think we both needed our separate space after what had gone on before. We needed that time apart. Those months apart taught us a lot about each other."

I could tell Franny wanted to delve deeper, bring up London, the kiss, old wounds, she was a journalist after all, gossip was her field, scandal and heartbreak must have been hard to resist. Franny glanced at her notes, her list of harmless questions.

"What did you find out about Max that you didn't already know?"

"That he'll never give up," I said, a little too quickly.

"That's a very romantic quality, I would say."

"I'm very lucky."

"Any plans to go back?"

"I enjoyed my time there."

"So, you do plan to go back?"

"I'm going to be so busy with filming and press and family." I took a sip of water.

"I'm sure our English readers would love to see you back there again. It seems they've taken you in as one of their own. I'm sure if it wasn't for a certain Kate Middleton then you may have been the future Duchess of Cambridge."

I didn't answer. Took a few more sips of water.

"You OK, sweetie?"

"I'm fine. I'm a bit away with the fairies today."

"Guys." She turned to her entourage behind her. "Could you leave us for a bit? Go out and grab us all a bite. Lilly, you want something? You didn't eat much."

"No, I'm fine thanks," I smiled, watching her staff as they let themselves out.

"Lilly, you don't seem yourself at all. Is it the set-up? Would you rather we do this somewhere else? I don't mind rescheduling to somewhere not so invasive."

"No, no it's fine. Having a shitty morning, that's all. Nothing major, promise."

"Are you sure? I didn't mean to grill you too much. I know I went a little off piste. And of course, Max is a hard subject to avoid right now. I'd be shot if I didn't come back with something Salter-related."

"No, the questions were fine. I'm just a little hormonal."

"I'll go and fetch you some more water." Franny got up, went over to my kitchen. When she came back I was in tears.

"Lilly, this is obviously not nothing."

"I told you. I'm just having a bad day."

"This is more than a bad day. You look exhausted. You look thinner than me too which can't be a good thing seeing as I'm practically Skeletor these days. Is it the press? Are they giving you a hard time again?"

"No, it's not them."

"Is it Max again?"

I didn't answer.

"It's Max, isn't it?"

I nodded.

"Tell me."

"There is nothing to tell."

"Lilly tell me."

And I did.

All of it.

About Max.

About Tom.

Everything.

Finally, I just broke, just couldn't keep it in any longer, I had to tell someone, turned out I chose to tell it to a journalist, one with an incredible memory and voice recorder I had to assume had been turned off.

* * *

The magazine came out a few months later, just before Christmas and true to her word Franny didn't print a word of what was spoken that day in September. I had to give her credit for that, what I told her could have made her a fortune, could have paid for her entire wedding day, but instead, as promised, she kept silent. She was far from quiet on the day though, cursed Max, threatening to take legal action into her own hands, offering solutions both then and in the months that followed. I wish I could say I took any of her advice, and I wish that my reluctance to fight Max in a courtroom, as Franny wanted me to, hadn't damaged our friendship, but I'm quite sure it had. And I wish she understood why I chose to stay, but she would never understand what Max was capable of, what his worst could look like and the damage it could cause.

You never know, if I waited long enough, once filming was done, once Max had got what he wanted from me, then I could run back to Tom, if he was still there, or still wanted me for that matter. I had to have a little faith at least, a blind faith perhaps, but faith nonetheless.

We finished the interview, I recomposed myself, Franny got the required answers needed to make her word count. As I said the article came out a few months later, just before Christmas. And when the reader saw the question on whether I'd ever go back to England, my reply was just those three little words, short and sweet.

I hope so.

Not the truth, but not a lie either.

I never did catch that bouquet, though I don't think she had me in mind when she threw it; she aimed it at women who actually stood a chance.

50

You wouldn't have thought we were about to go to the airport. Mum was having a lie down before all the excitement. Molly, now over her ordeal, was sat on a sun lounger in front of the pool, cutting card with scissors, sticking things with glue. She was deep in concentration, her lip curled towards her nose, as she put together the final touches to her welcome banner. Flight was landing in an hour, we were in no rush, though I still wanted to set off with plenty of time spare, so was already giving her ten-minute warnings of our pending departure.

I'd just finished writing to Dot, told her about our next destination, Mum's progress, Molly's dodgy tummy, a lot considering the size of a postcard, though the more I sent, the more I'd perfected writing small and to the point. The whole postcard thing had escalated, Dot made me promise I'd sent her one, so although she expected the first, she wouldn't have predicted all the rest that must have come through her letterbox. Now it was just part of the ritual, my running joke, leave a town, or arrive at one, the first thing I did was buy a postcard, I'd lost count of how many.

The sun was relentless today, I looked over at Molly, contemplated sun block, but she looked contented and bronzed, her skin just like her stomach had acclimatized to the new surroundings. What before would have made her burn or spew her guts now was not a threat. I felt like a bad parent, sat there with a bottle of Chang in one hand and my daughter broiling just in front. That was as stressful as it got around here, staying cool, keeping rehydrated, though I'd picked up worse habits, new and old. Technically, it was Mum's fault, claimed it was medicinal though all we'd smoked so far had cured little other than irregular bowel movements. But hey, to look at us, we'd never looked better, skin golden, waists thinner, wider smiles, we went to bed when we were tired, woke up when we weren't.

I had another quick look over my list, everything ticked and ready. This day had been marked in my diary for well over a month so it wasn't like I didn't know it was coming, I just didn't think it would be so soon, or ever happen for that matter. This was a huge deal, Mum said it wasn't, but it was, I wanted it all to run smoothly. So even with my feet dipped in cool water, shaded by palms, despite this I still felt a little on edge, like, although I was expecting smiles, how long those smiles would last, I wasn't so sure.

★ ★ ★

"Molly. Are you sure you don't need a wee?"

She was ignoring me, not deliberately, she was too excited, hopping about, counting things.

We walked through the automated doors, past the suitcases and trolleys.

"Still glad you've gone wigless, Mum?"

"I think so."

"Did you bring it with you in the end?"

"I'm gonna throw that bloody rat out on the street later. I don't even know why I bought the damn thing. Complete waste of money."

"Why did you?"

"Everyone else in my support group was getting one, so I kind of felt obliged to join in. It's the done thing. Get cancer, get chemo, get a wig."

"I prefer you bald anyway. It suits you. You must have the right shaped head for it. And I quite enjoy shaving your head. It was a strange experience the first time, but now I find it quite therapeutic. Quite erotic."

"Shut up, you fool," she said, punching me in the arm.

"Sometimes I forget how I look. It might be a bit of a fright to whoever hasn't seen me like this."

"You don't have to impress anyone, Mum. Just act yourself. Look how you normally look."

"What, bald and breastless? A double mastectomy is hardly a nice welcome after a long flight. Does it look like I've got breasts, Tom? I'm still not sure about these new bras, feel like a lady boy." She moved her chest towards me.

"I'm not answering that, Mum, on principal. Just relax."

"Sorry. Every now and again I have these little moments. Normally I'm fine with it, everything that has happened, but some days, like today, I look at myself and get a little upset. I blame mirrors. I avoid them at all costs. No hair and breasts makes a lady feel ever so unwomanly. This illness is so bloody undignified. "

"Daddy. I've counted five Christmas trees, and one polar bear." Molly was tugging at my leg.

"Wow. That's a lot."

"Santa Claus knows I live here?"

"Positive. You wrote him that letter, remember, saying where you'd be."

"But we keep going to new places all the time. How will he know where I am now?"

"He just does, Molly. His elves know."

"Can I write him a new letter when we get back?"

"Yes. But I'm sure he already knows. You were quite clear in the last letter that you weren't in England anymore."

"It might be Santa on the plane, Daddy?"

"No, I can assure you Santa is not on the plane."

"Why?"

"Cos firstly he would be on his sleigh, secondly it's not even December yet and thirdly you know who's coming, remember? It says on your banner."

We walked into the arrivals lounge, checked the flight details to make sure we were in the right place.

"You two thirsty?" I asked noticing the news stand behind us. "I'll grab us some drinks whilst we wait. Think we've got ten minutes till they land."

"Something fizzy for me, please. Nothing with sugar for Molly. It might tip her over the edge, I'll find us some seats."

I headed off leaving Mum and Molly to prepare the welcome banner as I joined the end of a long queue. The owner of the tiny kiosk wasn't coping well under the pressure of lunchtime trade, there were raised voices over something. Hard to tell aggression from affection in Thai. Either way I ignored it, took my eyes elsewhere, browsed crisps and magazines, picked up a familiar newspaper.

I hadn't read the news back home in a long while, but seeing an English tabloid I couldn't resist seeing how the place was getting on in my absence. I flicked the pages, a royal engagement, snowstorms, traffic chaos. Not much had changed at all, everyone keeping calm and carrying on.

I browsed the rail some more, cars, health, interiors, celebrity. I picked one up, leafed through the pages. Put it back, did the same with another, funny the things you miss and don't miss. It was a shelf full of upgrades, new engines, new phones, new kitchens, new bodies. Everything looked so alluring to a man who'd lived from his backpack the last three months. And even though I had no need for any of it, didn't mean I wasn't allowed to drool over things I'd never get to touch or own, that I would spend my whole life working out how to get. I put the magazine back on the rail, immediately noticing the front cover beside it. I read it again, had to do a double take to make sure.

Party dressing for under £150.
A decade of supermodels.
Predict your style.
How to dazzle in evening make-up.
A new Lilly. A Lilly in love.

I went to find the article.

"*Yai puan!*" said the man behind the till, pointing at the magazine still in my grip.

"Oh sorry," I said, giving him my leftover change, as I curled it into my rucksack and quickly walked back over to banner and child.

"They're here," Mum said. "Well, their plane is. Right Molly." Mum kneeled down next to her. "Look at your photo and tell me when you can see them come through the door. Keep your eyes peeled."

"There. There. There." Molly shouting and pointing.

She was right. It was Lou and Rose. Matching Christmas hats, matching silver hair, matching grins. The biggest of grins, the kind that bring fathers close to tears, as Molly ran towards them, jumping into their chests like she was hugging Cassie herself.

★ ★ ★

That evening we ate like kings, my treat, I took them to a little restaurant just by where we were staying, a place we knew was authentic, but westernised enough not to put them out of their comfort zone. They seemed to like it, ate all the food, which was a good sign, the night felt too celebratory to be bothered by menus or new cuisines, lots of toasts and cheers across the table.

Lou was on top form, he'd had half a bottle of wine to himself, spent most of his time with Molly on his lap. She was full of questions, and of course he was full of answers, they talked of Thanksgiving, about Disney World, about Cassie. I couldn't stop staring at them both, Lou had her eyes and mouth. Molly had her nose and chin, her hair too, two versions of my wife right in front of me. She would've loved this moment, the pair finally together.

★ ★ ★

Everyone was home now. The ladies were asleep, excused themselves, both full up and tired. A busy day of chemotherapy and jet lag, between the pair of them they could barely keep their eyes open by the time we got back to our rooms.

Sounded like Lou and Rose had been busy. Florida to London, stopped there a few days, did all things you'd expect Americans to do, saw everything that could be seen, loved every minute. Then to Bangkok, where it was made quite clear they hated every minute till it was time to catch a flight to meet us in Phuket. I was impressed with their stamina, a lot of air miles for a couple approaching their seventies, not that it showed. Cassie never really told me what they were like before, I expected quiet and frail, awkward handshakes. What I got was instant energy, instant family, hugs that said far more than they were supposed to, hugs that settled things. Molly was sat with Lou, cuddled up on the sofa with cartoons and duty free, half asleep, Lou not far off neither. Despite the sun outside the whole house was about to fall asleep.

"I'm gonna pop out, Lou. I fancy a walk," I whispered.

"We'll talk later," he mouthed over the babble of TV. "Once this one is in bed," he smiled. He looked so happy, grandfather and granddaughter together, as I grabbed my bag, opened the door, instantly stepping on beach.

★ ★ ★

Nai Yang was deserted, some boys mucking around in the sea, ankle-deep, a few fathers tying up their boats. I heard you could surf here, but I hadn't seen a wave or break since we'd arrived, everything here was still, even the wind knew how to behave. I'd never visited here first time around, there were always far more alluring places on the map than here, ones faster and louder. To look at the view now I was a fool to dismiss it, though most twenty-year-olds were foolish, or at least start foolish, it took a gap year to turn me from arrogant prick to someone half decent. Tonight, though, it looked damn near perfect, no umbrellas, no loungers, nothing to spoil the stretch of blue, a good place to think, grab some silence. I sat on the floor, kicked off my flip flops with eyes to the sky, before taking out the magazine curled and stuffed in my rucksack.

I should have never bought the damn thing, I thought, after reading it for a second time, should have left it at the news stand. Told me everything I didn't want to hear, her new house for all to see, how excited she was about her career, how happy she was. A part of me knew I shouldn't believe any of it to be an accurate reflection, but there would be some honesty, I just didn't know what was and what wasn't, which meant all of it blurred into truth.

Mostly it was about Max and her, love conquers all, second chances, made me feel sick, whatever he'd done, Lilly had fallen for it. Max was a pro at this, getting his way, I couldn't compete, though I expected better of Lilly, thought she was cleverer than that, stronger. Guess I was wrong.

There was a time a few months ago where I still believed that there was a chance for us. For most of that summer I still clung onto hope, even though Lilly had made it quite clear there was none, her silence gave very little doubt that, whatever we had, had reached its end.

I'd like to say I accepted it, that I let go and moved on, but I didn't. I rang her, messaged her, voicemails, rang her again, this went on for weeks. She never answered once, so all I had of her was what everyone else had of her, TV interviews, social media, what magazines printed. I became addicted to her, searched newsagents and websites, looked for answers, looked for her. It did me no favours, neither helped nor healed, just let things fester and rot. There was a heaviness to loving Lilly and for a long time I couldn't cope with the weight. The only thing that got me out of it was getting on a plane – travelling saved me, cancer too, to some extent. I had to be strong for Mum, had to focus on her, my issues had to wait, the priority was her. And it had worked, my life here was a different one, gave me a revived purpose, shifted attention away from Lilly and onto something new. And there was me thinking I was finally cured, able to move on. Seeing her again at the airport, reading about her and Max together again. It brought everything back, made me realize that I was never over Lilly. I'd just learned to hide it better.

There were stars now, festoon lights too. It was time to head back.

The next morning, I threw the magazine away. For whose benefit, I wasn't sure.

51

Lou had declared it a gentleman's evening, told the women that we were going out, no questions asked. It was a declaration he'd made before, weekly in fact, since he arrived a fortnight ago – gentleman's evening had become a sort of routine, however, Lou still liked to put on a show, make a big song and dance about men and men's need to drink and smoke and talk. But it was an unnecessary show of masculinity, neither Rose nor Mum bothered, in fact Rose in particular always looked overjoyed at the prospect of another night off from her husband, practically pushing him out the door every time. "And don't think you are sleeping in our bed tonight," she would say. "You know drinking brings out your snore." Lou didn't seem fussed, looking equally as thrilled by both the excuse to drink and a guaranteed bed to himself.

★ ★ ★

The barman brought over another tray, replacing our empty bottles with full.

"Not that I'm moving regardless, but this is OK, I assume?" he asked me, pointing at his feet up on the chair. "Isn't it rude to show the soles of your feet in this neck of the woods?"

"The barman has no shoes on, Lou. I'm sure your calluses haven't caused too much offence just yet." Lou smiled, reclined further back into his chair. This was a reclined evening, jazz in the background, or the Thai equivalent. The moon full and fat, the night windless, everyone and everything lethargic and laid back. I wasn't drunk this time, intentionally, I'd stuck to beer, the safer alternative, having learnt the hard way last time, though there was talk of whiskey later, so already I knew the night had potential to veer off course. Lou was knocking quite a few back as normal, twice as much as me, though he was twice my size, told me I drank too slowly. Not that my lack of speed had slowed him down too much, he was the seasoned drinker after all and I got the impression it would take something a lot stronger than foreign liquor to knock him off his feet, unless they sold horse tranquillizers behind the bar.

I'd never seen a man so happy and content. He looked how every retired man should look, spoilt with food and wealth and sunshine, eyeing up bourbon he shouldn't drink and women he couldn't have. The arrival of Lou and Rose was the second wind we needed, gave Mum a boost, made Molly think less of home. It wasn't like we'd even done anything amazing, just hung about the pool, took some nice walks, ate, drank, talked, nothing too strenuous, nothing ever was in Nai Yang. Mum was taking Rose to her hospital tomorrow, or Rose taking Mum, either way they were heading towards Phuket Town first thing, so although I was enjoying my wild boy's night, in the back of my mind I was already working out the best way to entertain Molly with a hangover and little sleep. Lou finished his beer. "If I was thirty years younger, Tom," he said, pointing over at the bar at high heels and not much skirt.

"I don't think age matters here. Just the size of your wallet."

"How big a dent?"

"2000 baht."

"Tempting," he said, counting the notes in his pocket.

"Might be best to check for an Adam's apple first. I suspect that might not be a girl."

"You forget I've been to most ports around the world. Adam's apples I can handle."

"Best to try all things at least once, hey?"

"That was my problem. I'm a devil when it comes to temptation. Sometimes once isn't enough, young Tom."

I took a gulp of beer, then a second. Though used to Lou and his tales of naval debauchery, I was still never quite prepared for awkward.

"You ready to move on yet, Tom?"

"What, to another bar?"

"No. Move on. Women?"

I shook my head.

"You've had no one since Cassie?"

I laughed. "Are we having this conversation, Lou, seriously?"

"Pretend I'm not who I am. Pretend we are just two guys at a bar chewing the cud."

"Well, to answer your question, no, I haven't."

Lou looked shocked, even a little disappointed. "Not even a fling? Bit of slap and tickle?"

"Should I have?"

"Each to their own, friend. Just don't leave it too long, hey. There's no shame in having that urge. We are men after all. Anyhow, it would be good for you to meet someone else. Fall in love again."

"Perhaps."

"You don't sound very convincing. You not want love again, Tom?"

"Course I do."

"Love is one of God's greatest achievements. I should know. You're talking to someone who's been married four times."

"Four times? Cassie never told me that."

"Here, have a smoke, Tom," he said, offering me a cigar.

"I'm fine, Lou."

"Go on."

"No, it didn't agree with me last time."

"I think the Jim Beam played a part in that too," he winked. "Cigarette then?" he took a pack out of his shirt pocket, and was already lighting one before I could refuse. He took a big suck of his cigar.

"I love women, Tom. My biggest vice I'm afraid." Giant

exhale, a wall of smoke, thick and sickly. "Wives and sweethearts, hey. May the two never meet."

"I can think of worse vices than women."

"What, like drinking and smoking?" he laughed, holding both vices in his hands.

"Falling in love four times. That's pretty lucky in one lifetime."

"Who said I loved all four? My first wife I loved but we were too young. The second was a hell of a lot of fun, she ended up with my best friend."

"Sounds a good friend."

"He was. Still is, we play a few holes at the Country Club every so often."

"You are very forgiving."

"I was never mad in the first place. He was welcome to her. I still miss her breasts though, they were something else. Anyway, he loved her more than I ever did, and when your relationship is built purely on lust then its days are numbered."

"What about your third?"

"The third I downright loathed. We lasted less than four months. She was evil, didn't take too well to being made single either. She was always little tapped, probably was the sex was so good, but after we split she tried to make my life hell."

"Why did you marry her?"

"That I don't know. She was a rebound, that lasted longer than it should. And I'm not great on my own, I figured it's better to be with someone you couldn't stand rather than being on my own."

"And then you met Rose."

"The beautiful Rose yes."

"What are the gaps between them all?"

"First was 1959, second 69, the third 1970, then Rose in 81."

"One in every decade."

"Never realized that. It wasn't intentional I can assure you."

"No more divorces planned I take it. I mean technically you are due one seeing we are in another decade."

"Not for me. I know when I've been dealt a good hand and Rose is as good as I'll get."

"You've been together longer than I've been alive."

"Not long enough. We'll celebrate our 30th anniversary next year."

"How did you meet?"

"A funeral actually. One of my close pals I served with at Seal Beach. He lived in Sarasota, so I flew across state to pay my respects, turned out his cousin was a young lady called Rose who ended up flying back with me."

"But then you ended up moving back?"

"She wanted to be back with her mother, be by her side through the dementia."

"Why didn't Cassie go with you? It always puzzled me why she stayed and you left."

"I offered it to her but she was happy and settled in LA. She'd just started college so it wasn't the best timing."

"And you were OK leaving her on her own?"

"At her age, I was patrolling brown water on the other side of the world. Cassie was more than capable of fending for herself, in fact I knew it would be the making of her."

"Must've been hard having to choose Rose over Cassie."

"I didn't choose anyone Tom."

"I don't think Cassie saw it that way. She always wished you'd moved back. She even thought having Molly would make it a more tempting offer. Think it upset her a lot when you didn't."

"If I could've come back I would. But Rose's mother was pretty sick by then, she wouldn't move away and I wouldn't have left her. Dementia is a bitch and horrible to watch up close. I wouldn't wish it on my worst enemy. If I get it I'd rather someone throw me over board."

"She died then I take it? Rose's Mum?"

"Around April time. Hence why we were so late responded to your letters. Rose was pretty broken up by it, spent all our energy and time getting her back to a good place."

"Feels like everyone is either dying or dead."

"Circle of life friend. I'm sorry we left it so long to get back in touch with you."

"That's OK. I'm sorry too. I had a lot going on, though that is no excuse for my behaviour after Cassie died. The way I treated you and Rose wasn't right."

"Hey don't beat yourself up. It was a difficult time for everyone."

We took sips of our drinks.

"Do you regret not being more in Cassie's life though. Staying with Rose rather than be there for your daughter."

"I didn't like it Tom. But sometimes you have to do things that don't sit right for everyone else apart from you. Sometimes you have to make decisions and I made mine. I know Cassie wasn't too happy with me about it, but she got over it. I take it Cassie must've talked to you about it?"

"Oh, many a time. Called you most names under the sun. Think she just thought you were selfish. Just wanted her dad back."

"I figured that. Cassie didn't talk to me for a good few years." He took another puff, blew smoke rings, perfect circles. "If you are looking for love Tom then Thailand looks a good place to start, love would be easy to find."

"I've got Molly and Mum. I need to concentrate on them right now."

"Sounds defeatist to me."

"No. Just realistic."

"What about this girl I've heard about?"

"Girl?"

"The American?"

"How do you know about her? Let me guess... "

"I'm sorry, it was my fault. I was being nosy the other night."

"What did she tell you?"

"Not a lot, all I know is, whoever she was, she's now left."

"That's the long and short of it." Lou inhaled then exhaled, I did the same. Smoking does that, adds a natural pause, gives you time to think and digest. We looked out, couldn't see waves, but we knew they were there.

"How old are you, Lou?" I said, peeling the label off my bottle.

"Me? I'm sixty-seven."

"You had Cassie when you were in your forties?"

"If we had been younger we would have had more. Probably my one and only regret that Rose never got to be a mother more than once."

"You look younger."

"The Sunshine State does that to you. Takes the years off. The most stressful life gets is having to decide whether to broil my grouper or have it in a sandwich."

"Sounds a nice way to live."

"The offer is still open to join us. You are more than welcome."

"I appreciate that, Lou. Think at the moment, wherever my Mum is, I have to be. Just the way it is I'm afraid."

"There's room for her, there's room for all three of you."

"I couldn't ask you to do that. It's too much. You and Rose should be resting and winding down, not taking us on."

"It would be a walk in the park."

"What, a jobless widower, a four-year-old, a woman battling cancer? That's a hell of a trio."

"Molly is blood, Tom. That makes you and your mom blood too. I'm not saying it will be easy, but the reward outweighs any hardship. We get to be grandparents, we get to watch her grow up. I'd take that over resting and winding down."

"It is a tempting opportunity, Lou. But we'll need some time at home after this, see what is happening with Mum."

"There's always a reason why not with you, Tom."

I didn't answer, best to bite my tongue.

"Why didn't you ever put a ring on my daughter's finger?"

I didn't answer. Took my eyes to beer bottles and ashtrays.

"Married in secret did you, you old dog?" Punching my arm, a little too hard.

"So secret that Cassie didn't even know." I pulled my chain from under my shirt.

Lou leant in, holding the two rings in his palm.

"Not that these are the real thing. I just thought it was the right thing to do after what happened."

"She would've loved them, Tom. Sincerely. That girl spent her whole life wanting to be married."

"Well, talking of big regrets, that was one of mine. Better late than never, though she deserved better than a gesture."

"So now you've done it, why still wear them?"

"Because." A bit taken aback. "I just do."

Lou raised his eyebrow.

"You think I shouldn't wear them?"

"You do what you need to do, friend."

"What point are you trying to make, Lou?" The beer starting to talk for me.

"I've had a lot of friends who I've lost, my folks, Cassie. I could keep trinkets and war medals and letters but what does it prove? Who is it helping? Certainly wouldn't be me."

"You've kept nothing of Cassie's?"

"Rose has kept a few things for me, that we brought back from LA. But they'll stay in their boxes as far as I'm concerned. I've got all the memories I need up here."

"It's not about remembering, Lou. I don't keep the rings around my neck to remember Cassie."

"Then what is it? A statement? Justification for staying single forever? A warning for other women?"

"It means Cassie died a wife and not a girlfriend."

"Cassie is dead. Anything those rings symbolize is for yourself, not her. To show you did the right thing."

"What would you do?"

"You've got a big beautiful ocean out there, Tom. Say whatever you need to say to Cassie. Say some nice words, get everything off your chest, then you wind up like you're pitching at Marlin's Park."

"It seems ritualistic."

"But it means you can move on, Tom. Find someone new. Commit without feeling guilt."

"I don't feel guilt, Lou. Least, not all of the time."

"Because if you truly loved this Lilly girl, you would've fought harder than what your mother told me. And you would've found out why she chose what she chose."

"I did fight for Lilly."

"How did you fight?"

"I rang her every day. I messaged her every day. I did that for over a month. Every day for a month."

"Doesn't sound enough to me, Tom."

"What else could I have done? She never replied once."

"You could have got up off your arse, Tom. Stopped being an armchair hero and gone and fought for her. If you loved her, you would have chased her, come hell or high water you would've fought for her. But you gave up. Why?"

"I couldn't chase her. I wanted to. I had Mum and Molly. I couldn't leave them."

"They could've gone with you."

"That wouldn't have been fair on either of them."

"How long are you going to use your Mum and Molly and Cassie as excuses, Tom?"

"I'm not. I'm just doing my best."

"Best for everyone else. But not for yourself."

"Lou. No disrespect but you hardly know me. You don't understand what I've gone through or am going through. In the same way, I wouldn't understand or try to understand the choices that you have made. You haven't got the right to judge me like this."

"I'm not judging you, Tom. I can assure you of that."

"I'm accountable for my mother and daughter, Lou. They come first."

"Did you love Lilly?"

"Course I did."

"Do you love her now?"

"Yes. I think about her every day. No matter what I'm doing or where I am. I think about her every day. Drives me insane."

"Then you should have fought harder, Tom."

Lou took a gulp of beer, nearly the whole bottle.

"I'm just giving you my two cents. Think on it. Do what you need to do, otherwise those rings will get heavier and heavier around your neck. Will drag you down, son. And I don't want that."

I didn't answer.

"But hey, it's not a decision you need to make now. No one should try and solve matters in the middle of the night. Especially when liquor is involved." He put his arm around me as we walked over to the bar. Whiskeys were lined up and talk turned to old tattoos and where to find new ones.

52

"I'm going to head back, Tom. There's no way she'll make it anywhere near midnight." Molly was in Mum's arms trying to keep her eyes open. "You want me to come?"

"No, don't be silly. You enjoy the rest of it."

"You sure? I'm pretty shattered myself. I wasn't planning on getting another drink after this."

"I'm sure. You stay. Have some fun without your mum and daughter around."

"I don't mind, Mum, honest."

"Tom. Be reckless. Get drunk. Be young. Make noise. That's an order."

I kissed her head, and Molly's too, watched them disappear into the crowd as I started to make my way towards the beach, through the waving arms and the painted bodies. I was the odd one out, everyone in groups and couples, family and friends, tonight was a shared experience. Not that I minded being on my own, in fact I preferred it that way, though companionship was easy to find here if you wanted it, friendship never too far away if you knew the right bar or street.

I took the last gulp of beer, thankful it was over. I wasn't enjoying drinking, felt like I'd drunk enough recently and already I was planning a January detox. It had been a strange week actually, we'd all felt a little lost after we'd dropped Lou and Rose off at the airport a few days before, getting used to the original dynamic, being three again rather than a team of five.

I was sure they'd enjoyed their time with us, they kept telling us they did. I tried to make their weeks with us as exciting as possible, especially as it got closer to them leaving. Took them out on boat tours, they even got to ride elephants, tried to give them the full experience, so they went home with items on their bucket lists ticked off. I think they were ready to go home, after a month away from their own beds I could tell it was the right time for them, they'd done everything they'd set out to achieve. I suppose everyone needs home eventually, except us of course, me, Mum and Molly, the vagabond trio, taking our bundles town to town.

Though secretly we weren't too far off either, what before had been a taboo subject, we were all now equally guilty of romanticizing – the colder shores of back home. And predictably we'd started having those chats, chats anyone who's carried a rucksack long enough resorts to when all conversation has dried up and the only thing to fill the silence was what would be the first thing you'd do back home, what would you eat, where would you go.

But at the same time, as much as we talked about leaving, staying was talked about as a similar type of fantasy. God, the other night there was even talk of us never going back at all, talk of me finding a career here, working out how far my degree could get me, talk of required qualifications and certificates. We were at a confusing time, past the halfway stage, money was becoming tighter, the novelty of white sands and sunrises was wearing thin, determined to cling on, but reluctant to let go. People are funny, we want routine, but we like spontaneity, we want new experiences, but we like familiarity, we want purpose, but we enjoy frittering away our own time. Perhaps that was why paradise should always be a holiday, little bursts of foreign worlds, enough spontaneity and experience to wet the lips, but not enough to make you want to stay.

We were due to go home end of February, two months away. That's when our lease would end, when our tenants would move out, and we moved back in. Thoughts of gravy, internet and baths would have to wait till then, unless we stayed of course, there was still enough time to change our minds. Least that was exciting, the not knowing, oceans and sand or ponds and mud.

Christmas was special though, having Lou and Rose here. Despite our location and climate, we did our best to recreate a little of back home. Rose was adamant we went to church, so Christmas Eve the five of us headed back South to Patong for mass. Not that any of us were religious, but it got us all in festive spirits, all the prayers and candles and the church itself. It was nice to see the other side, see it as a building filled with hope and redemption and cheer instead of tragedy and regret, which was how I'd always perceived churches having witnessed nothing in any that represented joy.

Managed to find a place that did a turkey dinner too on Christmas Day, not the best roast dinner we'd ever tasted, but worth the double fare to get across town. Opened some presents across the table, we only had a few each, not expensive or large, just small and heartfelt, presents that didn't need receipts and weren't written on lists.

What did I get? Mum got me a few hand-me-down books, classics I should have read but never had. Molly got me a string bracelet, chose it herself off a village stall, of course I put it on straight away and I'm still wearing it now.

Rose cried a lot, cried whilst Molly opened her presents, cried when Molly gave her a locket with her photo in it, cried when I gave Lou his leather cigar case. Fair to say Rose was in tears more than she wasn't. Mum cried too which was unlike her, when she opened her present from me, a pocket diary for next year. Hardly sentimental, think it was more inside what set her off, the dates and plans I wished for us all. Trips to Barcelona in Spring, walks to Barnard Castle in Summer, Molly's birthday, Christmas markets. I hoped she understood what it meant, not the gift, but the future it represented. I think she did, she hugged me hard enough. Promised me she'd do her best to live that long.

Even I nearly cried, I blamed Lou, he gave Molly one of

Cassie's old patch dolls, it wasn't pristine but it was boxed and obviously well loved. Said it was only for the most beautiful and most precious of girls, told her it was Cassie's favourite toy, pulled out a photo from his wallet just to prove it, Cassie and Molly looked near identical. Didn't know why that set me off. Well, I did know, seeing Cassie as a child made me realize how young I lost her and what things she'd never get to see.

I did try to persuade Lou and Rose to stay a few days longer, tempted them with tales of full moon parties and firework shows, but Pier 60 back home was the only way they wanted to welcome in the new year.

As you could imagine the airport was hard too, equally emotional, equally fully charged, lots of hugs, pats on the back, see-you-soons, don't-leave-it-too-longs. It was all very dramatic, Molly clinging to their legs, Rose wishing Mum her thoughts and prayers, her every finger crossed. Lou didn't say much, I think he found it hardest, he and Molly had grown quite attached, probably affected him more than he wanted to let on. I gave him my firmest handshake, my tightest grip. I thanked him for all he'd done, the advice he'd given, ended up being hugged, nose sniffs, men doing their best not to let emotions show.

"Calm winds and following seas, hey," he said in my ear, as they did their final wave before disappearing towards the runway.

I hoped Thailand had left its mark on them, like it had on us. Thailand had done its job, gave us all a new energy, life before had made us tired, when cancer came and Lilly left. This trip away if nothing else had made us stronger, made our eyes whiter, smiles bigger, our thoughts less heavy. Regardless of how unhealthy our bank balances would look at the end of it all, we knew those things alone justified any doubts we may have had initially.

I was on the beach now, found myself away from the one-night stands and loved-up couples, a full moon without the party, a sea I could only hear.

I looked up, though I didn't have to look too far, the sky felt lower tonight, ghosts of fireworks still hanging in the sky, a million lanterns, a million amber holes.

What a place to see in a new year, I thought, wondering why all my new years seem to start with trying to forget the one just gone.

But not anymore.

53

Someone was talking in my ear, not that I could hear, all I knew was he'd bought me a drink I didn't ask for, but one I drank just the same. I felt my arm being pulled, our camp was on the move, bodyguards were clearing a route, barging people who didn't need to be barged, as me and the girls were moved from black ceilings to one with stars. Without asking our new table was filled with bottles, gold-wrapped, jewel-encrusted, the shapes of eggs and skulls, the most expensive of alcohol. People had more money than sense tonight and whoever was paying for it was either doing it for self-promotion or to promote their interests. Though why should I have cared? Regardless of how pristinely it was packaged, vodka was vodka and gin was gin, no matter the dollars it cost when I downed it neat, it always tasted like I'd bought it at a gas station. The pool looked inviting, there was something about a pool at night, the way it glowed, lagoon-like and neon. I felt inclined to jump, though I didn't want to be the first, anyway I wasn't that level of drunk, no one here was, people looked controlled, no one making fools of themselves, people had the clock in the back of their minds, this wasn't the time for getting wet and no place for ruined hair and running make-up, not with midnight so close.

"We need more drink," she shouted over the music, already filling my glass. "We need hot men, Lilly.

"We?"

"Can't you just have them ordered up to us?"

"That's an abuse of power."

"What's the point in power if you can't use it? Look," she said, pointing at a group of guys just below our balcony. "Admit those guys are hot."

"You do like a shaved head and a tattoo. You're still not over *Prison Break*, are you?"

"What can I say? I like a convict. Please get your dogs to bring them up."

"As long as that's all I have to do."

"Come on. What's wrong with a bit of harmless flirting?"

I raised my eyebrows.

"Why should you care anyways? Max isn't here, he's not even in the state. You have a free pass."

"Max might not be, but half of Hollywood Boulevard is."

"OK, so you are out of bounds, Miss Prude. Means there is more for me. Gives the rest of us a fighting chance. Damn, these heels hurt," she said, grimacing as she fiddled with her ankles.

"You shouldn't be encouraging me to cheat by the way?"

"You don't think Max is doing the same?"

"No, I don't actually."

"You're kidding me. That guy is more poly-amorous than me. Come on, admit that guy finds it hard to keep his dick in his pants."

"Not anymore."

"And when is the last time he was in your pants?"

"Hey, don't be gross."

"I still need a little convincing on you two."

"Convincing of what?"

"All of it. And I'm not the only one. I think the whole of the planet agrees with me."

"And you think me flirting with strangers is going to improve that?"

"I think, why bother pretending?"

"I'm not pretending. We are not pretending."

We went quiet, sipped drinks through our straws.

Ten minutes later I was watching one of my hired helps invite hot strangers to join our party. I couldn't watch, I felt like some wicked tyrant, some evil queen, demanding pretty things for my entertainment and disposal. Frank wouldn't have stood for it, he would've made me do it myself, probably why I was brave enough to ask this time around. One of the few perks of Frank never being around as much, my life protected by a nameless bodyguard who'll take a bullet and fetch me things to flirt and toy with.

It was weird to think a few hours before I was in a family lawyer's office, talking family law funnily enough, now I was pointing at single men I couldn't have and didn't want. It was a wasted journey, too, the lady behind her big desk didn't fill me with either hope or fear, kept asking me questions I couldn't answer, which meant she couldn't give me any in return. To be fair I couldn't blame her, without understanding Tom's situation, without speaking to Cassie's parents, what else could she have told me apart from guesswork. All I knew was, as soon as I heard the words "court" and "probable" I knew I'd heard enough. Though it felt good to at least try, to feel I was putting up a fight, be it one I would lose, or die winning. Though I did panic as I made my way to my friends for pre-drinks, had this awful feeling that I'd been stupid, there were only so many lawyers and I'm sure Max knew most of them in town, the ones worth knowing anyway.

I felt my shoulder being tapped. Our takeaway order had arrived and one of them was walking straight in my direction, looking more edible the closer he came.

★ ★ ★

Nothing happened of course.

Some flirting, obviously, which couldn't have felt stranger – having to resist one decent guy in fear of upsetting the opposite. We chatted for a quite a while, most of the night actually, ended up arm in arm as we sang in 2011, talked about what strangers talked about at the start of a new year, regrets and resolutions, raising a glass to both our failures and forecasts. Turned out he was single, but only just, his relationship sounded as on-and-off as mine and Max's, so our complicated histories took us through a bottle of whiskey older than the two of us combined.

It did get a little awkward, as the night drew closer to its natural end, where the louder the music the more you were drawn toward someone to hear and be heard. Though despite our close proximity and the goading of both sets of friends, he still didn't make a move, as I said, he was a decent guy, said he doesn't make a point of upsetting boyfriends, especially ones that weren't there to fight their own corner. Not sure what I would have done if he had tried to kiss me, or leaned in, he wouldn't have had to lean in far, we were pretty nose to nose by the end of the night. I'd like to say I would have stopped him, I think I would've stopped him, still made me feel pretty awful. Flirting was flirting, harmful, the only people who say it's harmless are only judging the harm caused to themselves. And even though I'd done nothing wrong, I was close enough to see what a mistake would look like, probably why I felt so shitty in the cab ride home, like I owed someone a confession for my near miss of infidelity, the least of all being Max.

I guess this may have contributed to why, rather than going to bed like I should've done, instead I chose to redeem myself. And redemption, the drunk kind, the 3am kind, was never a good thing to search for.

Tried his cell first.

Then his house.

You would have thought I'd have had some idea how our conversation might go, planned what I was going to say if he answered, even have had the courtesy to make sure I wasn't ringing when they'd all be asleep, but I'd done none of those things. Just rang and rang and rang, until someone eventually answered, though I wished they hadn't.

It wasn't Tom, it was a woman's voice, not his mom's either, younger, a woman with a pretty voice and probably a pretty everything else. I was instantly jealous and instantly angry, Tom had moved on and why shouldn't he? Anyway, I hung up, threw myself into bed, shouted every curse word under my breath, mad at Tom, mostly mad at myself for being so fucking dumb and so fucking weak.

To think an hour before I'd convinced myself I could give up Tom, forget him and move on, quit him like everyone promises to quit things on New Year's Eve, lead a happier and more fulfilled year, get rid of all those addictions and vices, the things that make you hate yourself. But hey, what's another failed resolution attempt? I'm sure I wouldn't be the last, though mine didn't even make it to sunlight.

54

I'd always hated ironing shirts and luckily during my few professions I'd managed to avoid it most of my adult life, spent the majority of my working years in collarless jobs, short-sleeve jobs, ones with limited responsibility and tiny pay cheques, on the plus side it meant I very rarely saw an ironing board.

Today, however, was unavoidable, I wanted to make an extra special effort, so that meant a crisp shirt with no creases. The lady on reception had lent me what I needed and I carried it back to my room, iron in one hand, the other under my arm like a surfboard.

★ ★ ★

"You do realize there are such things as dry cleaners here?" she said from behind her hand fan.

"You could help, you know."

"My ironing duties finished the day you left school, I'm afraid."

"At least do the sleeves. Look at me, I have no idea what I'm doing here."

"Give it here, you daft so and so. I thought we'd taught you all these sorts of life skills," she said, as I handed her the iron. "What have you done to your trousers? You're supposed to follow the natural crease," she added, taking over. "Go get Molly's shoes on, while I try and salvage these poor clothes."

It had been a good week, a good few weeks actually. Mum was doing really well, chemo had ended, one last session of radiotherapy in a few days. The hardest parts were now over, and Jesus, had they been hard. I can still remember her lowest days, October was bad, a sinkful of hair, me and Molly washing her face when she couldn't do it herself, helping her find the strength to want to wake up, but those days had gone. The doctors sounded pleased, they were quite clear this morning that there was still a long road ahead, question marks they hoped to answer, some that they never would. They said we should be happy, that we were on the right path to recovery. They say 'we' a lot, I'd noticed, it was the same when Cassie died, like dying and survival was a team effort, maybe it was, they just wanted you to know that you weren't in it alone, which at first, when dying is new and unfamiliar, is probably what you need.

We'd gotten used to cancer now, settled into the drills and phases, pretended we understood what they were doing and why. All we knew was we trusted the hospital and over time, whereas before we'd be asking tons of questions, researching worst-case scenarios and alternative treatments, now we all just let the doctors do their thing, trusted the treatments were working, not knowing why things healed and fixed themselves, just happy that they had and only worrying if and when they didn't.

I think both Mum and I had changed these last few months, me especially, since that long chat I had to myself on the beach that night, put all my attention into enjoying each day, where before it had been written off before it'd started. I felt like a younger me, bit more caution to the wind, a bit more Captain Ahab. It was nice to have me back again. It had been a long time.

"I thought I said you couldn't open this till next week." Mum slid the shirt back on its hanger.

"It's the perfect occasion though."

"Means you won't have much to open on your actual birthday though."

"I'm not eight years old. I won't throw a fit if there aren't boxes stacked to the ceiling. What have you and Moll got planned for later?"

"Not sure. She's got her head set on staying up late, so who knows what she'll have me doing. Last time she painted my head, so God knows what I've got in store tonight. We're going to pop out in a sec, grab a few essentials for our girls' night in. Do we need anything? Water? Bog roll?"

"Both, I think."

"Anything else. Chocolates? Bunch of flowers for the lucky lady? Engagement ring?"

"I think just flowers for now," I said, as she and Molly took themselves off to buy provisions, and I looked for a tie I wasn't entirely sure I owned.

Her name was Emma by the way, the reason for my smart attire, and I'd lost count on what number date this would be, it was a lot, more than ten. We hadn't kissed yet, which historically would have been a concern, though Emma was a different type of girl than I was used to, not the first girl on the dance floor, not the crowd surfer; no, Emma was a lower volume girl, and I got the impression her kisses weren't dished out too freely. However, it was Valentine's, the air was different on Valentine's, hence the fancy restaurant, hence the need for an ironed shirt. Emma worked over at the hospital so we had met in various hot corridors and sticky waiting rooms whilst Mum was having all her checks. I heard her accent over her desk and felt curious to find out how it got so far away from home, not that she told me at first. Initially I took it personally, how quiet and reluctant to talk she was, but I soon realized her shyness wasn't just aimed at me. Funnily enough we went to the same university in Sheffield, knew the same places, trod on the same pub floors, got into similar debt. Over the new few months what first started as bumping into each other on the off chance, soon became a habit that I'd make sure to stop and say hello.

I wasn't sure why it took it so long to ask her out officially, Emma's shyness being hard to read, me being scared to jump in. But since that first date things had moved pretty fast, faster than I'd expected, with so little time left here, it forced us into spending a lot of time with each other, trying to cram six months' dating into two.

She'd even met Molly, unavoidable really, seeing as the hospital was our second home. Though Molly never questioned the new friendship, to Molly she was just another nurse, another white uniform, speaking a language she recognized as her own. I certainly never called her my girlfriend and didn't plan to either, there was no need to complicate things, not with me being due to go home any day now. Couldn't see Emma coming back with us, not based on a two-month relationship, she'd been at the hospital for over a year, chances were she wouldn't come back at all based on what she'd told me. She was settled here, hence why we could not go to that next step, which also took away any unwanted pressure to feel the need to commit. It was just fun, easy and fun, nothing else, we both knew it would end, we both knew not to get too involved, we were both honest about where this would go and how it would end. In some ways, it was probably better if we didn't kiss tonight. A kiss could change everything.

I should just wear a T-shirt instead, I thought, looking at myself in the mirror, worrying that the combination of shirt and trouser would be hard for any woman to resist, even the restrained ones.

"Still hungry?" I asked passing her the dessert menu.

"No thank you. But if you want to I don't mind sharing maybe."

"No, no. Probably for the best. Here is a whole new level of sweet. I want to go back home with most of my teeth."

"Forgot to tell you. So sad, my little Ying died this morning."

I took a minute to answer. "Ying's the one that always pinches my butt, right? You OK? Did you see her?"

"No, that's what's so sad. I saw her a few days before, but only in passing, we only had a few minutes to talk. She looked fine when I saw her, was in good spirits, still trying to get me to go on a date with one of her sons."

"How many sons does she have?"

"Three I think. I know the youngest is sixteen, so I assume she didn't mean him. Don't worry, I declined her offer. Told her I'd already found my Prince Charming."

"What did she say to that?"

"Said she was running out of time to find them a good wife."

"Do you get used to it? Making friends, losing friends?"

"I'm not used to it, no. It affects me more than the others, they know better than to get too emotionally attached. That's what I need to do, it's hard though, they look so lonely and frightened. I feel obliged to be a listening ear, just let them talk."

"You are a stronger person than me. I couldn't do it. Why did you come here? Why not England?"

"Lots of reasons, the ones you'd expect mostly. Though the real reason was England wouldn't have me."

"Why?"

"I'm not entirely sure. I guess I just suck at interviews."

"I know the feeling. You want more wine?" I said, already topping up both our glasses.

"I bet you aren't as bad as me."

"So, Thailand doesn't do interviews?"

"They do, but they are more interested in what looks good on paper. My English education and my Bachelor of Science degree looks a lot better than the real me up close."

"England's loss, I say."

"Thank you for these by the way," she said, wiping the corner of her mouth with a napkin. "They smell lovely."

"Well, it is Valentine's. I felt obliged to make a romantic gesture. I must confess I didn't physically buy them. I can't take the credit."

She laughed. "I knew that already, silly. Your mother told me she chose them."

"You two are becoming quite the tag team."

"I should introduce you to my mother. Make it even."

"Does she know about me then?"

"Of course."

"Oh," I said, taken aback slightly, counting the number of dates we'd been on in my head.

"She likes you a lot, actually."

"I'm guessing you must have embellished the truth."

"Not at all. She admires you for how you have taken on the role of single parent. How you've looked after your mother through her illness."

"You've told her about Cassie then, I take it?"

"She's my mother, Tom. I tell her everything. Think she is just excited I've met someone, she'd started to give up hope."

"You've not had many boyfriends?"

"I had one serious one through uni, but he cheated on me with a girl I was sharing a house with."

"That was nice of them."

"Ever since then I have wanted to be on my own, focus on my job. Thailand was a good excuse to be single."

"Shall we go outside, get some air? Seems a waste of a view seeing it from behind glass."

We walked out onto the terrace, a few other couple had the same idea, coffees and candlelight, the ocean just below our feet.

"You two find it hard being so far apart?"

"More my mother than me, she lives on her own, so this isn't ideal. She cried a lot at first, but we speak every day, well, we used to. We haven't spoken this last week."

"How come?"

"We had a disagreement."

"Over?"

"Over you, actually."

"Over me?" I said, sipping my wine. "What have I done?"

"It's more what I've done. Or what I was going to do."

"And what was that?"

"I told her I was planning on ending things between us."

"And she disagreed?"

"She most definitely disagreed," she smiled. "Shall we order coffee?"

"Emma, I thought we… "

"Tom, I like what me and you are right now. It's nice."

"So why are you telling your mum you are ending it? I'm a bit confused."

"I just got cold feet that's all. Worried you don't feel the same. Worried you are just going to fly off and leave me."

"Emma, we knew this was the situation. We knew I would go home. We knew it couldn't get serious."

"I can't help how I feel, Tom. I don't want to feel this way either, but I do."

I didn't answer, looked down at the decking floor.

"I take it by your reaction that you don't feel the same then, Tom?"

"I care for you very much, Emma. You know that."

"But not enough?"

"I didn't say that, did I?"

"I'm sorry that I'm telling you this, I just wanted you to know how I felt. I can leave if you want me to." She went to get out of her chair.

"Emma, sit down. Course I don't want you to go."

"I'm sorry, Tom. You have been honest from the start, and it is my fault for how I feel right now. It's just taken me so long to find someone like you. I just feel so angry I've let myself get like this."

Neither of us spoke.

"What do we do now, Tom?"

We stared at each other. She was petite, but she looked tiny sat there, eyes filled with tears, about to break, her world about to collapse.

Somehow, we ended up kissing. A kiss that shouldn't have happened, but did.

55

"Darling, there is nothing sweeter than the buttocks of a twenty-two-year-old."

"That specific, hey? I'm afraid twenty-two is even too young for me."

"I've gone younger, I assure you. You should treat yourself."

"I'm OK, thanks."

"Always knew this town was ageist." Marla put a cigarette in her mouth, held it between her red lips as she lit and inhaled. "You fine if I smoke?" already four puffs in.

"I'm surprised you even asked."

"I must be softening in my years."

"I hope I'm like you when I'm older," I said, my head inside new cupboards.

"Who says I'm old? Seventy is the new thirty."

"What does that make me then?"

"You're a Baby Jane in this game."

"The young don't tend to fare well in this industry."

"I can see why. The public eye is no place to grow up, all your mistakes for everyone to see. Though the old don't fare any better. Look at me and you, before and after personified, beauty before it turns bitter and twisted."

"How old were you when you first got into the game?"

"Started in Broadway in the late fifties. I must have been around eighteen or so."

"I bet you were a handful."

"Nothing of the sort, actually. I was the most Yankee virgin who ever walked God's green earth."

"Obviously that didn't last long," I smiled.

"For some women sex appeal comes naturally. For me it had to be worked at."

"How long did it take you?"

"Luckily not too long, otherwise my career would've been over before it started. Some of us aren't as lucky as you, darling."

"I've seen your movies, Marla. Stop acting uglier than you are."

"I'm all tits and make-up, sweetheart."

"That's not true."

"I always knew I wasn't the prettiest. Meant I had to work a little harder. Find a little niche for myself."

"And what niche was that?"

"I made myself interesting. I made myself a bitch too."

"You think that might work for me?"

"You're interesting, I'll give you that. You're too nice to be a bitch, I'm afraid," she said, moving on to her next cigarette. "Lilly. I want to thank you for this. Whatever you did to get me here, I applaud you."

"I didn't do anything, Marla. You got this role on merit."

She laughed, coughed, laughed again. "I'm old and dumb enough to know merit had nothing to do with it, merit rarely does, my dear. I know you pulled some strings and I'm eternally grateful. You don't know how much this means. To be given a chance to act again. To know the girls back home are all talking about me behind my back, wishing it was them you were giving one last swansong to."

There was a knock on the trailer door.

"Come in", I said.

"Ms Miller." A girl with a headset. "They need you on set in ten minutes."

"You tell 'em I'll be out when I'm good and ready. And get me a tea unless you want a corpse on your hands."

The girl apologized awkwardly, closed the door behind her.

"Always the bitch, hey, Marla?"

"It's what I do best."

"Even if you're not a bitch."

"Well, we are actresses, darling. Not being ourselves is what we are paid to do."

"You could tone it down once a while. Let them see the real you."

"Arse to that. I'll be breaking butts till the final curtain. Here, grab me another smoke and help me down those infernal steps of yours."

"Do you get nervous?"

"No, never."

"I always get first-day nerves, it's like school all over."

"Honey, they should be nervous of you, not the other way around."

"You haven't worked with Max," I smiled.

★ ★ ★

I sat back down on my chair, took a look around me. This would-be home for the next few months, probably the biggest trailer I'd ever had, definitely needed softening, a woman's touch, felt like I was in a spaceship.

I walked over to the sofa, it was all suitcases and bags, started unzipping things, attempted to put my belongings into the most logical places. Mom had helped me pack, one of her many talents, so far clothes went from suitcase to drawers without much fuss. I'd spent quite a lot of time with her actually, my birthday in Vegas, Thanksgiving obviously, Christmas too. Surprised my mom and sister with a girls' trip to Cancun, so we spent the last two weeks of January doing nothing but reading trash and drinking margaritas.

I surveyed the kitchen table, it was covered in good luck bouquets. I should have appreciated the gesture, I always did initially, after that it was working out how to keep them alive and fed, and with one vase and no natural light, I doubted it would be that long. Mom had even sent a bunch, signed it from her and

Dad, pretending they still came as a pair. Max sent me roses too, no message in that one, knowing Max like I did I bet his PA did it, and knowing his PA, I bet she didn't even tell Max what good luck was being sent on his behalf.

Max hadn't been too bad so far, bearable, left me alone for the most part. He dragged me out when required, an event or show, various types of spotlight. Had me dress up and smile so everyone could take their photos and ask their questions. To the big wide world, we were now an item, but in truth we barely spoke and so far, it remained the working relationship he'd promised me from the start. I wasn't holding my breath, with filming starting today it wouldn't surprise me if all that changed and my freedom was finally cut short. It was only a matter of time till Max wanted more than a trophy wife and demanded more than kissing cheeks on red carpets.

Not that I'd done much with my freedom so far, most of last year I stayed pretty low key, either in some flea market or department store buying cute things I didn't need but couldn't live without. I'd toyed with the idea of a kitten, a Savannah, something female and feline, just like her potential owner. But bought a houseplant instead, to see how good I was at keeping that alive before I looked after something warm-blooded.

I'd started dancing again too, not that anybody knew, managed to find night classes, so twice a week I had a mad dash across town. Felt good to dance again, didn't realize how much I needed it, how much it grounded me, gave me a definitive line between Goodmanson and Goodridge. There were times last year where I lost my way slightly, did things and took things I shouldn't have. Thought it might help, of course it didn't, alcohol and tablets never did and never would, not long term, as always, the cure becomes the cause.

I'd like to say it went unnoticed, my unravelling, when in fact everyone saw it, everyone had an opinion. Some people make mistakes and I made mine on the wrong night on the wrong road last summer. I got caught DUI, pulled over, handcuffed and put in the back of a cop car. It sounds worse than it was, the officers were nice enough, didn't throw me in a jail cell like protocol would've told them to, let me sit and sober up before they let me go.

Mom was embarrassed, Dad hit the roof, Max just laughed, Sally told me not to worry, said she would make it work to our advantage and that she did. The media went crazy, my mugshot on every channel, my apologies printed on every page. Behind closed doors my publicist classed it as a triumph and whilst publicly I was left to hang my head in shame, Team Goodridge were chinking the champagne glasses of a media campaign deemed successful and cheap. Somehow my shocking behaviour had been granted a positive spin and now I was being offered edgier roles by the edgier directors, the poster girl of 'good girl gone bad'. I didn't know what was more embarrassing, the crime or the reward.

The only thing that neither Sally nor Max's legal representatives could fix was the punishment and the judge didn't seem to like me much. Despite being my first offence, she still dished out a fine and community service with the Caltrans chain gang. God, that was hellish, spent ten days on Ventura freeway with trash tweezers and an orange hard hat, pulling weeds as I sweated out my redemption in the midday sun. And it was still not over, I was still to attend the rest of my prevention programme, designed to educate me on the dangers of addiction, and why I felt the need to be dependent on things my body shouldn't have. To be fair, the sessions so far had helped, the lady I'd spent time with was actually quite cool, certainly not judgmental, and what at first I had felt a waste of time turned into a mini therapy course. I told her about Tom, not names and places, not the full story, but enough to make her understand my downward spiral.

In a strange way, Tom indirectly played a part in my recovery; it took him giving up on me to get back on my feet. Slowly and gradually, fewer calls and fewer messages, till eventually contact from Tom stopped completely and rather than sadness, I just felt relief. That was when I stopped crying, that was when I started to sleep again. Got my life back in order, attempted to get back into some form of normality, though I realized quite soon my life never would be, the frenzy Max had created meant there was never a day where I truly felt normal.

I was that girl in the magazine, speeding in an SUV, pushing a camera away, hiding her face. It's not like I wasn't used to intrusion, I knew my life would be shared, I just didn't realize how much they wanted to take. My life was not my own, it was other people's and for the first time in my career I felt genuinely unsafe. I'd become aware of an internet I never knew existed, the dark web, full of twisted fantasies and threats. Even I knew things had to change and that my entourage would have to grow, for my own safety as well as for everyone caught in the crossfire. Quite simply I needed men on the ground, men who could be barged and pushed, men who knew how to read a situation, stop danger up close, but see it coming from far off too. I did everything I could to keep Frank, but in the end, it was him that called it a day. I offered him a promotion to make him stay, offered him more money, more responsibility, but his mind was made up. Tried to give him a full year's salary, healthcare, a gesture of how much I'd appreciated what he'd done. Typical of Frank, he declined both.

Sally told me he'd got a job in some store, security guard, patrolling the aisles, looking out for kids stealing candy bars. We message each other occasionally, I'd invited him down to stay a couple of times, but he always had a reason not to come. Made me sad I didn't see him anymore. We both said that nothing would change, when clearly it already had.

There was a knock on my door.

Same girl, same headset, similar request.

"Miss Goodridge, Max is asking for you. He wants you over at wardrobe."

"Tell him he can wait."

"He said it was pretty urgent." The girl went to grab her walkie-talkie.

"Don't worry. I'll be a couple of minutes. Sorry, I didn't mean to snap at you. I was seeing if I could be a bitch. Was it convincing?" The girl smiled, not sure she knew the appropriate answer. Her walkie-talkie crackled, she was being summoned elsewhere.

I sat down at my dressing table, the mirror and bulbs, made me feel immediately like work was about to start. I closed my eyes, took a deep breath. It was an unfamiliar sensation reprising the role of a character I'd played years before, especially a character that admittedly wasn't far too removed from my own self. Clearly, this was the only reason I was here today, the reason I was now an actress, not still working the graveyard shifts in a dance studio. Practically impossible for Max not to offer me the part, whatever he was searching for those many years ago, he found it in me the night we first met. And although I was young, had never acted, what he did get was the girl on his page, a ready-made character, all he had to do was aim the camera at me and hope I didn't try and act.

Problem was, I wasn't the same me I was back then. A lot had happened in between, not all bad, but not all good either. Where I was damaged before, now I'm not. Where I was fixed before, now I'm broken, they might not like the Lilly I'd become, and the Lilly everyone wanted may not be the Lilly they get this time around.

I sat down, one quick last check before I faced the world. There was a tiny box in front of me, full of little trinkets and photos, silly things really, things to remind me of home. I started to position them, sticking them around the mirror like a picture frame. I would need these memories, things I could cling onto when it got hard, remember why the hell I was here. And I needed to know that, as sometimes even I forgot, got caught up in it all. Every day I needed to know why I was doing this, why I had chosen Max. And no matter how much I enjoyed it, the money it made me, the places I got to see, the people I got to work with, every day I needed to remember why I was here and what Max had made me give up. I didn't regret what I did and if I had to make that decision again it would be no different. It was love and still is love. It took losing Tom to understand just how much I wanted him back.

I looked at the photos in front of me. Black and white like they were old, when they weren't old at all. My farmhouse, my mad hotel in the cliffs, my Tom. So sad, the only thing left to do was smile. For the thirteen days we had together, I would always be thankful. We deserved a better chance and Tom deserved a better ending than I gave him.

We both did.

56

A month passed and it was now nearly April.

Hair and make-up had just disappeared out of my hotel suite, so I was left to stare at the end product, marvel at my own breasts and fringe, wonder how they were being held up and what with. The dress was genius, sent by the designer himself, which I assumed I didn't have to send back. The jewellery was Harry Winston, that for sure I knew wasn't to be kept, just a loan, a big fat half-a-million-dollar loan. I looked again at myself, I looked amazing, a transformation I hadn't expected, I felt a fraud taking all the credit, between their three pairs of hands they'd somehow managed to turn me into a happy day again.

My life was exhausting, every day a chase, sometimes I escaped, mostly I got caught. I keep telling people that whatever we were trying still wasn't working, every day I was being mobbed and the numbers were growing as was the interest. There was never any respite, the world was turning claustrophobic, nothing good came from going outside. Sally said she was on the case, assured me the team were working out solutions, there was talk of me wearing a wig, turning blonde to avoid detection, there was even talk of finding me a lookalike, another Lilly Goodridge. Whoever she was, I already felt sorry for her, no one should be paid to be bait.

My world had turned ridiculous, the last few days especially.

First crazy thing was Frank.

Heard some pretty shitty news, I didn't know all the ins and outs but he ended up in a hospital with his chest again, so despite Max's attempt to stop me I decided to go and visit him, check he was OK. I'm glad I did, I thought it might be awkward but it wasn't, just like old times. Wished I could've stayed longer, but I was informed the police had been called, a riot of paps was causing chaos downstairs, getting in the way of ambulances, apparently knocked some sick kid to the floor. I thought some places were off-limits, turned out I was wrong. I got to talk to Frank I suppose, albeit briefly, brought him some flowers, grapes, crosswords. I never meant to cause him stress, that was the last thing I wanted to bring to his door.

So that was the first thing.

The second thing was that Jon rang me, completely out of the blue. We hadn't spoken since after the New Year, so it was nice to hear someone English again. It wasn't a long call, he rang to tell me he'd be in LA soon for our premiere, he sounded excited, early screen tests were positive, even my accent hadn't been ridiculed, which I was certain would have been regarded as woeful by every respectable critic in Hollywood. We were both excited about catching up again, it would be nice to see the gang, the friends I'd made, even Chris Rogan, God his face was everywhere right now too, fucking some pop star just like he was supposed to, his life was probably as ridiculous as mine right now. Anyway, Jon had some big news, told me worldwide release would not be long after the US, and calendar permitting I would be asked to attend as many premieres as physically possible, different countries and continents. Wasn't till I heard Jon say the words "Leicester Square" and "May 14th" that I realized what it meant and where that might mean I would have to go.

Look, I was a smart girl. I knew England wasn't Tom and London wasn't Tom. I knew I should not have associated the two together, but I did. Until proven otherwise, me getting on a plane and stepping foot on London's cobbles was as close to Tom as I was going to get, felt like Tom could just be a camera lens away again. Made me smile for a good few days, but it was a smile that wasn't to last long. Max messaged me eventually, he'd obviously been informed of the same news of my pending European vacation not long after me. He made his feelings about my return to England quite clear and he was clever enough to understand how my brain would be ticking and plotting.

I told Sally this, she laughed it off.

"Who does that arsehole think he is?" she said. "It has got nothing to do with him. You're contractually obliged to a different studio. You'll go to London; the film is set in England for fuck's sake."

I just asked her to do her best, do what she could. I was glad Sally had my back, one of the few that wasn't afraid to stand toe to toe with Max. In fact, I think she quite enjoyed the jostling for power and control, I think Max did too, he'd always liked a good fight, fights won without fists, fought in boardrooms and conference calls.

I hoped I'd get to go to London and that the tug of war between Sally and Max would end in my favour, however it was a slim chance. One thing I knew was, Max would do all he could to stop me and he would probably be successful, he normally was. I mean, look at what he'd done so far, I was a laughing stock, a walking calamity. I knew what everyone thought of me, I'd have thought the same thing if I was them, I hadn't read the news, been online, but I wasn't stupid. You get in and out of an abusive relationship once, you get sympathy. You go back to him a second time, you're on your own. Not that Max was abusive, I wasn't fearful of violence, he may have hit me once, but I'd hit him harder, and I deserved it, I would have hit me too. But I knew what Max was capable of and it was much worse than any black eye or bruised cheek. And that was why I did as he said, stood where he wanted me to stand, say what he wanted me to say, go where he wanted me to go, and stay away from places I wasn't allowed to go, I must have looked so weak. Who cared, let everyone whisper and gossip, give their opinions, write me off. I was willing to look the fool, time just to get my head down, see it through. Tom would've done the same for me, saved me if I needed saving.

There was a knock at my door. It was a knock I recognized, a perfect knock, always the same. I bet a hundred dollars that behind my door would be two Agent Smiths. I didn't know how many security guards Max must've gotten through, trust issues obviously, I barely ever got to know their names, as if that mattered, they just did as they were told, stayed quiet and kept me alive.

I put my wine down, grabbed my clutch bag, opened the door.

"Ma'am. It's time to go," they said as I was ushered down a corridor towards a limousine and the sound of high-pitched screams in the foyer.

★ ★ ★

"Admit this is all very agreeable, isn't it?"

"Agreeable?"

"This. All of it. It's not a bad way to live. Being wined and dined, being the brightest thing in the room. Everyone looking at us."

"And you want to be looked at?"

"Is ignoring fame your little rebellion? You look so cute when you're being the *enfant terrible*."

"You're no different, Max."

"I do love being famous. Once I understood how to take advantage of it."

"You don't act that way."

"You're not the only one who can pretend to be someone else."

"What, Max Salter, the loveable rogue? Is this a part you are playing?"

"I've always been the sinner, you should know that. Pretending I care is the hardest part."

"I take it tonight's heartfelt speech wasn't heartfelt at all then?"

"I don't have patience for victims."

"They are hardly victims. They are ill, that is not intentional."

"Lilly, don't be so naive. AIDS is a choice and no one is here tonight for AIDS awareness. I've just got the balls to say it."

"You've got no balls, Max. If you did you would've said all this over the microphone, rather than holding that girl's hand and pretending you gave a damn about her illness."

"She's just lucky I held her hand at all."

"Jesus, Max."

"Come on, Lilly. I was joking. You're laughing too. It was funny."

"I'm laughing cos you're so evil-minded it's absurd. You're like a fucking cartoon villain."

"The world needs big bad wolves, Lilly."

"Can we stop now? My legs hurt."

"No, not yet."

Max swept me slowly across the dance floor, strong and confident and gentle. He knew everyone was watching. This was a performance, to our audience it probably looked beautiful, romantic. Women probably swooned, men were probably jealous. I did my best to swoon too, to be swept away.

"Tell me this doesn't feel like a life sentence," he said, as I tried to ignore his aftershave. "I can think of harder ways to be in chains, Lilly. Look around you, it's hardly prison, I'm hardly the warden, am I? This is an amicable agreement."

"You backed me into a corner, Max."

"Doesn't mean you can't enjoy it. You may feel like trapped, but that isn't my intention."

"Max, you tell me where to go, what to say, what to wear. That sounds pretty trapped."

"You don't like the dress I had sent especially? The jewellery? I won't tell you how much it costs, or what hoops I had to go through."

"It's very nice, thank you."

"But?"

"But I can't be bought."

"Oh, but you can, Lilly G. I've proved that once already."

"Don't be mean or I will stop dancing with you."

"Sorry, I was teasing you. You know I love you to death. I always have, that's my downfall," he said, as w we continued to slow-dance.

This had been our fourth dance of the evening and despite the chains it was, as Max described, all very agreeable once we'd done the carpet, the wall of flashing bulbs, once we got inside where the canapés and champagne were endless and everyone was full of smiles and positivity. Although I was made to come and given no choice, it was a nice place to be held captive amongst the rich and successful.

It was for charity, too, not that Max cared which, it could have been any, he wasn't here to donate or for the auction, he was here to sell. He may have done a speech on stage, pledged his loyalty to the cause, he was here for one reason only and AIDS awareness was the furthest thing from his mind, Max saw dollar signs, not the sorts of dollars that cured things.

I was glad I couldn't see myself, me and Max dancing together, our bodies tight together, the sound of a swing band, the chandeliers, the taste of fizzy bubbles, men in white tuxes, men in velvet suits, women so beautiful it made me feel drunk, and everyone was laughing. Yes, Max was right, there were harder ways to be in chains, but they were still chains.

"I am serious, you know. I do love you. And you love me too, I'm sure of it," Ma,x said as I continued to dance ear to ear. "Do you think they do, though?"

"They?"

"People. The world," looking over his shoulder. "You think they all believe our story?"

"They'll think whatever we tell them."

"They're cleverer than you give them credit for, Lilly G. We need to raise our game."

"I don't follow."

"You could move in with me."

"No, Max. That wasn't our agreement. We aren't together. This isn't real."

"We need to make a statement of our intent."

"Isn't what I'm doing enough?"

"No, Lilly. Smiling and holding hands isn't enough. We are supposed to be in love."

"I'm doing my best, Max."

"Well, it needs to improve for this to work. Let me kiss you." He looked directly at me.

"No, Max."

"Why not?"

"No."

"There are plenty of cameras here. Give them something to salivate over."

"I'm not a prostitute, Max. As much as you probably think it of me."

"It's just a kiss, Lilly. We are supposed to be lovers."

"Love can be behind closed doors. Doesn't have to be in full view."

"We need to be believable."

"No, Max. I'm not kissing you."

"What if I said I wasn't asking, I was telling."

"Don't do this. Tonight has been nice so far. We are enjoying ourselves. Please don't ruin it by forcing yourself on me."

"I'm not forcing myself on you, Lilly. This is a business opportunity. I don't think I'm asking for much."

"You don't?"

"Please, Lilly. I want to kiss you, a small tiny kiss. Get all the tongues wagging. Be on the front page for tomorrow morning,"

"OK, Max. I will kiss you."

"You will?"

"If you let me go to London in May like I'm supposed to."

"No."

"Then I'm not kissing you. Simple as that."

"You think I'm a fool?"

"You let me go to London and you can kiss me however you want, in front of who you want."

"You turning into quite the game player, Lilly G, aren't you?"

"Do we have a deal?"

"Can I trust you in London?"

"I understand your threats, Max, believe me."

We stared at each other. The band started another song, my head rested on his shoulder, piano keys, crystal ceilings.

"Then we have deal," he smirked. "I'll allow you to go."

A small part of me wanted to tell him where to go. How dare he say such a thing, I thought. But of course, I didn't, I thanked him, stayed in his arms, let him sweep me across the dance floor.

"When do you want to kiss me? Now? Here?"

Max looked around the room. "Not yet. Later. We need more cameras."

"Well, let me know when you want me. I'm going for a drink."

"Not yet. The song's not over."

I went back into his arms, without argument or fuss.

"Good girl. Doing as you are told is not a weakness, Lilly. The opposite in fact. You remember that."

I realized at that exact moment that the only way I could ever beat Max was by being smart, being clever, tiny risks for tiny rewards, small wins – so small, Max didn't even think he'd lost.

PART FOUR

Home from home/Oct/Shot 902

57

Rain. Rain. Rain.

"You want wine with dinner, love?" Mum's voice from the kitchen.

"A small one. I'm driving later, remember," I shouted back through the walls.

I looked back out of the window. Recycling bins, a shed, a garden neglected, a lawn knee high. My phone buzzed, it was Emma wishing me good night, I turned back to my computer screen, watching Thailand upload itself.

Even as a child, I loved Dad's office. I'm told there was a time, just after I was born, when it was full of shoes and coats, a dumping ground for umbrellas and vacuum cleaners. I'd only ever known it as Dad's room, his little retreat, the little desk under the stairs where he'd do his school work, important papers and filing. Mum told me it was just an excuse to get away from her for ten minutes, to avoid watching soaps, to fill his evenings with art and gin.

Mum had barely touched it since he died, said she couldn't bring herself to, it was floor-to-ceiling Dad, it would be like tearing down a gallery. His pencil sketches, his alphabetized CDs, his carvings and sculptures, his windowsill of stones and geodes, his photos of a younger me, cuddling his hips, dancing in sunflowers. A perfect mess, a room only he could have had and one very hard to convert into anything else. I never appreciated how talented he was and for the most part I was embarrassed by him. Back then I just wanted a father like everyone else's. A normal one, one that liked football and beer, not a dad that relaxed to Chopin and sketched chubby nudes. I couldn't have been more wrong.

We'd been extremely lucky with our tenants, an excitable young couple, a pair of happy blondes, said we could leave Dad's office locked and untouched till we returned from travelling. That was nice of them, so nice we decided to make their rent a little lower. Not too low, just enough to thank them for the gesture, show them how much it meant. True to their word, when we returned, it had been left untouched, in fact the whole house looked as if we'd never been gone. Mom said if we ever travelled again, she'd make sure our tenants would always be lesbians, assuming all homosexuals would be as clean as the last pair.

I could hear banging, rolling pins and chopping boards. Mum and Molly were in the kitchen, there was yeast and flour involved, a mess which they always got into when they were cooking and baking. Mum thought it best, after the morning we'd had, thought kneading dough might make Molly smile.

She hadn't been great since coming home. Today she threatened to leave home, packed her tiny suitcase with a hairbrush and Calpol, said she was going to swim to America. It would have been funny, if it wasn't so heartbreaking, watching her get so upset, genuine tears and frustrations. All that time spent with Lou and Rose, all the talk of Cassie, so full of questions and no matter what answers we gave, she had never looked so lost and confused. Her head couldn't quite take it all in and although she could accept what happened, her heart didn't know how to cope with the enormity of it all. Luckily, she was never upset for long, a cuddle and a cartoon and she was back to her giggling and inquisitive self, though I wondered how long it would last till she packed her suitcase again and threatened to breaststroke across the Atlantic.

With a few minutes to myself I thought it a good time to transfer our photos of Thailand from camera onto the hard drive, and there were a lot of them, hundreds and hundreds, six months' worth, blurred ones, ones Mum took by accident, the ones with Molly's fingers over the lens, had to be brutal in my choices. But that would be a job for another day, I wasn't editing yet, tonight was just about getting them saved and filed away.

"What am I doing with all of this crap in here?" Mum leant against the doorway, looking floor to ceiling.

"You're supposed to say it's sentimental."

"Some is, the rest is just tack, utility statements and prehistoric computer consoles."

"People would pay a lot of money for this stuff."

"I still think we should order a skip," she said, looking through a shoe box full of computer mice and scart leads. "It will sad to see his artwork go though."

"Who says it has to go?"

"Me. I don't want it all."

"You could put them all in storage?"

"Cost a fortune. I'll see if his sister wants some of it. Hopefully she will."

"It wouldn't fit in her little bungalow. Dad's artwork is far from small."

"Might have to donate some. I'm sure I could find somewhere that would take them. Better to be in a gallery than in some dark cupboard collecting dust. I might give some to his old school, they've got plenty of bare walls and long corridors."

"You think it will be strange, Mum? Finally saying goodbye to the place?"

"I've been saying goodbye to the place for years. No, it's time to let someone else fill it with memories. I hope we sell it to a young couple, I don't like the idea of selling it to another old person. I want people to grow up in it."

"I don't think we can be that picky, estate agent said the market is slow, not much work around here, which doesn't help either."

"Well, we've till the summer. I'm sure we'll sell it by then."

"We could always rent it out again?"

"No. I like the idea of selling. It makes it more exciting, means we haven't the easy option of coming back. Means we have to make it work. Though I don't think Molly would be happy with any house at the minute."

"Unless it's Florida."

"She'll come around. Once we start looking at houses with us, once she gets to choose her bedroom, or run around new gardens." Mum looked at the computer screen. "That's pretty. Where's that?"

"Burgh Island."

"I'd like you to take us there one day."

"What, Burgh Island?"

"I'd like to see all of Devon, actually. Go to all those places you always talk about. Meet the infamous Dot."

"Can't see why not."

"Go in April or May perhaps, try to avoid the school holidays."

"That would be nice. I'm sure Dot wouldn't charge us much."

"And you wouldn't mind going back there?"

"Why would I mind?"

"I just thought with the whole Lilly thing. I thought you'd rather not go back."

"Mum. Lilly was like ten months ago."

"You've never actually showed me all of the photos from Devon before. I wouldn't mind one night having a look through them, if you don't mind, that is."

"I've just deleted quite a few, well almost all of them actually."

"That seems silly, Tom."

"Silly?"

"Just because it didn't work out doesn't mean you have to be so drastic. You and Lilly did happen."

"This isn't me being drastic. It's me being careful."

Mum raised her eyebrow. "I'm going to put the dinner in, check why Molly has been so quiet, that normally spells trouble. I've had to put a few of my boxes in your room. I've run out of space in mine. If you get a chance, have a look through, think some of it might be yours."

I nodded.

"And don't throw it all away. Put some in bin bags, keep me a little nostalgia please."

"I've only deleted a few photos, Mum. You know I keep stuff."

"Other people's nostalgia, not your own. Autographs of dead people. Posters for films I've never heard of."

"Mum, what's your point?"

"Try and keep some proof of your existence. I've hardly any photos of your travels, America, hardly any of Cassie, now you're deleting Lilly. You're allowed to own things you know, not everything you own needs to fit into a rucksack."

I went to answer, but got caught mid-yawn.

"What time do you start?"

"Got a couple of hours yet. Put Molly to bed then head out."

"Saturday night is no time to work."

"Saturday night is the only night to work."

"Didn't realize there was anywhere worth going to round here. It's all fields."

"That's the whole point, Mum. Otherwise people wouldn't need taxis."

"What time will you be home?"

"Normal time. Though it's raining so if it's busy I might stay out longer. I'll probably be back before it gets light."

"If it was up to me you wouldn't be driving that taxi at all. It's not like we need the money."

"We do, Mum. Thailand wiped us out. I know this is hard, but it gives us a little extra to play with, and means I get to see Molly."

"Means you spend most of the day catching up on sleep, walking around like a zombie. You'll make yourself ill. Humans were never meant to be nocturnal. You know it shortens your life, it was on TV the other morning."

"It suits me, Mum. You know I've never been able to sleep anyway."

"Don't know where you get it from, this love of the night time,

339

no idea how we've managed to raise Nosferatu. Sorry if I was too hard on you earlier, about the photos."

"That's OK."

"I was just concerned you were getting rid of Lilly for the wrong reasons."

"Not at all, the opposite in fact. I'm doing it to protect her. And us."

She kissed me on the head. "I'll check on Molly, check how much flour she has managed to keep on the work surface. I'm guessing not a lot."

★ ★ ★

Later was pretty uneventful, by a bit of luck I managed to grab a few airport runs, took me up to one in the morning. Decided to grab ten minutes, stopped in a lay-by, ate some cold pizza, watched the rain as I drank my coffee.

My phone buzzed in my pocket. Immediately I thought it was Emma, she normally sent me a message before she started work, wishing me a good morning when I was about to go to bed.

I checked my phone. A message, not from her.

"I think we need to talk," it said.

I very nearly replied, nearly even rang back. But I didn't, ignored it instead, finished my food, got back on the road.

However, there were more messages to come, lots more.

58

I'd given myself a Sunday night off, had a nice evening with Mum, talked plans and futures, feasible and unfeasible. Now everyone had gone to bed and I was left to ponder my bedroom ceiling again, my body clock on meter time, still not able to sleep.

I checked my phone, looked at what my friends had been up, scrolled through their photos and timelines. They'd all been busy, getting drunk, getting pregnant, having babies. Friends I never saw but friends just the same.

I'd another message from Emma, they were coming hourly, what she was eating, wearing, the weather. I much preferred hearing her voice and I'd told her that, but she said talking made it harder, so instead I got messages, to which I always replied, a kiss, or a like, something that didn't invite a response.

I couldn't blame her. This was new for us, and we chose to deal with it in our different ways. The messages were cute at first, but despite her good intentions they now felt a little desperate, like she was overcompensating. Emma predicted she would find this whole thing difficult, she'd never had a relationship like this one and neither had I, so we knew there would be some trial and error. I told her not to worry, a few days' silence wouldn't mean the worst, that we didn't have to communicate every thirty minutes to validate our situation.

On our last night together, Emma and I went out for our farewell dinner. It was a restaurant we'd been to before, by the sea, candlelit, food that tasted more expensive than it was. I'd purposely booked us a table in the corner, away from other diners, some privacy if things got too emotional, not that I thought they would, but I planned for it just in case.

I met her at the hotel reception. Emma looked stunning in her dress and heels, she always looked a world away from a tunic and clipboard. It was a night talked about for a long time, a night set in our diaries, counted down over days and weeks and we assured ourselves we would try to treat it like our first date rather than our last, but as we looked over our menus we realized ending a relationship couldn't be anything other than awkward, regardless of whether it was amicable and planned in advance. So instead I decided to order wine.

And the problem was the more bottles of wine we ordered the less absurd the whole long-distance relationship sounded. And what we both thought the end, wasn't really the end at all and despite the pending miles and time zones between us we agreed we would at least try to make it work, see where it could go, if it was worth holding on to, if one day it could turn into something else. Somehow the night had turned celebratory and rather than us both walking our separate ways as I planned we would, instead we ended up leaving together, back to her apartment, into her bedroom.

This was our relationship now, one that was supposed to end but didn't and hence the reason for Emma's constant contact. She was just worried, I could see why, worried it wouldn't work, that it would eventually fizzle out, that it was only matter of time. It was my job to reassure her that we wouldn't become pen pals, even when I had a job convincing myself most of the time.

★ ★ ★

Still awake, I decided to make myself of use, make my way through the stack of boxes in the corner that Mum had been asking me to sort out since we arrived back on English soil. It was a pointless exercise really, taking everything out, knowing full well I'd probably be boxing them back up when we eventually moved out. But Mum was adamant of course, didn't want to live like squatters, wanted the house back looking sellable. Felt like I was boxing things for boxing's sake, just making things neater, when I suspected wherever we'd end up, these boxes wouldn't be coming with us anyway. Wherever our new home would be, the aim was to travel light, be able to fit our lives in a few small suitcases. Still, it was something to do, something for an insomniac to focus on. I'm glad I did, otherwise I wouldn't have found what I did.

It had fallen out of a book as I moved a pile from a box to my bed. I was about to slip it back inside till I noticed my name and Molly's too. Whatever it was, it was half-finished, written in pencil scribble, words rubbed or crossed out. I should have just slipped it back where it came from, perhaps it wasn't meant to be found, something that should have been thrown out.

I looked at the date, 31st August, that was the night before we flew to Thailand. Before we all took the giant leap.

> *Well my darlings.*
>
> *This is my seventh go at this, think I'm losing the will to live (sorry bad joke)*
>
> *Not even sure why I'm writing this flaming thing. As you already know I'm never one for sentimentality or following other people's advice, so take it all with a pinch of salt, I won't mind if you don't take any of it on board, not that I'd know, being dead by the time you read it.*
>
> *But apparently writing a diary or farewell letter is all part of the cancer experience, like losing my hair, or a sponsored fun run. All part of coping with it, accepting cancer, accepting the possibility of death. Sounds a load of rubbish to me, death is death, no matter if I approve of it or not.*
>
> *Well here goes. Time for me to be profound and all-knowing.*

343

Molly darling.

What a beautiful girl you are. I wish I was able to spend more time with you, but I'm glad of the months we shared. Now I'm not sure how old you'll be when you read this, your dad will know the right time, but the three-year-old Molly that I knew was a girl filled with so much excitement and enthusiasm for the world. I hope that never changes, don't get disheartened, you may not become a princess or an Egyptologist. Chances are you might end up in some office staring at a computer screen like most people. Don't regard that as failure, our jobs don't make us who we are. Just because you're not an explorer doesn't mean you can't still explore. Keep asking those questions. And please don't use your mother's death or even mine as an excuse, it will make me so cross with you if you do. You've not had the easiest start and I wish I could give you all the answers but it isn't really as easy as that. You need to find a way to deal with it, which I'm sure you will, you'll be surprised how much sadness you can deal with, us humans are made of strong stuff.

I'm not going to sugar-coat things, Molly. Life is pretty shit sometimes. You just need to get to the end of it unscathed. The only thing to do is smile and laugh. The art is pretending to know what you are doing. There'll probably be a point where you might hate life a little. Some of it will be about things you can't change, some of it things you can. Just make sure you talk about it, your dad, friend, a professional, yourself, me even. Being a woman is hard and being a girl is even harder, from both sides, men can be cruel, but females can be crueller. You've been blessed with good skin, that's a start. I used to have good breasts and my mother had great breasts too, if you inherit anything from me let's hope it's that.

What else?

Love things or hate them. There should be no in-betweens. It makes life easier, it sounds cold-hearted I know but if it doesn't evoke a reaction, good or bad, then you haven't taken time to understand it fully. Trust me, I thought I hated Leonard Cohen, Margaret Thatcher, your grandfather even. Took me a lot of patience to fall in love with him, most things aren't one-dimensional, especially people, you need to peel back a few layers. To have an opinion you need to educate yourself first, then you'll know definitely if you love and embrace it, or hate and reject it. It's better to be passionate about something or someone. Don't be sat on the fence, or in the middle. Don't just sit and nod.

Look after your dad too. I predict he may need you more than you'll need him, don't tell him that, he acts strong but I do worry. He may never tell you this but he met someone after your mother died, her name was Lilly, you met her once. They loved each other, but it never worked out, you'll have to ask your father why, I still don't understand why myself. Maybe one day their paths will cross again, maybe he might meet someone else. I'd like him to marry again, someone to share things with. You might find that difficult at first, try not to give your new mother a hard time, it will be difficult for her too. You may not see it, but she is only doing her best, she's isn't trying to be Cassie, she's just trying to be your mum, even if you don't want one at the time.

Anything else? I think that covers it just about. I know it's not the conventional letter, if you get stuck, type in 'farewell letters' into Google, I'm sure that covers whatever normal advice dying people give to their loved ones. It's all a bit sappy if you ask me.

Just don't be sad. I'm not, a little scared perhaps.

I wish you a great life, Molly.

I love you. I don't know how much you will remember me, don't worry if you can't, I've taken plenty of photos of us. I hope from those you see how happy you made me. Please know I loved you. You were my best friend. Believe me when I say that, I've only had a few friends who I felt I could tell anything to. You were one of those.

I love you.

Kisses from heaven. Me and your mother will always be looking down.

Tom.

My little boy.

Thank you for everything. And I don't mean just recently, I mean from the day you were born, you only weighed just under seven pounds, a perfect little bundle. Of all my creations, my paintings, my sketches, you are by far my best work. Nothing has changed since then, I may pretend to be a rock, but the worry I had when I shushed you to sleep are the exact same worries I have now knowing I'll have to leave you on your own. I hope I've given enough guidance and resources to be able to fend for yourself, I'm sure you will, you've always been one who copes and adapts.

We both knew there was a chance this cancer would beat me and if you are reading this then I assume it has won. But that is life I'm afraid, and sometimes it doesn't seem fair, and I know you have had a hard few years with Cassie and now me. But it will get better, it always does.

I'm deeply sorry I haven't left you and Molly any money. Me and your father should have handled our finances better, but at least you can sell the house, must be worth a fair bit. Don't worry about any fancy burial for me either, I mean it, Tom. I don't want any fuss, I'd rather Molly have a couple of thousand pounds than have a pointless coffin or headstone. Take her to Disneyland, keep it for her driving lessons, or university. And I don't want to be kept in some urn on a fireplace, I'm not an ornament. Scatter me somewhere pretty. I'm sure you'll find me somewhere you know I would like, just make sure it gets lots of sun, you know I'm not one for shade.

Now in regard to little Molly. You are going to have to deal with some uncomfortable subjects, girls are complicated, both anatomically and emotionally. Without me and Cassie around, you'll need to be aware. Don't be frightened by the changes you'll see in her, things will happen down below and on top, keep an eye out. Please, please, please, get her a bra that fits her when the time comes, take her into town, Marks and Sparks, get her measured by a professional. She'll be really confused about what's happening to her body, be honest with her, educate her, don't let her feel embarrassed and don't let her go to school unprepared. Girls don't need much excuse to bully each other. Anyway, I'm sure you'll know what to do.

I want to thank you for all you've done these last few months, Tom, and don't for one minute think if I don't last the whole of Thailand that you are responsible in anyway. This is the best thing for us, Tom, gives me hope, makes me want to get up each day. I will have so many new memories to take with me, ones I never thought I'd have. I can't wait, not long now. How exciting.

Try to find something you love doing. I know your last two professions didn't sit well with you in a moral sense of the word. But you were good at it, I think you need something with that kind of speed, something to rattle your bones, keep you on your toes. Fireman, a policeman, dashing about the place. Just don't settle for something that makes you miserable. Jobs are about money, yes, but me and your father have had money, lost money and had it again. I preferred not having it, makes you work harder, live smarter. I don't want you back in some warehouse again, you'll be dead by forty if you do. You could always ring Vince, I wouldn't think any less of you if you went back to stalking celebrities, it was the happiest I'd seen you, though I guess Lilly had something to do with that.

Tom, I know you loved Lilly.

You loved her more than you ever loved Cassie. Don't beat yourself up about that, you can't help what you feel. Cassie was loved and I'm sure she knew that even at the very end.

I think we both know you should have gone after Lilly, you didn't do enough. You gave up too soon. Deep down you know that too, I can see it in your eyes, that part of you that wants to get on that plane, find her, fetch her back, but you won't because you use Molly as an excuse, you even use my cancer as an excuse and that isn't fair on either of us. If Lilly is the woman you loved and still love then you do what needs to be done and do it quick. Time to grab onto it with both hands. Or let go completely. Right now, you are doing neither.

I just want you happy, Tom. That's all. That's all a mother ever wants for her son.

If it takes me dying to let you go off and do all the things you need to do, then I can deal with that. What worries me more is if I survive, then you'll always have me as an excuse.

I love you, Tom. I've never told you enough times.

I don't know if any of this has helped you at all, or helped me.

I think it has, at least for me. I'm not writing this again that's for sure, can't waste all my day planning death, I've got Thailand to pack for, too much life still to cram in yet.

Love you both
Mum xxxxxxxxxxxx

★ ★ ★

Next day, I woke up just after ten, quick shower before heading downstairs.

"You want coffee?" Mum said, already pouring me a cup.

"Yes please," I said, giving her a hug she didn't expect.

"What's that in aid of?"

"Just because." I helped myself to cold toast. "Hello, Miss Molly. You have a nice sleep?" ruffling her hair. She nodded, mouth full of fry-up.

"Tom. You had a phone call this morning."

"Who from?"

"Vince of all people."

"How did he sound?"

"Impatient. He was a bit rude to be honest. Said you were ignoring his calls."

"He's left me some voicemails."

"And what did he say in these voicemails?"

"Nothing. Don't worry."

"With Vince, I always worry. What did he say?"

"Says he knows about me and Lilly."

"What do you mean he knows? Knows about what?"

"Proof we were more than just actress and paparazzi."

"And have you seen any of this proof?"

"Yes, he sent me a picture just so I knew he wasn't bluffing."

"What is the photo of? It's nothing rude, is it?"

"It looks far more incriminating than it was. I've seen it before. I thought it had been buried."

"And what is it that Vince wants?"

"An explanation first, I expect. Wants me to grovel probably, after that I don't know."

"Have you rung him back? I guess not."

"I was gonna sleep on it."

"And how long have you slept on this?"

"About two weeks."

"No wonder he sounded rude. Do you think this is wise?"

"Probably not no."

"And now you've had half a month to sleep on it, what is your next move? You are ringing him, I take it?"

"I deleted his number actually."

"Tom. Why?"

"Vince will do what Vince wants, Mum. Me ringing him won't change that."

"He might just genuinely want an explanation. He could be trying to help."

"Now he wants me to kneel. He wants me to beg for

forgiveness. It's just one of his power trips. If anything, it will boil down to the money he's lost and the money he might be able to make back."

"And what if he rings again?"

"Then I'll hang up. And you'll do the same."

"What does this all mean, Tom? It sounds like he's making a threat."

"I don't know, Mum. It could mean a lot of things."

"Do you think Lilly knows?"

"How would I know, Mum? I don't know where she lives. I don't have her number."

"I think you should take Vince's number," she said, taking it from her pocket. "You could be making things worse."

"Whether or not it will be worse will be down to Vince."

"You're sure this is the right move? You seem to be playing a dangerous game."

"I'm not playing any games. If Vince chooses to bring LA here that is down to him."

"What about Emma? Are you going to tell her about this?"

"No. Not unless I have to."

"Does she know about Lilly?"

"Of course she doesn't."

"Here. Take Vince's number. Keep it just in case."

"There won't be a 'just in case,' Mum. Let's eat breakfast, go for a walk after. Forget about Vince," I said.

"I'll keep hold of his number. Better to have it and not need it."

"No, Mum," taking it out of her hand. "We won't need it," throwing it into coal and embers, numbers becoming ash and smoke, knowing that all my silence would change was his tactics.

59

If I got asked one more time what it had been like working with Max again I was gonna fucking scream. I had to ask for a break in the end, took myself out on the balcony to calm myself, get back on point. Rogan was late too, supposed to be here hours ago, held up in traffic I heard, meant it was down to me to hold the fort. I saw Jon briefly when we arrived at the hotel before we were pulled in opposite directions and different rooms. He looked stressed and agitated, well we all did, we knew it was gonna be a long day, repetitive, invasive, worst thing was we had to grin and laugh, which occasionally was genuine, but for the most part it wasn't.

I did try though, I'm never rude, the least I could do was to make it remotely pleasurable. I'd heard of some actors and actresses who'd go out of their way to make it clear they didn't want to be there. I'd like to think I was a little less bitch than that, I mean we all had professions, mine was to answer and theirs was to ask. And I tried my hardest to answer, sometimes a little too hard, gave away too much to be honest. I knew my mouth had gotten me in trouble before so was pretty sure my mouth would do it again. Hopefully not today.

Max was the worst, he'd made journalists cry many a time, walked out on even more. Personally, I always thought he did it for effect, to make people more curious, to give them so little that they yearned to find out more. He was under the impression his best performance was behind camera, that was where he did his best work, what he gave in press junkets was just the scraps. I always thought Max was missing the point, it wasn't a game, it was just sales. Weren't we supposed to be promoting something? Technically we were sales people, trying to get arses on seats, balancing books, trying to justify our ludicrous salaries.

One night years ago, over wine and chocolate, I spoke to Franny about it, got onto the subject of rudest celebrities, which she was more than qualified to give her opinion on, especially when drunk and full of sugar. In fact, she had quite a clear opinion on fame and famous people, none very complimentary.

"Actors assume as they play interesting roles it makes them interesting people," she said. "And that they are always far more interesting than the person sat opposite them."

Biased, of course I didn't agree, though I saw her point. But there was blame on both sides, ask a dull question and you'll probably get a dull response, ask a lazy question, ask a personal question, the answer tended to match what came before. The best ones were the ones that didn't feel like interviews at all, just a conversation, two people having a chat, though that was rare, especially seeing as they lasted about ten minutes. Difficult for me and them to open up or reveal with so little time to do it in. I didn't envy the press, must be a hard task, a horrible game neither player was enjoying. One side trying to say as little as possible, the other trying to get as much as they could. I'd say today had been pretty standard, a few tried their luck, a few just wanted to have fun, a few knew exactly what buttons they were pushing. One asked about my DUI, I was clever enough to handle that, I'd been well trained on dodging the truth, and giving politician answers.

I noticed Sally behind the glass, waving me frantically back inside. I opened the door.

"Rogan is here," she said.

"Can't I stay out here?"

"Are you mad, girl? It's freezing being so high up. Even the sun is cold here."

"Pneumonia is OK with me. I'm surprised he has actually shown this time."

"Don't start all that again. It sounded a genuine reason when he cancelled before."

"More like he is so famous now he can pick and choose what media duties he has to attend."

"What is your problem with him?" she said, sitting beneath a heat lamp yet to be turned on.

"Long story."

"We haven't time for long stories, Lilly."

"Wonder which Rogan has shown up? Gentleman or arsehole?"

"I've never witnessed the latter. He has never been anything but pleasant, a little arrogant but aren't all men his age?"

"You do realize this is a bad idea? I told you and Jon this would probably backfire."

"Don't worry," Sally said, trying to turn on the heat lamp. "Everyone on both sides of the camera has been briefed. The questions will be tame at best."

"The questions might, but the answers won't be."

"Is there something you aren't telling me, Lilly? Did something happen between you and him that I don't know about? If there is then you'd better tell me now."

"Sally, nothing happened. We just don't get along. We never have."

"Well, you need to pretend to now. Bear in mind you are the movie's only love interest. It would be nice if the romance could look remotely genuine, at least for the next hour or so."

I nodded.

"You want something to chill you out?" Sally started to rummage through her things.

"I haven't got a headache, Sally. I doubt there is something in your medicine bag that cures me and Rogan."

"You'd be surprised what cures I'm capable of locating." She handed me a foil strip of tablets and an assuming grin. "Look, take two of these. I'll hold them off for five minutes, whilst you collect yourself."

"Cheers, Sally," I said as she walked back inside. I looked out across the skyline, a view I had been keen to leave but glad to see again.

60

The bridges, the Gherkin, the Palace, the Abbey.

Molly asked how many tube rides it would take to get back to our hotel. I didn't know the exact answer, tried to work it out on my tube map, it was a puzzle I was too tired and worn out to crack, decided to treat us to a taxi home instead, trying not to look at the meter.

"Looks like today has finally beaten her, Mum," I said, noticing Molly had fallen asleep between us.

"She's not the only one. Just because I survived, doesn't mean I've got nine lives." Mum flicked through her new book. "She's had the time of her life, though, me too actually. You been to Key West?"

"No, but I know of it."

She smiled at her page. "Looks a fun time."

"Full of eccentrics and hippies. You'll fit right in."

"You spoke to Emma?"

"I've messaged her a few times, but she probably hasn't got a signal."

"I won't be awake by the time she gets here, will I?"

I shook my head. "And that's assuming there have been no delays either end."

"I bet you're excited."

"More nervous, actually."

"Two months is a long time. I wouldn't be surprised if you drag her to the bedroom and have your wicked way with her first chance you get. Just don't be too loud," she said, nudging me. "I'm in the room next door, remember, and those walls aren't thick."

We stopped at more traffic lights, gave us time to admire the views. Road was a good way of seeing things, wasn't so good for getting anywhere. We'd barely moved, every other mode of transport was quicker than us. I glanced at the meter, it was already at twenty pounds.

"You have slept with her, Tom, haven't you? You can tell me, I'm your mother."

"Sometimes I swear you're controversial just to get a reaction."

"I'm just curious."

"You don't think we have, do you?"

"I don't know, you tell me."

"Well, we have actually."

"That's good news."

"You content now? Or do you want positions next?"

"And, how was it? I mean, being intimate with someone after Cassie. After Lilly."

"How much wine did you have over dinner?"

"I'm not drunk, Tom."

"Yes, we had sex. I shouted out Cassie's name. Then I burst into tears. Is that what you are implying?"

"Did you shout out anyone else's name?"

I picked up a newspaper from off the floor, a battered London Metro, pretended to read.

"I wish you wouldn't keep bringing Lilly up. Especially today of all days. And for your information, I never slept with Lilly."

"When you rang Emma to tell her we were going to Florida, admit a big part of you assumed it would be the end."

"Not really. I knew it could go either way."

"And what would you have preferred?"

"This, obviously. Her coming here, coming with us."

"That's a load of old bull, Tom."

"Mum, don't ruin today. It's been nice, don't turn it nasty just cos you are in the mood for an argument."

"Admit you thought Emma would finish it, and admit that you were hoping for that to be the outcome."

"Why would I want that?"

"Because your heart isn't in it. It never has been, it keeps dragging on because you are too cowardly to stop it. You thought Florida would be the final nail."

"Why are you telling me this now? She arrives in six hours."

"I've told you lots of times."

"And I always give you the same response."

"Tom, it has been a year. If it was going to pass it would have passed a long time ago. You are not being truthful to Emma."

"I thought you liked Emma."

"I do, Tom. Hence why I think it's cruel to lead her on, to lie to her."

"I haven't lied."

"You haven't told the truth either. She is crossing continents for you, Tom."

"Just because I don't love her now, doesn't mean I won't later. She is beautiful, caring, perfect for Molly."

"But she isn't Lilly."

"I don't want to be alone anymore, Mum."

"I don't want that either. But it isn't fair to drag the poor girl all the way to America when you are in love with someone else."

"America makes sense for us. Florida is the right thing to do."

"For us. Not for her."

"No, for all of us. Emma included."

"Well, as long as you know what you are doing," she said, returning to her book, as I turned back to my free newspaper, pretending I was reading when I'm sure out of my window was a better view. Maybe I'd seen enough landmarks for one day.

★ ★ ★

I heard sniffs and sobbing, crying that got louder the longer it was ignored.

357

"What's the matter, Mol?" I peeked round her door. "A nightmare?"

She shook her head.

"Do you want a little light on? Is it too dark in here?"

Again, no talking, another shake of her head.

I sat down on the edge of the bed and sat her on my lap, her head buried into my chest.

"Come on, Molly, what's up?"

"London is scarier than home, Daddy," talking through my T-shirt.

"Is it?"

"It's noisy."

"Wasn't Thailand just as noisy?"

"Do you think Mummy will be cross at me?"

"Cross at what?"

"Cross because Emma is coming to live with us?"

"Course she won't, silly. What's making you think that?"

"Well, I wouldn't like it if I died and you let another girl sleep in my room."

"You don't have to worry about things like that." I ruffling her hair. "Do you not want Emma to come?"

"No."

"No, you don't? Or no you do?"

"I do want her to come."

"Then Mummy won't be cross. She would be happy as long as you were happy too."

"Will one day Emma be my Mummy?"

"These are big questions for this late at night, little miss."

"Shall I call her Mummy yet?"

"Not yet. Just Emma is fine."

"When is she getting here? Soon?"

"Not till later."

"I'm going to stay awake till she gets here."

"You need to close your eyes."

"Can I have a midnight feast? It says twelve, look," she said, pointing at her glow clock.

"Not tonight. We haven't any food anyway."

"Can I watch cartoons?"

"No, Molly. Time for sleep."

"Can Emma wake me up when she gets here?"

"OK, deal," hoping to God she wouldn't last that far.

"Night, Daddy."

"Night, fart pants." I closed the door, already predicting this wouldn't be the last I'd hear from the girl determined to greet our late-night arrival.

★ ★ ★

I too did my best to stay up for Emma, camped out in the front room, remote control, newspapers, magazines, cans of Coke, mini-bar peanuts. Watched a pay-per-view movie that was as long as it was bad, tried to tidy up all the crap on my phone, a spring clean, deleting photos, culling old acquaintances, friend-requesting new ones. Most of what I got rid of was Vince.

Through March and April, I don't know how many phone calls and voicemails he must have left me, I lost count. He was persistent, I'll give him that, but in the end even he must've worked out I wasn't going to play ball, his last message just said I'd made the wrong move, whatever that meant. Whether that was genuine concern or a threat, I couldn't tell, better to expect either. Mum kept asking what I would do if the truth came out about me and Lilly for the world to see, what plan I had if the worst was to happen. Again, Mum had forged her own conspiracies, thought I was welcoming the prospect of me and Lilly being thrust together again. She was wrong, wrong about a lot of things actually. She's always thought she knew how I felt and what I wanted. I wasn't saying things were ideal and sometimes I was conflicted, but one thing I'd always tried hardest to be was realistic. Lilly left and Emma didn't and that was why Emma was the future and

Lilly was the past. Forget who I love or loved more, it made no difference.

No, I couldn't guarantee that Emma and I would work, but I could guarantee if it didn't, it would be nothing to do with Lilly. That was a promise, if our relationship fucked up, it would be our own fuck-up and the only people to blame would be ourselves.

Don't get me wrong, I was nervous, Florida felt a big enough risk, bringing Emma only made it riskier. I knew it was hardly the done thing to move your new girlfriend into your in-law's house. But Lou welcomed the prospect, in fact he downright instigated it and quite frankly wouldn't have it any other way, no matter what other suggestions I put forward. Now there was no more planning, houses had been sold, possessions boxed. Dad's stuff had been donated and given away, a couple of neighbours took a few sculptures, we kept a few small ones, the library, the college where he taught were happy for half a dozen canvases. In centuries people might wonder how and why one man's art could take over one tiny village, I hoped they made it more romantic than it was too big and expensive to take anywhere else.

I heard the hotel door, a quiet knock. Opened it to find Emma looking both tired and relieved, gave her a big hug, took her suitcase through, made her a herbal tea. We didn't stay up long, it was late enough already, went to bed, woke up the next morning strangled by her arms and limbs, Emma cuddling me from behind, like she never wanted to let go. We were still getting used to each other's space and intimacies. We'd only shared a bed a handful of times, both of us had slept alone for so long we'd forgotten the etiquette, hadn't quite worked out who cuddled who, hadn't even worked who slept on what side. Probably why it still felt a little awkward, why neither of us slept too well, why deep down we still longed for our own beds. I'm not sure why I'd lied before when Mum asked if we'd slept together, though technically I hadn't – we had slept together, just not the way Mum had implied and not the way I insinuated when I answered.

61

Next day, after Emma had gotten back some of her missed sleep, after she'd washed the twelve-hour flight out of her hair, I thought it best to get out of our stuffy hotel rooms and get us all some city air. Didn't have any real set agenda, headed to the centre, in search of whatever it had to offer. Molly was on tour-guide duty having already spent the last few days in palaces and dungeons. I was trying to stay enthusiastic, several nights on a thin mattress had ruined my back, it took a coffee-and-cake pick-me-up till I was ready to embrace a new day. It wasn't too difficult to embrace, not a grey cloud in the sky, tourists lapping up every green space, every cafe with an umbrella stand, ice creams, beer and lime wedges. London was at its best and I showed it off as if it was my own.

"Looks like my daughter intends to buy the whole of the city." Emma pointed in front as Molly and Mum browsed more Union Jack tack.

"We better be careful. I have a feeling her new bedroom could be a shrine to Britannia."

"Do you think she will miss England?"

"Once the excitement wears off, yes. I'm sure there'll be a comedown."

"You could pack some things to take with her. That's what I did when I first left for Thailand. Little reminders to tide me over on my down days."

"You had down days? You don't seem the sort."

"Not many, but yes at the start especially. I missed my mother a lot at first."

"Friends?"

"Not really. I had a few friends back home, some from university, but they were never close enough to make me miss them. I've always been used to my own company. The lone wolf, my mother calls me."

"Even lone wolves can get lonely."

"I'm never lonely, Tom. Just a bit funny about crowds. Being small and quiet I tend to find it quite intimidating, tend to get barged over, find it hard to get my voice heard. I'm not odd, am I?"

"Not odd, everyone is wired a little differently. I wouldn't be ashamed or embarrassed about it. My dad was similar, he was much more comfortable in his own space, in his own little world. Have you packed enough of Thailand in your suitcase just in case?"

"Everything I'll miss about Thailand are things I couldn't pack or take with me. And deep down I always knew it wasn't home. I always knew it wouldn't be where I'd settle."

"You sound like me. My travelling days are over, want to find somewhere and stay put."

"Me too." I felt my hand being squeezed tighter.

"Hope I don't start letting myself go," I said. "Put two stone on and start listening to James Blunt."

"What's wrong with James Blunt?"

"A lot is wrong with James Blunt, Emma. Too much to go into."

"You don't think we'll get fat, do you? I do worry about how they eat over there."

"We won't go obese. If we do, we'll get fat together, that way we'll be declining at the same speed. Might be a bit quieter than Thailand though. Clearwater is the mobility scooter capital of the world. Though Tampa isn't too far away if you fancy a pulse from time to time."

"I quite like the quiet, actually."

"You won't get bored, I hope."

"Not of you or your family."

"Good." Giving her a kiss, forgetting she wasn't always comfortable being affectionate in public.

Molly came darting over.

"Daddy, what's happening over there?"

I looked through the people, a small crowd, staff positing metal barriers, media setting up cameras. "Seeing as it's Leicester Square, I'm guessing Hollywood has arrived."

"Can we go and see, Daddy?"

"We can take a quick look, yes."

Emma held back, her arm stiffened. "I don't know, Tom. It looks like people shouldn't be over there, seems busy. Molly, you might get squashed."

"I won't," she said clinging onto my other arm. "Please, Daddy."

"A quick look won't hurt," Mum said. "Never know, we might see someone famous."

"I doubt it," I said. "They normally don't start till it's night-time, I'm guessing they are setting up for later. We'll have a walk over. Don't worry, Emma, I promise no one will get squashed or trampled, especially you."

"You guys go. I'll stay here. I'll have a look around the shops. I don't mind."

"Emma, you'll be fine. I'll look after you, I promise."

"OK, Tom," she said, taking a deep breath, squeezing my hand a little tighter, smiling like she always smiled, like it was for someone else's happiness rather than her own.

"What is the first thing you want to do when we get to Florida?" I asked the table.

"Eat more ice cream," Molly said, laughing hysterically. "Kick Lou up the bum."

"Molly, don't play with your food. And sit on your chair properly, please," Mum said, not looking best pleased with her granddaughter. "Me, I want to eat buffalo shrimp with blue-cheese dressing. Followed by she crab soup, followed by molasses bread. Eat everything I've read about."

"Thinking with your stomach as always, Mum. Emma, you?"

"Just looking forward to it all, really. Probably go to the beach. Oh, and the Walt Disney castle. Or is that a bit predictable? What about you?"

I sipped through my straw. "Me, I want to go for a drive. Take Lou's car out, get to know the place, find my bearings, work out where things are." I looked down at my dessert, hardly started and I was already defeated. "Help me with this cheesecake, Emma? I'm not making a dent here."

"I can't even finish my tiramisu, let alone yours. Besides I don't like cheesecake, remember?"

"What? You like James Blunt. You don't like cheesecake. I can't see me and you lasting."

"You don't mean that, do you?"

"Please tell me you like normal cheese though. I can't trust anyone who doesn't like cheese. Answer wisely, this could be a deal breaker."

"I like cheese, well not all cheese. I don't like Stilton."

"I can live with that, I suppose. You OK?" noticing her yawn. "Jet-lagged?"

"A little, yes."

"I'll get the bill, head back, have an early night."

She smiled. "I'll pop to the lady's room."

"Can I come?" Molly jumped up.

"Of course, you can," she said. "Give that face of yours a wipe. You've got more ice cream on your mouth than in your tummy," she said as she took Molly's hand, made her way through the busy restaurant, weaving past giant pizza plates and waiters grating parmesan.

For a moment, Mum and I didn't speak, concentrated on our desserts.

"Tom."

"Can I try some of your *panna cotta*?" I said, taking my spoon to her plate.

"Tom."

"I prefer yours to mine."

"Tom."

"Mum, I know what you are going to say," I said, avoiding eye contact.

"It means she'll be here, doesn't it?"

I nodded.

"What are you going to do?"

"Nothing."

"Nothing?"

"How can I go?"

"Because of Emma?"

"What do you expect me to say? Oh, Emma I'm just popping out to see the woman I still love, I'll only be an hour."

"You could make up another excuse."

"Even if I did want to go. You assume Lilly wants to see me."

"She might."

"She doesn't. She never answered my calls. She's back with Max. The last person she'd want to see is me."

"I don't care if she does or doesn't. I want you to see her because I want you to get those answers you were never given. Get that closure you need to move on with your bloody life."

"And what plausible excuse could I possibly give to Emma?"

"Just say an old friend wanted to catch up with you for a few drinks."

"Let's say I did go, which I'm not. How would I even get close enough? This isn't some farmhouse in the middle of nowhere, this will be heavily policed, security will be tight."

"You've gotten close before. Closer than anyone else has ever got. You're a smart boy. I'm sure you'll figure it out."

Just then we noticed Emma walking back, Molly in her arms, as we switched the conversation back to something light-hearted, calamari or cancer, anything but Lilly.

62

The worst was over. Panic attacks subsided. I was en route, nothing anyone could do about it now. I'd spent the last hour being talked to, grilled by Sally, advised by publicists, warned by PR guys, all huffing and puffing as they became experts on meteorology, studying change in wind speed, forecasting cloud movements, contemplating the skies outside. All day London had predicted showers, so what umbrella and how to use it had taken over my last three hours. Now in the car, looking out my tinted windows, it was a worry over nothing, the threat of heavy rain was an empty one and wet hair looked a tragedy Team Goodridge had narrowly avoided. Not sure what all the fuss was about, wasn't like I'd be camped out in it like most of those poor fans and paparazzi and it would take more than heavy drizzle to put me out of this good mood.

I always looked forward to premieres, made me remember what my profession was, forget all the bullshit that comes with it and just sit in a movie theatre and be entertained, watch actors and actresses and made-up stories become reality for a couple of hours. Closest I get to feeling a rock star or a big-time ball player too, the build-up of knowing hundreds and thousands were about to scream my name. The fact Tom might be here may have been a reason for my big smile too, in fact I'd been smiling since I first woke up this morning.

We weren't moving fast, though traffic rarely did in London. I could already hear the noise, the cheers and whoops, so we must have been close. I took out my mirror from my bag, one final make-up check, checked my cell for the first time today, message from Mum reminding me Ringo was at the vet's, reminder from Max reminding of where I was and what I wasn't allowed to do.

I replied to both, told Mum to give him a kiss from me, told Max I'd get Tom to say hi. Of course, I regretted it instantly, I thought it would be funny, thought he'd know I'd only said it as a joke, to make him squirm. Quickly I sent a second reply, making sure he understood the gesture was meant as a joke, worried Max was already plotting his retaliation. I bet he hated every second of this, the one thing he had no say in, even he couldn't meddle in me fulfilling my media obligations, made even better by the fact he was back in LA, not by choice of course, commitments he was unable to decline or delegate, otherwise he would've been here right beside me, strolling the red carpet, arm in arm, forced smile and gritted teeth.

I hadn't told anyone, but I very nearly drove to Tom's house. I had a rare day off, told myself there was no chance Tom would be in London, decided to make a mad dash for it, got my concierge to secretly get me a car and driver, drive me halfway up the country before I had a reality check and told him to turn back around. I wasn't thinking straight, thinking with my heart, not with my head.

Filming with Max was nearly over as well, he'd promised once the film was made I could do what I wished, in fact he encouraged it, said it would make the media go wild. Though that was before, being with me every day had made him territorial again, made him jealous. I got the feeling nothing would change once the filmed wrapped, in fact I expected it to get a whole lot worse. Hence my urgency, hence my erratic thinking.

Problem was, the mood I was in, being here, being caught up in all the euphoria, the less concerned I was about what punishment would come mine or Tom's way. A dangerous mood to be in, a mood that had repercussions, both good and bad. But I couldn't live my whole life this way, a constant threat over my head, my life always able to be bargained and bartered with. Besides I was running out of time, tomorrow was another airplane, tomorrow might be too late.

Even now I still couldn't work out why Tom meant so much to me, how I knew I needed him. It wasn't complicated, I know sometimes love can be, but this wasn't. Tom made me wake up happy and go to bed happy, look forward to what was coming next, be satisfied with yesterday, no man had done that before.

The car stopped.

The driver told me we'd arrived, not that I needed telling.

Deep breath.

"Time to shine, Lilly," I said under my breath as the car door opened, noise and flashes hit me like a wave, a wall of faces when I was looking for only one.

63

I looked at my watch. I was a mess, head in my hands, staring at an ugly carpet, working out what to do with my hands. I'd have been smoking too, if I hadn't already given up.

The rest had gone to bed hours before, I had Mum to thank for that, she orchestrated the yawning and early baths and hot milk so Molly was in bed before it got dark, with Emma and Mum following not long after. Despite being clear that I had no intention of going, Mum still planned for it, got rid of reasons not to, hoping it would be enough to make me reconsider. I was glad of the time to think at least, to have my own company, be away from Emma so I didn't feel so fucking awful having to smile and lie, whilst mother and son plotted my potential escape.

I was genuinely lost for words when I saw Lilly's face on that first billboard and realized what it meant, I'm surprised I kept it together, more surprised Emma didn't notice, in fact I don't even think she'd heard of the movie or its cast. Jesus, it was still awkward though, could've been a lot worse. Molly didn't recognise Lilly's poster thank God, too preoccupied by all the excitement of banners and fans. Mum just gave me a look, a look that said it all, though she knew better than to say anything out loud. Mum asked me on the tube ride home if I had known Lilly would be here, if this trip to London was premeditated, I assured here it wasn't, which was the God's honest truth, though I could understand why she'd asked, most coincidences weren't that believable, this one included.

It would be easy to go. Leicester Square wasn't far, a straight line from Euston, just over a mile away, walkable even.

I looked at my watch again.

Then again. And again. Every couple of minutes.

64

I looked everywhere, stayed on the red carpet longer than I should, let myself be photographed, let people stick microphones in my face, answered their questions, even let myself be rained on when everyone else rushed inside, let my hair get wet, my arms, my dress, everything Team Goodridge told me not to do. Inside I sipped champagne, made conversation, all of the time I was checking doorways, looking over people's shoulders, excusing myself for no reason other than to climb steps, get high enough where I could see across the hundreds of guests, scan the room, check every face. Even as they called us in, as we got to our seats, as the lights dimmed and the title music played, even then, rather than digest the film, analyse my performance, appreciate the script, all I could do was search, look at fire exits, at the back of heads, searching for Tom, when all I could see was a black room and a glowing movie screen. I was at the bar, flute glasses had turned to cocktails, cocktails were about to become shots. Jon was to blame, he was the catalyst for all the drinking, said we deserved to enjoy ourselves, said getting 'sozzled' as he put it was completely acceptable, implying it may not be with the others. Can't imagine he wanted our media campaign to turn into a worldwide booze tour. I suppose Jon was right though, we did deserve one night to cut loose, though most of the praise should have gone to him and his editing staff for what they pulled together up there for all to see. The movie looked and read so much better on screen than it ever had on paper, and that included me, I found it all very nostalgic hearing my awful accent again, all those greens of England, oceans I was still just as fond of as I had been before. The end even made me cry, even though

I knew what was coming, though sometimes that was worse, like even though your body braced itself, it was still gonna hurt just the same. I wasn't quite sure where we were, wherever we were it was gorgeous all round, awesome view, hot bar staff, beautiful drinks, it couldn't have been that far from Leicester Square, as I was only in the car for a matter of minutes between being dragged from one bar and dropped off at another. Somehow, I was alone, I'd lost the girls or they'd lost me. I checked over my shoulder, they were on the dance floor en masse, slut dropping and dancing dirty. Few more shots and I wouldn't be far behind them. "Yo, Goodridge in the house," said a voice behind me.

I turned around, I didn't mean to look so shocked.

"You stopped giving hugs these days or what?" his arms spread out.

"I thought I'd be the last person you'd want a hug from."

"You're my favourite person to fall out with, you know that," he said, grabbing me off the floor.

"You drunk?"

"Only a little. Not as much as Jon. That guy is hilarious, keeps pinching my ass. What you reckon?"

"To what?"

"The movie."

"I liked it. You?"

"I'm surprised I managed to stay awake." He leaned his bicep against the bar.

"It was a lot more fast paced than I thought it would be. Especially as we all did was drink tea and stroll gardens."

"I enjoyed watching me and you up there."

"I bet you did. Quite the convincing couple. Well, not our accents, but the rest of it."

"Our accents were a joke. That's the last time I go British."

"Why did you even take on the role? It was like the exact opposite of a Rogan movie."

"Not my idea, trust me. My manager thought it would make

my IMDB look a bit more varied. Y'know, something animated, something serious. The dude's not my manager anymore anyways so I'll be in a loincloth or blowing stuff up soon, don't you worry."

"Do you mind that? Being the hero all the time?"

"I just wanna get paid in the easiest way possible. You wanna drink?"

"I'd love one, thanks. I'm glad we've finally got a chance to properly talk just me and you."

"Oh," he smiled, like I was flirting when I wasn't, as he ordered us some drinks.

"Just wanted to say I'm sorry for what happened before."

"Before?" watching as the barmaid pretty much flopped her breast in his lap.

"Before. When I invited you back?"

"Oh that. Dude I haven't even thought about it."

"I shouldn't have led you on like that. That was wrong of me."

"Hey man, stuff happens. I was mad at the time probably, but I'm easy on shit like that."

"I don't know what I was thinking."

"You don't have to explain yourself, Goodridge. It's cool. Though you may be the first girl to turn me down. I'm not used to that sort of rejection."

"Don't worry, it was nothing to with you, promise. I had a lot of stuff going on then. There was a guy, it was, well it was complicated."

"Let me guess. The guy at the restaurant that night, right?"

"That was him, yes."

"What's the deal with you and him? He was on set too, wasn't he?"

I nodded. "I guess what I'm saying is, I know that me and you haven't always seen eye to eye. But can we just put a line through it? Start over?"

"Works for me. Shall we drink to that?"

"We shall."

"Let's make a toast."

"Only if you make it. I'm awful at them."

He raised his glass, I raised mine too. "Never above you. Never below you. Always by your side."

"Rogan, that is so cheesy," I laughed.

"Something my old coach used to make us say."

"Well, cheesy or not, I like the sentiment," I said as we downed our drinks and ordered more.

"Where is the guy, anyway?" Rogan said, sucking his lime wedge.

"Which guy?"

"The guy. The one in the restaurant. The complicated guy."

"Still just as complicated."

"I saw him earlier."

"Where? Here?"

"No," sucking another lime wedge. "Back at the movie theatre."

"Where, inside?"

"No outside in the crowd. Only briefly. Well I think it was him."

"Did he say anything?"

"Nope."

"How comes I didn't see him? Why didn't he call my name?"

"Goodridge, everyone calls out our names. I thought I heard you were back with Max?"

"Rogen, you are being serious? You saw him? You are not screwing with me?"

"Why would I screw with you? I saw him."

"Look I gotta go. Can you… "

"Don't worry, you go. I'll cover for you."

But I was already gone.

65

Not quite sure of where to be, I quickly realized I'd made the wrong choice. I was too far away, there were far too many bodies in front of me, too many yells and cheers. The energy was building, fans starting to get territorial over their position from the front, barging and jostling for a better view. It was mostly women, young girls, Rogan fans, screaming and crying, puppy love and puppy yelps. I looked across the sea of heads, the paparazzi piled in row after row like a football team roster, that was where I needed to be, there was fewer of them, they were closer, more chance of being seen or heard.

Right Tom. Think.

I checked my clock, I still had time, a few limos had arrived but not people I recognized, probably producers and cinematography, small-part cast members. I'd brought my camera, found some old press pass in my camera bag on the tube ride here, Vince gave it to me when the whole adventure started, said it could be useful to get into places we had no right being in, turned out Vince was right. The shot pulled off, managed to elbow and fight my way across to the other side unnoticed, by sheer luck security were momentarily preoccupied with some altercation in the crowd, meant I could slip past, quickly sandwich myself between other paps, shoved my camera in front of my face, pretended I was taking photos, now it was just a case of waiting.

Jon was first to arrive, though not many recognized him, it was only when more well-known actors and actresses started to step out onto the red carpet that the screams and shouts erupted, especially Rogan. He was on the carpet a long time, chatting to fans, talking selfies, signing chests, before making his way over to the press area. I took photos of course, joined in with the melee of flash bulbs and shouting. I could've sworn he noticed me, for one brief moment we crossed stares. I nearly said something, wanted to shout out, not sure what, anything so he might tell Lilly I was here. But I didn't, he was handed an umbrella and ushered inside.

Lilly was last to arrive, the main event, and the mood of the paps around intensified. The smell of money was in the air, any previous camaraderie or friendship had been forgotten, everyone in it for themselves, knowing she was the one who'd make standing in the rain and cold worthwhile. The crowd exploded when she stepped out of her limousine, as she waved and greeted the fans around her. She took longer than most, slowly making her way round the crowds, making sure every fan got their few seconds, took her time, even with the rain, she made sure the audience could walk away with a memory or memento. I had a horrible feeling she would run out of time, not to mention the weather, the rain had worsened and the film would be starting soon, I kept looking at her team behind her, they looked concerned, kept checking their watches, talking into earpieces. As she started to walk over, towards me and the dozens of cameras, I knew this was it, I wasn't sure what I'd do, but I would do something. I had to.

Then I heard a bang. Ringing in my ear. Things went blank.

66

When I came to, there was blood. I patted my head, again more blood, not a lot but blood nonetheless. I looked up and there stood Ludo, a smile that wasn't friendly, offering me his hand, telling me Lilly had gone inside.

Strangely, I wasn't mad, fighting him wouldn't solve anything, let him pick me up instead, even walked with him through London. I was just exhausted, failure was exhausting and Ludo was right. I'd fucked him, so he'd fucked me. I didn't begrudge him his tiny revenge, just bad timing of when Ludo decided to seek it, the worst timing.

The reality was, my chance was blown. I didn't have a plan B. I didn't know how else to get inside. I didn't even have her number, just some vague memory of the last three digits, from all the times I'd ignored and deleted her calls before. Instead we found the nearest bar, somewhere I could let my wounds heal and Ludo could buy us both a strong drink. Get home, forget Lilly, forget tonight, but not till I'd had a few more drinks, something to get rid of my headache, stop everything from hurting.

"You married, Ludo?"
"She live back home."
"Kids?" taking a mouthful of Guinness.
He nodded. "Girls," holding up four fingers.
"You've been busy. Guess you don't see them much."
"I see enough."
"You must miss them."
"My wife not so much," he grunted. "She break balls."

"How long you been together?"

"Twelve years."

"And how long you been doing this? Chasing celebrities?"

"Two years, I think."

"You still enjoy it?"

"I don't think about enjoy. It gives money. If I do this few years longer, then Ludo give up, go home rich, get fat, let my five women look after me." He took a big gulp of beer. "How's head?"

"Sore."

Ludo laughed.

"You still haven't apologized," I said, rubbing my head.

"Ludo not sorry that is why." He took a handful of nuts. "You fuck with my money. I fuck with your money."

"Well, I guess we are even. I'm sorry I lied before. Sent you off on those wild goose chases."

"I sorry I make you bleed. Ludo hit harder than should."

"You couldn't have picked a worse time."

He laughed. "Ludo picked perfect time."

"How long is she in London for?"

"She go tomorrow. Midday I think."

"You following behind her, Ludo? America?"

"No. Too far. I work Europe. Have friend in America. He take over."

"What is going on with her and Max? Last I heard they were getting pretty serious. Is he here in London?"

"Max here. Arrive today."

"At the premiere?"

"No premiere. He somewhere else."

I took a few more sips of my drink, it was too thick, half of it left, should have ordered something I could have finished quicker.

"Have you heard any rumours?"

"Rumours?"

"About Lilly? Have you heard about her with anyone else?"

Ludo looked confused behind his beer. "Ludo hear nothing."

I looked around the pub, it was quiet and late, I was nearly out of questions. Ludo wasn't asking much back. I needed to get some sleep, get my head back into reality, back on Florida, work out how to explain a head wound when as far as they knew I hadn't left our hotel room.

"Thanks for the drink, Ludo. I better start making tracks."

"Stay one more. I pay. You finish drink."

"I better not. Early start tomorrow."

"I tell you more about Goodridge," he smiled.

"Honestly, I better go."

"Tomorrow? See you at airport?"

"You wave her off for me." I picked up my stuff. "Good luck, Ludo. Hope you earn that big pay cheque someday. Hey, go easy on Goodridge."

Ludo stood up, offered me his hand. "You good man, Thomas. I don't like you. But you are good man."

"See you around."

Just then my phone buzzed. I looked down. Had to double take. Make sure I wasn't seeing things.

Three digits.

Three digits I'd ignored for over a year, but three I wouldn't ignore tonight.

67

In the panic to arrive on time, I'd arrived too early. It was agony and waiting felt cruel, bare knees, open toes, my body brittle, my bones ached like I could be snapped. A friend at the party lent me her coat and despite the body of fur its warmth wasn't enough. The champagne had made me brave and hot-bloodied, both had started to wear off just when I needed them the most.

I was already concocting the various lies I may have to tell the next day if and when my absence was questioned. Rogan said he'd cover for me, though I didn't know how much I could trust him, though to be honest he'd been cool so far, helped sneak me out, grabbed me a car, didn't ask too many questions, didn't try and talk me out of it.

I was still a little out of it, the last half hour had been a blur, adrenaline had subsided, reality was taking hold, I was starting to wonder what the hell I was about to do or say. I hadn't expected Tom to answer seeing as he never had before, I very nearly hung up out of sheer shock. Had to think on my feet, think of where we could meet, away from everything, somewhere I could get to in a city I barely knew myself. Tom didn't say much, agreed we needed to talk, asked me where and when, like I'd planned that far ahead.

God, I was petrified. I wasn't prepared for face to face. Talking on the phone felt safer, I could hang up, he could hang up, at any point we could both escape. Meeting up like this, being able to see him up close, see what damage I'd caused, how much he hated me and how much I still loved him. It felt far too intimate.

The park was quiet, lifeless, stood under a street lamp on a street corner, in designer gown and floor-length furs. I was more prostitute than princess and I would have laughed if my jaw wasn't froze shut by cold, laughter would have helped stopped the nerves. Funny I should choose this place of all places to meet, though not really, the only place I knew close enough to escape or flee, not that I would need to. I looked up, power lines, buildings so huge they made the sky look possible. I should have been more scared than I was out there in the dark and although I felt some fear I wasn't fearful for my safety, just scared he wouldn't show, but even more scared that he actually would.

Suddenly I heard something, the sound of iron gates being rattled, bushes and twigs being disturbed. I kept looking, maybe it was nothing, the wind and shadows playing tricks with me, just like they were supposed to. But then I saw him, watched as a silhouette landed on its feet, I had to stop myself from running to him, instinctively it felt the right thing to do, to sprint toward him, and him to sprint to me, but he didn't run and nor did I. His walk was slow, his shoulders slumped, his body awkward. I caught glimpses of his face going in out of light and dark, he was hard to read, it changed with every step he got closer, from relief to anger, to happiness to disappointment. Like he didn't quite know the appropriate emotion, torn between whether to slap me or never let me go.

68

"Hi." I smiled, letting him know this was a happy invitation, not the opposite, not that it worked. He looked as uncomfortable as I felt.

"I'm sorry. Should have found somewhere indoors, with an open fire and good whiskey," he said, trying to lighten the mood.

"You caught me off guard when you answered. It was the first place I thought of." He seemed unconcerned about where he was, more concerned with why.

"Just making it clear. I didn't know you were here. Me being in London at the same time was not deliberate. I wasn't following you. Just some bizarre coincidence."

"I'm just glad you are, Tom, and that we finally get to talk. I think there are things that need to be said between… Oh my God what happened to your head? You're bleeding." Instinctively I went to touch him.

"It's nothing," he jolted back, like it would do him harm if I came too close. "Why am I here? What happened between me and you?"

"I can't tell you all of it. I wish I could," I said, sitting down, as he did the same.

"Then tell me what you can."

"It was for the best, believe me, I did it to protect you."

"Protect me from what?"

"From having your life turned upside down."

"Lilly, I could've handled myself."

"You wouldn't have handled this, trust me."

"You were an unknown once, Lilly. You assume I couldn't cope being thrust into your world, but I could. I was prepared to go that far."

"I know that. But I wasn't protecting you from fame, Tom."

"Stop speaking in riddles and just tell me the truth. What were you protecting me from?"

"I know you want an explanation, but I can't give you one."

"Then this is just more games. Don't screw me over again, Lilly. I barely survived the last time. Took me a long time to get my head clear of you, took me a long time to get back up. I loved you. I thought you felt the same."

"I did. I do."

"Then what changed?"

I went blank. It would have been so easy just to tell him, and even though I'd taken a big enough risk by both of us being here, I knew telling the truth was a step too far.

"What is it you want from this, Lilly? Friendship? My forgiveness? You don't deserve either." He stared right at me, he looked strangely triumphant, like this had been rehearsed in his head many times over, like it was a relief to finally say it to my face.

"I'm sorry for how things ended, Tom. I really am. I promise you it wasn't what I wanted either."

"You are making no sense. I remember the words you told me. They came from your mouth, Lilly, no one else's. You ended it. And the way you ended it was brutal and unfair."

"I didn't have a choice."

"From what I can see, you had a choice and you chose to walk away. You chose the easy option."

"Easy? You think walking away from you was easy? It was one of the hardest things I've ever done and every day I have to try and tell myself it was the right thing. I know it doesn't seem that way to you. But don't think for one second that I don't think about you. I miss you. I want you back, Tom."

I looked at him. It was the first time his eyes had softened. He stepped closer.

"You're with Max."

"Not for long, I assure you."

"A lot has changed since last year, Lilly"

"I'm sure it has. It's been a long time. My God, how is your mom?"

"She is fine."

"I thought about her all the time. Has she still got...?" I paused purposely.

"No, that's all over and done with. She won't get the all-clear for another five years, but looks like she's beaten it."

"And Molly? I sent her a birthday card."

"Thank you. You didn't have to be so generous."

"Did she spend it on anything nice?"

"No, not yet, we've only been back in the country a little while."

"Where have you been?"

"Thailand." He looked apologetic, like he shouldn't have been allowed.

"How cool. I'm jealous. How long were you out...?"

"Lilly, I've met someone else."

"Oh." I felt winded. Took me a few moments to find my breath, think of some words.

"I had to move on."

"Of course."

"You left me, Lilly. Left me in every which way possible. And I might have been able to cope with it if I had known the reasons behind it, but I never got a reason and I wasn't able to cope with it."

"What's her name?"

"Does it matter?" Tom paused.

"I was just... "

"Her name is Emma."

"Is it serious?"

"Yes."

"Do you love her?"

He took his time to answer, too long.

"Yes, I do."

"More than you loved me?"

"What do you want me to say? That I loved you more? The fact is, she stayed and you didn't. We have a life planned, a future. You never gave me that."

"But what if I can now? What if I stay? What if I can promise us a future?"

"I don't believe you, Lilly. I don't trust what you will do next. I wish I did, but I just don't."

"And how can I change that? How can I make you trust me again?"

"I don't know." He shrugged.

"Do you want to be with me again, Tom? Can you see a future? Me, you, your mom, Molly."

"That is all I ever wanted, Lilly. That's what I thought our future was. Then you went to New York and that all changed."

"Then let's do it. Let's start over. Here. America. Anywhere, I don't care."

"Lilly, just because it's all I ever wanted, it still doesn't change things. I'm with Emma now."

"But you love me more than her."

"That isn't enough right now."

"If it isn't, why are you here? Why did you show up tonight? To the premiere? Here? You know deep down that me and you had something."

Tom didn't answer.

"Tom, I'm flying back tomorrow."

"Lilly, I can't…"

"Please, Tom. We might never get this chance again."

"Lilly. I'm…"

"I've thought long and hard about us and I thought I could get over you, but I couldn't and it doesn't sound like you got either me either."

"Lilly, your life is a whirlwind. I don't want it. I don't want that life for me for or my family. We have had enough chaos."

"I can't help who I am and what I've become. You think I want chaos. I want the same things as you. You know I want out of this, I've told you how trapped I feel. I want you and your family and everything that comes with it."

"I can't just ditch her and the plans I've made based on promises that I know you won't be able to keep. Promises you made me before."

"I can't tell you who you should be with. I can only tell you how I feel. I love you, Tom, more than her. I need you more than her."

"I need to go. I need time to think this through. I wasn't expecting this."

"Come see me tomorrow. Please Tom, before I go."

"Is that an ultimatum?"

"Meet me here again. Please Tom. I fly just after lunch, but I can find some time to sneak away. You message me what time and I'll be here, promise. Meet me here, same place. Eleven."

We both started to step away from each other, about to go our separate ways.

"Lilly." Tom turned back to me. "Are you sure you want this? Me? Us?"

"Isn't it obvious?"

"Nothing has ever been obvious with me and you, Lilly."

And he smiled, a sad smile, like his heart was neither broken nor fixed, like he knew someone was going to get hurt, he just didn't know who.

69

On the tube, I thought about Lilly. On the walk back to the hotel, I thought about Lilly. Even as I undressed myself, I thought about Lilly, stared at the bathroom mirror and tried to stop myself thinking about Lilly.

I wish I didn't feel so excited. It should have been an easy decision, but it wasn't. What she told me was everything I'd wanted to hear, what I'd always wanted. Lilly was a whirlwind and she was chaos and she was dangerous, and I should never want those kinds of flaws. But to me they weren't flaws, they were what I loved about her in the first place and more importantly what I used to love about myself. And you know what, I think my family love that too, both Mum and Molly have that same impulsive streak, where adventure and uncertainty was what kept the smiles on our faces.

Lilly assumed I wanted her to change, that I wanted her to calm down, to settle, to give up. I would never ask her to do that and she wouldn't be the same person if she did. She was perfect and thought I did my best to hide it, to be mad and angry, the only thing I wanted to tell her was I loved her and that would never change. Lilly was strong and beautiful and talented, but she was fragile, she was complicated, she needed someone to look after her. That person would always be me.

I didn't know how I would break it to Emma. It would be painful. It would be one of the worst things I'd ever had to do. Mum was right, America was the right thing to do, but Emma wasn't. And it was better to be honest now, not let it get any worse, she didn't deserve this, any of it. Emma was strong, beautiful and talented too and she needed someone, but that someone was never me, I think she probably knew that too.

I turned the lights off and went to check on Molly, see if she was OK.

Fast asleep on a single bed I found them both, curled up, nose to nose. Emma's hand cradling Molly's little head, the same way Cassie used to when Molly was sick or scared, the same way any mother would be with their child. Affection I never thought I'd see again, affection I had no right to rip apart.

70

That was a lie what I said to Tom. I said it wasn't, but it was an ultimatum. If he didn't meet me tomorrow, then I'd have to assume that would be the end. If Tom didn't know by tomorrow, he would never know.

Back at the hotel I tried to get warm, got straight into bed, clothes and all, pulled the duvet over myself and tried to work out tonight, tried to remember what was said, try to decode his reactions, the way he looked at me, try to understand what he might do next.

Suddenly there was a knock at my door. You can tell a lot about a knock, this one told me whoever was behind it was coming in regardless of whether I chose to open the door or not.

"Hello, trouble."

"What the fuck are you doing here?"

"Nice to see you too."

For a few moments, I couldn't speak.

"You are supposed to be in LA."

"And you were supposed to be at an after-party. Seems we both got a little lost tonight."

"Have you been following me?"

He didn't answer, started to make himself comfortable, took off his suit jacket, unfastened his bow tie.

"Max, we made a deal."

"And I have let you come to London, haven't I?"

"It was supposed to be on my own."

"We both knew what you were up to. And so far, you have proved me right," he smiled as he made his way to the kitchen, poured himself a whiskey. "Did you seriously think I would let you come here on your own?"

"LA was a lie then? You have been here all along?"

"Not all along. I arrived this morning, thought I'd surprise you at the party but I was informed you had gone AWOL. Don't worry, I've had my spies watch you whilst I was engaged. Seems you've been quite the busy bee around town haven't you, Lilly G?" he threw an olive into his mouth. "Don't look so worried. This has gone so much better than I'd predicted. So much more interesting than I ever would have envisaged."

"And what was your prediction? Tom?"

"The lovely sweet and innocent Tom. I wonder if he'll show tomorrow. Will it be her? Will it be you? It's quite the finale, isn't it?"

"How do you know… ?"

"Of course I know, darling. I have eyes everywhere, even at this late hour."

"Who?"

"Who is of no concern." Max sat himself down on the couch, crossed his legs, throwing more olives into his mouth.

"It's Sally, isn't it? She's the mole?"

"Poor Lilly. You don't trust anyone these days."

"Vince then?"

Max clapped. "Quite the sleuth."

"I don't understand."

"You're not supposed to understand. All you need to know is, this has worked out perfectly. Now stop pacing and sit down." He patted the seat next to him. "We need to talk about tomorrow."

"I'm not fucking sitting down. Get out!" pointing to the door.

"Tomorrow I want you to meet Tom."

"How do you know he will show?"

"Of course he will show. He's as predictable as you, probably even more so."

I sat down. "Max, what do you want?"

"I want you to meet with Tom tomorrow. I want you to have this happy ending. Do you think you could kiss him?"

"Why do you want that?"

"Isn't it obvious?"

"No. This whole fucking thing is not obvious."

"A story needs balance, Lilly, good and bad sides, but an audience needs to empathise with both, root for either, make them undecided."

"And you think this is how you seek empathy? Making me into the enemy?"

"You catch on, finally."

"I hate you."

"I know. I'm good at this, aren't I?"

"What if I leave now? What if I never see Tom again?"

"Do you still need to ask? His mother may have survived but my legal team have enough dirt on her son to make her wobble again."

"I don't believe you."

"Only one way to find out."

He was smirking.

"What makes you think Tom would kiss me? He probably hates me."

"Kiss or slap. Either wins for me. Just don't make it obvious. I don't want it to look too staged."

"Will someone else be there? Some fucking camera lens?"

"Why of course. There has always been a camera."

I walked over to the champagne bottle, found a glass.

"Has Vince always been in England? Was he here last year?"

"Vincent does as he is told. He has been equally intrigued by your relationship with Tom. He's been waiting a long time to get a picture of you two again."

"Again?"

He smiled, undid his tie, put his feet up.

"What do you get out of this, Max?"

"Not me, them out there," he said, pointing out of the window. "Keep them on their toes. Keep it interesting."

"I'm not a fucking movie, Max. I'm not some fucking *Truman Show*."

He laughed. "Oh, but you are."

"I thought you loved me?"

"I do. I still do."

"Then why this?"

"Movies have become unnecessary, too expensive. Reality is more fun."

"This is my life, Max. I'm not yours to own. I don't care if you sell photos of me and Tom. I don't care if you want to try and take Tom's child from him. We will fight back and fight harder than you ever will."

"There is no need for threats, Lilly. You can have your moment with Tom, but you will come back to me."

"Fuck you."

"Heroes, villains, villains, heroes. It will always change and revert, but eventually you will end up with me. That has always been the plan."

"I hate you."

"That, I have become used to. But I love you, Lilly, more than Tom. You are mine."

"What if I don't see Tom tomorrow? Your plan is screwed."

"Screwed?" he laughed. "You have no idea, do you? You think I haven't covered every eventuality?"

"I could just run away. From Tom, from you, from everyone."

"I can already see the headline. It would be quite the search and rescue, wouldn't it?"

I started to cry, felt myself struggling to breathe.

"Hey, hey, don't worry." He put his arm around me. "This has a happy ending, don't worry, but like most good stories it will just take a bit longer to get there."

I'd run out of words. I had nothing left.

"I love you, Lilly."

"This isn't love. This is sport."

"You may not think it, but I do. I know it's hard to see right now, but trust me I will look after you, I will treat you better than anyone else ever could." Max took my face gently, held it in both hands. "You will be safe with me. I only do these things to benefit us, what I do will make us timeless and I assure you we will both end up happy, I promise that."

"Get out, Max."

Max got up, stood by my side. "After all this blows over, maybe we will try for that family you always wanted, hey?" He kissed the top of my head. "Now get some sleep. Big day tomorrow. Tom finally gets his girl." He smiled as closed the door behind him.

I knew he meant every goddamn word.

★ ★ ★

I met Sally downstairs, she offered me the remains of the coffee and grapefruit, I downed one and picked at the other. The waitress came over and as quickly as I asked, brought over a plate of eggs, yellow and steaming. I assumed Sally was mad at me, pretending to read world affairs when really this was just a deliberate show that she was angry with me. She was obviously pissed about the night before, my sudden disappearance, I was already working out my responses for when she finally decided to say her piece, which she most certainly would.

"I heard you weren't feeling too great last night?" She peered over her newspaper, checking my face. "You look fine to me. A somewhat miraculous recovery, hey?"

"Sorry, I had to shoot off, had the most awful headache."

"Headache? I heard it was your tummy." She closed her paper. "Something you ate, apparently."

"I don't know what was wrong with me, my stomach was in knots, my head was even worse. I think I'm due on any day now."

"It's not that, I assure you, Lilly."

"And how would you know my menstrual cycle?"

"Calm down, misery guts. I only know because yours is the same as mine, and mine was a few weeks ago." She smiled, sipping her tea. "Means our erratic emotional states are synchronized."

"Sorry, I didn't sleep well. I didn't mean to bite."

"Don't worry. You've a good nine hours to catch up on sleep when we get on that plane."

"I hope me leaving early last night didn't upset anyone?"

"No, all your media duties had been done, all that you missed was idiots getting drunk and deluded. Was Rogan still mad with you?"

"We made up, actually."

"Good. Glad you got all that shit resolved before we cross the pond. I can't have you two terrorizing every capital we visit. You all packed?" she said, checking her cell.

"Nearly."

"You need a hand. I haven't got much on this morning and you know I'm never happier than when organizing luggage, be it mine or someone else's."

"I'm pretty much done. Anyway, I may have to pop out."

"Where?"

"Just out. I won't be long."

"I might come too. Get a bit fresh air before we get cabin fever later."

"No, it's OK."

"You sure you don't want my company? We could do a little retail therapy."

"No honestly, I'm good."

Sally looked curious. "Where you off to, Miss Goodridge? Why all this secrecy?"

"I am allowed time off, you know. Not everyone needs to know my whereabouts every single minute."

"Sorry I asked. I thought it would be nice to spend some time together. It's not because I have to be with you, it's because I want to."

I nodded and smiled. "Ignore me. I'm in a bad mood."

"Well I've got something that might cheer you up. Fuck, I shouldn't really be telling you."

"Well, you have to tell me now."

"I suppose I do. Well, try to act surprised when he tells you."

"Who tells me what?"

Sally leant forward. "Max let slip that he has booked a surprise trip for you both."

"Where? When?"

"I don't know for sure, next month."

"When did he tell you this?"

"This morning. He was down here as early as me. Looked damn pleased with himself too."

"He's staying here?"

"I assumed he spent the night with you, hence his big grin?"

"Did he say anything else? About me or last night?"

"He didn't stay long, said he had a meeting with a treadmill. Hey, I bet he's taking you somewhere exotic and I bet you will need a passport. I'm a little jealous to be honest." She leaned over to steal some croissant. "I'm going to head back upstairs to get my hand luggage ready. Make sure I've enough to keep me medicated and entertained. Enjoy wherever you're off to. Just make sure you are back here for twelve as our cars will be out front." Sally stood up, picked up her bag and cell. "Oh, and if Max decides today is the day for his big reveal, make sure you act surprised."

She left me to eat my grapefruit alone, so sharp and sour my eyes threatened to water.

★ ★ ★

About an hour later I sent Max a message saying Tom wasn't coming. Told him I'd heard nothing all morning, sat watching my cell, watching the clock, pretending to pack. Whatever Max predicted wasn't going to happen how he'd planned.

I sent Max a second message, just after eleven, told him I was

394

going back to my hotel. That it was stupid, stood in the middle of a park, same corner, same cold. Told him it was pointless and that he should have listened when I said I didn't want to take part in this, that I wasn't his bait. Tom was never coming and being here only made it ten times worse. Told Max to tell whoever was watching or hiding away behind a tree somewhere to stand down.

Third message I told him I was definitely leaving, that I would miss my flight if I waited any longer. That Sally was leaving me angry voicemails, if he was going to meet me here, he would have done it by now, he wouldn't leave it so late. And each time Max gave the same short reply, each time more assured and arrogant that he would show, as I battled with either outcome, knowing either would elate him and destroy me regardless. Still didn't mean I wanted Tom not to show, just to see him, to know he picked me, even if our triumph would be short-lived, at least it meant we had each other, which was something we'd never been allowed to have before. I just wanted Tom to save me, I could deal with what would come after, I couldn't deal with doing this on my own, even if we were then sacrificed and Max got his way.

I looked over at the gate, then at the time; seconds felt too quick, minutes not long enough.

Please, Tom. Don't leave me, Tom.

Please.

71

"You've barely touched breakfast. Something the matter?" Emma put her hand on my leg.

"Just not hungry," I said, putting on a smile that wasn't mine. "What do you fancy doing on our last day?"

"I'm easy. I wouldn't mind seeing Portobello Market, having a little browse. I'd like to be able to give my mother a little something. She likes her little knick-knacks, things to put on shelves and cabinets." She took a sip of coffee. "She is dying to meet you. She is counting the days till next week." Another sip. "Are you sure you are OK?"

"Sorry, still got a headache."

"Well banging your head on a door will do that, silly. I told Molly to tidy away her shoes, I knew they'd be a death trap. Shall we wake them up? It's such a lovely day."

"No, leave them. I'm sure they'll be up soon." I looked at the clock, the same clock I'd looked at since I got up. "I might go for a little walk, actually."

"I could come with. I feel like I still haven't seen enough of London."

"I need to pop into the bank, actually," I said, scrambling for a legitimate excuse. "Boring stuff really. You stay."

"I'd rather come with you. Feels a waste of a sunshine being cooped up in here."

"Honestly, I won't be long. You stay."

"Oh well, I'll start having a bit of a tidy, start packing our things away, save us a job for tonight. After, we could find somewhere nice for lunch. I also need to buy myself something warm and knitted. I doubt Florida is hot all year round. How long will you be?"

"Not sure," I said heading towards the door. "Half an hour, an hour."

"OK, darling. See you soon. Let's hope this walk gets rid of that horrid migraine, hey," she said, kissing my head like she was trying to cure it herself.

72

"Dad, is this a gem stone?" showing me her cupped hand, a green pebble.

"No, darling. It's most likely glass. Probably a broken bottle."

"But it's not sharp like glass."

"No, because it's probably been in the ocean for the last thirty years, you know how sandpaper works? Well, it's a bit like that. All that time tumbling around in the sea and sand has turned it from sharp to smooth."

"Could have been a message in a bottle, Dad?"

"It could have been. How comes you keep calling me 'Dad'? I thought I was 'Daddy'?"

"I'm grown up now," she said, more concerned by the contents in her hand. "Can I keep this glass?"

"Yes. See if you can find some more." She ran off with her bucket in one hand.

Even though it had only been a few weeks since we got back from London, as a little surprise I drove us all down to Devon. To be fair, I did promise Mum, told her I'd take her as soon as the weather brightened, before Florida, before we never got the chance again. I'd have been lying if I said I was a little apprehensive about my return, there was part of me that liked having the memory for myself. Mum was genuinely surprised, she never thought I'd bring her, always said I'd keep Devon just for me, but there you go, sometimes I even surprised myself. It had turned out to be a weekend of firsts all round. First sunny weekend in months, Molly's first time in a wetsuit, first time on a surfboard, first time trying to get out of a wetsuit, that was interesting, caught her first crab, ate her first crab, disliked the taste of her first crab.

The place hadn't lost any of its charm and I fell in love with it all over again, we all did. Introduced everyone to Dot, she and Mum talked all things butter and baking, became instant partners in crime. Tripod even looked pleased to see me, not that it showed, I'm sure most dogs wagged their tails, though Tripod wasn't one of those dogs.

Took everyone to the Oyster Shack as well, Molly liked the shack, but not the oysters, at least she tried them both. Dot and Alfred had a good time, a little too good, I blamed Mum for how tipsy they both got and how much lobster we over-ordered. Drove out to the farmhouse too, didn't go inside, it looked busy, whoever owned it was doing renovations, scaffolding, walls being made higher. Mum and Molly insisted I still gave them the grand tour, so I took them for a quick look at where I used to work, my office under the tree. I was more embarrassed than proud, being paparazzi was hardly a profession to be proud of, not something to show off and parade. Strange seeing the house again, so much had gone on, sometimes I forgot how much.

The only place left was Burgh Island, so on the last day I made sure we'd see it before we went home, shame the weather wasn't great. Built sandcastles in the rain, ate scones in the car, drank flasks of coffee under umbrellas. Luckily the clouds cleared and we finally got to feel sand, say our goodbyes to one tide before we welcomed another.

"I miss your father today."

"Funny. You never normally mention Dad."

"I never normally think of him. Does that sound awful? Just every now and again. Things I know he'd have hated to miss. Molly learning to draw, horizons like these, just begging to be painted."

"How many times did I make him read that old Jacque Cousteau book?"

"The one in Italian?" she laughed. "Wasn't much reading as far as I recall."

399

"Don't remember him ever drawing or painting the sea, actually."

"No, your father never did. He tried a few times but always said he couldn't do it justice, never liked his end product. Might be why he loved the sea so much. The one thing he couldn't put down on canvas, a sort of stalemate."

We both looked in the distance towards it, lit up, a pathway of dunes and puddles, as the two tides, left and right, did their best to meet in the middle, cover a million footprints with sea again.

"Should we all be more nervous?"

"You can't purposely feel nervous."

"What about you-know-what?"

"It is what it is. It's out there. What can we do about it now?"

Mum took a big breath through her nose. "I will miss England. I will miss the seasons. I will miss my garden and my birds. Everything else I could quite easily leave behind. Can you promise me something when we get to Florida?"

"What?"

"Would you let me live on my own?"

"On your own?"

"Not straight away of course. But once I've found my bearings, I want to find somewhere just for me."

"Why?"

"Because you need your own space. I need my own space."

"Molly would be devastated."

"I wouldn't move miles away. But I think it's for the best. A son shouldn't live with his mother for as long as you have. You need to fend for yourself now. The three of you need time to grow as a family."

"And Lou and Rose, of course."

"Well, five then. Don't take it personally, Tom, me wanting to move out. It's with the best intentions."

"It seems drastic, but if that's what you want to do, I can't stop you."

400

"Not drastic, Tom. I think we would start driving each other up the wall. We both need our own lives. And can you promise me something else, Tom?"

"Jesus. What now?"

"I'd like another grandchild soon, if that's OK. Whilst I've still got upstairs and downstairs working. Before I lose my marbles." She pointed to her feet and then her head. "I'm getting on now. I want to be a grandmother whilst I've still got all of my faculties." I didn't answer. I didn't think I needed to. "Shall we head back?" Mum asked. "My bones are cold."

"Probably best, get us all an early night before we head home."

"Can you believe it's all come around? In a few days, the house will be someone else's, no more village, no more pond, no more rainy afternoons. Dot said she'd let us raid Alfred's drink cabinet. Few ports before bed, hey, means I can sleep in the car on the way back." She started to collect Molly's things, put bucket and spades back in bags.

"I might take a quick walk to the island if that's OK, whilst the tide is out, take a few more photos up close."

"I'll keep an eye on Molly. Don't be too long, remember Dot is teaching your girlfriend how to make her infamous bacon and onion roll, we'd be disowned if it was over-steamed. Who's that over there? He looks like he isn't here for the view. Could be harmless."

"Probably not the greatest idea coming here with all that's going on."

"You weren't to know, Tom."

"But I did know. Here, the farmhouse, they are all out of bounds."

"You think he's alone?"

"No, there's another one over there."

"Where?" looking around.

"I won't point, but just over my left shoulder. They got here just after us."

"Bloody vermin."

"Still not used to our new fame, are you, Mum?"

"I'll never get used to it."

"I prefer this. I prefer the truth being out."

"Out. It's bloody everywhere. I don't know how you stay so calm with all this."

"Calm about what?"

"Everyone talking about you. The chaos of it all."

I didn't answer.

"You go and say your farewells. Sorry for bringing it up. I don't want to ruin your moment. I know how much this place means to you. Even if the moment isn't as private as it should be."

"It's as private as I'm gonna get from now on," I said, starting to head towards the island, trying to ignore that I was being followed, being watched, my photos taken, though already imagining it on the newsstands, jealous I wouldn't be the one who took it myself.

Burgh Island deserved its front cover, I didn't. The hotel in front, still as white and majestic, the tide either side like a middle parting, an orange sky not yet squashed purple. A man and his memories, walking towards his end and his beginning.

73

"You keep taking deep breaths," I whispered. "I never knew you were scared of flying."

"Flying I'm fine with. It's what's meeting us on the ground I'm scared of."

"I should be more nervous than you. Try to get some sleep."

"It's impossible to sleep on planes."

"Try telling those two," I said, pointing across to Mum and Molly, sleep masks, catching flies.

"We'll be OK, won't we, Tom?"

I smiled, no answer required.

"Can we just camp out in our hotel for a few days? Lock the doors, eat junk, watch movies?"

"Sounds good. Though I'm not sure Molly will approve of being confined indoors, not with Disney on her front doorstep."

"You still happy that I'm coming with you?"

"Course I am." I put my arm around her. "What makes you say that?"

"Just over-thinking."

"You fancy watching something? May not be the biggest screen but I'll let you put your legs on my lap." Fiddling with the remote, pressing buttons on the hand rest, as the air steward asked if we'd like anything. "What shall we watch?"

"You can choose, Tom. Just nothing with a sad ending," she said as she sank into my chest, a smile I couldn't see, but one I knew was there.

AMERICA

Clearwater/June/Shot 1109

74

He'd fallen back off to sleep again, a deep sleep, his arm across my chest, a snore I was still getting used to. We should have been out of bed by now, room service was half eaten but that wouldn't be the case for long, we planned on spending the next few hours making our way through it, and there was a lot of it. For the millionth time, we'd decided to watch *Totoro*, it was the right movie considering, appropriate for mornings as slow as these, like reading the most exquisite book without the need for words. What could I say, I'd always been a sucker for a subtitle, an even bigger sucker for anything anime. Whenever I watched Japanese cartoons I instantly felt too cool for school, made me feel I was in a Sega game, an instant nostalgia, ten years old again eating fruit loops before school.

In England, I got kind of obsessed with Japan all over again, found a huge book on the kitchen shelf which I'd skim through as I'd waited for whatever was bubbling away on the Aga. Page after page of stunning mountains, temples and palaces, pink cherry blossoms. Everything looked so peaceful, like the whole country had been taught to whisper. When I was little I wanted to be a samurai, but rather than the sword I'd asked for, on Christmas Day Santa brought me ballet shoes and I was forced to be the little girl I always pretended not to be. I asked my mom once why Japanese people had slanty eyes and the answer she gave meant I would never ask again. Though I wasn't making an insult, it was genuine curiosity to find out how I could get them too, how I too could look like the girls in the cartoons, everything petite and perfect. I wanted to look different, I wanted people's heads to turn.

I think in a past life I'd have been a geisha, beautiful but sad, talents sold to the highest bidder. I read a lot about them, they'd lived a hard life, but it was a comfortable one. I'm sure if you were to ask one what they'd prefer, to go back to obscurity or stay as that exotic caged bird, I was sure none would want to fly away. But what could I say? My fascination with tortured women lives on, give me a stunning girl whom I could both envy and pity and I was hooked.

Now my obsession had turned permanent and I may have done something a little out of the blue, a bit crazy, completely unplanned. Well, not necessarily, I'd thought about it for years, I knew it was something I would eventually do, I just didn't know when and most importantly I didn't know what. It took just over six hours, sat there in some tiny little studio, laid horizontal as things buzzed and stung. I'm pleased with it, stupid or brave, I let the tattooist do her thing, her body was pretty much neck-to-toe Orient. I gave her free rein, pointed at various parts of her body and told her what I liked. She looked pretty fucking hot, prettier than me, I think I may have formed a little girl crush, think I may have briefly flirted, till my arm throbbed and I had to focus my attention on the ceiling fan, let my eyes water and my mind wander.

No one had seen it yet, spent the last few days in jumpers and sleeves, rubbing it in cocoa butter and watching it scab, before my grand reveal. I expected it would not go down well, I could already hear Sally's voice, my mom's eyes roll, my agent's frown line. But hey, what could they do? It was my arm, not theirs. Though it wouldn't surprise me if somewhere, on the two-hundredth page of some form I'd signed, it says I'd broken some rule, I'd have to get it lasered off before I was sued for breaching contract. Suppose I better enjoy my secret whilst it lasted, before I had to explain and justify why I chose to make myself less marketable. I was sure my half sleeve meant I crossed a lot of boxes on why I shouldn't be picked for a role, though on the flip side it ticked a few on why

I should. But hey, I've spent a lot of years pleasing people before myself, normally the ones who didn't need or notice it. Time to be a little selfish for a change, do something just for me, without permission or challenge.

Only one person had seen it so far, and I thought they might be angry, not at the tattoo, but the fact he hadn't been pre-warned or involved, instead he said it was beautiful. I find myself staring at my new friend, my little geisha girl tucked away just under my armpit, both sharing a similar expression, not quite a grin, but not quite a frown. You could tell my new twin was a Goodridge.

I was hungry. My stomach rumbled. I looked at him again, he looked too peaceful to wake up just yet. Give him five minutes, I thought to myself. I was a little annoyed to have woken so early, it was a rarity that either of us had the opportunity to wake up naturally, without alarms beeping or doors being knocked.

God we'd barely been home, passing ships, which was mostly down to me, well all down to me. Clocking up the air miles, spending most of my time in hotel rooms the size of the Staples Centre. Though I couldn't be too mad, yes, I wished I could stay in one place, spend time with the people I wanted to rather than the ones I was forced to, credit to him he never made me feel guilty, in fact he encouraged it. So, I got to see some of the wonders of the world, got to speak to fans I never thought I had. Fans that spoke another language but still knew how to scream my name, got to stay in the prettiest places too, doesn't look like letting up either. I'd seen my schedule for the next few months, so knew we should soak up all this calm before the storm hits again. Make sure we take advantage of lazy days like these and not feel too guilty if we don't fill them with culture and activity. Be able to sit in front of the TV, little walks, swim, read, eat and cook what we wanted and when we wanted. I'm OK with busy now, try to plan, make my free time count. Though some of us don't find it as easy to wind down. I guess when life is a hundred miles per hour, it can be hard to slam on the brakes, but I'm working on him, trying to teach him the art of doing fuck all, when most girlfriends wouldn't dream of encouraging that.

Though a strange thing had happened to me when I returned back to America after my time on Europe's finest red carpets. One, I realized I could never give up being an actress, I was in too deep to get out and I was too famous to be forgotten about. Even if I ran and hid, moved to the other side of the world, then I would still not be free, people would always be watching.

Secondly and most importantly, I learnt to accept being an actress and accept what came with it. I was past blame and past working out people's motivations, trying to figure out who was with or against me. I watched as people did their talking for me and perhaps I should have been more worried than I was, question their decision-making, now I just had to learn to trust them. It was clear that my career was out of my control, but rather than be angry and bitter, now I sort of embraced it, rode with it as opposed to challenging and kicking out. Let my crazy life stay crazy.

I suppose you could say I worked out how to be happy finally, took me a couple of self-help books, recommended by Mr Snore beside me, took little bits from each, worked out my own version of what advice I needed and what might work for me. The Goodridge method. It wasn't that complicated, just made sure I saw the people who counted, took time out to do things that made me smile, reading too. Being in the air so much, stuck on tiny jets with nowhere to go, rather than movies or internet, I preferred disappearing behind a book, the bigger the better. American books actually, again another recommendation from Mr Snore. Not American literature, books about America, the different states, try and get to know a little more than how good our airports are, understand our culture and our history. I sounded like a grown-up, Mom would be so proud.

Believe it or not I'd started doing a little volunteering work again, shelters and food banks, big cities and not-so-big cities. So whatever media campaign Sally had me do, whatever part of the map they put me in, rather than just camp out in plush hotels and VIP bars, instead I found places that needed an extra pair of hands. Turned out there was a lot of those places, every town had its problems and there were always people who needed someone to lean on. It was a win–win, good for me, good for them, so far no one had noticed Lilly Goodridge and were content with just me, more preoccupied with when they would get their next meal rather than who'd be serving it to them.

This wasn't some marketing campaign either. I tried my best to keep my new hobby a secret, not sure what else I could have done, I'd told no one, made myself unrecognisable. But my generosity that was supposed to be pure and selfless, becomes a KTLA breakfast headline, photos of me and the downtrodden, like it was some PR set-up, but who cared, hey? The poor got fed and more people got to read how Obama is still faraway from fixing America. But that's another story, I tried not to focus on things I couldn't fix anymore, put all my energy into things I could.

And that had been the hardest thing. Understanding what was broken and what was beyond repair. Took me a while to work out the difference. Might even take me a little longer.

75

"Ladies and gentlemen, boys and girls. Welcome to my jolly trolley, my shiny tram on wheels. My name is Tom and I'll be your driver today. How are you all? I want to see bigger smiles than that, guys. Come on, days like today don't come around often. Now straight off the bat I know what you are all probably thinking. Milk-skinned, sunburnt, funny accent. Hardly who you would typically be expecting to be driving you around this beautiful city of Clearwater. And I tell you, it is beautiful. But my job today, ladies and gentlemen, isn't just to be your driver, think of me as your concierge on wheels, so any questions about what we see, or where you need to go to or get off, then just let me know. I'll be the one in the flowery shirt getting us all lost – I'm kidding. So, guys, leave your car where you are and let's get this bus moving and the air con blasting."

It wasn't a bad way to earn a living. It was only my third week on the job, Rose had a friend of a friend that hooked me up. The boss didn't pay much attention to my detailed CV, said she wasn't one for formalities and protocol. She was lovely, and like every old lady in Clearwater, she instantly embraced you like an extension of her own family, treated the work I did like I was doing her a favour, hugged you like she owed you one in return.

Originally my intention wasn't to hang around long behind the wheel, it felt like a backward step, had my eyes set on a career in journalism, wild dreams of working for the *Tampa Bay Times*, writing for Pulitzer prizes. I sent them my résumé but heard nothing back and didn't expect I would, instead I toyed with the idea of taking a night course, getting some academics behind me, at least that was the plan.

I never expected to enjoy this job so much, didn't expect to get on so well with the customers and staff. Yes, the salary wasn't as large as I'd hoped and wasn't a future that would set the world on fire, but at the moment I could hardly complain, no stress, flexible hours, health care. I went to bed happy and woke up happy, Mum said that was always her litmus test, albeit simple, I agreed that people made life more complicated than it needed to be.

Mum had been the happiest I'd seen her, sunshine had always suited my mother, pottering round gardens with gloves and a glass of red. Despite beating cancer, she still soaked up every available sun ray and was content to turn herself into a leather couch. She and Rose had become best friends and Lou was now a man doted over, two women at his beck and call. I joked about a love triangle, he laughed, said they were overrated, speaking like a man who knew, which he probably did.

Despite her warnings, Mum was still living with us, and showed no particular rush to change that, she talked of her own place, but a month or so of being looked after meant the eventual move date had changed from October, to November, and now there was even talk of the new year. It wouldn't surprise me if she never left, in fact it wouldn't surprise me if I never left either. It was an easy place to sink into, Lou and Rose kept their home pristine, kept the fridge well stocked, pool Ph at optimum level, hard to walk away from show home to squalor. Still, Mum said she would stay till Molly had become settled. To be fair, Molly settled to the pace of life just as quickly, spent most of her time in a hammock with Lou or chasing Rose with the water hose. Though she would get a shock when September came around, no more lazy mornings and beach picnics. In a month she would start kindergarten, so I was already predicting tears, mine as well as hers.

Emma had decided to go back home, just for a short while, missed her mum. None of us were prepared for what happened after London, the world finding out about me and Lilly, including Emma. I was surprised she stood by me, most women wouldn't have, though she very nearly didn't. There were a lot of raised voices, a lot of late-night discussions, think she was just mad I never told her, that she had to find out at the same time as everyone else. Wasn't the best timing either, the day the news dropped was the day before we went to visit Emma's mother, so as you could imagine the warm arms I expected was instead a cold front.

Life became manic after that, constant phone calls, hassled and harassed. After the first few photos hit, more came out, then some more and by the time Devon came around the story of poor boy meets rich girl was a fairy tale every woman and daughter wanted to read more about. And the way the photos came out made it movie-like, the photos came out in order, from surfing to holding hands, from meeting Mum to riding sea tractors. Every photo was another episode and without hearing mine or Lilly's side, the world remained unfulfilled by the gaps in between and thirsty for an ending or explanation.

I was everywhere, so was Lilly, so was Max, but the audience wasn't satisfied and hence why I was being offered silly money to say my piece, go on talk shows, speak to editors. Of course, I could've wallowed in it, milked it for all it was worth, made my fortune, even used it to get me some fancy job with some big-time newspaper or magazine. But instead I hid, laid low, disappeared for a while, hung out at Lou's, tried to stay silent till they'd given up, which I knew they never would.

Even before the media intrusion it was clear that out of all of us Emma would find it the hardest. She wasn't used to not working and despite attempting to get work back in the medical field all her attempts so far had been unsuccessful. I told her to enjoy her time off, kick back and take advantage of not having to get up for the twelve-hour shifts she was used to. But though she tried to sunbathe, to swim, to take walks on the beach, doing nothing didn't quite sit right with her. Then of course there was the press invasion and from day one at the airport the camera flashes had been relentless and everywhere she went she was often followed by people asking her questions about a girl she hadn't even met.

She would be back, not sure when, but she would be back. We talked on the phone still most nights, things were OK, it was a period of adjustment for all of us, I told her things would get better, it would just take more time. For now, it was just a case of making a life here, getting on with things, blending in, which wasn't easy now I was suddenly Clearwater's newest celebrity. But it wasn't that bad, meant the passengers sometimes asked me for a photograph or signature, the brave ones even asked about Lilly, not that I ever answered. Though from the little exposure I'd had so far, I could see how fame could drive someone mad, moments were not my own anymore, pushing Molly on a swing, a jog in the sand, learning to fish with Lou, there was always a camera not too far away. Though I could hardly complain could I, and I'd be a hypocrite if I spoke badly of the people behind the lenses, seeing as I'd done much worse in a previous life. They were just trying to earn a decent living after all, just like the rest of us.

Though the media was camped outside my front door, only one person actually chose to knock, funnily enough. It wasn't me who answered, if it had been I wasn't entirely sure I would've let them in, though it wasn't the first time Vince had turned up unannounced and uninvited and still be welcomed inside.

At first it was all smiles and handshakes, introductions to a family he'd met before and a family he hadn't. Lou and Rose were over-friendly, I didn't have any friends, so Vince being the first he was now considered instantly one of their own. Despite any resentment my mum had for Vince she didn't show it when he stood in front of her with his big bleached grin, gave him the same hugs and smiles she did the first time she welcomed him into her arms. And once drinks had been offered and poured, eventually I excused myself and Vince, as my family dispersed to different rooms of the house and Vince and I took ourselves outside to the garden.

"Is this the part where we hit each other as hard as we can?" he said and for a very brief moment it felt the right thing to do, slug it out, till we were satisfied with the punches we'd given and taken. But of course, we didn't.

Instead we both said our side, he asked about Lilly, how we came about, I told him very little, though he was still impressed, even a little proud, called me a little devil, whatever that meant. I asked him about Lilly too, how long he'd known about us, or if he'd known all along, which he said he hadn't, the first he heard was when Max returned from London with a bruise on his cheek and a concern Lilly was enjoying the company of someone new. Things started to make sense the more he explained, turned out Vince arrived just before Lilly whisked me off back home to meet Molly and Mum. He was behind us ever since then, followed us to Mum's village, followed us back, followed us to Burgh Island. I asked him if he was the Silver Merc, not that I needed to and not that he answered, it was obvious.

I could've asked him why he double-crossed me, why he went behind my back, but it would have been a wasted conversation. Plainly and simply, Vince would do any job as long as it paid the most, his choice wasn't based on ethics and morals and loyalty. The truth was, Max paid more, lined his pockets more than I ever could have hiding behind bushes.

Why the messages, though? I never understood why he got back in contact when we first got home from Thailand. Why the reveal? Why the threat? If it even was a threat. Why tell me he knew about me and Lilly? What did he want to happen?

Vince just said it was a moment of weakness, said he thought I should know what shit storm was coming my way even though neither me nor him had any control to stop it. I tried to get to the bottom of how much he knew about Max and about Lilly, figure out how she went from loving me to loving him. He just smiled, said he didn't ask things he didn't need to know. Max was ruthless, that was all he said.

After that we reverted back to small talk as we strolled poolside, my life in Clearwater, his life back in LA, no matter the fortunes he chased and spent, his world was always full of problems, as was mine. It was a strange visit, not quite sure why he showed up when he first arrived or even after when he left. He wasn't there to apologize, that was for sure, and he never asked for one from me in return, when in truth we both probably deserved an apology of some kind. I was glad he came, meant I was no longer in Vince's debt, didn't have to worry about owing him or worry what he might do next. In the end, we left on good terms, handshakes at the door, a friendship I thought dead and buried, which more than likely would stay that way, but at least it was settled and squared up.

As he left, as was about to climb into his big shiny SUV, my head filled with unresolved questions, things I should have asked, that I might not get the chance to ask again.

"Vince?"

"What's up, buddy?" he said, about to close the door of his car.

"He didn't send you, did he?"

Vince smiled. "My days working for Max are over, don't worry."

"Why?"

"Let's just say I've earned enough."

"And Lilly?"

"What about her?"

"Is she all right? Is she OK?" assuming they'd even met.

Vince paused, took his time.

"I haven't met many celebrities I've ever felt sorry for, Tommy."

I waited for him to finish, like he was about to say more, or wanted to say more, but he didn't. And with that he was gone, a honk of his horn and a wave out the window.

★ ★ ★

More weeks passed after my encounter with Vince. Emma was back any day now, flights booked, suitcase packed. The day before she was due to arrive an agent called, one who'd rung me before, told me again why I needed him when I was sure it would be the other way around. This time the offer was bigger, twice as big as the last time. I turned him down, obviously, just like I'd done before, though each time it was getting harder to refuse. The money they were talking, the deals they were throwing at me, life-changing offers, would set me and Molly up for life, pay for college, pay for her first house. Felt like eventually they'd get their way, that it was only a matter of time till they had me in front of a live audience, giving my confession, or Lilly giving hers. Like neither of us really had a choice. Like the world wanted us back together again, to watch us fight, or watch us fall back in love.

In the end, they'll always get what they want.

76

I turned over and looked at Max again. Mr Snore.

He had gotten greyer, more wrinkles, but he had grown more handsome, hours spent in the gym had turned his body from thin to sculpted. He slept with a smile, a face of a man that had won and was still winning, but this time it felt like I was winning, too. He had treated me differently since London and rather than feeling fearful I felt protected. Like Max knew what he was doing, that it was all under control, I just had to enjoy the future he had mapped out for us, understand any bumps were deliberate and eventually they would run smoothly.

Max had slowly and surely made me fall in love with him again and trust that he would keep me safe, forgive him for what he did, understand he was doing it for us. This may not be my future but it was a future filled with ambition and grand ideas. We did things together again, we talked about the countries we wanted to visit, the films we'd love to make, how our lives may look in thirty years' time.

I got up to the bathroom, turned on the taps and watched the marble turn the water black. Barefoot and half-naked, I wandered across the suite, it took a while, lots of rooms, too many chairs and too many tables for just me and him, not to mention a grand piano. I took a book from the bookcase, flicked through the pages just to check it wasn't just for show, made me jealous my library back home was so small, realising that was something I would have to fix, though Max assured me that when his house had been built we would have a whole room dedicated to our books and movies and art and photos.

From my balcony, Tokyo looked like the future. High-rise buildings always made me feel uneasy, both looking up or looking down, partly down to Mr Bin Laden. But mostly because it made me the world look far too crowded, like the planet was too small and we had no choice but to live in the clouds. And it was certainly not the Japan I dreamt about when flying half a day to get here.

Max had promised me tomorrow I'd get to see a different Japan besides foreign fashion houses and foreign traffic. Max asked me where, I said somewhere quiet, temples, little rivers and bridges, tiny men catching fish, somewhere unspoilt. Max laughed, said there aren't many places that people hadn't spoilt, but he would do his best to find me Mr Miyagi's house. It was nice to see the funny side of Max again, for so long most of his smiles came from my demise, but now it was a laughter shared, at least for now. And even though I was always ready for what he might do next, both good and bad, it seemed less and less that Max's plans involved my sadness. So, for now until Max decided otherwise, I was being lavished and pampered in all the ways a girl should, though my decision to accept Max's gifts and affection came at a price. Friends that were once close weren't so any longer.

Franny was the angriest, said Max was just fattening me up before slaughter, think she took it personally I didn't listen to her revenge tactics. Kate was a strange one, although close to Max still and although we'd never actually fallen out, our friendship was a Facebook timeline and all I saw now was her child go from newborn to baby on my cell screen rather than in person. And Frank, well Frank and I had not directly spoken since he came out of hospital, though just after news broke of mine and Max's reconciliation he sent me a message telling me to be careful. I rang him back but he never answered and I guessed he never would. I could imagine his face, his look of disapproval, his sigh and sniffs. So apart from a few that had no choice, only a few stood by my side, family, Sally, Marla. All I could do was listen to them and trust my own judgement, do my best to be careful. I went back to the bathroom and stopped the running tap, our black pond was full.

Out of the blue, Max bought me a house in England, I knew it well, big garden with fields of lambs, a ghost upstairs, an Aga perfect for warming socks. I asked him why, an unusual gift, one that was premeditated, but he answered like I'd opened just any other present, a watch or piece of jewellery, not the keys to a house and a romance that I've been trying to lock away ever since.

Max was unconcerned, gave off the impression I was more in love with the big white house than I was ever in love with the romance outside. Max had grown in confidence when it came to my emotions, he was honest and understood that a little bit of Tom would always be in my thoughts, that was why he felt no danger in buying it, saw it as a house, bricks and mortar, not anything that happened between its four walls. We hadn't been there yet, not to England or the house, too busy, plans were to spend some time there over the holidays, when it was cold and white, when the river looked like glass and the fire could roar day and night. I wondered what I'd change, or not change even, all those pictures on the wall, remove their memories, fill it with our own.

I asked Max on the plane here who the owners were, who that family was in those photos, all blond-haired and blue-eyed, the ones I used to stare at and aspire to. Turned out it was a divorced banker with debts and diabetes. Max was under the impression there were kids and a wife somewhere, joked they were probably the reason for the quick sale and early grave, apparently it was the man who lived next door. I didn't tell Max I'd met him, the man who gave me eggs, who always waved when he saw me, he was always happy to help whenever I needed a spare barbecue or help diffusing a smoke alarm. He wasn't the man in the photos, he may have been once, but the man I knew looked old and lonely, not commanding a yacht or cuddling wife and children like their smiles would never fade. It shouldn't have made me as sad as it did and even though I didn't even know his name, I mourned him like a friend. Made me realize photos never show the full story, only show a brief moment, not what came before or after. Perhaps that was the key, perhaps that's why we smiled for the camera, to prove we were all having a good time, evidence that we'd lived a fruitful life, even if we hadn't before or since.

I looked back over at Max once more, his stirring, about to wake. We'd made love last night, it was starting to feel less awkward, I was stopping letting my mind wander, kept my thoughts on just him, not abortion or past loves. I don't think Max noticed, too caught up in the moment, his eyes shut, biting me, kissing me, Max always knew how to provide pleasure and climax for both him and me. I didn't need to fake, not the end part anyway, just the start and middle when all I could think about was what a bad human being I was. Like it was wrong, like every time I was intimate, it was an insult to the memory of what came before. I was sure that would pass, that as time went on it would hurt less and less.

I went to wake Max. We had a busy day ahead of us, wine-tasting, party on Max's friend's boat, only a select chosen few, there was talk of dignitaries being on board, a prince or king. My dress was already hung up, my jewellery was being delivered at lunch. That was me, billionaire yacht by day, soup kitchens at night. It was nice to be so far away from all the noise coming from America, Japan had paparazzi, but not the sort to be bothered by a love triangle on the other side of the planet, so for the most part they left us alone.

I'm not going to say my heart didn't break when Tom didn't show up, but I understood his decision to choose her over me. He didn't want the life I offered, didn't love me enough to take the gamble, maybe he just hadn't forgiven me for what had gone before. A very small part of me smiled when he didn't show, knowing Max and Vince were somewhere watching, they may have had a Plan B, but it softened the blow knowing things hadn't turned out exactly how they'd wanted. But it was only a very small part of me that smiled, the rest of me was broken, waiting there as long as I did, checking every face to see if it was Tom's, waiting till the very last minute, until I couldn't wait any longer. The plane home felt long, though Sally gave me enough sedatives to help me cross the big pond in one piece.

I'd like to say things were easy after London, but they weren't. The photos of me and Tom were released and the world got to see me cheat on poor little Max. But it wasn't that bad, I was used to looking glum and apologetic. I was worried more for Tom, wondered what damage it had caused to him and his family, I hoped they came out of it unscathed, that they could get on with their lives. Credit to Tom, from what I read, wherever Tom was he kept what me and him had silent, tried to let news wash over, tried to keep quiet till everyone lost interest, which so far, they hadn't.

Me, well my infidelity had only added to my image as the rebel with or without a cause, and now I was being offered the edgier roles by edgier directors. No longer the girl next door, I was the brunette you wouldn't fuck with, whose sexuality was questioned, with loose morals and a wild spirit. I was now suddenly a bitch and a fierce one and I'm sure my new tattoo would only make things worse, make me even more of a head fuck. It made me laugh, I was none of these things, a head fuck for sure, but wasn't everyone in Hollywood? Max was clever, and my role as villain and his as hero was a triumph. His plan had worked all along, his masterpiece, it was only after Tom didn't show that I realized it was better to be on Max's side than against him.

Not bad, I thought, looking at myself in the mirror. My hair messy, eyes still puffy from sleep, nothing a bath and a Bloody Mary couldn't fix. I turned to my view again, my view from the top, a view more sky than city. Max made it hard to be unhappy, he made sure my life was filled with amazing things and amazing people and amazing views, meant no matter how I felt, I was always appreciative, grateful to be in the world he'd given us.

423

My Mom still keeps asking if I'm happy. Sally too. People must assume I'm not, regardless of how much I laughed and smiled.

I am happy, honest. That is what I tell them.

I am happy.

Honest.

Maybe one day just those first three words will be enough.

But hey, as four Welshmen I saw on a poster once sang, "*La Tristesse Durera.*"

Scream to a sigh.

THE END

Burgh Island/June/Shot 1081